Shrouded

in

Blackness

Shrouded in Blackness

Norma Jeanne Karlsson

Shrouded in Blackness

Edited by Progressive Edits

Cover Design and Layout by
Ellie Kay Bockert Augsburger
Creative Digital Studios
CreativeDigitalStudios.com

Cover Images by
© cristovao31 / Dollar Photo Club
© creative_stock / Dollar Photo Club
© ChaosMaker / Dollar Photo Club
© triling / Dollar Photo Club
© jirikaderabek / Dollar Photo Club

Published by It's Publishing
PO Box 14402
Parkville, MO 64152
www.normajeannekarlsson.com

ISBN: 978-0-9911873-5-5
ISBN e-book: 978-0-9911873-4-8

Table of Contents

Dedication...

To the people who forgot to fight for me. It's because of you I can fight for myself. And it's because of you I'll always fight for others.

Acknowledgements

The journey of *The Blackness Series* began as a solo mission with a few people at my back for support and encouragement. It has now grown in such a way I'm a bit blown away when I sit down to think about it, much less write about it.

As always the beginning of my thanks starts with my husband. You've given me this gift without question. When I had a story rolling around in my head you're the one that said write it. You gave me the final push to do something that has fulfilled me in a way I don't think either of us believed it would. I can write about love and connections built in unconventional ways because you taught me that. You showed me how to love when it was the last thing I wanted to do. I'm not lucky...I'm honored that I get to share my life with a man like you. Thank you for everything you give me, teach me, unveil to me, experience with me...and for loving me like I deserve to be loved.

My children are too young to know what they give me in life, but it makes it no less important. Unconditional love was a new thing to me when I became a mother. I can't imagine going a day without it now. You give me strength through your hugs, smiles, kisses and love. You are my highest priority in life, my greatest achievements and my best rewards. It's your laughter that brings me through the tough moments in life. It's your tears that rip at my soul when you're sad. It's your smiles after I've wiped away those tears that cement my assertion that being a mother is what I was meant to be in life. It's your love that inspires me to make every day a little better for you than it ever was for me. I love you, boys.

My mother is forever the person that can make me laugh until I have tears streaming down my face, cramps in my cheeks, pain in my stomach and love in my bones. You give me reprieve whenever it's necessary in my life. I can always count on you to weather the storm right along with me, cursing the waves as we struggle through. I can write about tears being shed in laughter and love because you've shown what that is and how good it can feel. You give me every bit of everything that you can without question or hesitation when needed and for that I am forever grateful. You love me with pride and admiration that warms my soul at every turn. Thank you for fighting to become the woman you are today and allowing me to blossom into the woman I've strived to be. I love you so very much.

As best friends go I've got the kind that everyone should wish for and I hope someday are able to find. As two teenagers we formed a bond through tragedy and survival, fun and recklessness, love and loss...and bathtubs. Chris, you've always been right where I need you. Whether it was by my side at my wedding or bursting into a room you weren't allowed in while I was giving birth...you've been there. You're the person I call when I want to share my highs and lows because I know they matter to you as much as they matter to me. You've made me feel worthy and important in life when I didn't feel those things much less believe them when you fought to convince me. You're that piece of good in me like the piece of good Shannon offers the people in her fictional world. You're my light. Love you...and then some.

When you move to a new country where you know absolutely no one you hope you'll find at least one person that can offer you friendship. I've found an outstanding woman who's given me that and so much more. Thank you Ruth, for being a support and an ear for me share with. Your concern and genuine intrigue with my life and my family has given me so much comfort I can't begin to describe it for you. Your words of support combined with some great afternoons filled with laughter and joy have filled me when I was otherwise empty. You've made this homesick girl feel at home. I love you dearly.

An editor is what you began as, but you're my friend now. Friend isn't the right word…Amanda, you're my everything as I write. You're my sounding board, my cheerleader, my critic, my inspiration and my escape. SIB would not have been written if it weren't for you, truly. This was your wish. This is the story you wanted. Kieran was the man you wanted to learn about. So this is for you my dear. Thank you for the support you offer. At any moment I begin to question or hesitate you're the first person to have my back, pumping me back up and surging me beyond where I began. I love you, lady. I can't wait to see where we go from here!

Ellie, Ellie, Ellie! Sometimes you just click with someone in the world and that's what we've done. Your art speaks for me in ways we both know I can't even begin to articulate. You're patient and considerate with me and for that I'm beyond grateful. Your art is such a small part of what you mean to me though. What an outstanding friend you've become. Fridays are my new favorite because I'm so damn excited to chat with you. I haven't dated in a while, but friendship dating you has been a blast! This relationship goes beyond Photoshop and stock photos. It's about sharing, laughing, storytelling and love. Thank you for being just the amazing person you are. Loves and hugs.

To the bloggers and reviewers I don't really have the words to articulate how much you all mean to me. It's your words of praise that have reached readers and encouraged them to enter the world I've created. Kel at Literary Nook, Pam at Racing to Read and Michele at Insane About Books you ladies have a special place in my heart. You have given me such kind words and support since BTO. I take the things you write to heart and weigh your criticism as I move through *The Blackness Series*. Thank you for your support and interest. I hope you'll continue on this journey with me.

Finally, you dedicated readers. What do I say? Thank you seems too small to encapsulate my gratitude. Whether this is the first book of mine that you've read or you've been with me since the beginning, I'm greatly appreciative of you. I think the thing that knocks me back the most are the emails I receive. I started writing with the hope that my words would touch at least one person and I'm beyond amazed I've done that. Reading your stories of pain, struggle, survival and perseverance make me humble and honored. I hope more of you continue to find a little light in my stories and even more in life. Please continue to share with me as we move forward on this journey together. Happy Reading!

Shrouded in Blackness

Chapter 1

Quinn

Do you want to know what heaven feels like? It's this right here. Standing under a steaming hot shower head, dousing my grime-covered body in droplets of freshness. After a week and a half of being out there with nothing more than a wet wipe to do a basic rubdown in a public bathroom, this is pure ecstasy. My muscles are releasing tension as each second ticks by. My skin is breathing deeply through each pore as the water drags away the filth. My lungs are being cleansed by the steam mixed with the scent of some cheap generic soap that may as well be the most high dollar body cleanser the world has ever seen. I never thought soap could mean so much to me, but at this point in my life I live for soap.

I don't know how long I've been standing here, but my fingers are pruney to the point of pain. Time to move this along. I stick my hand under the pump attached to the wall and fill it with an industrial, green-colored shampoo-conditioner-body wash combination that has a manly fragrance. I don't care. I scrub my inky raven hair into a sudsy pile on top of my head. A feat really, considering it reaches my waist at this point. That happens when you don't cut your hair for eight years.

I brace my hands against the cracked, grey, used-to-be-white-twenty-years-ago tile and let the fluffy mound on my head set while the water scalds my back. I'm covered in goosebumps from the sting and I relish it. I use the pump combo soap again to scour my body clean.

I buff so deeply that it's red and welted. Clean. I won't be able to come back for another week and a half so I'm making it count. Now that I'm covered in foam from head to toe I step back in the searing heat and rinse myself slowly.

I hear something and halt my movement instantly. I've become hyper aware of every sound in the last eight years. I can hear a rat take a shit I'm so highly tuned in. I wait for thirty paced breaths. I've found in that amount of time if something's actually making a sound it'll make another in that space of time. The breaths come and go without another peep so I return to rinsing. I shave everything with the cheap one-blade BIC Ian gives me every week while I'm here. He leaves me the razor and a towel without fail, and the soap pump is always full as well as the lotion pump out in the changing area.

Ian Brogan is the closest relationship I have in this world. Seven years ago, he came upon me and decided to insert himself into my life. I fought and bitched like crazy until I realized he didn't care what my opinion was on the matter. So, the then-sixty-two year-old with the body of a man twenty years his junior and a face always masked in some form of pissed off became...my everything. He watches out for me, feeds me when I allow it (or so I tell myself), and lets me come here whenever I want to clean up.

Ian owns and operates a gym of sorts. It's really an old warehouse that he converted into a training center for fighters in the 1970s. Not boxers: fighters are what he and his crew train. Fighters that are vicious, lethal men who no one wants to cross in the dark of night or even on a bright sunshine-filled day. Some of the men he's trained have gone on to fight professionally, but most stick to the underground bare-knuckle fights that have been going on for centuries. I met Ian after one of the fights he hosted here. I was out back in an alleyway when some guy, who had bet on one of the fights and lost and then got rip-roaring drunk, decided he wanted to make my acquaintance. It didn't take long for the guy to realize that my five-foot-nothing, barely hundred-pound frame was not in the mood to be acquainted with him or his "skin flute," I believe is what he called it. Instead, I introduced him to a swift knee to his musical instrument.

Ian had been watching the guy because, well, that's what Ian does. As I unmanned the prick, Ian watched from afar before approaching me cautiously. He complimented me on my skills and tried to start up a conversation which I quickly shut down and disappeared into the night. I didn't see Ian again for months but when I did, I was in a worse situation and Ian didn't watch from afar. Needless to say, after our second encounter I was more willing to talk to Ian Brogan.

After shaving and rewashing myself, I cut off my heavenly shower and wrap myself in a towel. The only problem with using a men's gym is that I have to use men's towels. I flip my hair over and wrap it up turban-style with one towel before I dry my body and then wrap the other tiny one around my waist man-style. Walking into the changing area, I slather lotion anywhere and everywhere. It's another industrial product that smells manly and, again, I don't give a shit. It feels silky with a bite on my raw skin that I welcome.

The dryer isn't done with my clothes yet so I sit on the bench and wait. I dig through my worn and holey backpack to find a book I've been reading. There's a lady at one of the shelters I hop around that gives me books. I think she runs a program to educate homeless people. I don't pay her much mind other than to collect books

3

when I see her and then take off. I never stay anywhere more than a few hours. Moving makes me invisible. You can't catch something that isn't there. Life lesson learned early.

I hear a noise out in the gym and begin counting my breaths. Ten breaths in and I hear the noise again, louder. I slide my hand into my bag and grasp my knife. Ian gave me his Yarborough knife after our second encounter. He taught me how to use it and I perfected my craft over the last several years. Oddly, in my life I haven't had to use my knife skills all that often. I wish I could claim I have a steely disposition and feel no fear but right now, I feel sick to my stomach and my hand has the slightest tremor as I prepare myself for whatever I'm about to meet.

I stand up silently and move in the direction of the noise. It sounds like someone is moving something across the mats in the grappling area. Ian left before I got in the shower and won't be coming back until later. I know it's not him. He would make himself known before jacking around in the gym. I reach the door to the locker room and wait to hear the sound again. Five breaths and the same dragging noise mumbles through the glass and wood door. I'm wearing a damn towel around my waist. Not my idea of combat clothing, but it'll have to do. Sometimes fighters come in to train at night, though Ian doesn't allow it when I'm here. It's not a fighter out there. The gym is in a rough neighborhood, but Ian Brogan possesses enough of a reputation that no one would think to rob him. It could be someone like me out there, looking for a warm, dry place to sleep for the night. Whoever it is, I'm about to find out.

I push the door open slowly and peer through the crack, seeing the back of a man dragging something from the far end of the gym toward me. I can't see what he's dragging or what he looks like. There are only a few running lights on so he's mostly shadowed. He's broad in the shoulders and a good foot taller than me. I'll have to surprise him to maintain the upper hand. When he's about twenty feet away from me, I step lightly into his path. As he's about to run into me, I take my opportunity.

"Don't move," I warn menacingly as he comes to a halt. Before he can turn around I press the tip of my blade in the center of his spine. He stays stock still at the sensation.

"Down on your knees," I order. He complies quickly, keeping his hands raised on either side of his head. With him on his knees, he no longer has a size advantage over me. I stay silent for a long moment and then rip his head back with my left hand on his forehead, crushing it into my bare chest and pressing my blade to his fully-exposed neck.

"What are you doin' here?" I ask in a whisper.

"You could ask nicely without the blade, girly," he responds in a cocky tone. Yeah, that's not going to work with me.

"I could just slit your throat and go back to reading." I press the blade into his skin, drawing the slightest glimmer of blood.

"Okay. I'm here for Ian," he responds more respectfully, not even wincing at his wound.

"Ian's not here and fighters aren't supposed to be here right now, so try again." I pull his forehead even harder, avoiding his eyes with my hand covering his brow.

"I'm here for Ian," he repeats in a calm tone. Why is this dude not afraid I'll kill him?

5

"We seem to be havin' a communication issue. Ian's not fuckin' here. So why are you?"

"He asked me to come by. I'm here." He shrugs. He SHRUGS! I'm a little mindfucked right now.

"You can wait outside for Ian if you want. Not in here. I'll walk you out." Those words sound nice, but my tone is far from it.

"Ian didn't want me to wait outside. He asked me to meet him in his office. I'll go up there," he says flippantly. Death wish for sure with this guy.

"You'll stand up. I'll keep my blade at your spine. You'll go outside. Ian gets here he can decide what to do with you. Tell me you understand and I'll let you up."

"I understand. Do you always walk people outside with your tits out?" I see the corners of his mouth turn up and realize this guy thinks he has the upper hand and is quite possibly some freak who's turned on by knife play and a half-naked woman. I bet he's hard right now.

"I don't have time for this shit. Easier to kill you and let Ian clean up the damn mess. Nice talkin' to you," I say in a completely civil tone. I move to drag my blade across his throat.

"QUINN!" Ian screams from the door into the gym. I snap my gaze to him as he runs toward me. I halt my execution based on the crazed look on Ian's face; he doesn't want this mess in his gym.

"Quinn, let him go. I asked him here. He's a little early. Let him up," Ian orders softly, trying to placate my mood. I hold his gaze a moment longer before releasing my captive. He stands up slowly with his back still to me as I cross my left arm across my boobs so he doesn't get a free show. I'm covering the essentials but there's a lot spilling over and under my arm.

"Quinn, you okay?" Ian asks as the other guy turns around. I get a good look at his face now. He is definitely a fighter. There are scars under his eyes, above his brow and one just brushing his top lip. His eyes are a murky blue and there is a bump on his nose from a break at some point. Square jaw and deep lines around his mouth, he's a lethal killing machine. I'd know that face anywhere. Even his espresso colored hair, that's not long enough to style with product and not short enough to be buzzed, looks angry and perfectly disheveled.

After studying him, I realize that even though his face is worn and marred he's gorgeous. Aren't they all? Not that I give a shit. He could be a Calvin Klein model and I wouldn't react. A woman in my position can't...ever.

"I'm fine," I reply confidently to Ian. I am fine. This is not the first time I've been in this situation and this won't be the last. The life I live on the streets demands that I be this person. I've had to become her...I like being her.

"You wanna go get some clothes on?" Ian prompts. I nod and turn on my heel to return to the locker room. Once inside, I check the dryer and my clothes are finally done. I pull on my underwear and bra before covering myself in long underwear, cargo pants, a black thermal, a hoodie and my biker boots. I fold the other two outfits I have, which are much the same, and stuff them in my bag with my book and a few food items I have with me. I slide my blade into its sheath and attach it to the back of my pants. I flip my head under the hand dryer, getting as much moisture out of my hair as possible. After a long while, my hair is almost dry. I check myself in the mirror and see cold, lifeless crystal blue eyes staring back at me. Good to go.

Chapter 2

Kieran

"Sorry 'bout that," Ian apologizes after G.I. Jane enters the locker room.

"Quite the welcoming committee," I snark, reaching up to inspect my wound. It stings, but it's nothing I haven't dealt with before. I step around the tire I was dragging through the gym before that tiny ninja attacked me.

That chick was impressive. I didn't even know she was in the room before I felt her blade in my back. I know one other person with skills like that...Shannon. I've got to be the only motherfucker in the world to meet two women with abilities like that. This one's different from Shannon though.

Shannon Kelly is a woman I've admired and loved since she was seventeen. I met her after a piece of shit and his buddy conspired to rape her at a college party my cousin, Brian O'Sullivan, was having at his house. Once Brian and his roommates were done with the rapist and his pal, I cleaned up the mess. One of the best nights of my life.

When Shannon was eight, her father, the former State's Attorney, was killed in a hit carried out by the mob ordered by a crazy fucking politician here in Chicago. She was in the car when the hit was executed and her uncle faked her death to keep her safe. This is a fact we just learned when the same crazy fucking politician had Shannon kidnapped to get information from her about the hit and other incriminating evidence he believed she had about him and his connections to organized crime. It was a shitstorm within a clusterfuck to get her back safe and sound. But she's back now and facing a new landslide of whacked-out.

Shannon's uncle was some sort of super-soldier and he trained Shannon from the time she was little to become her own version of a killing machine. And that's what she is. The fight that Shannon has is innate, intuitive. Her abilities are so ingrained it comes as easily as breathing to her. I swear she's calmer with a gun in her hand than she is taking a bubble bath. This chick with the knife to my throat has been forced to be what she is. It makes her no less deadly than Shannon, but somehow softer. There was a tremor in her hand as she held the blade.

"Quinn can be a bit much. Sorry, Kieran," Ian says looking at the slice in my neck. "Let's clean that up." I nod and we head to the locker room as Quinn comes out.

"Thanks, Ian," she says politely, moving past us like I'm not in the damn room.

"Quinn, don't take off. We need to talk," Ian orders in his gruff voice. She turns and offers him a glare that's piercing and cold. Her eyes are ice blue surrounded by long dark lashes. Her long hair is pure black and contrasts her pale skin. Her lips are plump, full, bow shaped pillows. Highest ass cheek bones I've ever seen and a perfectly small, sloping nose. She can't be more than an inch over five feet and ninety pounds soaking wet. This chick is a knock out. Fuck me running.

"Ian," she growls cutting her eyes to me. If looks could kill I'd be in tiny pieces dotted around the gym.

"Christ, Quinn, you almost slit his throat. Don't fuckin' leave," he bites out and stomps into the locker room leaving me with my would-be murderer.

"Sorry about scarin' you," I apologize in a kind tone, as kind as my whiskey and tar voice can be.

"I bet," she quips.

"I'm Kieran Delaney," I offer, moving my hand out in front of me. Her knife is out and at the ready before I can take a full step toward her.

"Whoa, whoa killer. I was just introducin' myself."

She studies me for a long time before returning her knife to her back. This chick is high strung!

"You still fight?" she asks pointedly, nodding toward my haggard face.

"Rarely, mostly just arrange fights, manage fighters, shit like that." I have no idea why I just told her that. I don't usually tell perfect strangers that I'm a criminal two seconds after being threatened with a knife. If she's here with Ian, she knows the business, so it shouldn't be an issue. She's obviously not a cop. What's the harm?

She doesn't respond, just bores into me with those crystal blue eyes. Ian breaks the tense stare down as he comes out of the locker room. He approaches me and wipes the blood away with an antiseptic wipe and then slathers ointment over the wound. It'll leave yet another scar and a pretty good story to follow it.

"Quinn, you gonna quit lookin' at him like that any time soon?" Ian questions her with a stern tone.

"I'm ready to head out, Ian. I'll see you around sometime," she dismisses him and avoids the question.

"Quinn, hold up," Ian says, almost defeated in tone. I've never heard that tone from him in the last almost twenty years I've known him. Who the fuck is this chick?

"Go on up to the office and crash on the couch. No one'll bother you. You can get a good night's rest. It's snowin'."

"I'm good. Thanks, though. It was nice to get cleaned up a bit." With a ragged sigh the old man drops his shoulders and watches that tiny thing walk out the back door into the alleyway.

"She live close by?" I ask, knowing there's no way she does. There's nowhere near here to live.

"You could say that," Ian replies in a grunt, rubbing his mostly bald head vigorously. "That girl is a pain in the fuckin' ass!"

"I noticed." I chuckle a bit thinking about calling Shannon to tell her about my assault. She'll laugh her ass off and she could use a laugh right about now.

"She's gonna freeze to death one of these nights." Ian's comment pulls me out of my chuckle and I scowl.

"Why would she freeze to death?"

"She's homeless. Sleeps on the streets most nights. Sometimes she goes to shelters, but it's rare. Even rarer I can convince her to stay here, but she'll only sleep on the couch in my office. Won't even consider one of the bedrooms." Ian's staring at the backdoor like she'll magically appear if he keeps his eyes locked there long enough.

She's homeless? She'll definitely freeze to death. It's February in Chicago and she's a fucking twig. My stomach rolls with discomfort at the thought. That's a sensation I've only had a handful of times in my life, always surrounding Shannon and her safety. Shit.

"Where will she go tonight?" I growl. Ian quirks an eyebrow at my tone. I'm shocked as hell at it too.

"Don't know. She won't tell me where she goes and I've never been able to keep tabs on her. She's like a fuckin' ghost out there."

"I'll be right back."

I make my way out the back door and see her tracks leaving the alleyway in the freshly fallen snow. As I follow them, I pick up my pace a little. She's got a few minutes head start on me, but she's short and I'm covering her tracks quickly. I get to the street and see her a block and a half down. My car is parked in front of me so I hop in and roar in her direction. It's almost 1:00 am and we're in the old packing district. She's the only person on the street. I come to a screeching halt on the sidewalk right in front of her. Quinn stumbles a bit but has her knife drawn as I scissor out of the Camaro.

I tip my lips in a cocky smile. I can't help it. Seeing her all riled up makes me smile. I'm a sick fuck and I don't claim to be otherwise.

"Get in," I say nicely.

"Fuck you," she responds harshly.

"Maybe some other time, Shorty."

"How 'bout I fuck you with my friend here," she nods at her knife, "and we call it even?"

"As nice as that sounds, I'm not into that weird shit you chicks read in crappy romance novels. Get in the car," I say a little more sternly.

"You deaf?"

13

"Look, I can see you're hell bent on bein' tough as nails and all that but come the fuck on. It's cold and snowin' and blowin' like crazy out here. Don't be stupid and get your ass in the fuckin' car."

"Wow. You're seriously determined to get stabbed tonight. Unfortunately, I don't feel like gettin' messy so just move along, Kieran," she sneers my name.

"Get. In. The. Fucking. Car."

She starts walking away backwards with her knife still aimed at me. She's not wearing gloves so her hands are probably starting to ache from the cold. If I can wait her out until they're numb I can get the knife from her. I could get it now, but I'd probably hurt her and I don't hurt women.

"Quinn," I warn. "If you make me chase you it's not gonna be pretty."

"If you chase me I'll try to make your death as clean as I can so you can be as pretty as you are now in your casket."

She's still moving backward as she threatens me. I'm getting annoyed now and a little bored. I can only be held at knife point so many times in one night and I think I've hit my threshold. Quinn notices my patience is running thin and tips a knowing smirk at me. She is sexy as hell.

I quickly advance on her and grab her wrist as she thrusts the blade toward me. Too easy to disarm her. It took half a second. My side shrieks in pain as Quinn plunges a smaller blade just under my ribs and stares me in the face as I gasp in a deep breath. I stumble back and fall to the ground, shaking my head in disbelief.

She squats down and washes the blood off her smaller blade with the snow on the ground, stands up without looking at me and walks off in the same direction she was originally headed. That's the last vision I have of Quinn before I pass out on the sidewalk like a pussy.

Chapter 3

Quinn

I move quickly down the sidewalk before beginning to wind and weave myself between buildings and alleys. I know Kieran's not coming for me, but I need some distance. When I've put a good three miles between us I stop at a dumpster and puke my guts out. My whole body is shaking from head to toe like I'm having a seizure. I wish I could be as cold and unfeeling as I want, but I'm not. I don't want to kill or threaten people, but I do it and I do it well. When I have to act out as the animal I've become I always get sick afterward. A little piece of me dies every time and is expelled in vomit.

Once my stomach is settled I press myself between two brick buildings, dragging my bag at my side. Only someone my size or smaller could fit in this crevice. After I smash my way through I find the small clearing at the back. The two buildings should have been attached when they were built, but some idiot decided to build them side by side instead. The dark, smoky brick building is about ten feet shorter than the light grey one leaving a small area for me to hide out where another building backs up to it. It's like living in a grain silo.

I spend most of my time here. I've never seen another person try to get back here and my stuff is always left alone. I still don't spend more than a few hours at a time in my silo, but I generally come back once a day to sleep. I'm protected from the elements with a tarp I've attached overhead and I'm safe with a heavy wooden door I dragged back here years ago that I use to cover the small entryway.

I drop my bag and heave the heavy door into place before I unwrap my foam mat and sleeping bag. These two items were expensive and my one splurge I allow myself every few years. I'm not homeless due to circumstance; I'm homeless because it's the only way. I had choices years ago when this all started and I didn't like my options, so I chose a new one...alone.

There are parts of my old life that I miss. Family and friends are at the top of that list until I remember the people that I thought were my family and friends turned out to be something completely different. I didn't grow up in a suburban wonder filled with picket fences and puppies. I grew up in a criminal family, a connected family. My father dealt with finances for organized crime my entire life. My mother's entire family was part of an Irish gang that ran drugs and guns.

So my upbringing was different from most. My parents kept me sheltered from everything in the "normal" world. I wasn't rolling around on the floor while junkies were snorting lines off my coffee table or anything like that. But people gave me a wide berth in the streets just based on my name alone. The only friends I had were children who were connected to the same crime families as mine. It was insular and confining, but I always felt safe and loved...until I wasn't.

I snuggle into my subzero sleeping bag and zip myself in, burrowing my slight body down as far as I can. The walls around me break all of the wind so I only have to battle the cold and snow which I've found is pretty easy at this point with the right gear. I'll sleep for about four hours and then I'll move again. I'd love to know what a good night's sleep feels like. I can't even remember. It's best not to remember.

I wake up to the sound of scratching at my door. I begin to measure my breaths, but the sound comes again before I can draw a single lungful. I scramble quickly out of my sleeping bag, clutching my knife, and move to the door. I lean my head against it. Crying. I hear a baby crying. I quickly heave the door to the side and stumble back at what I find.

A little boy covered in filth and hardly any clothes, clutching a tiny baby wrapped in newspaper to his chest.

"Please help my sister," he squeaks, handing the baby to me. I look down the long gap between the buildings and see nothing but falling snow. Turning my gaze back to the boy I pull him into my space, drag the door back in place and grab the baby from him.

"Where's your mom?" I ask him as I unwrap the newspaper.

"She's taking a long sleep in heaven. She told me to find you and you would help," the boy responds. I furrow my brow as I think about what he just said and examine the baby. She's a newborn, still bloody, with her umbilical cord attached and closed off with a shoelace. She's squealing weakly and turning a little blue from the cold.

I keep her in the crook of my arm and dig through my backpack for clothes to wrap her in. I pull out my hoodie and wrap her snugly before climbing into the sleeping bag with her clutched to my chest. I hold the edge up and indicate with my head for the boy to climb in. He's got to be freezing too. He scampers to me and snuggles himself into my arms alongside his sister. I hold them close to me for a long time before I start to doze off myself.

I wake up when the baby wiggles beneath my hand. She's hungry. I have no way to feed her. I need to get them to a shelter or a hospital. It's too cold to drag them around the city with me to get them safe, though. I need to ask this boy some questions to see what I'm up against.

"Hey bud," I say quietly, rubbing his back. His skin is warm to the touch which is a whole lot better than what it was a few hours ago.

"Yeah?" he squeaks, peeling his eyes open.

"My name's Darcy. Can you tell me your name?" I whisper because the baby's back asleep.

"Jack. That's Ashling," he says, pointing a boney finger at his sister. Two Irish names. I tuck that piece of information away for later.

"What happened to your mom, Jack?"

"She did something bad. Then Ashling came and mom told me to find you. She said that you wouldn't hurt us and you wouldn't let the bad guys get us. Then she went to sleep and got really cold so I left and found you." This kid has seen too much of the world already and he can't be that old.

"How old are you Jack?"

"Six."

Jesus Christ! That's too damn young to have watched your mother die and take care of a newborn. There are adults who couldn't do that. I pull him into me and hold him for a long while.

"I don't think I knew your mom, Jack. I know I've never met you. How did you find me?"

20

"I used to watch you in the park sometimes. My mom did, too. You don't take the bad medicine and you don't let the men touch you. When I asked my mom why she couldn't be like you she said she didn't know how to be that way," he says honestly with a shrug. He doesn't seem to miss his mom. I'm guessing she wasn't much of a mother for him to miss.

"Mom made some of the men mad before Ashling came. She told me that they wanted the baby and that I had to make sure they didn't get her. You won't let them get her will you, Darcy?" he asks with a small amount of terror in his eyes.

"No, Jack. I won't let anyone get either of you," I promise confidently. "Let's get up and find somewhere warm. You think you're up for a walk?" He nods and climbs out of the sleeping bag.

Jack said he's six but he's a bag of malnourished bones. I wouldn't have thought he was more than three until he spoke. He has on two different shoes that are riddled with holes. His pants are thin and threadbare, two sizes too small. The shirt he's wearing looks like a pajama top, thin stretchy jersey with the Incredible Hulk on the front. It's also too small. He has no coat, gloves or hat. He might as well be naked out here. And he's dirty and smells like you wouldn't believe. There is so much dirt caked on him, I can't be certain what color his hair is. His eyes are bright blue, almost the same as mine. This is a good thing because if I can pass him off as mine I won't get as many looks as we move through the streets this morning.

I lay Ashling down in the sleeping bag and crawl out. Digging through my backpack I find the wet wipes, a granola bar and my last hoodie. I tear open the bar and pass it to Jack who attacks it like a shark. When he's done, which is about ten seconds after I give it to him, I pull him over to me and start washing his face. I can tell by the look on his face no one has ever done this for him. A simple act that mothers do every day for their children, Jack has gone six years without experiencing. As I wipe the dirt away tears spill over, running down his cheeks. I offer him a sad smile and keep rubbing away the tears and the grime.

Once I have his hands and face as clean as I can get them I pull the hoodie over Jack's head and pull the hood up, securing it tightly with the strings. It reaches his knees, but that's a good thing because his clothes are covered in blood and afterbirth. With most of his body covered and just his eyes popping out beneath the hood, Jack really could pass as my son.

I take Ashling out of the wet hoodie and wrap her in my remaining dry thermal. I bag the wet and dirty clothes in a plastic sack, shoving it to the bottom of my bag. Then I put Ashling in the backpack, zipping it most of the way up until only her head is poking out. I put the backpack on backwards so it's hanging from my chest and then zip my coat around it. No one will be able to see Ashling and she'll be warm. I also have my hands free to hold onto Jack and access my knife if needed. It's almost four miles back to Ian and he's the only person I can go to. If I killed Kieran last night, I may no longer be welcome, but I have to take the chance. I need more information on who these kids are in danger from before I make any other moves.

"All right, Jack. It's a long walk where we're goin'. If you need a break you just say the word, okay?" I reach my hand down and he wraps his tiny fingers around mine tightly.

"You won't leave me, right, Darcy?" he asks in a whimper. I crouch down in front of him, supporting the backpack with one hand. His giant blue eyes shimmer at me, holding tears at bay.

"I promise I won't leave you, Jack. I will keep you and Ashling safe. You can trust me. I need you to do something for me, though," I say softly, trying to convey with my face that I'm as trustworthy as he needs me to be. I may be willing to maim and murder to keep myself out of fucked up situations, but I'd do more than that to keep these kids safe.

"What?" he asks sheepishly. I can only imagine the tasks the people in his life have asked from him. The wariness on his face tells me there's beyond-dark shit lurking in his mind. I offer him a comforting smile and run the back of my frigid fingers down his still dirty cheek.

"If anyone asks, you tell them I'm your mom. When we're around other people, you call me Mom, not Darcy, okay? It's the best way I can keep you safe, Jack."

He regards me for a moment before responding.

"Okay, Mommy," he whispers and reaches around my neck for the tightest hug I've ever received. He called me Mommy...not Mom. Jack called his mother Mom. I don't know if he's using a different word to be respectful or if the softness I've shown him has won me that title. I don't give a shit, either. When he said that word, something bloomed in my chest that I haven't felt in my adult life...hope.

Chapter 4

Quinn

It took three hours to make the journey to Ian's gym. There's over a foot of snow on the ground, making it a rough walk. We had to stop for Jack a lot and I carried him on my back for the last mile. My arms are shaking and I'm starting to feel exhaustion take over my body. I'm fighting through it though, because I need to be on my toes right now. I've never come to Brogan's during the day and I can tell it's busy inside. There's no way to contact Ian so I have to just go in and find him. Walking into a gym full of training fighters at noon on a Saturday seems really stupid right now, but I have no other options. I need to hide Jack as much as I can, so I improvise.

"Jack, I'm gonna take off my coat and I want you to climb on my back. When I put my coat back on I want you to snuggle against me and hide in that big hood, okay?" He nods as his little chin chatters loudly.

Jack quickly climbs on my back and helps me get the coat around us. I struggle to fit the coat around Ashling, but after four tries I get it zipped up. I pull the drawstring at the bottom of my coat as tightly as I can and Jack relaxes down into the edge it creates. I have my arms free this way. The coat won't hold him long, but it will be enough to find Ian without much issue.

I push the door open and I'm smacked in the face with the smell of blood and sweat. Jack is completely hidden under my hood so I know he won't see anything

25

traumatizing. I walk quickly toward the stairs that lead to Ian's office, hoping that he's in there. I make it no more than a few steps before a glistening mountain of man steps in my path. I have access to my knife, but I can't really fight him off here in the gym where I spy at least thirty other men. Play it cool.

"Where you headed?" he asks, looking at the weird bumps protruding from my front and back. He studies me long and hard before returning his eyes to me with a questioning gaze.

"I'm here to see Ian. Is he up in his office?" I use the sweetest, most polite voice I can muster and flash him the sexiest smile I can fake. I'm not adept at either, but I'm improvising.

"I'll take you to him," the mountain responds, staring at my back again as Jack wiggles a bit. I act like there's nothing to be seen and start walking toward the office again.

"He's not up there, sweetheart. Follow me," he orders and grabs my hand. I want nothing more than to snatch it back and knee him in the balls for touching me, but obviously I don't. The mountain winds and weaves through the gym as all eyes focus on me, many glaring, others just curious. I step a little closer to the mountain to avoid eye contact with any of them.

Finally, the mountain stops outside a large metal door and knocks twice loudly. Jack jumps at the sound and I rip my hand from the mountain to steady Jack on my back. The mountain looks down and gently peels back the hood to reveal Jack. I quickly spin around to keep Jack shielded by my body and the wall that's now at my back. I grasp my knife in my cargo pocket, readying myself for whatever is going to happen. I know I can't fight him, but I could play the super-crazy-knife-wielding lady card.

"Mommy," Jack whimpers.

"It's okay, Baby. Everything's okay," I console him, keeping my hand on my still hidden knife while staring down the mountain. The mountain looks concerned and a little freaked out that I'm hiding a child under my coat. Ashling starts to cry and the mountain's eyes bug out of his head. Yeah, we're quite the sight.

"Are you okay?" the mountain asks with sweet concern in his voice.

"I need Ian," I say in a feigned sob. If I know anything it's that men don't do well with emotional women. His eyes flare and he pounds the door again. After a few beats I hear it slide inches off to my right.

"What, Connor?" Ian growls.

"Girl here for you, boss," Connor replies, indicating in my direction with his big green eyes.

The door moves a little and then Ian spots me.

"Quinn. Christ, Quinn, are you okay?" His voice is panicked as he grabs my shoulders, staring into my icy blues with his honey glazed eyes. I nod sharply as Ashling lets out another scream. Ian's brow furrows at the sound. He reaches out and unzips my coat just enough to see her head and sucks a breath sharply between his teeth.

"Mommy?" Jack says in a shaky voice. Ian takes a step away from us at the sound of Jack's voice.

"Jack, we're fine. Uncle Ian's here now," I say, staring Ian down, trying to get him to play along and catch on quick.

"Connor, clear the gym out and then come back here with Owen," Ian instructs harshly, never looking away from my face.

"You got it, boss," Connor responds and turns on his heel back into the gym area.

"Come on," Ian growls at me, leading me through the metal door. On the other side I realize it's some type of therapy room, tables and medical supplies everywhere. I head to the first table and lean against it so Jack is supported and I can get my coat off. Once I peel us out of the coat I quickly spin around, pick Jack up on my hip, and he snuggles into my neck, placing one little hand on his sister's head.

"Quinn, sweetheart, what's goin' on?" Ian asks in an almost pained voice.

"A lot, Ian. I need you to help me. I'm sorry to come here like this in the middle of the day. You don't owe me any favors, but I don't have anywhere else to go. Will you please help us?" I plead. I fucking plead, because if he says no I don't know what I'll do.

"You know I'd do anything for you. What do you need?"

I feel my whole body relax and I lean against the table behind me. Jeez, I'm tired.

"I need a lot, but right now I need baby supplies, clothes for Jack, food and a shower."

"Done. I'll send the boys out to get stuff when they come back here. You're safe here, Quinn. I'll be right back."

Ian slides the metal door open before slipping through it and pushing it shut with a soft click of the latch. The gym sounds quieter now than when we arrived, even behind the closed door.

"Mommy, I thought your name was Darcy," Jack murmurs into my neck.

"It is, Jack. My name's Darcy Quinlan, but people call me Quinn. You doin' okay?"

"I need to go to the bathroom."

I push off the table and move to the back of the room hoping there's a bathroom back here. There are two doors at the end of the room. I choose the one on the left. When I push it open it's pitch black, so I search for a switch with my hand. A click sounds within the room and a lamp illuminates the room.

"You come to finish the job, Shorty?" Kieran calls out from a bed at the end of the room. Shit!

"Is there a bathroom back here?" I ask blankly, avoiding his question. Kieran sits up on his elbows and takes in my appearance of being covered in children. He doesn't answer, just points at the door across from his bed. I step in the room and quickly make my way to the door. I go in with Jack and flip the lock. He does his business and then reaches up for me to carry him again. There's a large tub-shower combo in here so I decide to get him clean first.

"Wanna take a bath?" I ask through a huge smile.

"What's a bath?" he asks curiously. My stomach drops as I realize this child has never had a bath. He doesn't even know what one is.

"I'll show you."

I lead him over to the tub and turn on the taps, getting the water nice and warm before plugging it. As the water fills, Jack's beautiful blue eyes get huge with wonder.

"It's like a fountain," he whispers, turning to me with a giant smile.

"Can you get out of your clothes on your own? I can step outside if you want." I don't want to make him uncomfortable. I don't really know the rules about naked kids and strangers, but I'm guessing I should give him some privacy. Jack pulls my hand roughly, glaring harshly at me.

"You promised," he growls.

"Jack, I'm not leavin' you. I was just gonna give you some privacy if you want it." He furrows his brow and I realize the concept is lost on him. "Are you okay if I stay in here while you take a bath with no clothes on?"

"You won't let those men in here to hurt me right?" he asks, turning his gaze to the ground, embarrassed. I quickly tip his chin up to look in my eyes.

"No one will ever hurt you again," I say in a fiercely protective growl.

"Okay," he whispers and the edge of his mouth curves, puckering a cute dimple. I smile and rub my thumb across it. He quickly peels out of his clothes and I see my fears for him come to life. There are scars on his body from what I'm guessing are cigarettes being put out on his skin. He has rashes all over from not being washed regularly. There are bruises of finger prints on his arms, legs and hips. If I ever find who did this to him, I'll slit their fucking throat.

I pull myself together and help him climb in the bath. The relief and excitement that beam from him brings tears to the back of my eyes, but I squash them quickly.

"This is so cool!" he squeals.

"I know!" I respond with the same amount of enthusiasm.

I pull Ashling out of the backpack. She doesn't look good. She's limp and her skin is yellowing. I need to feed her. There's a soft knock at the door and Jack jumps, throwing his body into the corner of the tub, shielding himself as best he can.

"Jack, you're safe. It's just Uncle Ian," I coo softly. His gaze leaves the door, but he doesn't move.

"Yes," I call out to the knocker.

"Quinn, you okay?" Ian questions.

"Kids needed a bath. We're fine. I really need to feed the baby, Ian. She doesn't look good. Can you get me some bottles and formula really fast?"

"I already sent Owen and Connor out to get stuff. I'll tell one of 'em to hightail it back. Should I call someone?"

"NO!" I yell making both kids jump. "No, don't call anyone," I say softer.

"Okay. Can you tell me what size clothes Jack needs?"

I look at Jack who has gone back to sliding around in the bathwater which is now a dirty grey color.

"Four year old size stuff," I guess. I have no clue.

"On it. There's towels and stuff in there. Just come out when you're all done."

"Yup."

I take Ashling over to the sink and warm the water up. Once it's warm I wet a washrag and clean her all

31

over. I don't know if I can submerge her so I don't risk it. She wakes up and starts rooting around. I stick a clean wet rag near her mouth and she sucks it back. I'm sure I shouldn't be giving her water on a rag, but it's all I can do right now.

As she suckles away her little eyes open up and they're the same piercing blue as Jack's...and mine. It's like they were sent to me on purpose. I don't believe in stuff like that, but damn if that's not the feeling I have coursing through my veins right now.

I wrap Ashling in a towel and go back over to Jack. He's as happy as a clam in this tub. Best thing my eyes have seen in eight years, maybe in my entire twenty-six years of life, actually.

"Hey, Jack. Let's let the water out and give you a shower. Then we can eat," I prompt, expecting a fight. He nods happily though. I drain the tub while he watches the water funnel down with amazement on his face.

"I like it when you call me Baby," Jack admits quietly. I smile broadly as I turn the showerhead on.

"Okay, Baby," I say softly and his face lights up brighter than the sun. I squirt some soap in his hand while supporting Ashling up against my chest with one arm.

"Scrub-a-dub," I instruct. He goes about scrubbing and wincing as the soap stings his rashes, but he never complains. He rinses off and I make him repeat the process one more time, helping him scour his scalp. His hair has a slight curl and it's shaggy around his face. It's been cut before or, I should say, hacked. I'll cut his hair later. Now that it's clean I can tell his hair is almost as dark as mine. Ashling's fuzzy head is also sporting dark curls. If someone out there is trying to send me a sign that these children belong with me, I'm starting to get it.

I turn the water off and gently pat Jack dry before wrapping him like a burrito. He looks up at me and I know he wants to be carried so I gather him up on my hip and stride out of the bathroom, both kids in my arms. I may be small, but I'm strong. I could do this all day if it brings them half the comfort it seems to.

I open the door and I'm met with the naked chest of Kieran Delaney. His ripped pecs and arms are covered in tattoos, mostly Celtic designs. There are a few scripts, though I don't chance trying to read them. A bandage stained with bright blood covering the wound I inflicted on him glares at me from beneath his ribs. I feel bad now, or I would if I had the energy.

"Need a hand?" Kieran asks softly. Jack nuzzles into me tightly.

"We're good," I reply in a soothing tone meant for Jack.

"Why don't you set them in the bed while I grab you all some soup?"

I hold his murky blue gaze for a long time before nodding. Why the hell is he being nice to the person that left him for dead twelve hours ago? My guess is he's plotting some type of revenge, though I can't imagine him actually harming me or the kids. Still, I don't trust him.

Kieran leaves the room and I climb in bed with the kids. I lay Ashling in my lap and pull Jack underneath my arm as I rest my back against the headboard. The room is basic beige with white linens and a honey-hued, wooden queen sized bed. There's a matching dresser next to the bathroom door with a TV on it. The bedside table is whitewashed with a lamp. Like I said, it's basic but comfortable.

I close my eyes for a moment when I hear Jack's light snoring. Just a few minutes of rest.

Chapter 5

Kieran

Quinn showed up here an hour ago strapped down with two kids like a fucking Sherpa. I didn't know she had kids and her body in no way indicates that she just gave birth. I'm at a loss here because the look in her eye is that of a protective mother bear. Jack clings to her as if his life depends on it, but that baby doesn't look good. Quinn probably didn't have any prenatal care and gave birth in an alleyway somewhere. No wonder she stabbed me instead of getting in my car. I'm a fucking prick, but tell me something I don't know.

I walk back in the room and all three are sleeping huddled together in the same space half of me would take up in the bed. These kids look just like their mother. Ice blue pools for eyes and raven hair. Fucking breathtaking. Jack wakes up when I set the tray of soup down on the dresser near the end of the bed. His piercing eyes cut to me and he further wiggles into Quinn's side. He's afraid of men and I'm a scary-looking man.

"Hey, Jack," I whisper. He starts to shake but holds my gaze like a brave little man. "You hungry? I made some chicken noodle soup for you and your momma. I bet if we're real quiet I can turn on some cartoons while we eat."

His eyes cut to the TV and then sharply back to me. He thinks I'm trying to bribe him so I can hurt him. My stomach turns at the thought of why he fears that.

"You excited about bein' a big brother?" I ask as I grab a bowl of soup and sit on the end of the bed with my back to the three of them. I turn on the TV and lower the volume to a slight hum before turning on some old-school cartoons. Jack doesn't respond so I go about eating and watching cartoons. My side is killing me, but I'm too stubborn to let that affect me. I changed the bandage after Quinn eyed it earlier and looked like she wanted to stab herself. She was protecting her kids...I don't blame her for stabbing me. I'd stab me too.

I feel the bed move behind me and keep my eyes trained on the TV. Wile E. Coyote is getting his ass handed to him as usual. Jack appears at my side, wary to get too near me. I lean forward, grimacing in pain, to grab him a bowl of soup and realize the bowl is damn hot and too big for him to hold.

"This bowl's real hot, Jack. I'll hold it and you feed yourself, 'kay?" I whisper while watching Roadrunner smash Coyote with a boulder. I chuckle and hear Jack giggle. Best fucking sound ever!

He scoots a hair closer to me and spoons a bite into his mouth. After the first spoonful the kid gets up on his knees, leans over the bowl and goes at it like a champ. Two minutes pass and he's scraping the bowl clean. I place the empty bowl back on the dresser and wince when I sit back a bit.

"You got a bad booboo, Mister," Jack says quietly.

"Yeah. I'm okay though." *Your mom stabbed me* didn't seem like the appropriate response. "You think your momma would let you have a cookie?" I finally turn to look at him and my breath hitches when I meet his eyes. This kid is gorgeous. That sounds like the girliest damn thing I've ever thought, but he is. He's still wrapped in a towel and shaking a little. I don't know if he's cold or scared.

"You cold, bud?" He nods. I want to scoop him to my side, but I'm pretty sure that'll get me stabbed again. I stand up and go into the bathroom to grab another towel. When I come back he's watching every step I take, cautious and curious.

"I'm gonna wrap this extra towel around you and then you can give me the wet one from underneath," I explain, taking a tiny step in his direction. His husky-like blue eyes cut through me, but he makes no move to avoid my advance. I reach around him, gently wrapping him in the dry towel and then quickly turn my back to give him privacy.

"Thanks, Mister," his voice shakes.

"I'm Kieran," I say before I turn back. He's holding out the wet towel, snuggling further into the dry one. I throw the wet one on the floor in the bathroom and then snatch a plate of Oreos from the tray before sitting down in my original spot. I hold the plate out the same way I did the bowl and Jack takes one quickly, giggling at the TV. He scoots closer to me as I peel an Oreo apart.

"Don't break the cookie!" he scolds under his breath.

"This is the best way, see?" I say, showing him the creamy inside before licking it clean. Once I have only the chocolate left, I dunk them in a glass of milk and pop them in my mouth. His eyes bug the fuck out and he takes another cookie, mimicking my way of eating it. When he's ready for the milk I see his hesitation because I'm resting the glass on my thigh. Before I can raise it for him he scoots against my side and plunges one half of the cookie in.

"See, the goal is to get it mushy without it falling off in the milk. It's like a game," I inform him. He concentrates hard and pulls out the cookie at what I recognize is the last second before disaster and pops it in his mouth. "You're a pro, Jack." He beams the brightest smile my eyes have ever seen before helping himself to another cookie and snuggling tightly into my side. I can't help it, I pull him closer with my arm around his shoulders and I feel him relax a fraction when I don't try to do some sick fucked up shit to him. When I find out who hurt this kid I'm beating him to a pulp and then feeding him his own dick before I piss in his gouged-out eye-sockets.

Jack finishes the plate of cookies in quick measure just as Ian, Owen and Connor walk in the room. He immediately cowers into my chest as they enter.

"You're safe here, bud. None of those guys are gonna hurt you. I promise," I whisper into his hair. I cut my eyes to the guys, warning them to tread lightly around this kid and they nod in acknowledgement.

Connor Doyle is a beast of a man. He's six-foot-three, 250 pounds of ass-kicking brutality in the ring. Never been beaten...never will be. Outside the ring, the guy's a pussy cat. His green eyes are in pain just watching the kid's reaction to him being in the room. Connor has a kind face with only one scar marring his right eyebrow and a buzzed blond head. He's the kind of guy that will walk your grandmother home just because.

Owen Doyle, Connor's younger brother, is a bit rougher. He's the mirror image of Connor other than he has brown eyes and no scar. Owen wouldn't walk your grandmother home, but he'd watch her at a distance until she made it there safely. They're good guys.

"Hey, Jacky," Ian calls out. "You like the Incredible Hulk?"

Jack looks up into my face for reassurance and I offer him a kind smile, letting him know he's safe.

"Yes," Jack whispers.

Ian walks over to the bathroom door and holds up a grey hoodie with the green man, himself, on the front. Jack perks up and gazes intently at Ian in anticipation of some bribe for pain. Rage bubbles within me again for the trauma this kid has endured.

"I got you some clothes. I'm gonna set 'em in the bathroom and you can go in alone and put 'em on. We'll wait out here to see how awesome they look."

Ian glides in the bathroom, flipping on the light, and comes back out a few seconds later with nothing in his arms.

"Kieran?" Jack questions his safety again with just my name.

"It's all good, bud. I can't wait to see the Hulk on you." He hesitates a moment and then scurries into the bathroom and locks the door. I drop my head in my hands after he leaves, willing the fury I have to calm the fuck down.

"Kid's terrified." Connor points out the obvious.

"No shit," I grunt, standing to join them near the door into the therapy room.

"So that's why she shanked your ass last night." Owen nods at my now-seeping bandage.

"I didn't know she was tryin' to get back to her kids. I feel like a fuckin' prick...more so than usual," I say as Ian pulls my bandage off and replaces it with a fresh one.

Ian found me passed out and brought me back here. He called a doctor that rolled in and stitched me up before I crashed in the back room. The blade she got me with was maybe three inches long and didn't do any real damage other than draining me of a lot of blood. The doctor gave me a transfusion, so all is well.

Owen and Connor start unloading the ridiculous amount of bags they have with them and I notice a snowsuit for the baby.

"You're not lettin' her take those kids back out on the streets are you?" I ask Ian in disbelief.

"Don't know that I got a lot of say in that one, Kieran."

"Fuck that shit. I'm not lettin' her outta here with those kids unless it's to a house with heat. Over my dead fuckin' body is she leavin' on her own."

"That can be arranged," Quinn's soft voice calls from behind me. Fuck.

"Where's Jack?" she asks sternly, cradling the baby to her chest and swinging her legs off the bed.

"He's gettin' dressed in the bathroom," Ian says gruffly.

"Thanks," Quinn responds, nicer than her earlier tone but only by a little bit. "Can you make Ashling a bottle?"

"Don't know nothin' about makin' bottles, Quinn. I'll hold her and you can do it. We got every kind of formula and bottle they had. Didn't know what we were doin'."

"I'll get her dressed quick first. You think you could trim her umbilical cord for me?"

Ian's eyes get big at the request, but he nods in agreement, moving into the therapy room to get some medical scissors. Ian comes back in the room with some weird plastic clamp thing and the scissors. I grab the diapers, wipes and a stack of clothes, following behind Ian back to the bed. Connor and Owen are hot on my heels.

Quinn lays Ashling down on the edge of the bed and unwraps her gently. The baby doesn't look good. Her skin is ruddy and she seems dehydrated, not that I know shit about babies.

"She's not lookin' good, Quinn," Ian whispers.

"Let's just get her dressed and fed," Quinn dismisses.

Quinn tags the wipes and diapers out of my hands and sets about wiping and diapering. She seems to know what she's doing so I just watch. Once Ashling's butt is covered, Ian slides over and clamps the plastic thing an inch or so above her belly on the umbilical cord which is easily a foot long and tied off with a shoe string. Ian cuts the excess and hands the remaining bit to Owen who quickly gets rid of it like it's going to bite him. Pussy.

Quinn grabs an outfit and hurriedly dresses Ashling in it. It's an all-in-one outfit for a boy. It's black with Brogan's emblazed on the front in Kelly green. The fighters put their boys in them as a sign of respect to Ian and his gym. Just as Quinn finishes the snap under Ashling's chin the bathroom door opens.

"Mommy," Jack calls quietly from the doorway, "I can't get the button."

"Okay, Baby," Quinn coos before striding over to him to button his jeans. "There you go. You look pretty good with the Hulk on your chest."

"I'd say that's the best the Hulk has ever looked," Connor compliments.

"You think?" Jack asks, dumbfounded by Connor.

"Yeah, I do."

"Cool." Jack tips the edge of his mouth and a small dimple appears. Quinn runs her thumb over it before standing and coming to collect Ashling. She scoops the baby to her chest and Jack reaches his scrawny arms up to be carried, too. Quinn's too little to be toting around two kids after giving birth a day ago. She pulls Jack up and sets him on her hip effortlessly.

"Kitchen?" she asks Ian. Ian lifts his chin for her to follow. The kitchen is in the room next to us, but you have to go through the therapy room to get there. We all follow Ian who grabs five bags of bottle-making shit on his way. When we get in the small kitchen, us guys start unpacking the bags waiting for instructions from Quinn.

"Says you need to sterilize the nipples in boiling water for two minutes," Connor reads the side of one of the bottle packages.

Quinn sets Jack down and starts rummaging for pans before Ian steps in for her. He fills the pan with water and sets it on the stove. Quinn spins around to the table and starts reading the formula package. I'm guessing she breastfed Jack and doesn't know how to make a bottle. Formula would be expensive for a homeless girl. She was maybe fourteen when she had him by the looks of her. She can't be over twenty years old.

After reading for a minute, Quinn's stomach rumbles something fierce.

"Hungry?" I ask kindly. She glares her icy blue eyes at me. She thinks I'm fucking with her.

"When's the last time you ate?" Ian demands at her side.

"Yesterday, I think."

"Fuck me," Owen says under his breath and moves quickly to the fridge. He pulls out stuff for turkey sandwiches and makes her one with speed and precision a Subway employee would be jealous of. When Owen puts the plate in front of her she pushes it in front of Jack for him to eat it.

"I fed him already," I inform her. She cuts her eyes at me again.

"He taught me how to eat magical cookies," Jack beams up at her. Before she can pull a knife on me for feeding her kid weed-filled cookies, which is what Jack made them sound like, I tell her, "I just taught him the proper way to eat an Oreo."

Quinn runs her fingers across his dimple again as the pan begins to boil. Ian drops the nipples in the water and we all stand and wait. As us guys are watching nipples boil, Quinn grabs a bottle that has no bottom and sticks a trash bag-looking thing into it. That's a weird fucking bottle. She scoops some formula into the bag and waits. After the two minutes pass Ian pulls the nipples out laying them on a clean dish towel next to the sink.

"Put the water back on the stove for me," Quinn instructs Ian softly. She moves to the sink and fills a measuring cup with water and then adds it to the powder. She shakes the shit out of it once she has the nipple screwed on tight. Moving to the stove, she plops the bottle in the water and stares at it. After a minute she pulls the bottle out, shakes it, and squirts some on her wrist. I guess she's happy with the temperature because she pulls out a chair and flops into in.

Quinn lays Ashling down across her chest and traces the nipple across the baby's lips. At first nothing happens and I feel panic creeping up my spine. If this baby won't eat, something is definitely wrong. Quinn tries again and Ashling thrashes her head back and forth a few times before pulling the nipple into her mouth and sucking greedily. The room relaxes.

Owen picks up his sandwich and holds it in front of Quinn's mouth. She leans forward, takes a bite and moans a little which makes my dick twitch. I'm an asshole.

Owen keeps feeding Quinn as she feeds Ashling. It's a pretty cute sight. All of a sudden, Jack is at my side. I sweep my arm around his shoulders and pull him into me. He's warm, finally.

"Can we go watch some more TV, Kieran?" he whispers.

"You'll have to ask your momma, bud."

"Mommy, can I go watch TV with Kieran?"

Quinn pins me down with her eyes, trying to figure out my game. Don't have one, sweetheart.

"Sure, Baby. We'll leave once you're done."

"Hey, Jack," Connor calls from next to me. Jack looks up at him, horrifyingly scared. "I bought us *The Avengers* to watch. The Hulk is in it. You think I could join you and Kieran with my brother Owen and we could watch it out on the big screen in the gym?"

Jack looks up at me with his big blue eyes for some guidance.

"It's a really good movie, bud. I think you'll love it," I encourage.

"Okay. Cool."

Connor just did something amazing for Jack. He took the pressure of being in a small room with unknown men out of the equation. The gym is a huge open space where Jack won't feel so enclosed, hopefully making him feel safer.

I pull my hand off Jack's shoulder to leave the room and Jack threads his hand into my palm. I grip him tightly and head out to the big screen. Connor and Owen follow a distance behind us, talking loudly so Jack knows right where they are. This kid is safe with us and now we're going to prove it to him.

Chapter 6

Quinn

As the door closes behind Owen, Ian starts in on me.

"Whose fuckin' kids are these?" he growls.

"Mine," I say defiantly.

"Bullshit and you know it."

"They're *mine* now and that's all that fuckin' matters, Ian."

"So you're gonna live on the streets with a newborn and a four year old in the winter?" he asks, disbelieving.

"Jack's six. He's small and malnourished."

"No shit. So you're just gonna keep him in that state, then?"

"I'll figure something out."

I have no clue what I'm doing. I didn't know how to do the diaper so I just copied the front of the package. I didn't know how to make a bottle so I read the instructions. I know there's no book on how to raise kids on the streets, though. I need a plan and quick.

"Quinn, it's February in Chicago. This baby doesn't look good already. How in the hell are you gonna make this work?" Ian scolds in his harsh gravelly voice.

"I promised Jack I'd keep him safe," I whisper as Ashling finishes her bottle.

"You need to burp her now," Ian instructs me. I know that.

"I know, Ian," I admonish him.

"You can stay here with the kids as long as you need. I'll keep the guys outta your hair. There aren't any fights scheduled this week. Just training."

Ian's wrinkly face is a mask of concern and pissed off. He always looks pissed off, so that's normal. I seem to be the only person that sees him concerned. I know he cares about me and would do anything for me, but even the great Ian Brogan can't keep me safe. He recognizes I'm about to fight him and says, "You owe these kids warmth. They've had a few hours with you and you've become their world. Give them a day of normal before you decide to drag them into the back of an alley again."

"Okay. But Ian, you have to keep the fighters away from us. No one can know we're here. I don't know what's goin' on, but Jack said his mother died and someone's lookin' for him and Ashling."

I continue to pat Ashling's back as Ian's face goes from perma-scowl to enraged. As you can imagine, the owner of an underground fighting gym has a vicious temper.

"So you're tellin' me there's someone out there in the streets lookin' for these kids and you mean to go out there and try to keep them safe and alive on your own? You're not that fuckin' stupid. There's no goddamn way I'm lettin' you back out there now. I'll put out some feelers and try to figure out where these kids come from and, until then, your ass stays here. Don't you dare try to fight me, Quinn, or I'll tie your ass to the bed," Ian growls.

He's right (that sucks). I can't pull knives on people with Ashling in my arms or Jack on my back. I should try to get them to a shelter, but I can't do that now. I may have only had these kids for a few hours, but they feel like mine. Call me crazy or delusional; I'll take on the title proudly. I have a large amount of money in a safe deposit box that I could use to buy us a little house and live off of. It's my father's money really, but he doesn't need it anymore. Problem is, I have no identification to access it. Also, walking into a bank and retrieving money from Patrick Quinlan's safe deposit box will raise more red flags than a hooker becoming a nun. I need to stay invisible. That's the only way to keep me and these kids safe.

"I'm too wiped to fight with you. I'll stay the weekend and figure something else out. I can't be here longer than that. It's not safe for you or us," I whisper as I rub sleeping Ashling's back.

"I'll take that for now. Quinn, I can keep you safe. Let me keep you safe, please."

Ian reaches his leathery wrinkled fingers to my cheek rubbing with the gentle caress of a loving parent. He's the only man who's ever touched me like that in a long time. It warms my soul.

"Okay," I acquiesce. He smiles broadly and drops his hand from my face and then scoops Ashling from my arms.

"I bought you some clothes, soap, hair shit and some toiletries. Why don't you go hop in the shower and I'll take Ash to her first action movie."

Seeing Ashling cradled against Ian's broad chest makes me realize she's really small. I start to worry about her health even more.

"Ian, do you think she looks smaller than normal?"

"Yeah, sweetheart. She's probably a little premature. Her breathing's okay, but she looks a little jaundiced. I'll have the guys get on the computer and see what we should do. If she needs a doctor I've got a guy I can call that'll keep quiet. Don't worry. You promised Jack you'd keep him safe, now believe me when I say I'll keep you safe. Go get a shower."

"Okay. Come get me if the kids need me."

I stand up and stretch my sore muscles. Being a mom is hard on your body, apparently. I move to the table and rummage around to find all the stuff Ian bought for me. It's too much. I'll never be able to carry all of this with me and he knows it. He was planning on keeping me here the moment I walked in with those kids hanging off my body.

"Thanks Ian...for everything," I whisper as I leave the room without looking at him. I'm feeling emotionally overwhelmed at this moment.

I peer into the gym to see Jack jumping around in front of the guys, acting out scenes from the movie. He looks so happy and I feel tears prick the back of my eyes. How can I force him to live on the streets with me after offering him this taste of normal? He deserves all of this and more. I'll clear my head in the shower and then come up with a plan to get my money. If I have that cash I can move us away from Chicago. I could take us across the country and better ensure our safety. It would mean leaving Ian, but he would understand once I explain.

I've never told Ian why I'm homeless or really anything about me. He's never pushed for the information, either. He's taken me at my word and left me to my own devices for the most part. Anyone who

50

has come across me in the last eight years could tell with one glance I'm a closed book. You're not getting anything out of me and if you push you'll never see me again. Ian respects my silence.

I move into the bedroom and then the bathroom. I crank up the hot water and let the room fill with steam as I peel my filthy clothes off. As I step into the stream I relish the burn just like I did last night. I can't remember the last time I had a shower twice in a twenty-four hour period. I'm back in my heaven. I don't take as much time as I usually would. I can take as many showers as I want while I'm here so I don't need to cling to every second of cleanliness.

I pour a huge palm full of milk-and-honey scented shampoo in my hand and lather away. I'll never be able to go back to the industrial combo again. My lungs inhale the fragrance deeply as it fills the air. I rinse and repeat like I'm in a TV commercial. Bliss.

I slather my head with matching conditioner and tear up at the realization I've not conditioned my hair in eight years. While the conditioner sits on my hair, I scrub my body with a loofa poof and a body wash that matches the fragrance of the hair care products. It smells like a honey farm in here. I scrub and buff every inch of skin and let a few tears finally fall. I'm relieved and terrified all at the same time.

What if I put the kids at further risk? Shit, I didn't think about that. I can't be the reason something bad happens to them. I need to get out of Chicago fast. I'll stay here the weekend and figure out a way to get into the bank. Ian will help me. I'll tell him my story and he'll help me get out of the city.

I rinse off my hair and body quickly and climb out of the shower. I dry off with the small towels and wrap my hair up in another one. I pull on clean underwear and a new sports bra Ian bought. Black yoga pants and a skin tight, pale blue, long sleeved shirt with some fuzzy socks and I'm good to go. I don't know where Ian shopped for me, but all the clothes are comfortable and fit me perfectly.

Ian also got me a blow dryer so I set about drying my hair. It's so long it takes forever to get dry, but once it does it lays flat, sleek and shiny from the conditioner, curling in soft rings at the end. I see a glimpse of the girl I used to be as I wipe the mirror clean. That girl is gone now, only her face remains.

There's a soft knock at the door.

"Yes?"

"Jack needs to go to the bathroom," Kieran calls from the other side.

"'Kay."

I scoop up my dirty clothes and open the door to be smacked in the face again with a shirtless Kieran Delaney. Good God, I'll never get used to that sight. I quickly avert my eyes by looking down at Jack.

"Hey, Baby. You go ahead," I coo. Jack wraps his arms tightly around my waist before moving into the bathroom. I close the door and hear a soft click as he locks it. Good boy.

"Thanks for...well...uh...thanks for helpin' out," I stutter and stumble with my words as I move around Kieran, keeping my gaze on the floor. I've turned into an idiot.

"Jack's a good kid. It's not a problem." Kieran moves to the bed and flops down, patting the spot next to him. I roll my eyes at his invitation. Sure, watch my son and

I'll hop into bed with you while he's in the bathroom. I don't think so. My son? Yeah, my son.

"Quinn, I'm sorry about last night. I didn't know you were tryin' to get back to your kids. Ian didn't tell me. I wouldn't have been like that if I knew. I'm an asshole, but I'm not that bad," Kieran says quietly, holding my eyes with his. This scary man is so gentle with me and the kids that it's throwing me off my game. I know I can't trust him. Kieran Delaney has a reputation that even I know. He's a talented fighter and has a way of getting information about any-and-everything. It's rumored he was a hit man for the same gang my mother's family ran, but I don't know for sure. I'll not be asking.

"I'm sorry, Kieran. You caught me at a bad moment. I'm not usually that stabby," I lie. I am sorry, but I'm always that stabby. I let my eyes wander to some of the script running around his chiseled torso. Just beneath his heart is *Dílseacht* ("loyalty" in Irish) with a strange four-leaf clover that looks like a Celtic knot dotting the *i*.

"Like what you see?" Kieran purrs. Yes. Who wouldn't? Not telling him that though.

"You speak Irish?" I avoid his come on.

"Nah. My grandparents did, so I know a bit. Do you?" he asks, rubbing his palm over his chest and the dilseacht tattoo I was just admiring. I force myself not to watch his hand.

I do speak Irish. Both of my parents were from Galway and spoke mostly Irish in the house. I'm definitely not telling Kieran that. Thankfully, Jack comes out of the bathroom before I have to lie.

"Mommy, Connor ordered us pizza!" Jack exclaims, hopping up on the bed next to Kieran.

"What kind of pizza did he order?" I ask with a smile on my face as Kieran sweeps an arm around Jack's shoulder.

"I don't know. He said it was the best in the city. You think it'll be good, Kieran?" He turns his big blue eyes up at Kieran's rough face.

"It'll be awesome, bud." Jack beams a smile at Kieran, puckering his dimple. Jack shifts his gaze back to me before announcing, "I got the prettiest mommy. Don't you think, Kieran?" I feel a flash of red creeping up my cheeks as I quickly spin around and pretend to be busy sorting my dirty clothes.

"She's gorgeous, Jack." The timbre of Kieran's voice vibrates in my chest and makes my cheeks flame that much more.

"I'm gonna go start some laundry. I'll be right back," I say quickly and flee from the room. That was fucking uncomfortable.

I take my time loading the laundry and getting my face back to a normal color. No one has called me gorgeous in the last eight years who hasn't wanted to rape me in an alley. It feels amazing to have a man say it just because he believes it's true. I'll take that compliment today. It feels good and I could use a boost right now. I'll need every good feeling I've got to make my way through what I'm planning to do.

Chapter 7

Kieran

Holy fucking shit! Quinn is a goddamn knockout. I thought she was before, but I know it for certain now. I don't have the words or the appropriate amount of blood servicing my brain (because it's in my cock) to describe how stunning she is. Her raven hair is smooth and shiny with little curls that skirt her waist. Her blue shirt is about two sizes too small based on the tight cling to her perfect tits. Who knew a girl that small could rock boobs that big? And those black pants sliding over her round hips and cupping her firm (I'm assuming) ass...I could die a happy man.

Unfortunately, she seemed horrified that I noticed and ran out of here like her hair was on fire. She just gave birth, not that anyone could tell, and I'm eye-fucking her in front of her son. I am a class act all the way. Shannon would take my balls for doing something like that. Quinn's not Shannon though. Quinn seems scared and vulnerable. I've never seen Shannon anything but rock solid and ready to blow someone's head off. But both of these women have a fight in them that is sexy as hell.

"Hey, Kieran?" Jack asks quietly, pulling me and my perverted dick back into reality.

"Yeah?"

"Would you teach me how to fight?" he asks, barely above a whisper.

"You're pretty little to learn how to fight, bud. Maybe in a few years."

His brow furrows and I see a spark of anger behind his icy blues. He is his mother's son.

"If I know how to fight, no one can hurt me again," he says in a growl. Okay, now I'm pissed and feel like growling back. I'm not pissed at him, obviously, but I feel the need to pound on something.

"I won't let anyone hurt you again, Jack. I promise you that," I say in a harsher tone that I wanted.

"You can't keep us safe," he scoffs pushing away from my side and climbing off the bed to face me. "My mommy says we're leavin' and you're not comin' with us. She has to take care of Ashling now so I have to take care of her. That's how it works."

"Jack—"

"You don't know how it is! If they find us they'll hurt us and take Ashling. That's what she told me!" Jack screams as tears stream down his face.

"Hey," I say calmly and reach toward him. He steps out of my reach and stumbles over a bag on the floor, crashing onto his ass as Ian enters the room. He pins me with a lethal gaze as he approaches Jack.

"Jacky, you okay?" Ian soothes, crouching down to him. Jack heaves himself into Ian's arms, almost knocking the old man on his ass. Ian's too tough for that, though.

"They're gonna kill us!" Jack wails. Ian holds him tightly to his chest and stands up with him shushing and rocking back and forth.

"It's okay. You're gonna be okay," Ian soothes. Owen and Connor walk in, probably having heard Jack's

56

hysterics. They both glare at me like I'm the fucking cause. I return their stares and that brings that shit to a screeching halt.

"Will you teach me how to fight?" Jack sobs to Ian. "If I can fight I can keep us safe this time."

I feel like I'm going to puke and, based on the looks on the guys' faces, I'm not alone in that sensation. I swear to everything on this planet I'll find out who hurt Jack and make him pay in the cruelest way I can imagine. Maybe I'll call Shannon and let her work her magic on the motherfucker. That's a fate worse than death in this world and she could use an outlet right about now.

"Jacky, can you tell me who hurt you?" Ian asks the question that we all want answered.

"No."

"Do you know who he is?"

"Yes."

"But you can't tell me?"

"No."

"Why not?"

"Because he's a bad man. He'll know if I tell and then he'll hurt us again. I promised I wouldn't tell."

Jack's crying is under control now, but his slight body is still trembling. I can feel myself pumping my fists and bouncing my knee. I need to hit something hard and soon.

"Jacky, you're safe here. I promise you that. I won't let anything happen to you, your momma, or Ash. If you tell me who he is I can make sure he never bothers you again." Ian's tone is sweet, but the look on his face is murderous.

"No, you can't. I want my mommy," Jacks says as he slides down Ian's body and then runs from the room to find the only place he feels safe...his mother's arms.

"Goddamn it!" Ian roars and plunges his fist through the wall. Good man.

We all sit in silence until Ian Brogan gets his wits about him. He may be pushing seventy but he's not to be fucked with...ever.

"I convinced Quinn to stay the weekend. It was like pullin' teeth, but she agreed. That means you three got a little over a day to bring me the piece of shit that tortured that kid. If there's some asshole out there tryin' to find them you should be able to find him," Ian growls.

"On it, boss," Connor answers and ambles out of the room with Owen at his side.

"I don't know her story, Kieran. It's not good. No, it's probably fucked up beyond belief, but I love that girl. I've been watchin' out for her for almost eight years now and I'll be damned if some motherfucker out there will hurt her. You pull every fuckin' string you've got and I'll owe you."

"Ian, you won't owe me shit. I'm glad you put your fist through the wall before I did. I need to go at the heavy bag...now. I'll call every low-life contact I've got and I'll find the guy. Why'd she only agree to the weekend?" I ask, standing up and moving to the therapy room.

I start wrapping my hands so I don't fuck them up too much. I'm hoping I can ruin them on some dude's face sooner than later.

"She doesn't feel safe in the gym when the fighters are here. I don't feel safe, either. She's too goddamned pretty for them to leave her alone. You know how those assholes are. Even if I gave a standing rule for her to be left alone, some dickhead would still try to get at her," Ian says in a snort.

"So put her up somewhere else."

"Quinn won't do it. Plus, I don't want her on her own with those kids. The baby's sick. She's got jaundice based on the shit Owen read on the Internet. I need 'em safe and this is the only place I can manage that on my own."

"I'll take 'em with me." The words are out of my mouth before I really think them through. Did I really just offer to take a young woman and her kids home with me? Sure the fuck did.

"Thanks for the offer, but I don't see Quinn agreein' to that," Ian grumbles.

"I don't give a shit what she agrees to. I'll strap her down and tote her ass with me. Jack is fuckin' scared outta his mind. Quinn's good with a knife on her own, but with Jack and a newborn…no way. She's not goin' anywhere alone."

I finish wrapping my hands and Ian slides some MMA gloves over my hands. I move into the gym to find Connor and Owen grappling on the mats. Apparently we all needed an outlet. I stalk past them and heave my fists into the heavy bag, causing it to take a wide swing. Ian grabs the bag and steadies it with his body as I go to work. I imagine the face of the sick fuck I'm about to hunt and allow my fury to unleash. If he hurt Jack, that means he hurt Quinn too, because there's no way in hell she would she let harm come to her son. That fuels me even further into the zone of untapped violence.

When my arms are like limp noodles I finally stop. I'm dripping with sweat and my stab wound feels torn wide open. I accept the pain. I find peace in this type of pain. As I step back from the bag I feel a small body leap onto my back as a blade is pressed to my neck.

"What did you do to my son?" Quinn seethes in my ear. "If you hurt him I swear I'll fuckin' gut you."

"Quinn," Ian warns, but he makes no move to intercede.

"I didn't hurt Jack. He asked me to teach him to fight so he could protect you. He got upset when I told him he was a little young to learn to fight," I explain softly.

Quinn's whole body is shaking and her breath is ragged. She's hanging on by a thread at this point. She's probably hormonal, too. Never a good time to piss a woman off.

"You didn't hurt him?" she asks with tears in her voice. Ah, fuck, if she starts crying I'm done for.

"I didn't hurt him," I soothe and run my hand along hers until she releases the knife to me. She slides off my back as I hand the weapon over to Ian.

I turn to face her and she collapses into my chest and sobs. I scoop her tiny body off the ground and carry her up to Ian's office. I'm guessing the kids are in the bedroom and they don't need to see their mother have a breakdown. Once we're in the office, I sit down on the world's oldest black leather couch and hold Quinn in my lap. She's still crying and has her arms wrapped tightly around my neck. I pull her closer to me—not that it's possible, since she's in my lap—and shush her while stroking her hair.

"There is no anguish of soul until one has children," she murmurs into my neck. An old Irish proverb I've heard more than once from my mother.

"Quinn, you're safe here. No harm will come to you or your kids. I promise you," I soothe into her raven hair.

She tips her head back, her ice blue eyes glistening from the tears. I rub my thumb across her cheeks to wipe away the stains. She looks terrified, just like Jack did earlier. I feel my inner caveman coming to life. I feel a primal need to take care of this woman and her children even though she clearly doesn't need me to. I think that's the most amazing part. I hate needy, clingy, weak women. I want a woman that can stand on her own and do her own dirty work, but lets me do it for her. I want Quinn to let me do this for her.

"Come home with me. Let me take care of you and the kids. Ian said you won't stay at the gym past the weekend and I can't bear the thought of you and those babies out in the streets. Please, for me. Come home with me," I plead. I fucking plead with a chick who has tried to kill me three times in one day to come home with me like my life depends on it. I've turned into some kind of pod person.

"I just threatened to kill you and you want me to be your roommate? Are you insane?" she asks, disbelieving. Not that I blame her, because I sound nuts.

She moves to slide off my lap, but I constrict my arms to hold her in place. She slants her stunning eyes at me for a moment until she realizes I'm just holding her. I'm not going to hurt her. Then her face goes soft.

"It's because you tried to kill me three times in the last day that I want to you to come home with me. I don't want you to feel like that. I can't explain why, but I feel a primal fuckin' need to keep you safe. If you're in the streets it'll make that harder on me, but I'll still do it. I'm not a good man, Quinn. I'm guessin' you know this based on how you treat me and that's okay. Most things you hear about me are true. I've beaten and killed men. I've hurt people for money. I've done plenty of other shit that I'll share with you if you wanna know. But I've never hurt a woman or a child and I'd die before I ever would.

"I met a girl like you a long time ago and she didn't need anyone to keep her safe, either. My cousin and his friends found her in a fucked up position and inserted themselves in her life. It got better once she allowed them to take care of her...to free her of that burden of shouldering it alone. I know I can be that for you if you'll let me, Quinn. Let me."

She studies my face for a long time before responding.

"Do you still know that girl?" she whispers.

"Yeah."

"Is she safe now?"

"That's a loaded question, sweetheart. But I'll tell you this. She's never alone in this world that's tried to chew her up and spit her out more times than any one person deserves."

"You love her," she says appreciatively.

"Like my own flesh and blood."

"Okay," she whispers, cuddling into my chest and nuzzling her face into my neck. I feel my whole body relax. Thank fuck.

Knock, knock.

"Sorry to interrupt but Ash's screamin' like a wild woman down there," Owen says sheepishly as he eyes our position.

"Shit! Sorry, Owen," Quinn calls, jumping out of my lap. She gives me a sad smile and then sprints down the stairs.

"That looked cozy," Owen snarks.

"Fuck you, man. She needed some comfort."

"Didn't know your dick was comfortable. Mind if I try it out?"

"You're a sick fuck. Stay away from my junk," I say, standing up and cupping my crotch. "It's more than you can handle."

"I'll take your word for it. You get her straightened out? I thought she was gonna cut your head off," he mutters, rubbing his blond head.

"Me, too. She's movin' in with me so I guess shit's straightened out," I say nonchalantly.

"She's movin' in with you?"

"Yeah."

"She's movin' in with you?"

"Fuck, is there an echo in here? Yeah, Quinn's movin' in with me."

"Willingly?"

"Jesus. Yes. I didn't hold *her* at knifepoint, remember? I told her about Shannon and she seemed to open up to the idea of lettin' someone else take care of her."

"You told Quinn about Shannon? They're pretty fuckin' different, Kieran. Shannon's...well, Shannon.

Quinn needs something more than what Shannon needs. You know that, right? Just because the girl's got mad knife skills doesn't make her the lethal wonder woman that Shannon is," Owen says sternly.

"I know what Shannon is, asshole, and no, Quinn's not her. But she's got the same fight. And she needs someone to take care of her for a while."

"And Kieran Delaney is gonna be that man? You're not Brian O'Sullivan."

"Fuck, thanks for the vote of confidence. I know I'm not my cousin. I'm not claimin' to have a clue of what I'm doin'. I told Quinn who I am and she didn't bat an eye. She comes from our world, Owen. It doesn't scare her. You don't think I'm up for the job why don't you offer your services?"

That suggestion makes my stomach roll. I don't want Owen or anyone else taking care of Quinn. I'll analyze that on a different day because I know he won't offer to do it.

"Nah, man, you go ahead with the knight-in-shining-armor routine. Just don't fuck it up. I'll have to beat your old ass," he says jokingly with a tinge of seriousness.

I offer Owen a chin lift and move past him to find Quinn and the kids. *I'm not Brian O'Sullivan.* No shit I'm not Brian. I made sure he was nothing like me when we were growing up. He was like the little brother I never had and I protected his ass, always. Still do. What Brian and his boys did for Shannon is different from what I'm offering Quinn. Okay, not really, but I know what I'm doing (sort of). Quinn needs someone to look out for her and I'm good at that. If there's a prize for looking out for people I'd fucking win it hands down. I need to call

Shannon. I could use her voice in my head right about now.

Chapter 8

Kieran

"Kieran Delaney, I'm not your one phone call, am I?" Shannon answers, snarky as ever, flexing her attorney muscle.

"Nah, I was just hopin' for a quick round of phone sex before I set out for the night," I snark right back. Her raspy laugh fills the line and I relax into the couch in front of the big screen.

"What's up, cousin?"

"Chick stabbed me last night and I asked her to move in with me," I say in a tone like I'm talking about the weather.

"Well, that sounds like a good Friday night. My kinda girl. What did you do to deserve gettin' stabbed?"

"You think I deserved it?" I feign offense.

"Oh, fuck off Kieran, if you got stabbed you probably got off light."

"True. I stepped in where I wasn't wanted. She made herself clear and I didn't listen so she made herself clearer with her stealthy blade skills. Tell you what, Shannon, she's not you, but she's got skills."

Shannon stays very quiet for a long while before responding.

"If she has skills like me then she's been somewhere pretty fucked up in life. She okay?" Shannon asks softly. This is the reason I love this woman. She can bust your balls better than anyone in the world, but when shit's real, she knows it.

"She will be," I state confidently.

"You makin' sure of that?"

"Yeah. It took some convincin', but she agreed to let me take her home with me. I told her a little about you, Brian and the guys. It seemed to help. She can take care of herself, but right now she could use a little help."

"God knows I know how that is. Be gentle with her, Kieran. It's hard to hand over your life to a stranger even if you're doin' what's best. It wasn't easy for me and the guys in the beginning. We all had to learn how to live like this. The love's always been here, though."

"I know. I'll be gentle. It's easy with her. She reminds me so much of you, yet she's completely different. I feel like a goddamn caveman, wantin' to protect her and her kids."

"She's got kids?" Shannon asks in a gasp.

"Two. A little boy named Jack and a baby named Ashling. I know what you're thinkin'. But I can do this, Shannon. She needs it and I can do it."

"Don't tell me you know what I'm fuckin' thinkin' when you clearly don't have a damn clue!"

I've just been handed a Shannon Kelly smack down.

"Sorry," I say quietly.

"I think you'll be great with her and her kids. I know you'd do anything for me. You've done everything for me lately and I'm forever in your debt for that. I can't give you any advice as far as kids go, though. I've got my own issues with that, as you know. Be the good man I know you are and you'll be fine. No punchin' walls when you get mad. No smokin' around those kids. No drinkin'

68

whiskey like a fish. No fuckin' random hos on the couch. No fightin' in front of any of 'em. Keep your shit together and all will be well."

"First, you don't owe me shit! Say it again and I'll fly to Kansas City and kick your skinny ass. I'm fuckin' sorry for bringin' up her kids with what you've got goin' on with Kellerman. That was insensitive of me," I apologize. Shannon's man, Dylan Kellerman, got his ex pregnant before he and Shannon got together. His crazy-ass ex decided to use their unborn child as leverage to get Kellerman to move in with her or else she threatened have an abortion or claim that he beats her. So Shannon's in Kansas City while Kellerman's living in hell in Seattle with his cunt ex. Kellerman's trying to find dirt on the bitch so that he and Shannon can get the baby away from the loony tune. It's a fucked situation.

"Don't worry about it. I'm not made of glass." That's the understatement of the century.

"I'm still sorry. And as for your rules, I'm not an idiot. I'm not gonna act like an ape with a woman and her kids in my house. I'll lay low for a while and just hang out with 'em until she figures her shit out."

"You need anything from me, Kieran?" she asks all sweet and warm. Kellerman is a lucky motherfucker to have this woman.

"Just needed to hear your sweet voice. Punch my cousin in the nuts for me. Love you," I finish tenderly.

"You need anything for this woman or her kids, you call me. I'll do anything I can. Love you, Kieran."

We hang up and I take a minute. Shannon's right, I've got to get and keep my shit together if I'm going to bring Quinn and the kids home. Shannon didn't even ask for Quinn's name. She never pushes until it's needed. Love that woman.

I walk into the bedroom and find Quinn and the kids curled up together, sleeping in the bed. It's a serene sight. I have the urge to climb in with them, but I don't feel like getting a knife pulled on me again today.

I quietly make my way into the bathroom to take a shower. I reek! I heard Connor and Ian go up to Ian's office, where I left Owen, before I called Shannon. I'm sure Ian's ready for us to start looking for whoever or whatever is threatening Quinn. Knowing that she's coming home with me gives me added focus on the task at hand. If I don't have to worry about her, I'm free to worry about finding someone to kill.

Let's be clear—I kill people. Not regularly, but when needed I have no issue taking a man's life. The people I've killed have been the scum of the earth. I don't say that to absolve myself of the sin, it's just the facts. I don't murder rich people to steal their Cadillacs. I kill people who would end my life just as readily if given the chance. I feel no remorse for the lives I've taken and I sure as shit won't be bothered by taking the next one. I hope like hell my next victim is the monster that hurt Jack.

I climb out of the shower clean and smelling spicy from my body wash. I rub my tattoo beneath my heart and settle myself down. I've got a temper. Just thinking in the shower was enough to get me riled up. I breathe deeply for a few minutes until my pulse slows and my head clears.

I sling the towel around my waist and pull the door open to run smack into Quinn.

"We've gotta stop meeting like this," I tease. Her cheeks flame and she averts her gaze to the floor.

"Sorry. I need to pee," she mumbles.

"I'll just wait out here with the kids."

She nods and scurries past me into the bathroom, locking the door swiftly.

"Hey, Kieran," Jack murmurs and looks up at me with sleepy eyes.

"Hey, bud." I move over to the edge of the bed next to him. He sits up as I sit down.

"Sorry I yelled at you and cried," he apologizes staring at his hands. I tip his chin up with my finger and look into his red-rimmed, pale blue eyes.

"You don't have to be sorry for either of those things. I should have listened better before I answered you. I'm sorry. And you never feel bad about cryin'. If you need to cry, you cry. Don't hold that back from anyone," I say kindly.

"Mommy says we're gonna stay with you for a while. Is it my fault? I'll tell Mommy it's my fault and she won't make you do it," he says with panic in his voice. This kid's breaking my cold, dead heart.

"I want you all to come home with me. And yes, it's your fault. I like bein' around you so much that I can't let you go." I beam a broad smile at him and he relaxes.

"You got lots of tattoos. The bad man has tattoos, too."

Easy, Kieran. Ask these questions the right way.

"Do you remember any of his tattoos? What they looked like?"

"One of 'em. He had a bull on his chest where you have those swirly things." He points at my right pec that's covered in an intricate Celtic knot basket weave. I smile and nod, keeping my growing fury at bay.

"Did the bad man talk funny?"

Jack waits a long time before he nods once. That's all I need to know. Motherfucker! A bull on your chest in the Russian mob is the mark of a hit man. I'll have him in my grasp within hours.

"You hungry, Jack?"

"I ate some pizza while you were fightin' with Mommy," he says nonchalantly.

"I wasn't fightin' with your momma, bud. We were just talkin'."

"You made her cry," he says, offering me a glare.

"I didn't make her cry. She was just upset. That happens sometimes with girls. They get mad and they cry. Don't ask me why because I don't understand it either. I would never make your momma cry, bud," I promise, though I know I shouldn't. I usually make women cry, except for Shannon. She makes me cry, but that's another story. I'll try my damnedest not to make Quinn cry if it means Jack won't look at me like he is right now. Less than a day and this kid's got me wrapped around his finger. Never fucking expected that in this lifetime.

"I don't want Mommy to be sad."

"Me neither." I wait for a second and let that sink in for both of us.

"I've got a bedroom for you at my house. You can have it all to yourself," I say happily, trying to change the subject.

"I've never had a bed before. Can Mommy and Ashling fit in it with me?"

"I'm sure they could, but your momma will have her own room and I'll get Ash a crib. You can have your bed all to yourself," I say excitedly but falter when I see Jack's face. He's scared.

"I've never slept alone. Well, the bad man left me alone after...but I didn't sleep." He shudders. Holy fuck, if this kid tells me one more horrible thing I'm going to grow horns and go on a devil's mission.

"Tell you what. If you don't wanna sleep alone you don't have to. You can sleep with your momma. If you wanna try the bed out first, that's fine. If you don't wanna try the bed out at all, that's fine. Whatever you wanna do is okay. You're never gonna have to do something you don't want in my house."

"Okay," he says sweetly, showing me his dimple.

"Kieran, can you hand me some clothes from that bag on the floor?" Quinn calls from the cracked opened door. She must have taken another shower because steam is pouring out of the bathroom.

"Sure." I hop up off the bed, hanging onto my own towel. I dig around in the bags and pull out some blue sweat pants and a white long sleeved T-shirt. I see underwear and a bra in the bag so I grab them too. I walk to the bathroom and wait for her to open the door a little more so I can hand them to her.

"I'm naked," she says in a whisper.

"I figured you didn't take a shower in your clothes."

"The towels don't cover...well...everything."

"I won't look. I'm closin' my eyes right now," I say loudly, trying to make light of the situation. She did have her naked tits smashed against my head last night, though she was in attack mode then.

I hear the door creak and then the pile of clothes is snatched from my hand. The door shuts quietly and I open my eyes. I turn around and Jack is looking at me like I'm crazy.

"You don't like lookin' at naked ladies?" he asks, furrowing his brow. Wow, this kid is hitting me with all the tough questions.

"I only look at naked ladies that want me to look at 'em."

"The ones you pay money to?"

Holy shit! Am I really explaining hookers to a six-year-old?

"I don't pay the ladies."

"So their pimps beat you up?"

My jaw is on the floor. And I have the slightest urge to laugh.

"No one beats me up. And I don't pay ladies because I don't...uh...It's that...well...sometimes a man and a woman...they uh..."

I scrub my hands over my face, praying for some divine intervention. Ian, Connor and Owen walk in, saving me just as Quinn comes out of the bathroom.

"Mommy, Kieran gets to look at the naked ladies without payin' 'em money and their pimps don't beat him up! Isn't that cool?" Jack jumps up from the bed excitedly. "He must be really tough because pimps don't mess around."

Connor and Owen smother laughs with coughs, Ian glares at me and Quinn raises her eyebrows to her hairline.

"He must be, Baby," Quinn coos at him, still looking at me with crazy eyes.

"I'm gonna head to the locker room and get dressed now. Can I talk to you guys a sec?" I ask the men who are still fighting off the chuckles. Dicks.

I walk out of the room quickly, hoping I don't feel a knife in my back. Once we're all in the locker room I drop my towel and pull on a clean pair of boxer briefs from my gym bag. When the guys come into the changing area, Ian rips my wet bandage off roughly and then slaps a new one on even harder. He's pissed.

"Think Jack's a little young to learn about hookers," Owen scolds through a smile.

"I didn't teach him shit. He was the one schoolin' me on the ways of the world," I defend myself.

"How's that?" Ian growls.

"Quinn needed some fresh clothes after she took a shower and I closed my eyes so I wouldn't see her naked as I handed the clothes to her. Jack wondered if I liked to look at naked ladies. You can imagine where the conversation went from there."

"Jesus Christ," Connor moans.

"Yeah. It was sad and hilarious all at the same time," I grumble. I pull a long sleeved black thermal over my head and dark jeans over my ass.

"Anyway, before Jack taught me proper hooker etiquette, he gave me some information on the bad guy."

"What?" Ian asks excitedly, still a little pissed.

"He's got a bull tattoo on his chest and talks funny," I explain with a menacing growl.

"Fuckin' Russian mob," Owen scoffs next to me.

"I'll find him by tonight. I'm headin' out to hook up with some guys. Call you when I know somethin'."

With that, I stride out of the locker room and into the gym which is filled with Jack's laughter. Quinn's on her back flyin' the kid around on her feet making airplane noises. I walk up behind them, snatch Jack off her feet and start to run with him hoisted over my head making louder (better) noises than his mother was. He squeals and laughs as I run and run.

When we get back to Quinn she's beaming a full-toothed smile at us. I bring Jack to rest on my shoulders and stare at his mother. Drop-fucking-dead gorgeous. She's wearing sweats, not a stitch of make-up, her hair's in a messy pile on top of her head and she just gave birth. I've never seen a woman look better. Do I tell her this? No. I act like a dick.

"You shouldn't be exerting yourself so soon after Ash. If he wants to play rough get one of us guys," I admonish her and watch her glowing smile turn into a dagger-throwing glare. I'm a prick.

She takes two sharp strides toward me and reaches up at Jack without so much as a glance at my face. Jack immediately leans down to her and she rips him roughly off my shoulders, catching me in the back of the head with his knee. He curls around the front of her like a baby monkey and she flips me the bird before stalking away. What can I say? I've got the touch when it comes to my people skills.

Chapter 9

Quinn

Kieran Delaney makes me want to stab him more often than not. Why the hell did I agree to move in with him? I'm a crazy person, that's why. When he was holding me to his chest and talking about his friend who's like me I melted. He was so sweet and sincere that I turned into a pile of goo in his lap and agreed to move in with him. Fucking idiot!

He's already bossing me around like he thinks he's my father. That shit is not going to fly with me. Once I get to his place, I'll quickly put my plan into action so I can leave. Maybe I should just stay here at the gym. Jack will be bored, but I can take him out during the days while the fighters train. That's a better idea that spending time with Kieran. I'll end up murdering that man.

I put Jack in *Avengers* pajamas and feed Ashling another bottle before tucking them into bed. They've had an eventful day and fall asleep quickly. I lay down beside them, trying to fall asleep, but it never comes.

Hours later, as I lay in the dark room with my new kids, I hear banging around in the gym. I know the guys are still here because they told me they wouldn't leave so I'm not scared. I am curious what the hell they're doing so loudly at 4:00 am. I fed Ashling another bottle an hour ago so I think she's good and asleep for a while. Ian and I weighed and measured her this evening. She's an ounce shy of five pounds and seventeen and a half inches long. I asked Jack if he knew when Ashling was supposed to be born and he told me in "marsh" which, I'm assuming, is March. She's at least three weeks early but probably more. Ian agreed to have his doctor come tomorrow and check her out. Her skin looks better, but I want to be sure she's healthy.

I climb out of bed slowly and grab my knife out of my backpack hidden under the bed. Safety first. I creep out of the bedroom into the therapy room, hovering in the doorway where I see some lights on in the gym. I listen attentively to locate the sounds reverberating through the building. They're coming from the locker room.

Using my ghost-like skills I glide through the space quickly and stop at the glass and wooden door. There's yelling and grunting going on in there. If I walk into some creepy sex scene I'm going to puke. I've seen enough weird on the streets to last me a lifetime. I push the door open and am hit with the smell of burning flesh and muffled screams. This is the moment a normal person would turn back...I'm not normal. I slip through the locker area and stop dead in my tracks in the shower area.

Ian, Connor and Owen are standing behind Kieran who's putting a cigar out on the cheek of a man's who's been tied to a chair. I'm horrified and mesmerized all at the same time. When Kieran's done using the man's face as an ashtray, he picks up a pair of sheers and begins pruning the man's fingers slowly, making him feel every millimeter of pressure before the bone snaps.

"I'm gonna cut off every piece of you that touched that kid," Kieran seethes, and the picture before me becomes crystal clear. That's the man that hurt Jack. He's naked and tied to a chair. He's been beaten to shit. Connor's knuckles are dripping blood. Owen's shoes are covered in blood. Ian's holding something in his hand that looks a lot like a dildo. I'll leave that one alone.

Fury blinds me as I rush forward, slamming Kieran out of my way.

"*An raibh tú ag Gortaítear mo mhac?*" I seethe, pressing the tip of my knife to his stomach. The man's eyes bug out as I realize I just asked him if he hurt my son in Irish. I don't give a fuck if he understands me or not.

"Did he?!" I roar.

"Quinn," Kieran tries to soothe me.

"Goddamn it, Kieran, fuckin' tell me!"

"Yes."

I raise my blade and slam it down, severing the pedophile's dick from his body. I reach up and rip the duct tape from his mouth, taking a shit load of skin with it. He opens his mouth wide to release a scream, but I fill it with his dick. I lean in close to his ear whispering, "*Féach tú i ifreann.*" See you in hell.

I plunge my knife into his stomach and drag it to his throat, watching the life seep from his red-rimmed grey eyes. He was soulless to begin with. I just helped the process along. I remove my knife from his throat and thrust it into each eye for good measure. Then I spit in his face. I could go on all night, but I have children to get back to.

I spin on my heel and head to the sink without looking at any of the men around me and begin cleaning my weapon. I'll be forever indebted to Ian for giving me his Yarborough knife. It's a Special Forces knife that I'm sure I shouldn't have, but right now I couldn't be happier to have it my possession.

As I wash the blood away, I feel the bile rising in my stomach. If there was one death I wish didn't make me sick, it's this one. No such luck. I drop the knife, run to a urinal and puke up the entire contents of my stomach, retching and dry heaving the last of it before strong arms lift me from the ground.

Kieran carries me into another area of showers, away from the corpse. He cradles me to his naked chest as he turns on the taps. Searing hot water washes over me as he steps into its stream. Kieran lowers my feet to the ground and grabs the hem of my shirt pulling it off my body. He reaches around my back and unclasps my bra, pulling it roughly from my chest. His foggy blue eyes are boring into mine with pain and fury combined. He jams his thumbs into the waist of my sweats and drags them down my body along with my underwear.

Once he has me naked he pulls me into his chest so viciously that my chin snaps shut causing a great deal of pain, but I remain silent. I hear him pumping the industrial combo and then he begins to vigorously scrub my head. I don't move. I don't speak. I barely breathe. I'm not afraid of Kieran, but I know he's hanging on by the barest strings of a thread.

He roughly fists my hair, wrenches my hair back and starts rubbing soap all over my face. I close my eyes to avoid the sting. When he's done, he moves us further into the stream, rinsing me clean. The water is so hot I feel my skin blistering on my back, yet I remain silent and allow the pain. Kieran pulls out of the water again and fills his hand with the industrial combo. He scours my entire body other than my crotch, which he skirts around effortlessly. His hands are calloused and rough, sharply abrading my skin. When he's content with his cleansing, he pushes us into the stream, washing the death from my body and my soul.

80

I spin him around so he's in the stream and fill my palm with the soap. I fiercely pull his head forward, lathering his entire head and neck before forcing his chin back up and into the flow of water. While he's rinsing, I undo his jeans and remove them along with his boxer briefs. I'm beyond relieved that he's not hard. What's happening between us isn't sexual, it's primal.

I fill my hand once again with soap and scrub his skin harshly, dragging my nails down his flesh, scraping the torture from him. I avoid his crotch with the same respect he showed me. When I'm exhausted from washing him I push him into the spray one last time.

As the last of the murder disappears down the drain, Kieran cuts off the water. He scoops me up into his arms like a baby and carries me into the locker room. He sets me down, then pulls a towel around my body and dries every inch of my skin, again avoiding between my legs. He wraps one towel around my shoulders, another around my waist and finally one around my hair. Kieran quickly runs a towel over his own body before dropping it on the floor. He reaches in a duffle bag next to me and pulls out a pair of black of boxer briefs. Once he has them over his hips he swings me off the floor into his chest and stalks out of the locker room.

He steps lightly into the bedroom and tags one of the bags with clothes in it, supporting my body with one arm. Kieran enters the bathroom and shuts the door with a faint click before flipping on the light. He sets me down and rips the towels from my body. Rummaging around in the bag on the floor, he holds out a pair of terry cloth shorts for me to step into. Once both my feet are in, he roughly drags them up my hips. When he stands up, he yanks the towel from my head and shoves a long sleeved T-shirt over me. I push my arms through on my own.

Ignoring the mess on the floor, Kieran reaches behind us and flips off the light. He scoops me off the floor and walks us out of the bathroom. When we reach the edge of the bed he crawls in with me in his lap before laying down on his side, keeping my back pressed snugly to his front. Kieran reaches across my body and pulls Ashling into my chest, followed by Jack. I wrap my arm around both kids and Kieran lays his arm on top of mine. He threads his fingers with mine and squeezes them almost painfully. I squeeze back for a long while until he begins to release the pressure.

He pulls the three of us even tighter into him and I drift off to sleep, feeling safe and protected for the first time in twenty-six years.

I wake up to the sound of Ashling whimpering against my chest. None of us have moved from the sheltered embrace of Kieran. His body is relaxed and warm behind me and I'd love nothing more than to stay enveloped by him, but duty calls.

I move to lift his arm off of the three of us and he snarls, clutching firmly onto my hand. Okay, the passive move is not going to work.

"Kieran," I whisper and nudge him a little with my elbow, getting absolutely no response.

"Kieran, I need to feed the baby," I say louder and rock my whole body against him. His grip strengthens on my hand again. What the hell is it going to take? Ashling screams out in frustration and Kieran's entire body goes rigid before he sits straight up.

"She's hungry and I couldn't get you to wake up," I apologize. He scrubs his hands over his face, trying to wake up before he hoists me up, drags me across his lap and sets me on the floor. He reaches over and gently cradles the baby to his chest before offering her to me.

I grab the diapers and wipes, quickly changing Ashling before heading to the kitchen. Before I'm out of the bedroom Kieran whispers, "Bring the bottle back in here to feed her." He may be whispering, but his tone and gaze let me know that was an order. I nod and continue on my path.

I'm not big on being told what to do, but I can see Kieran is battling with himself still. I can appease him for a while. I make quick work of the bottle and return to the bedroom. Kieran hasn't moved a muscle since I left. I pass Ashling over to him and he lays her near the foot of the bed with the bottle next to her. He grabs me under my arms and sets me next to him, covering us with the duvet. Reaching down, he gathers Ashling in the crook of his arm and pops the bottle in her mouth. Kieran holds the bottle with the hand of the arm that's cradling the baby and reaches across me with his free one, pulling Jack's sleeping body into my lap. Once he's happy with Jack's position, Kieran pulls me under his arm securely and rests his hand on Jack's head. I'm back asleep in minutes.

Kieran

I only thought I was a caveman before. I don't have a fucking clue how to describe what I feel right now. I'm full of rage and pain in a way that I've only experienced once before in my life—seven weeks ago.

Shannon was kidnapped by the Mancini Crime Family. When law enforcement couldn't find her, my cousin, Brian (her roommate for the last thirteen years), called me to see if I could help. I worked an angle that had us to her in a matter of hours. Unfortunately, we were ambushed and Shannon was shot four times. I watched her seemingly lifeless body carried past me that morning as she was placed in a medical helicopter. I felt this way when that beautiful woman passed by me on the stretcher. Pain and rage that carries no name, only feelings.

This time is worse. This time I caused it for myself. This time I feel like a monster.

When Quinn shoved me out of her way, I swear I thought a Bears linebacker had entered the locker room. She knocked me flat on my ass. The ferocity in her eyes as she spoke to the pedophile was...petrifying. The Irish that dripped off her tongue was oozing with disdain. The Russian didn't understand her and she knew I did. I couldn't lie to her. These are her kids and the predator's life was hers to take, but I didn't want that for her.

When she killed him, it was poetic. He deserved exactly what she gave him and I can honestly say I couldn't have done it better. Quinn's hand never trembled, her voice stayed clear and her vicious gaze never faltered. Then it was over and she crumbled. Quinn's not Shannon. Shannon killed a man while she was held captive and it didn't faze her, never will. She was trained to kill and remain emotionless. It's a skill pretty much no one has, but she does. Quinn felt that murder and will carry it with her always. These are the things nightmares are made of.

So I acted like a Neanderthal and stripped her naked to wash the blood and death from her skin. I couldn't stand the sight of him on her. When she did the same for me I almost cracked. I was rough with her in a way that she didn't deserve, but I had only so much control. It wasn't until we were in this bed and I had all three of them in my arms that I could take a deep breath. I was smothering beneath the emotion and guilt until the warmth of their bodies offered me a pocket of air.

We only got a few hours of sleep before Ash needed to be fed so that's what I'm doing...feeding the baby with Quinn and Jack asleep, nestled into my side. I can breathe.

Now that the baby's back asleep I slide down the headboard, keeping her over my heart. I pull Quinn down next to me. I have to move Jack, so I sit back up a little and drag him onto my stomach before laying back and scooping Quinn onto my chest. Taking a deep breath, I fall back to sleep covered in everything that's important to me.

I wake up to the sounds of whispered voices.

"He'll let me go once he wakes up, Baby," I hear Quinn coo.

"He's holdin' you so tight. Doesn't that hurt?" Jack asks from farther away than I want his voice to be.

"I'm fine," she reassures him.

I realize I'm the topic of discussion as my hand is gripping Quinn's shoulder firmly, too firmly. I quickly relax my hand and peer down at her.

"You're like wakin' the dead," she says through a small smile.

"Yeah, I poked your booboo and you didn't even move," Jack says brightly.

"Sorry," I whisper.

"Jack's hungry," Quinn says, gazing into my eyes with her icy blues questioning if I'm okay, if I'm done being a caveman. I force a broad smile.

"I'm hungry, too," I lie. She spots the lie, but nods in understanding.

Quinn crawls out of bed and Jack wraps himself around her like a monkey. They walk out of the room, giggling at something I don't catch because I'm too busy waiting for them to come back. I realize I'm capable of movement and climb out of bed with Ash. She sleeps like the dead, too. Good girl.

I tag a pair of shorts out of the storage unit in the therapy room and struggle to get them on one-handed but finally manage. Connor, Owen, Ian and Jack are sitting at the table when I walk in. They're all laughing at something Quinn just did and she's rolling her eyes. As I amble in, my men cut their eyes to me in knowing glances. We're all struggling. Not because of what we did, because of what we saw. I could sleep like a baby after what we did, no problem. Sleeping after watching Quinn gut that animal, I would have had sweet dreams.

Sleeping after watching Quinn heave into a urinal and the aching bleed coming from her eyes, that shit will haunt me for the rest of my life.

I sit at the table in a trance, willing myself to pull my shit together. When Quinn sets a plate of pancakes in front of me, I snap out of it.

"You want me to take her?" Quinn asks sweetly.

"I'm good," I respond in the first normal voice since last night.

"What do you want on your pancakes?"

"Peanut butter and syrup," I say with a smile at Jack.

"Ooh, me too, Mommy," Jack says excitedly.

She curls her cute little nose up at me, but slathers five pancakes with peanut butter and syrup for me and then does the same for Jack. He doesn't get five like me, though. We all sit quietly, eating a really great breakfast.

"Who died?" Jack asks quietly.

Connor and Owen's eyes bug out and Ian coughs up a lung as he chokes on his pancakes.

"What do you mean, Baby?" Quinn asks, concern all over her face. I know Jack didn't witness anything last night. Owen guarded the door after Quinn came in and stood watch at the therapy room until I brought Quinn back.

"You're all so sad and quiet. Usually means someone died," he says with a shrug, stuffing a too-big bite in his mouth.

"We're just tired this morning. Ashling was up a lot last night," Quinn lies convincingly.

"Wanna watch *The Avengers* again?" Jack asks Connor, full of excitement, spitting a little food as he talks.

"Nothin' I'd rather be doin', little man," Connor says with a full mouth.

"Do you think you could watch the kids so Quinn and I can do some shopping this afternoon?" I ask the guys.

Jack shoots his eyes to Quinn and back to me.

"Remember I told you I need to get Ash a crib? Need your momma's help for that. I also need to get car seats for you two so we can go home tonight. You okay hangin' out here with these boring guys for a while?"

Jack's blue eyes hold mine for a long while, searching for the lie, but they don't find it.

"Mommy?"

"If you want me to stay with you, I will. Kieran can do the shoppin' on his own. He'll just buy ugly stuff," she teases.

"You won't let anything bad happen?" Jack asks Ian.

"Never," Ian says sternly, leveling his honey eyes at the boy.

"Okay, but I'm not changin' Ash's diapers," Jack announces as he stands up from the table.

"Aw, man," Owen feigns disappointment. "No fair."

"Oh yes, it is. She's my sister for life, but we're leavin' here tonight so you won't see us anymore. Then we'll leave Kieran's and never see him anymore. Take the chance while you got it."

Jack finishes his gut-check and walks out to the gym, throwing a ball around without a care in the world.

"Sorry about Jack. We've never stuck anywhere too long," Quinn offers her apology to the men across the table.

"Well, that's done now. Right?" Ian growls.

"Don't know. What you guys did last night...I can't thank you enough. When the time is right, I can tell Jack he's safe now and that's priceless to me. I'll never be able to repay you for that. That was just the tip of the iceberg, I'm afraid. I have bigger demons haunting me than one pedophile. But you cleared out Jack's boogie man, so thank you," Quinn whispers, her gaze on her hands.

My heart clutches at the realization she's still going to run. She's not safe yet, not by a long shot, given her current state. Fuck! Okay, new plan. Find out what the threat to Quinn is so I can keep her. Jesus, I sound like a serial killer. After last night, I'm not letting her go without a fight. No goddamned way.

I've been sneaking outside the whole time they've been here to grab cigarettes and I'm in desperate need right now.

"Goin' for a puff," I say, handing Ash over to Quinn.

"You smoke?" she asks with a furrowed brow and a bit of a scowl.

"Yeah. Not in the house, though."

"'Kay." She shrugs and turns her gaze back to the baby.

I head to the locker room to grab some clothes. It's been cleaned from top to bottom, no remnants of last night to be found. Connor and Owen dropped the body back in his neighborhood. It'll send a message, but it shouldn't get back to us.

I strip out of the shorts and pull on grey sweat pants, a white V-neck, and a black Brogan's hoodie like Ash is wearing. I put my black leather jacket on, then my sneakers and head out the back door into the alley. I tap a cigarette out of the package and spark my Zippo. That first drag is heaven. I take a few more before I let my mind wander.

How can I keep Quinn safe if she won't tell me what's haunting her? I'll have to manipulate her with the kids' safety. She'll do anything for them and I'll convince her she's putting them in harm's way by allowing the threat to remain. It's a dick move, but I've got limited options at this point. I finish the cigarette and light another off the butt. I could finish half a pack if I'm not careful.

When I finish the second cigarette I make my way back into the gym. I'm stopped by a familiar face.

"Collin?" I yell across the gym. My cousin, Collin O'Sullivan, a cop, is standing in the middle of the gym talking to Connor and Owen. Ian's coming down from his office and Quinn's standing in the doorway of the therapy room, shaking from head to toe, holding Ash tightly to her chest, her gaze fixed on Jack who's in front of Connor and Owen, smiling broadly at my cousin.

"Hey, Kieran," Collin calls out in a friendly tone. I make my way to the group, saddling up next to Connor. I slide my hand onto Jack's shoulder and pull him in front of me as Ian joins our group. Jack looks up at me, noticing my tension, and reaches his arms up. I scoop him up and he wraps around my front like a monkey the same way he does with his momma.

Collin's eyes bug out at the vision of me holding a kid. I stifle a laugh at his reaction.

"Think we can talk alone for a sec?" he asks once he rearranges his eyes in his head.

"You can use my office," Ian offers.

"I'll meet you up there," I say and turn toward the therapy room. When I get to Quinn at the doorway and she scurries into the bedroom. I shut the door once we're inside and set Jack down on the bed.

"Don't worry. He's my cousin. No big deal," I soothe Quinn.

"Okay," she replies softly, trying to rein herself in.

"Your cousin has a badge. He showed it to me." Jack's eyes are wide with wonder.

"Pretty cool, bud. You watch your sister for a second while I go talk to your momma about some boring grownup stuff, okay?"

"Sure. Can I watch TV?"

I look to Quinn and she offers me a slight nod.

"Yup," I say, turning on cartoons and dragging Quinn into the bathroom. I turn on the tub to drown out our voices.

"Quinn, everything's fine. Take a breath for me," I say sweetly. She takes a few deep breaths and then dives into my chest. I wrap my arms around her until she stops shaking. Once she's calmed down I tip her chin up with my finger.

"I promised to keep you safe. I'll keep you safe. Trust me?"

"Yes," she responds immediately and my heart zings to life. That cold dead rock in my chest pounds so hard it hurts. I run the back of my fingers down her cheek and stare into her dazzling eyes.

92

"How old are you?" Yes, this is a weird moment for me to ask that question, but it tumbled from my mouth before my brain could shut it down. She rolls her eyes at me.

"Eighteen," she says with a sweet smile. At least she's legal. And there's the prick I know and love. I cannot be thinking the thoughts I've been having about an eighteen-year-old. Time to shut it down old man. This girl is officially off limits!

"Jesus, Kieran, I'm fuckin' with you. You look like I just kicked your puppy. I'm twenty-six."

I scowl at her and release her from my grip.

"Not funny," I growl. "Stay in here with the kids until I come get you."

I stalk out of the bathroom and smile at Jack before I head up to see if my cousin is here to arrest me. Wish me luck!

Chapter 11

Kieran

When I open Ian's office, I find Collin sitting on the couch I held Quinn on yesterday. Today it doesn't look quite as inviting. Collin's a tall guy, a few inches over six feet. He's got dark hair like me and Milk Dud eyes. All the O'Sullivan boys look the same, and from what the ladies say, they're good looking. My uncle, not really because he and my dad are first cousins, Stephen O'Sullivan, is the Bureau Chief of the Bureau of Organized Crime here in Chicago and his sons are the spitting image of him. Collin and his younger brother, Hugh, are homicide detectives, while Brian is an attorney in Kansas City with Shannon and her gang of protective brothers. We are a strange, tangled web of relationships that skirt legal and illegal, killers and saviors.

"What's up, cousin?" I ask with a smile touching my lips. Collin looks up at me from his phone and grins. He's not here to arrest me. I feel the tension leave my shoulders as I plop down on the couch next to him.

"Talk to Shannon lately?" Collin asks.

"Yesterday. Why?"

Collin's brow is furrowed in concern. Fuck, if something happened to Shannon, I'll lose my shit.

"Brian called this morning. She's not doin' good. Said she's lost a shit load of weight. I'm worried about her.

95

We're all fuckin' worried," he groans and throws his head back on the couch.

"She's not good at wait-and-see. Shannon's like a dude—action first, questions later. Waitin' around for Kellerman's gonna take its toll. Somethin' else wrong with her?"

"She's fine on the phone. She laughs and gives me shit like always, but that light is dim. I feel like we're barely hangin' on to her." Collin scrubs his hands vigorously over his face.

"My parents are headed down next weekend. They can't take it anymore. Ma says she's gonna force feed her all weekend," he finishes in a grunt.

"Shannon's gotta get through this thing her way, Collin. She was kidnapped, tortured, almost raped, fuckin' shot to shit and then her man was ripped from her arms on Christmas morning. Give her some time. She's not made of glass. Shannon's tougher than all of us put together. She's good," I say encouragingly. I'm the only one that knows Shannon also had to kill someone while those fuckwads had her. I know because I make it my business to know everything. I haven't told Shannon that I know. It's her secret to hold as long as she wants.

"You ever love someone so much it fuckin' hurts?" Collin asks with pain in his voice.

"Shannon," I respond swiftly.

"If I thought she'd be safer in Chicago I'd drag her ass up here and keep her in my house. Fuckin' hate havin' her in Kansas City away from me. I know Brian and the guys have her covered, but I want eyes on her."

"She's better in Kansas City. It's her home. Go see her, man. You know she'll be happy to look at your ugly mug all day long. Give you some peace of mind."

I clap him on the shoulder and he finally picks his head up and looks at me. Shannon's his sister for all intents and purposes. He's at war with himself to not be a caveman when it comes to her. Shannon is not Quinn and would not take kindly to caveman behavior, no matter how well intended. Collin knows this, hence the struggle.

"Got a body this morning," Collin says, changing the subject.

"So you're not just here to talk about your hot sister?" I snark. "You get bodies in your line of work, cousin. What do you need from me?"

"Body is Vasily Rostov. Hit man for the Russians. His widow says you dragged him outta their house around midnight," Collin explains with a brow raised.

"Dude was a piece of shit with a lot of enemies. I didn't know him though, only by reputation." I shrug.

"You drag him outta his house last night?"

"Fucker had a taste for little boys too. Did you know that? Liked to kill people for money and then torture kids. Someone did the world a favor, endin' his ass," I grunt.

"So you're avoidin' my question and givin' me your reasons. Not here to arrest you, cousin. I know about Rostov...you don't see me sheddin' tears for him. I need to know if your name comin' up is an issue. That widow's runnin' her mouth to any and every ear that'll listen, meaning all the Russians are meetin' now to surely plan your beheading."

If only I didn't have issues hurting women. Goddamn it!

"You got a way to swing this in someone else's direction?" I ask, knowing I can do it myself but it'll take time that I now don't have.

"Already did. Russians have some beef with a small street gang. I may have dribbled some information that I thought could be helpful. Just doin' my duty," he says with a wink.

"Street gang deserve that kinda heat?"

"They help traffic women and kids. Whatever they get they fuckin' got comin'," Collin growls. I offer him a chin lift.

"So...wanna tell me why you got a woman and two kids hidin' downstairs?"

"No."

"You need help, Kieran?"

"Got it covered."

"Call me if that changes."

Collin stands up and I follow. We shake hands and he pulls me in for a man-hug-back-slap.

"Nice work on Rostov," he compliments in my ear.

I pull back and offer him a giant smile. He laughs while we exit the office. Collin says his goodbyes to the guys, who are just standing around waiting in the gym, and leaves.

"All good, boys. Gonna go check on them," I say, indicating my chin toward the back. Ian eyes me for a moment and I offer him my cockiest grin, causing him to smirk and shake his head. I'm a pain in the ass. I know.

I amble through the therapy room and hear Jack squealing and giggling beyond the bedroom door. When I walk in, Quinn's on her back flying him around on her feet making crappy airplane sounds. Ash is sleeping on the bed wearing a new outfit that's hot pink. I liked her better in black.

I snatch Jack off Quinn's feet and swing him around a few times before plopping him on the end of the bed. His blue eyes are shimmering with joy.

"Gonna head out now, bud. You still good stayin' here and watchin' your sister?" I ask softly.

"Yup," he replies, popping his *p*.

"Good boy. You wanna hang out in here or out in the gym?"

I know he doesn't want to be in a closed-off room with the guys. Even though he trusts nothing will happen to him.

"Can we watch *The Avengers*?"

"You bet." I pluck him off the bed, holding him against my side, before scooping Ash up to my chest. I walk them out to the gym where Owen is setting up the movie already and Ian is carrying a bowl of popcorn to the couch.

"Little man," Connor calls from behind us. "We got candy, soda and popcorn. You ready to do this?" He offers Jack a mischievous grin.

"Cool," Jack responds and slides down my body, running toward Connor, who picks him up and sets him on his shoulders. I smoothly pass Ash to Ian as Quinn comes up beside me.

She's wearing green cargo pants, biker boots and a black hoodie with the hood up over her head.

"Be good," she says softly to Jack who launches himself off Connor's shoulders, down into her arms. It was a steep fall, but she catches him with ease.

"Love you, Mommy," he says softly.

"Love you, Baby," she coos, running her thumb over his dimple. After a moment, she hands him back to Connor who holds Jack high above his head and starts running through the gym. Jack laughs in delight.

"Let's move," I instruct with my hand on Quinn's back. She quickly walks to the door, stepping away from my touch. Yeah, she's pissed at me. Well touché, honey.

I let her in the Camaro and then quickly climb in before speeding down the road. The silence in the car is tense. Quinn's whole body is pressed against the door, her hood still up and with the angle of her body, I can't see her eyes. I'm losing my will to be irritated at her joke earlier.

I pull up at the two-car garage behind my house a few minutes later.

"Need to switch cars. You wanna see the house now? Get a feel for whatever furniture we'll need and whatnot?" I ask gruffly.

"'Kay," she says blankly. This isn't the Quinn that I've been with the last two days. This is the Quinn I met with a knife to my back. I've fucked up and I haven't even done anything yet. Shannon would beat my ass.

Quinn hops out of the car and waits for me to lead the way. We head through the garage to the back yard, up the deck, and through the back door. The house is an average, pale brick family home, paid for in cash a few years ago.

The back door opens into a large kitchen-dining-living room. I gutted the place after I bought it and knocked down every wall that I could. I like the open space. I put in a fully upgraded, high-end kitchen with stainless steel appliances and quartz countertops with black cabinets. Dark hardwood floors run the length of the space. The living room has a charcoal suede-effect sectional with two matching chairs facing a fireplace. I spend most of my time in the finished basement in my recliner staring at my sixty inch flat screen.

Quinn walks through the house slowly, glancing around at the light grey walls which hold a lot of photos from my life. She runs a finger down the length of the dining room's walnut table before entering the living space. She turns toward the hall that leads to the bedrooms and waits for me to lead the way again.

I open the first door on the right. It's an empty ten foot by ten foot bedroom. I haven't had any use for it so all that's in here is the new carpet I had laid.

"This can be Jack's room," I mumble. Quinn looks around the space briefly and then waits for me to move it along.

I open the next door on the right which is the main bathroom. It has double sinks, and a soaker tub with a shower overhead. Quinn steps onto the travertine floors and glances at the black marble vanity. She waits again without a word.

I open the next door on the right. It's a bigger bedroom than Jack's with a queen cherry wood sleigh bed, matching bedside table and dresser. There's room in here to fit a crib and it won't be cramped. Again, she glances around, but says nothing. I press my hand in the small of her back and feel her knife saddled against her skin. She flinches away from me, walking to my bedroom door at the end of the hall. I push the door open and she takes one cautious step in.

My room is a large extension off the back of the house. It has a black four poster California king against the wall to the left. The entire back wall is made of glass, looking out onto the deck. I can open the wall completely in the summer. I don't have much furniture in here other than two bedside tables and two dressers that came with the bed. I'm not an interior decorator. Matching takes the work out of it for me. I walk into the room and open the door to my ensuite. Quinn follows and glances around quickly at the double black marble vanity, jetted tub and separate walk-in shower. I walk through the bathroom and open the attached dressing room. She doesn't follow, just peers in the door from where she stands. I shut the door and move past her back into my bedroom. When she comes out she doesn't meet my gaze, just waits.

"You wanna have this fight now and get it outta the way?" I snarl. Quinn slowly brings her head up. I'm expecting to see fury and instead I'm met with remorse and anguish. I take two strides to her and hoist her up to my chest by her armpits. She wraps her arms around my neck while I constrict around her back.

"I'm sorry," she whispers. I hold her snugly before placing her back on her feet.

"When you said you were eighteen, the only thing I could think was that meant some sick fuck had raped you at eleven or twelve and left you to raise Jack on your own on the streets. After what we had just gone through, it was too much for my brain," I explain softly.

"I wasn't thinking, Kieran. You looked at me and asked how old I was outta the blue. I knew you thought I was young, everyone does. It was a mistimed joke. Nobody hurt me," she mumbles the last part. I don't believe that for a second.

"So you had Jack when you were nineteen?"

"That would be the correct math."

I notice she doesn't really answer my question, but I don't push. She'll tell me when she's ready.

"His dad around?"

She shrugs.

"Ash's dad around?"

She shrugs again.

"You gotta give me something, Quinn."

"They're mine and I'm alone. That's all I've got to give you," she says quietly, looking at her hands. "Everything okay with your cousin?" She changes the subject.

"Yeah. It's all good. You doin' okay after everything?" I ask cautiously.

Her head snaps back up with a curious gleam in her icy blue eyes.

"Are you okay?" she asks with an edge in her voice. She thinks I'm belittling her.

"I didn't want that for you. I got no problem with what me and the boys did. I'd do it again in a heartbeat. But I'm fuckin' strugglin' with you," I grumble.

"I've been takin' care of myself a long time. Don't worry about me," she says dismissively, which pisses me the fuck off quick.

"Don't. Do. That," I order grasping her chin, roughly forcing her to meet my gaze.

"Take care of myself?" she grinds out sarcastically.

"You know what I fuckin' meant. Don't dismiss me. I'm standin' here tellin' you the truth. I expect the same in return." Her face goes soft and I release her chin. She keeps her head angled up at me. I'm more than a foot taller than her so she has to look up a long way to meet my eyes.

"I always puke afterward. It doesn't mean anything. I don't feel bad for what I did to him. That's a first for me. I wish I could shut off the emotion and act like nothing happens but I can't. But last night is not bothering me. AT ALL. Thank you for what you did. Thank you for lettin' me do what I did. Thank you for holdin' me all night with my kids. It's the safest I've felt in eight years." She gasps and throws her hand over her mouth at the last sentence. Guess she didn't mean to say that.

"I'm sorry I was rough with you last night. I was hangin' on by a fuckin' thread. I needed his blood off you. I needed you in my arms with your kids. I don't know how to explain this other than to say I need to protect you more than I've ever needed anything in my life. Is that okay? Please tell me that's okay, Quinn."

"It's okay," she whispers and offers me a small smile. I grin back.

"The basement's finished, just one big room with a TV and a few recliners. We can put toys and shit at the other end and make it a playroom for the kids. Let's get movin' so we can get back to Jack," I say lightly.

"You don't have to get us anything or change your house. We'll only be here a few days. We can all sleep together in your guest room. We'll be fine in there. I just need a little while to line a few things up."

"Fight one done and now on to fight two. You're not just stayin' here a few days. Those kids deserve a house, warm meals and beds. I'm not lettin' you take 'em out in the streets again. You told me you've got demons out there and that means the kids aren't safe. Sorry, Shorty, but I'm not sendin' you off on your own," I growl.

"So you're just gonna go from criminal bachelor to what, fake husband and father? How quick before we're in your way and I'm out on my ass again? You've been good to us, Kieran, but I live in the real world. I know this has an expiration date. And based on the look on your face when I just said the words 'husband and father', I'm guessin' that date's sooner than later. I get it, we're a lot to take on. I don't expect anyone to do it. I've got a plan that'll get us outta your hair and keep us off the streets. I just need a little time to figure it all out."

"Okay," is the only response my mouth produces. My brain is working overtime to figure out half the shit she just said. First of all, yes my face turned in a strange twist when she said fake father and husband. I'll analyze the flip my stomach performed later.

Whatever she's got planned is a bad idea. I can tell. I know a good plan when it's swimming in someone's head. Her plan is shit. I may have to tie her to a bed to keep her here after all. I'll be damned if I let her carry out some harebrained mission she's created on limited sleep after giving birth and committing sensational murder. Quinn's out of her mind to think I'd be down with that. I'll play along for a few days until I can pin her down.

"We still need some stuff for the kids. Even for just a few days."

"Sure," she says with a shrug.

I press my palm into the small of her back and she doesn't move away from my touch this time. She lets me lead her from behind through the house and out the back door. I could use a cigarette right about now, but I'll hold off. I also need to hide all of the booze in the house before Jack gets here and lock the gun safe in the basement.

I put Quinn in the SUV and head toward the baby store nearest to my house, according to the GPS. I need the assistance because I've never been to a baby store. Quinn has her hood back up and is pressed to the door again. I can't take it so I reach across and pull her tiny frame toward me. I grab her hand, interlacing our fingers and rest (pin) her arm beneath mine on the console. She doesn't fight me at any stage, just keeps her gaze faced forward. This is better.

We drive in silence for the entire ride. This silence is less tense than before, but it's not completely comfortable, either. I suppose driving to a baby store to buy things for your kids for the first time ever is a bit overwhelming for Quinn. It certainly has my ass in a daze. This is the shit couples do at happy moments in their lives. A part of me wishes that's what Quinn and I were doing, instead of the reality that faces the criminal and the homeless girl.

Chapter 12

Quinn

Kieran pulls up in a large shopping area with stores and restaurants all around. There aren't a lot of people out, but the crowds are building. I just want this to move along so I can get back to the kids. I'm worried about them. I'm worried about Kieran's hot cop cousin. I'm worried about Russians coming for retribution. I worried about being alone with Kieran any more than I have to be. He's doing the right thing by me and the kids, but I can see on his face he's uncomfortable.

I don't want to wear out our welcome before I can get some identification and a plan in place to access my father's money. I haven't had time to think it through, but I have an idea that might work. It means having to be visible again, which I swore I'd never do. I'll need Kieran. He'll have to keep the kids safe for me.

We walk in the store after Kieran finishes his cigarette in the parking lot. Things are tense between us. It's better now that we talked, but shit still isn't right. Maybe it never will be. Committing murder together doesn't seem to have been a bonding experience.

I thought I'd have nightmares and feel unbearable guilt after gutting that monster, but I don't. I feel something that's a mix of relief and fear. If I were on the streets, I would feel more settled. Living at the gym and now moving to Kieran's is way outside my comfort zone. You'd think having walls and massive fighters around me would bring me peace and it does a little. But more than anything, I feel vulnerable taking their help.

I just want to get the money and get the hell out of here. Buy a cabin in the woods where I can see anyone coming for miles. Then I'll feel safe. I wasn't lying when I told Kieran how I felt in his arms last night. Stupidest damn thing I could have told him, like he needs me clinging to him right now. What he did last night with the washing and the holding was some primal base-brain behavior. I know it didn't mean anything more than what it was. The resulting safe feeling I had was the intention, so I refuse to feel bad about it. I'm just never bringing it up again.

We walk through the automatic sliding doors and come to a screeching halt. Holy-baby-products-two-stories-high! I'm overwhelmed. How much stuff can a baby need? I can't do this. I start to back up and leave when a perky girl in a pink polo painted on her giant tits comes bounding up to Kieran.

"Hi, I'm Kylie. Can I help you find anything today?" She beams like sunshine at him without a hint of acknowledgment of me. I'm pretty much hiding behind him at this point so that could be why.

"Babe?" he calls over his shoulder at me, I'm assuming.

"Yeah?"

He reaches his hand back in my direction, waiting for me to come to his side. I wait for a moment, uncomfortable in my surroundings as well as with the perky cheerleader.

"Quinn," he growls when I don't move. I roll my eyes and step to his side without taking his hand. He drops it and stuffs both hands in his pockets.

"We need a bunch of stuff," Kieran says sweetly to Kylie.

"I can help with anything you need," Kylie says suggestively like I'm not standing here. I don't give a shit. He's not my...well, anything. But, really? Get some class.

"I don't doubt that," Kieran purrs. Jesus, this is getting uncomfortable. Intense eye-fucking has now commenced and I feel like a voyeur. I turn my gaze to the floor and wait it out. I need to get out of Kieran's life so he can go back to girls like Kylie.

I can't stand here anymore so I walk toward the sign that says car seats. When I get in the aisle, my heart pounds with force at the never ending choices before me. Why I thought this would be simple, I don't know. There's an area with infant seats so I start there.

I look for the cheapest one. No point in spending a bunch of money. I'll get a better one later. I find the least expensive one for eighty bucks and grab the tag to retrieve it from the counter. I move over to the big car seats next. Jack's six, but he's small. I weighed and measured him last night after Kieran left. Jack weighs forty pounds and is forty-three inches tall. Based on the charts everywhere in this store, he's the size of a four year old, like I thought. I'm excited when I find an even cheaper car seat for him that's sixty bucks. I've got enough cash on me now that I can pay for it.

Back in my silo living quarters, I buried a metal box with all the cash I took with me eight years ago. My father kept that box under his bed, so I grabbed it before I ran. It had ten thousand dollars in it. I've spent about fifty on myself per month for the last eight years. Having money and being homeless don't go together. It attracts unwanted attention so I go without most of the time, eating at shelters and missions, buying only when I absolutely have to survive another day. I keep a few hundred in the lining of my backpack at all times, though. I should be able to pay for myself today.

I move over to the baby carriers. If I could have my arms free, it would make life so much easier. I find one for thirty dollars and grab it off the shelf. Then I come upon the strollers. That would be helpful. There's an ugly orange one that has a normal seat in front and bench seat behind it for big kids, the description informs me. It also says that you can put the car seat I'm getting for Ash in the front to make a travel system. Whatever the hell that is.

"Can I help you with that?" a deep voice calls from behind me. I reach in my pants for my knife as I spin around and find a sweet-looking kid in the same pink polo as Kylie, only his fits him.

"Maybe," I respond, releasing the grip on my knife. I can do this.

"This is a good one if you have two kids. Your older one can run around or ride along. Helps to stop the fits that come from exhaustion, you know?" Doug says. I'm thankful for name tags at times like this.

"That would be nice," I lie. Jack would never have a fit from being tired. He's lived a different life from the kids Doug and the rest of the people in this store are used to.

"Best part is, this is a floor model so it's on sale for fifty percent off," he says through a sweet smile.

"I'll take it," I respond, beaming him a large smile.

He starts folding the stroller down while I watch, hoping to be able to remember the process. Once it's collapsed, he stands back up and reaches his hand out to me.

"You want me to ring those up for you too?" he asks. Ah, he wants the tags and carrier I'm holding.

"Thanks."

"How old are your kids?" Doug asks as we make our way to the counter.

"I have a three day old and a four-year-old," I respond coolly. I probably should have lied completely, not just about Jack, but I'm not really on my toes right now. Where the hell is Kieran? Probably in a public bathroom banging Kylie.

Doug rings me up and I hand over a lot of my cash, grimacing a little and then letting it go. Another kid brings the car seats up to the register and it's time to go. Kieran is still nowhere to be seen. I have his keys in my pocket because I sat in the car while he smoked. I guess I'll go to the SUV and wait.

Doug follows me out to the SUV and loads the back for me. The tailgate is too high for me to grab and close it. When I jump a little to reach it, I miss and slip on a patch of ice. Doug throws an arm out and catches me behind my back before I bust my ass.

This, of course, is when Kieran appears around the back of the SUV, finding me in Doug's arms. Kieran's face fills with rage as he balls his fists. I cut my eyes to him in a warning to back the fuck off.

"Thanks, Doug." I smile sweetly and stand up straight. He lets me go, steadying me a little first.

"Thanks, Doug," Kieran mocks from behind him.

Doug spins around quickly, in shock that someone is standing there talking to him. Then the men stare each other down for a moment before Doug speaks.

"You okay here?" he asks me softly, perceiving Kieran as a possible threat to me.

"I'll be fine as long as I don't take up ice skating," I joke, trying to break the tension. "Thanks again for your help."

He smiles broadly at me.

"I hope all of this works out for you. Come back if you need help installin' your car seats. We have a service. Congratulations on your baby. You look great, by the way," Doug says moving past me with a wink. I feel my cheeks flame bright red at the compliment. And then what do I do? I giggle. That's right, I giggle like a little girl, which makes my face grow shockingly red.

"Have a good day," Doug says through a chuckle and pats my arm walking around the opposite side of the SUV from Kieran.

I follow in Doug's path before climbing in the passenger seat. Doug looks over his shoulder and throws me a two finger wave and I offer him a giant smile. Kieran slams the back of the SUV shut, cutting off my smile as the vehicle bounces from his force. He climbs in the driver's seat and slams that door even harder. Okay, Kieran's pissed at something. Maybe Kylie wasn't a good lay.

"Don't. Fuckin'. Do. That. AGAIN!" he roars in my face. I close my eyes and will myself not to grab my knife. It's a battle.

"You wanna tell me why you're screamin' in my face like a crazy person?" I ask calmly before opening my eyes.

"You walked off from me, leavin' me with that nightmare, Kylie. Once I scraped her off I couldn't find you. When I did fuckin' find you, you're in some douche bag's arms," he growls.

"I was givin' you privacy, or at least alone time, with Kylie and your eye-fuckin' session. I went to buy the things you instructed that I purchase. I then came to the SUV to load the stuff in the car and slipped on some ice, when Doug caught me you walked up. I didn't do anything so back the fuck off, Dad," I sneer. I tried staying calm. It's not working.

Kieran breaks into a menacing evil laugh. This version of him is scary and I'm considering climbing out of the SUV when he starts it up and peels out of the parking lot.

"You're so fuckin' lucky you're a girl," he scoffs after we ride a few miles in painful silence.

"You're lucky you're drivin'," I counter, not taking kindly to the threat.

"This isn't gonna work, Kieran. Take me to the gym and then go home alone. I'm not fightin' with you in front of my kids. It's not worth it. They've been through enough. They don't need this shit too."

"And whose fault is that, Quinn? I didn't force you to live on the streets with your kids and let them get worked over by a pedophile. That's on you, Shorty," he seethes.

Kieran pulls up at a red light and I hop out of the car before I slit his throat. We're only five miles from the gym. If I run, I'll make it in forty minutes. I cut through lanes of traffic and then slip between buildings and alleys, Kieran's screams fading in the distance.

Chapter 13

Kieran

I have beyond fucked up and I have no clue what to do. Quinn flew out of the SUV and disappeared like a ghost. I drove around for twenty minutes trying to spot her, but never did. So now I'm sitting outside the gym waiting for her.

Let me clear something up...I was not eye-fucking Kylie. I was attempting to be nice to get us some help. When Quinn ran off, that girl turned into the scary chick that gives men nightmares. I didn't expect Quinn to shop on her own and leave me there. I figured she was finding a distraction to rescue me from the claws of clingy. No such luck. I finally got away from Kylie by telling her I needed to find my wife. Kylie paled at that and let me go.

I made my way around the store twice and couldn't find Quinn, so I went out to the SUV thinking she got overwhelmed in the store. Then I find pretty boy holding her in his arms. I saw red. And to top off my fury, she giggled at him. I've never heard her giggle. She gave him that and I lost all common sense. I said horrid shit to her and chased her away. I need help.

"Hey, Kieran." Shannon's sweet voice fills my ear.

"I fucked up," I admit in a defeated voice.

"That didn't take long."

"No shit."

"How bad?"

"Bad."

"Kieran," she sighs. "Tell me."

So I launch into the whole story from last night to right now. Shannon's silent until I finish.

"Holy fuckin' shit, Kieran. I don't even have words. Good for her. Fuck, I'm jealous I didn't get to see her in action. I've had fantasies about doin' someone like she did the Russian. But you said she's not like me and that shit'll fuck with her in one way or another. If she says she's fine she probably is right now, but this just happened. Two months from now the nightmares could creep up on her. She needs to talk to someone. Someone you can trust not to turn her in. It's important, Kieran.

"Now for your bullshit. Are you completely fuckin' stupid? Don't ever again in your life say something like that to a woman who's lived the life you think she has. You haven't got the first clue what happened to her son or how. God forbid somethin' worse was happenin' to her while that little boy was tortured, you inconsiderate prick! Rein in that temper of yours and do it quick. You run her off and you know you're puttin' her in danger."

"I know," I huff.

"You want her?" Shannon growls.

"She just gave birth, Shannon," I admonish.

"Answer the fuckin' question this time."

"Yeah. Okay, yeah. She's gorgeous and soft. She doesn't need me to, but she lets me take care of her. A woman like you'd drive me insane. I need someone like Quinn," I admit.

"No shit. You couldn't begin to handle me. You pulled some shit on me like you just pulled and there'd be a bullet in your head. Good for her for not slittin' your throat. Though from what you said, I'm guessin' she ran to keep herself from doin' just that. Are you really ready to jump in and be partner and Daddy? That's a lot, Kieran," she finishes softly.

"I feel better when they're with me. I feel like I'm more than a criminal and a fighter. I feel sick for what I did to her today. You know me Shannon, I don't give a shit about anyone. Other than you."

"Then you treat her how you treat me. You weren't in my life for ten years and in the last seven weeks, you've done any and everything for me and never been cruel. I'm easier than she is so give her softness, Kieran. Give her what you've given me. And if you want her you do it right. Tell her and don't act like a caveman because some kid's helpin' her after you deserted her. You do this and it's a lifetime commitment. There's no goin' back."

"You think I can do it? I'm not changin' who I am, Shannon. I can't. I'm not a good person. Probably safer for them to let 'em go," I say defeated.

"Of course you can do it. If you're not a good person then neither am I. So weigh those words carefully. What you did last night was gruesome, but it was honorable in my opinion. You're a good man with twisted morals. That doesn't mean you deserve any less happiness in life. Make this right and be happy. Someone in our family needs that right now," she says in an emotionally exhausted voice.

"God, I'm an asshole. You doin' okay? Collin said everyone's worried about you. That you're not lookin' good."

"I'm fine. I just want my man and the baby home," she whispers.

"It'll happen. I feel it. You need me for anything, just say the word."

"I will. Go find your woman and fix your monumental fuck-up. I love you, Kieran," she finishes tenderly.

"Love you, too."

As I hang up I see Quinn out of the corner of my eye running down the alley toward the back door. I quickly scissor out of the SUV and run to cut off her path. When she sees me her face falls. She's tired from running and her eyes are filled with anguish. I did that. Time to take my punishment.

"I'm so fuckin' sorry, Quinn. I didn't mean what I said. I was pissed and tryin' to hurt you and I succeeded. I'm an asshole. I'm a monster. I'm a criminal. I have a nasty temper. I don't deserve anything as good as you in my life, but I want you. I want you so bad, Quinn, it fuckin' hurts. I know that's fucked up because we just met and have gone through some crazy shit, but there it is. I don't care that you have kids and just gave birth. I want you even more because of them. Please come home with me and let me take care of you. All of you. Forgive me," I say as sincerely as I can muster.

She regards me with her icy blue eyes for a few moments before taking two steps toward me. She squares her shoulders and takes a deep breath.

"Fuck you, Kieran Delaney. You don't know me. You know shit about me. You don't even know my name. Stay away from me. Stay away from my kids. You come near me again and I'll do a better job than I did last time. Get outta my way," she seethes, stalking past me through the back door and slamming it behind her.

Wow. I was not expecting that. I figured she'd be a typical girl and fall for my admission of wanting her. Shit! Okay so in real life, women don't just change their mind because some smooth-talking man says the right thing. Good note.

I hear my tailgate open and walk back out of the alley. Connor and Owen are unloading Quinn's stuff when I walk up. Owen hears me, pivots on his foot and lands his fist in my jaw with a crushing blow. I spit blood in the snow.

"Feel better?" I sneer.

"Not yet," he says, rocking back, landing a blow to my ribs. He continues to work me over for a few minutes before he's content with my state. My nose is bleeding, my brow is split, spilling a red river into my eye, at least a few ribs are bruised and my jaw is swelling. I never fought back. I deserved what Owen handed me and more.

Connor just kept unloading the SUV as I took my beating like a man.

"Feel better now?" I ask in a heaving breath.

"Yeah. What the fuck did you do to her?" he growls.

"Fucked up," I admit, spitting more blood into the snow. I pull my hoodie and T-shirt off before pressing it to my brow to stop the flow of the bleed. I need a couple stitches.

A car pulls up behind mine, stopping all three of us. The doctor climbs out of the car, eyeing us suspiciously. He approaches me and pulls my T-shirt from my face.

"You're a pain in the ass, Kieran. Come on," he complains, pulling the gym door open.

I follow behind the doctor while Owen and Connor fall in step behind me. Ian, Quinn and Jack are sitting on the couch while Ashling is lying across Quinn's arm drinking a bottle. Quinn doesn't look up at me as I pass. Jack does, though.

"Kieran, you got more booboos. Did the pimps get you?" he asks, concerned.

"Nah, bud. I just had an accident. I'll be back in a minute," I say softly.

Ian offers me a scowl and Quinn continues to act as though I don't exist as I pass them and make my way into the therapy room. The doctor stitches me up in no time and sends me off to clean up. When I come back into the therapy room everyone is in there while the doctor looks over Ashling.

"When were you due?" the doctor asks Quinn.

"In March sometime. I'm not sure an exact date," she responds sheepishly.

"That's all right," he responds kindly.

"Is she breast or bottle-feeding?"

"Bottle."

"Eating well?"

"About four ounces every three hours," Quinn responds, seeing me for the first time. She quickly looks away and concentrates on Ash who's lying on a therapy table in front of the doctor. He's got all the baby's clothes off and is examining her thoroughly.

"That's good. She's definitely jaundiced. I'll take some blood and check her bilirubin count to see if she needs phototherapy. At this point it's important to keep her hydrated. Overall, she looks healthy though, Quinn. You did good," he compliments her sweetly. She nods but doesn't reply.

The doctor pulls out some supplies to take Ash's blood. He cleans her foot and then pokes her with a tiny needle in the heel. She screams and throws her arms up. Jack flies at the doctor, yelling and punching him in the back. The doctor doesn't react as I pull Jack off and hold him to my chest. Jack starts beating on me and I allow it.

"Jack, the doctor's just takin' some blood from Ash to make sure she's okay. Calm down, bud," I soothe in his ear. I hear a sob break from his chest and he collapses against me. I shush and pat his back, locking eyes with Quinn. She looks broken. She doesn't have enough arms to comfort both kids at the same time. I offer her a small smile, but her gaze remains on her son's back.

The doctor finishes quickly with Ash. He tapes gauze over her wound and Quinn scoops the baby to her chest, kissing and shushing her.

"I'll get these labs back in a few hours, Quinn. Take care," the doctor says as he packs his things away and leaves the room.

Quinn quickly dresses Ash then crushes her into her chest again. She stalks toward me and Jack leaps into her extended arm. Quinn walks in the bedroom door and slams it shut with her foot. She never so much as breathes the air around me. I've lost her, just when I found her.

Chapter 14

Quinn

There's a fight at the gym tonight and I need to find somewhere to take the kids. Ian and I have a pretty good routine. He helps me get the kids ready in the morning and then I leave for the day while the fighters train. Ian has stopped all evening training for now which surely pissed some of them off, but no one argues with Ian Brogan.

When I get back we eat dinner together, watch some TV or a movie and then get ready for bed. The routine is good for the kids. I take them to parks during the nicer days. It's early March though, so those days are few and far between. I haven't taken them to any homeless areas or shelters for fear Jack will be recognized. We walk to nearby pubs and shops most days. Jack asked if he could go to school and I told him he can next year. Ian looked up a homeschooling program online that I'll start with Jack once we're in our own place.

Things are good, except my plan to get us free from Chicago isn't moving forward...at all. I can't get any kind of identification. I've tried to procure a few forgeries but they've all been too poor quality to work. I'm afraid to get one legally. The people looking for me have connections all over the city, underground, in offices, in politics, in the gutters and any place else they can pay people to be. They're everywhere.

We rode the L today for a long time. Jack loves the train. He keeps his face pressed to the windows, pointing and commenting on everything he sees. He's happy and we're safe for now. I'm nervous to rock the boat too much by removing the boundaries I have in place to keep us safe. I went to the silo that used to be my home and cleared everything out. I've got four thousand dollars to my name. I can't make a new start with that amount of money. I could get a cheap apartment here on the South Side, but that, again, requires giving people information. So I'm stuck living in the gym until I can find a high quality forger to get me passable identification.

"Quinn, I don't want you in the streets with the kids at night," Ian huffs as I zip up Ashling's white puffy snowsuit. Jack's already in his bright blue one trying to pull his gloves on by himself.

"I can't be here. It's not safe for them. You know that as well as I do," I whisper so Jack can't hear me.

"Where are you gonna go with them?" he urges.

"Millennium Park. We'll have fun. Don't worry about us." I attempt to ease his concern.

"I'll text you when the last fight starts."

"'Kay."

I load Ashling into her car seat and then put it in the stroller. Jack hops on the bench at the back and the three of us set off into the Chicago night. We hop on the Red Line and head to Millennium Park to be a normal family.

It's almost midnight and I haven't heard from Ian. He sends me out with his phone any time we leave. It's not like him not to text. I feel a trickle of panic creeping up my spine as I approach the gym with the kids. I have

Ash asleep in the carrier and Jack's asleep in the stroller seat, the car seat is wedged on the bench. I push the stroller to the alleyway and park it. I can hear voices inside so I crack the door open to check it out before walking in.

"Tell us where they are!" a man roars and punches Ian in the face.

Ian's tied to a chair in the middle of the gym. There are at least eight men standing around him while one guy uses him as a punching bag.

"You have something that belongs to us and I want it back," the man seethes and crushes Ian's face again. I don't recognize these men or the man's voice. I shut the door silently and run with the stroller to the end of the alleyway. I can get away from here quickly if they spot me. I frantically pull the phone out and call Connor. I get his voicemail. I leave a panicked message and try Owen. Fucking voicemail! I call them both again with no answer. Shit, shit, shit! I push his number and almost hang up before he answers.

"Yeah?" his tar and whiskey voice crackles through the phone. I freeze at the sound. I haven't spoken to or seen Kieran in over a month. I never planned on seeing him again, if I'm honest.

"Ian?" Kieran questions loudly. There's a lot of background noise like he's at a pub or a party.

"Kieran?" I whisper.

"Quinn? Hang on, I can't hear you," he yells. "Hey, I'm outside now. What's up?"

"Ian's in trouble," I keep my voice low.

"What?! Where are you?"

"In the alley behind the gym. There's about eight guys in there roughin' Ian up bad. I can't take 'em on myself. I've got the kids with me."

"Don't. Move," he growls. "I'll be there in three minutes." I hear his Camaro beep and then the line goes dead.

I pull Ash out of the carrier and lay her next to Jack in the stroller before moving the stroller behind a dumpster that's pushed away from the brick wall. I yank both my knives out and wait. I hear the roar of Kieran's engine and then see his headlights, followed by another set. Kieran jumps out of his car while Connor and Owen jump out of the other one. They sprint toward me. Connor pulls me into his chest roughly.

"You guys okay?" he growls. I nod.

"Wait out here. Hide back there with the kids," he instructs and moves to the door. Kieran throws it open loudly as I crouch behind the dumpster, knives at the ready. I pity the motherfucker that tries to get these kids from me.

I hear Kieran roaring and threatening the men, though I can't make out his exact words. The back door is open a touch, but I don't dare sneak a peek. Now there's grunting and scuffling—someone is fighting. This goes on for a while before I hear a single gunshot. I hold my breath and wait for more, but I hear nothing. No sound, no murmurs, no whispers, just the silence of the night around me and the peaceful breathing of my sleeping children.

I wait until I feel like I'm going to pass out from the anxiety when I hear footsteps. I clutch my Yarborough and listen as the steps crunch closer and closer.

"Quinn," Kieran calls out softly. "I'm comin' around the dumpster alone. Don't stab me."

I wait with my knife at the ready. I only hear one set of footfalls, but I'm taking no chances. A few breaths later, Kieran's in front of me alone. He's covered in blood and his knuckles are bleeding. That's the only scratch on him from what I can tell, though.

I quickly stand up and stow my weapons.

"You're comin' home with me," Kieran whispers glancing at the kids. "Owen and Connor are takin' Ian to the hospital. Don't worry, he's just banged up, but he needs a hospital. It's not safe to be here right now. Let's go in and get your stuff. The kids need to get to bed."

I want to scream right now. I want to stab someone right now. I want to hurt that man that hurt Ian right now. But I can't do anything. So I nod and push the stroller into the gym.

The chair Ian was tied to is empty and there's a large pool of blood on the floor a few feet from it. Otherwise, the gym looks normal. I feel a chill run up my spine. Those men were here for my kids. I move with purpose to the bedroom and start packing up all our stuff into Brogan's duffle bags from the therapy room. Once all our clothes and the kids' toys are packed, I empty the bathroom. I walk out dragging bags while Kieran stands watchfully near the kids.

"Go out to Ian's car and get Jack's car seat and Ash's base unit for hers," I instruct Kieran in hushed tones. He moves quickly at my request. Four giant bags of stuff later and I'm standing on the curb while Kieran loads the Camaro with the car seats. Once he has them in I put the kids in and fold down the stroller. Kieran stuffs two of the duffle bags in the passenger floor board then places me gently in the seat. He runs around back and loads the stroller and the other bags. The trunk closes with a soft click and Kieran has us pulling away a few seconds later.

We ride in silence the few miles to his house. When he pulls in the garage I release a small breath I didn't realize I was holding. Kieran jumps out of the car and runs out of the garage toward the house. I guess I'm on my own. I climb out of my seat and hoist the heavy bags off the floor, setting them next to the car. I walk around to Kieran's side of the car and pull Jack out of his car seat. He's heavy, dead weight when he's asleep. I go back around the car and struggle to get Ash's car seat off the base unit but finally manage.

As I walk out of the garage onto the paved stone path leading to Kieran's brick house, he races down the stairs off the deck. He's now shirtless, his hair wet, wearing very low slung sweat pants and no shoes.

"Sorry, I needed to clean up real quick," he apologizes in a whisper before scooping Jack off my chest then grabbing Ash's car seat. He makes that look too damn easy.

Kieran walks into the guest bedroom, setting Ashling on the floor before laying Jack in the bed. He gently covers him up and then creeps out of the room, pulling me with him. He stops in the living room, grasping me by the shoulders, searching me from head to toe with his eyes.

"You're not hurt, right?" He's concerned and soft right now, but I've learned that's a rarity with Kieran Delaney.

"I'm fine, Kieran. I was hiding, remember?"

"I know." He eyes me a moment longer before saying, "I'll go grab your stuff."

Kieran pulls on a pair of sneakers and then heads out the back door. I love Kieran's house. It's open and wide yet warm and inviting. I would love to get the kids a house like this with a yard they can play in.

I see a picture on the wall that catches my eye so I move closer to it. It's Kieran flying Jack around the gym. They both have huge smiles on their faces; I can almost hear the laughter. I smile at the memory of them doing that the weekend we spent with Kieran at the gym.

"I love that." Kieran's voice at my back startles me. "Sorry, I didn't mean to scare you."

"It's okay," I say quietly, not looking at him. "He's gorgeous."

"Yeah, he is," Kieran agrees. My son is a stunning boy. He's gained a few pounds and looks a little taller already. I'm guessing by the time he starts school in the fall he'll almost be caught up.

"I better get back to the kids. Thanks, Kieran. We'll be outta here tomorrow." I don't look at him as I walk past. I push the guest room open, pull Ash from her car seat and climb in bed with Jack. With both of them in my arms I fall asleep fast.

Chapter 15

Kieran

Quinn's here in my house. I can't fucking believe it. When she called tonight I almost fell over. Just hearing her voice soft and scared made my stomach flip. When I saw her in the alley my heart stopped for a few seconds. I've missed her and the kids so much I'm not sure how I've functioned.

I haven't been back to the gym since the day we fought. Ian threatened to kill me while Connor and Owen extended me the same offer. I didn't stay away because of them, though. I stayed away because of her. The pain I caused her that day was unbearable for me to witness in her eyes every time she looked at me. It was worse than her stabbing me. Quinn was amputating my soul with her icy blue eyes. So I left her alone like she told me to.

I spent two days with Quinn and since I've been away from her, I've been lost. I didn't know it was possible to care about someone that fast, but it is. Now that she and the kids are in my house, maybe I'll sleep tonight. I can already breathe easier.

I need to figure out what those fuckers at the gym tonight want with the kids. They were hell bent on getting Ashling and Jack. I knew those boys. They're part of a street gang that usually run guns and drugs. I have not a clue why they want the kids. I beat the shit out of the leader in the room. Punk kid named Tommy O'Rourke. After I beat him bloody I shot him in the knee just to make myself clear. My name carries enough weight that I wasn't worried about being clear, just needed to be sure I was heard. What they heard was a lie. A lie I now have to convince Quinn to go along with. I told them that her and her kids are mine.

That information in the street should spread like wildfire. By morning, Quinn and the kids will be known to the criminal community as protected and untouchable. If someone comes for them now, they'd have to be completely insane. Problem is, the lie only works if Quinn agrees. She's not speaking to me. Shit, she's not even looking at me, so this will be fun.

I lock the house up tight and then head to my bedroom. I pause at their door, listening to the sound of them breathing and snoring. It settles my soul. After a few minutes I enter my bedroom, pulling off my sweats, and climb in bed in my underwear, storing my gun beneath my pillow. Tomorrow is make or break for me. I hope like hell this works out.

I wake to the sounds of screaming and fly from my bed with my gun in my hand. I burst into the guest room and flip on the switch that controls the lamp in the corner. Jack's in bed crying and rocking himself, alone. I set my gun on the dresser and quickly move to him.

"Jack, it's me, Kieran. You're okay, bud," I soothe, leaning close to his face. Jack's eyes fly open and he hurls himself into my chest as Quinn flies into the room.

"Baby?" she calls in an alert tone.

"You left me," he cries.

She comes to the bedside and leans down near his face.

"I didn't leave you. I was feedin' Ash. I'm sorry you were scared," she coos. She turns her gaze to me and I understand she wants her son. I set him on the bed and take Ash from her arms. I stand up and leave the room to finish feeding the baby as Quinn pulls Jack into her lap on the bed. I snatch my gun on the way out and put it back in my room before heading out to the main room.

There's a bottle thrown on the floor dribbling formula onto the hardwood. I tag it one-handed and pop it in Ashling's mouth while I sit on the couch. She's so much bigger already. Her cheeks are a little chubby and her inky curly hair looks longer. The weight of her in my arms feels like heaven. If I could hold Jack and Quinn right now, my world would be perfect.

As if on cue, Quinn comes in the room carrying Jack.

"He wants you," she whispers. I pat the cushion next to me and she flops down. Jack lays his head against my chest, but keeps his body on Quinn. I wrap my arm around her shoulders, pulling her tightly into my side. She tenses under my touch and I don't care right now. They're here, that's all that matters. The three of them fall asleep in minutes and my cold, dead heart beats to life once again.

Once they've been asleep for a while I carefully peel my body away from Quinn and Jack. I swiftly deposit Ash in my bed and come back for the other two. With Jack lying on Quinn, I scoop them up together, moving fast down the hall to my room. Once I'm in my room I place them in bed near Ash. I climb in behind them, wrapping them in my arms, securing them to my chest the same way I did weeks ago. I fall asleep in mere moments with a grin on my lips.

I wake up to a firm ass wiggling against my crotch. My eyes fly open and I realize it wasn't a dream, they're actually here.

"Mornin'," I murmur into Quinn's hair.

"Sorry," she whispers. "I'll get them outta here in a minute."

I guess there's no time like the present. I gently push Ash and Jack away from Quinn and then turn her in my arms to face me.

"We need to talk and I'm takin' advantage of the fact that you're unarmed and your kids are asleep a few inches from us," I whisper. She narrows her gaze at me but remains silent.

"The men at the gym last night are part of a street gang that I know. They were there for the kids. I don't know why. I beat the shit outta the guy runnin' the show and blew his knee out for good measure. In order not to get shot by the room full of men that were with them, I told a lie. A lie that not only kept me safe, but that will keep you and your kids safe, too," I explain quickly.

"What lie?" she grumbles, still scowling at me.

"That you and the kids are mine."

I just let the words hang in the air. A bevy of emotions pass through her eyes before she settles on confused. I can work with confused.

"That information will have made it to every criminal organization in Chicago by now. No one will fuck with you or the kids. As long as they believe you're with me and that those kids are mine, you won't be in danger. But they have to believe it, Quinn. No more walkin' the streets all day and avoiding people. You'll have to be seen with me regularly, with the kids, too. Everything has to seem real. We can come up with a back story together. I told them you were stayin' with Ian because I was in the dog house, which isn't entirely untrue. Tell me what you're thinkin'."

"I'm thinkin' you're a real prick most of the time. I'm thinkin' no one has ever said more cruel things to me than you have. I'm thinkin' Jack loves you and I hate that. I'm thinkin' when you're good to me there's nothin' better in this world. And I'm thinkin' about whether I should stab you or kiss you," she finishes emphatically.

"I am a prick most of the time. I'll spend every day I can tryin' to make up for the awful things I said to you. I love your kids and I'm thrilled that they love me. I'm the best me I can be when I'm with you. And—" I smash my mouth against hers. She hesitates for a moment and then kisses me back, running her tiny arms around my neck, pressing her soft body against mine. I plunge my rough, scabbed hands into her hair and slant my mouth to allow more access. A small moan escapes Quinn's throat and my dick twitches.

Gently, I lick across the seam of her mouth and after a torturous few moments she allows me access. I massage my tongue against hers drinking in the taste of her soft sweet mouth. It's better than I imagined. I nip her bottom lip and she growls, yanking my hair almost painfully. I trail my hand down her back and palm her ass roughly, rocking my hard dick into her stomach. I'm dry humping a girl in my bed like a teenager and it's the best feeling in the world.

We tangle our tongues until I can barely catch my breath. I move my mouth from hers and trail my teeth along her jaw up to her earlobe. I gently flick it with my tongue before pulling it with my teeth.

"Oh," Quinn moans quietly. I'm going to come in my pants.

I roll her body beneath mine and sneak a quick glance at the kids. They're both out cold.

I kiss and suckle my way down her neck to her collarbone as I push my hand beneath her T-shirt. I cup her tit, a perfect handful, kneading the soft flesh. Her nipple is peaked as I run my thumb across it. I take the lace cup down and feel her smooth skin beneath mine for the first time and moan deep in my throat. I capture her mouth with mine again, pulling and pinching her nipple as I slide my body between her legs. She arches into me further as I grind my hips into hers.

Her breath hitches and I know I'm hitting her clit. I increase the friction and roll her nipple harder. She begins to shake and writhe so I pick up my pace. I'm so close. Quinn scratches her nails down my back as I thrust my tongue in tandem with my hips. She arches so far off the bed it almost knocks me off. Quinn pants short, sharp breaths and then comes squealing in my mouth, shuddering from head to toe. Two more strokes and I blow the biggest load known to man.

Panting and sucking in air, I collapse on top of her, burying my face in her neck. She giggles. That should be the soundtrack of my life. It's the best fucking thing these ears have heard other than Jack's laughter.

My come is soaking through my boxer briefs onto her stomach and I love it. I have gone full caveman and feel like I've marked her as mine. I want to reach down and rub it in her skin, but that's a bit much. So I just lay here and let it seep into her on its own.

"I guess you decided on the kissing instead of stabbing," she whispers, running her hands softly up and down the back of my head.

"Uh huh," I grunt. Oh God, I sound like a fucking caveman. She giggles again.

"I'm gonna go clean up," I murmur into her neck. I pull my hand out of her shirt and kiss her swollen lips twice before I push off of her. I hop in the shower, quickly washing off. In my dressing room I pull on a fresh pair of boxer briefs and black sweat pants before heading back to my little family.

When I come back in the room, Jack and Quinn are sitting in the bed talking.

"Hey, bud," I call as I walk to him.

"Hey, Kieran," he says with a giant smile making his crystal blue eyes squint.

"Can I talk to you about somethin'?" I ask him as I sit on the edge of the bed facing both of them.

"Sure."

"Some things are gonna be different now and I want you to understand," I start off. He nods and furrows his brow in concentration. Quinn looks much the same. I smile at both and continue. "You're momma and I are gonna be together now. And you're all gonna live here with me. It's my job to keep you safe. Part of keepin' you all safe is people knowin' I take care of you."

"Okay. You want me to tell 'em you take care of us?"

"Kind of." I pause for a moment. "I want you to call me Dad or Pop or whatever other word you wanna use," I say softly.

"Mommy?" Jack looks freaked.

"Baby, it's okay. Kieran's helpin' us. He's gonna take care of us for a while and this is part of it. When we're at home you can call him Kieran if you want. But when we're out of the house we need you to call him somethin' else," she coos.

I fucking hate that she just said I was going to take care of them a *while*, but I squash the irritation. She's trying to help her son with a big change.

"Can I call you Daddy?" he asks sheepishly. I know he's a little old to call me that, but he's never been able to call anyone Daddy. He deserves that experience.

"Yes," I say emphatically. He looks back and forth between Quinn and me a few times, thinking everything through.

"Okay, Daddy," he whispers with a grin on his lips and my heart skips a beat. I'll never forget this moment as long as I live.

"Okay, bud. You hungry?"

"Yes. Do you have pancakes?"

"No, but what if we go out for pancakes? How about that?" I ask, peering at Quinn. I can see the tension in her face so I pull her to me and kiss her forehead. She melts against my chest.

"Cool. Do I have to wear my snowsuit?"

"Nah, we'll take the car."

"Mommy, we get to go in Daddy's car!" he squeals and jumps off the bed.

"Thank you," Quinn murmurs in my neck.

"No. Thank you." I tip her head back and kiss her lips long and sweet.

"Gross," Jack says, making us laugh against each other's mouths.

We pull away from each other as Ash starts to wake up. Once we're all dressed and Ash has eaten her bottle, we climb in the Camaro and head to The Original Pancake House.

Chapter 16

Kieran

I've never done this before. Yes, I've eaten pancakes in public, maybe even with a woman once or twice, but never this. My woman under my arm, Jack on my shoulders and Ash in her car seat, clutched in my grip, walking into a restaurant to have breakfast with my family feels fucking amazing.

Once we get a table, I see a few guys from the neighborhood eyeing me cautiously. I offer their table a chin lift like I would any other day and turn back to my menu.

"Daddy," Jack whispers.

"Yeah, bud."

"That man's starin' at me," he murmurs, hiding under my arm. I look up, ready to pound someone's head in, to see my father striding toward my table. Fuck me!

Carrick "Rick" Delaney has spent his life as a thief. He's a good thief, only busted once. I get my criminal interests from his genes. He's shorter than me and starting to thicken in the middle. His hair is more grey than dark brown these days, his hair line pushing back more every year. I've got his eyes, in color and in observation abilities, and his are working me overtime as he saddles up to the table.

"Son," his gravelly smoker's voice reverberates a little too loud for the venue.

141

"Pop," I say with a hint of warning.

I shift my gaze to Quinn, who's piercing me with her icy blues. Her hand is grasping her knife beneath the table. I can't see it, but I can tell by her posture.

Pop pulls up a chair to the end of the table, acting the part of comfortable family member. I'm thankful for his ability to go with anything right now, but Quinn and the kids are unnerved by his presence.

"I've had an interesting morning," he says, eyeing Jack beneath my arm.

"I'm guessin' that's true. This isn't the place to talk it through, Pop. I'll call," I growl under my breath. The table of neighborhood boys is now gawking in our direction.

"Your mother wants you over for dinner tonight."

"No problem," I huff.

"I'll let you get back to breakfast. Six o'clock, she's makin' shepherd's pie."

With that, he stands, nods at the gawkers and leaves.

Jack uncurls slightly from my side as Quinn lets out a shaky breath.

Our waitress comes to the table for our order before I can calm everyone down. After we order I can feel their tension easing a bit so I don't say anything. We can talk at home.

"I need to get some groceries," Quinn breaks the silence. "Your kitchen is empty."

"Not much of a cook, Quinn," I snort.

"Neither am I," she admits sheepishly. It's not a surprise because she hasn't had a kitchen in eight years.

"I like grilled cheese sandwiches," Jack announces.

"Me too. I like 'em with tomato soup," I say through a grin.

"Mommy says she'll cook me anything I ask her for, but I don't know a lot of different food."

My heart sinks a bit, but I brush it off.

"Well I know lots."

"You do?" he asks with a bit of glee in his voice.

"Sure do. Your momma and I'll figure out some new stuff for you to try this week. It'll be an adventure."

"Cool."

After we polish off breakfast, where Jack ate the exact same thing as me again, we head to the grocery store and buy enough food to feed a small army. Jack giggles and laughs the whole time as I point things out to him in the store. It's like he's seeing the world for the first time. I hate it and love it at the same time. Quinn grins and shakes her head at us, but never comments.

Once we're back home and all the food is put away I take Jack and Quinn into his room. I push the door open and Jack squeals with delight. Quinn falls against my side as she gasps. I did this the week after Quinn told me to leave. I don't know why I did it, but I needed to.

The walls are covered in huge removable stickers of every comic hero I could find. The single bed has *Avengers* bedding. There's a large circular rug in the middle of the room with a Marvel Comics collage. He has a pine dresser and bedside table with a Thor lamp. One wall has a storage unit filled with toys, books, games, puzzles and anything else I could find that I thought he'd like. It's a perfect room for him.

143

"I get to stay in here?" Jack whispers, his eyes darting to every surface.

"It's all yours, bud."

Jack walks around the room, running his hand across the walls, toys, dresser and finally his bed. He turns his gaze to me with tears streaming down his cheeks and I feel tears prick the back of my eyes. He flies across the room, wrapping his arms tightly around my waist. I pull my arm off Quinn's shoulder and pick Jack up under his arms. He wraps around my front like a monkey, squeezing the life out of me. Finally, after a few calming breaths, he pulls his face from my neck and looks into my eyes.

"You won't leave me, right?"

"I won't leave you, Jack," I state emphatically.

"You won't let anyone hurt me?"

"No one will *ever* hurt you again."

"You won't make Mommy cry anymore?"

"I'll do my best not to make your momma cry," I say, knowing I'll make Quinn cry again at some point. I'm still an ass, but I'm trying.

"You're the best daddy ever," he whispers and lays his head on my shoulder. Trying to avoid turning into a blubbering idiot, I glance down at Quinn who's apparently fighting the same urge. I kiss Jack's hair and set him down.

"You play in here for a while. I'm gonna talk to your momma out in the living room."

"Okay."

Jack scampers away, pulling puzzles off the shelves. I pull Quinn from the room by her elbow, leading her to the living room. I flop on the couch and yank her down next to me. Ash is on the floor sleeping in her car seat. All is well.

"So you met my dad," I start off with a chuckle.

"Kieran what you did for Jack...I'll never be able to thank you enough. It's everything I've ever wanted for him," Quinn whispers, gazing up at me.

I brush my thumb across her cheek, placing a soft kiss on her plump lips. She still can't weigh more than a hundred pounds, but there's more weight on her. She's softer against my side than she was weeks ago.

"I have everything for a nursery for Ash in the basement. I couldn't do pink so I did yellow. If you don't like it we can take it back. I'll have to clear out the guest room to fit everything I got. If you don't want that I'll just set up the bassinet in there and you can take the guest room. It's whatever you're comfortable with," I say encouragingly. I'm not forcing her into my bed. If she wants to be there it'll make my fucking day, but if she doesn't I'll understand and be patient.

"Let's start with the bassinet," she whispers, pulling her face away from me.

"Quinn, there's no pressure. I'm not gonna force you to do something you're uncomfortable with. As long as you three are here, I'm happy."

I tip her chin up and capture her mouth with mine, teasing her lips with my tongue. She threads her fingers through my hair, pressing her mouth to mine. A growl thunders in my chest as she parts her lips and whispers her tongue across my bottom lip. I slant my mouth and take the advantage, plundering her mouth with my tongue. Quinn moans and arches her back with pleasure vibrating over her skin. I run my hand down her rib cage when a squeal breaks the mood.

"Someone's awake," I mumble against her lips.

Quinn smiles and pulls out of my arms. While she unhooks Ash from the car seat I go to the kitchen and make a bottle. I bring the bottle back to Quinn as she's bouncing Ash in her lap, making goofy faces at the baby. Ash is staring with her bright blue eyes in wonder at the crazy woman.

I get to the couch and take Ash from Quinn and pop the nipple in her mouth.

"I can do that, Kieran," Quinn admonishes, fussing with the baby's forever-falling-off socks.

"I've missed a month."

She nods and lays her head back on the couch.

"So your parents?" she asks warily.

"My dad's a thief. Has been his whole life. Did a nickel when I was a teenager. Only time he's been caught and that's 'cause someone ratted. He was a decent enough dad. Never hit, never cheated, always kept a roof over our head and food on the table. Ma's a seamstress, works outta the house. She wanted a big family, a shit load of kids, but only got me and miscarriages. So she fusses over me as much as I can stand."

"Are they gonna have an issue with us?"

"Nah. Ma'll be happy to have kids to fawn over. Dad's easy enough. They just wanna know what's goin' on with us. Don't worry. They'll love you all."

"Okay. So what's goin' on with us?"

"What do you mean?" I ask with a scowl.

"We need a story, Kieran. Homeless family, murder, only knowin' each other a few days is not a good story," she says pointedly.

"They'll know the kids aren't mine. I can't run that story past them. I'll have to tell them a close version of the truth. Tell 'em we met through Ian and can't live without each other. Let them fill in the holes on their own."

"They'll think I'm a whore and a gold digger," she whispers.

"Don't," I growl fiercely, making Ash jump. "Don't fuckin' say shit like that...ever."

"What else are they gonna think? I saw the look on your dad's face. He thinks I'm runnin' a con and usin' my kids as bait."

"Okay so we tell 'em Ash is mine. I fucked up and was a dick like usual. You're givin' me a second chance."

"I can't do that to Jack. If you claim Ashling, he's left out. That's cruel for no reason," she grumbles.

"Quinn, I'm tryin' here. I don't wanna do anything that'll upset anyone. If I could convince 'em they're both mine I would. As far as I'm concerned they are mine. That's all that matters."

"They're not yours, Kieran. This isn't gonna work. I appreciate what you're tryin' to do, but this lie is too much to pull off. The people you're scarin' off are gonna find out sooner or later. I need to get the kids outta here before it causes you any more trouble." She's panicking and it's pissing me off. I close my eyes and take a few deep breaths before I say or do something stupid.

Quinn hops up off the couch and busies herself in the kitchen. Once Ash is done with her bottle and back to sleep, I lay her on the couch and run down into the basement. I grab the bassinet and a baby monitor. I quickly set everything up in the guest room and carry Ash back. Once she's settled and the monitor is on, I close the door quietly. I peek in at Jack who has ten puzzles put together on the floor before heading back to the kitchen.

"Whatever your brain is tellin' you...stop it," I command coming up behind her while she washes already clean dishes. I wrap my arms around her tiny waist and constrict.

"It's tellin' me to run. That it's safer for all of us," she says dejectedly.

"Well your brain is fuckin' wrong. You runnin' with two kids is not safer than meetin' my parents. My parents aren't gonna have a problem with you or the kids. If you want me to tell them both of the kids are mine, I'll do it. I'll own the lie. Whatever makes you happy. No one in the street is gonna think it's a lie. I have a pretty foul reputation with women."

Quinn spins in my arms and glares at me.

"Told you I'm an asshole, Shorty. I've never had a real relationship other than a few steady fucks. That's the cold hard truth. People out there know that, too. So if I say I've got a woman and two kids, it'll be a shock, but one they'll pay attention to. I'd never claim somethin' that wasn't mine."

"Funny, 'cause that's what you're doin'," she scoffs.

"I'm tryin' to be nice, but you're makin' it really fuckin' hard," I growl, leaning into her face. "You're mine. They are mine. Say somethin' different again and we're gonna have fuckin' problems. Tell me you understand."

"I understand," Quinn whispers.

"Good."

I press a hard kiss to her lips and let her go. She releases her knife behind her back and turns back to the sink. I definitely make her feel stabby.

"Connor texted and Ian's gonna be in the hospital until tomorrow. I know you wanna see him, but I think it's better to hold off until he's outta there." I change the subject and let my anger roll off my shoulders.

"Is he okay?"

"Just banged up. Nothin' that old man can't handle. Connor says he's pissed and barkin' at the nurses every chance he gets." I chuckle at the thought of Ian with his perma-scowl growling at nurses.

Quinn snorts but doesn't comment.

Buzz, buzz.

"Yeah," I bark into the phone.

"Kieran, you could use some manners when your mother calls," Clare Delaney chastises me.

"Sorry, Ma."

"Your father says you'll be here at six."

"That's the plan," I grumble.

"I just wanted to be sure. Well, I have dinner to prepare. I'll see you tonight. Love you," she hums.

"Love you too."

I hang up and glance at Quinn who's starting to make sandwiches for lunch.

"Told you she fusses over me. Just makin' sure we're still comin'," I explain.

Quinn offers me a sweet smile and focuses on the turkey in front of her.

"Daddy, you wanna build Legos with me?" Jack calls from his room.

"You bet," I yell back. I place a soft kiss on Quinn's neck and go build the biggest Lego tower known to man.

Chapter 17

Quinn

Pale yellow thin sweater, tight (due to my recent weight gain) dark jeans and a pair of white canvas sneakers Ian bought me. This is what I'm wearing to meet Kieran's parents. I have no idea if I look appropriate or if I look like I'm trying too hard. I've never met anyone's parents.

I had a boyfriend from the time I was fifteen until I left. I'd known him and his family my whole life so I didn't have to meet his parents. I didn't have to try with them. This is different.

I'm leaving my knives in the car tonight. I don't think I should be armed to meet parents. Probably sends the wrong signals.

Kieran knocks on the guest bathroom door for the fifth time.

"My mom's gonna have a cow if we're late, Quinn. Let's move," he grumbles.

I wish I had some make-up. I could hide behind some eye shadow and foundation. I could make myself look my age instead of like a teenager. No such luck. I take a deep breath and leave the bathroom.

Kieran's walking out the backdoor holding Jack's hand and carrying Ash in her car seat with the diaper bag over his shoulder. It's the cutest thing I've ever seen. Kieran's wearing dark loose jeans, a navy long sleeved T-shirt, brown leather boots and his leather coat. On his own, he'd look badass. Toting kids and a diaper bag, he looks like a DILF. I giggle to myself and follow them out of the house.

I lean in the backseat of the SUV and hook Jack in his car seat while Kieran loads Ash in on the other side. Kieran bought the most expensive car seats he could find during the weeks we were apart. They've been set up in his SUV just waiting for us, according to him. I smile as I climb in the passenger's seat.

"You look gorgeous," Kieran breathes in a lust-filled voice.

"Sorry it took so long," I apologize, ignoring his compliment.

Kieran eases out of the garage and drives us to his parents'. It's less than a mile away so it's a quick ride. We could walk it with ease. If I didn't drag my feet so long this afternoon we could have walked this evening. Next time...if there's a next time.

I've been warring with myself all day. Everything in me is telling me to run for the hills. I'm scared. I don't know how to do the happy family thing. People are going to start asking questions about me and the kids eventually and I don't have the answers yet. I don't know if I ever will. I've gotten by so far by letting people come to their own conclusions.

I've gone from invisible to highly visible in a few short hours and it's freaking me out. No one knows my name and I've been gone long enough that the people looking for me won't be looking for a Quinn. But they will find me at some point. I need to trust Kieran when he says he'll keep us safe. I know he'll try his best. I don't know if his best will make a difference when they come for me.

I slide my knives under my seat and climb out. The Delaney house is red bricked with flower beds on the sides of the path leading to the front door. The front door bursts open when we hit the bottom stair leading to the porch. A slight woman with her deep chocolate hair up in a messy bun, wearing a pale blue sweater and a pair of chinos covered with an apron fills the doorway.

"Get those kids in here outta the cold," she orders quickly.

Kieran pushes me ahead of him and I slide past her with Jack on my hip. The family room I'm in is warm and inviting with walls covered in knick-knacks and pictures. There's a small fireplace roaring at the far end with two couches on either side. The house smells like food and hickory. A small smile ghosts my lips.

"Your dad's downstairs catchin' the last of the game," she says to Kieran before shutting the door.

"I'm Clare," she says softly, extending her hand to me.

"Nice to meet you. I'm Quinn and this is Jack and Ashling," I respond kindly.

"Well, let's get you all outta your coats and fill your bellies," she says with a smile.

I set Jack down, crouching before him, and unzip his coat before pulling mine off. Kieran takes them from me. I shift over and take Ash out of her car seat, removing her from her fleece cover-up. She snuggles into my chest and Jack climbs onto my side as I stand up.

Kieran reaches to take one of the kids, but I move out of his reach. Jack's nervous and so am I. We feel better when we're together in each other's arms. I follow Clare into an open kitchen dining area that's light and inviting with white cabinets and butcher block counters.

"I hope you're hungry," she calls from the stove where she resumes whatever she was doing before we got here. I walk up to the breakfast bar and Kieran pulls out a wooden stool for me. With a large heave I get myself in the seat and settle Jack on my lap.

"You know I'm always hungry, Ma," Kieran responds, pressing a kiss into my hair before sitting on the stool next to me.

"Jack, I'm makin' a special dessert for you. I'm meltin' some chocolate—you think you could help me out? Maybe taste it to make sure I got it right," Clare's tone is warm and inviting.

Jack's head pops up off my shoulder and glances over to Clare. She smiles at him, then returns to stirring her pot. Jack looks up at me and I offer him an encouraging smile. He grins, slides off my lap and walks over to Clare's side.

Clare reaches down to Jack, picking him up under his arms and plops him on the counter next to the stove. He watches everything she does with a gleam of curiosity covering his soft features.

"All right, Jack. Tell me what you think?" she asks in dramatic fashion. She spoons a small bite of the concoction she's making into his wide open mouth.

"Mmmmm, that's yummy!" Jack exclaims, running his tongue over his lips searching for more.

"It's my favorite, too," Kieran's father bellows from behind them. He darts around the other side of Clare, sticking his finger in the pot, then brings it to his lips dramatically. Clare swats him with a wooden spoon as he smiles mischievously at Jack. Jack snickers and looks up at Clare with puppy dog eyes and she quickly complies with another spoonful in his mouth.

"All right now, you two. I'll finish this up and we can start on dinner," Clare says, popping Jack back down on the floor. Jack looks around the kitchen a bit and then climbs into Kieran's lap. Kieran swipes his thumb at the corner of Jack's mouth, removing chocolate, and then licks his thumb clean. Jack crinkles his nose and giggles.

"I'm Rick," he states, reaching his hand across the breakfast bar toward me. I take his hand in mine briefly.

"I'm Quinn and this is Ashling. You've met Jack."

"You are some kinda pretty, young lady," he says with a whistle. My cheeks flare at the compliment. I give him a sheepish smile before looking to Kieran for a little help. He simply beams at me.

"Ten more minutes and everything'll be ready. Quinn, can you and the kids come downstairs for a minute? I wanna show you something," Clare says as she removes her apron and messes with the oven.

"Sure," I reply nervously. Jack climbs out of Kieran's lap as we follow Clare down to the finished basement. We walk through a large open rec room and then into another large open room filled with clothes, fabric, sewing machines and other things meant for creating clothes.

Clare moves over to a table and picks up a few things before coming back over to us.

"Now, I had to guess based on what Rick told me, but I think these should work," she says, crouching down in front of Jack. She holds a bright blue canvas jacket up to him, checking the size against his chest. It's gorgeous and makes his eyes even more impressive. She slides it over his shoulders and smoothes it down the front with her hands.

"Perfect! What do you think?" She looks up at me.

"It's really beautiful, Clare. Thank you."

"Cool," Jack offers. "I'm gonna go show Daddy." He takes off up the stairs. Clare freezes for a moment then schools her features before standing and holding out a small white dress with pink accents.

"She's probably a little small for it yet, but she'll grow into it," she says with tears in the back of her hazel eyes.

"It's really amazing. I can't believe you do all this," I say in awe of the things around the room.

"I learned to sew when I was a little girl. Makes me happy to create something with my hands. What do you do?"

And the questions with no answers begin. I figure I'll tell as much of the truth as I can and then wing it.

"I'm home with the kids for right now." It's true.

"It's nice to have that time when they're little," she coos, running her hand over Ash's head.

"How did you and Kieran meet?"

"Through Ian Brogan."

"Ian's a good man. How do you know him?"

"He's a friend of the family." And so the lies begin.

"Are you close with your family?" she asks with a little hope in her voice.

"I'm not. I haven't seen them in a really long time, actually. Been on my own since I was seventeen." The truth is just easier right now.

"Well, you've got great kids so you must be doin' all right," she says with a genuine smile on her lips. "Let's get upstairs and eat some dinner."

I nod and follow her back up the stairs. Kieran and Rick are sitting at the table while Jack regales them with a story from one of the comic books Kieran got him. Jack can't read yet, but when I read to him he absorbs every word.

"You think I could read one of those comic books with you some day?" Rick asks as we join the merriment.

"Sure. My mommy reads 'em the best, though. She does all the voices and sounds."

"It's quite entertaining," Kieran teases. I roll my eyes and lean into his side. He kisses my hair and his mother wipes a quick tear from her cheek.

"All right. Dinner's ready. Let's sit down at the table. Quinn, honey, do you wanna lay Ashling down?"

"I'll hold her. Thanks, though."

We all sit at the table and eat a glorious shepherd's pie with homemade bread. Most of the conversation is led by Jack and his stories. We laugh and smile while we eat like a normal family. It's a comfort I've missed. I didn't realize until this moment how alone I've been in this world for the last eight years. As emotion clogs my throat, I fuss at the baby until she wakes up. Not the nicest thing to do, but it gives me a distraction. I hop up from the table and head into the living room to change her and get a bottle ready.

Laying her down on the floor, I gaze around at the walls filled with love and memories. Pictures from trips and family holidays decorate the walls and tables. There are a few with Collin (hot cop cousin) and, I'm guessing, his brothers because they all look the same. Kieran grew up in the same world as me with crime a part of his every day, yet he had something I didn't. He trusts the people he comes from. His family is built on loyalty, dílseacht. Mine was built on lies and deceit.

When I'm done changing Ash I gather her up and peruse the pictures more closely, getting glimpses of Kieran as a boy. I can see the hard edge that he has now developed over time. It wasn't always there on his face. It came during his teenage years, probably when his father was in prison. I turn to the last wall of photos which are older and mostly of Rick and Clare when they were young and first together. They look so happy and full of life. Then I see a familiar pair of eyes looking back at me in a picture tucked a little behind a few others.

With shaky fingers I lift the frame. My father and Rick are standing next to each other, each with an arm around the other's shoulder, smiling at the camera. They were young, in their early twenties. They look like they don't have a care in the world.

I reach a finger out and trace my father's smiling face. I don't know if I ever saw him that happy in all my years with him. I'll never see him that happy now. I close my eyes and try to commit his features to memory. Having this vision of him in my mind is better than any that I currently have to look back on.

I gently return the frame to the shelf and go back to the kitchen. I have to be careful with anything I say to Kieran's parents now. If they knew my father they'll put the details together quite easily.

Clare helps me warm the bottle and I retake my seat at Kieran's side as everyone eats dessert. I feel sick to my stomach at this point so I politely decline, focusing all of my attention on Ashling and Jack.

When everyone's done eating we head into the living room to talk. Jack bounces around for a while before settling into my side and falling asleep, crashing after eating too much sugar. The weight of his body against mine feels like an anchor to reality that I need in order to make it through my life right now. I need these kids as much as they need me.

"So you wanna fill us in on what's goin' on?" Rick asks. Kieran is on my right holding Ash to his chest with me tucked under his arm, his warm hand resting on Jack's sleeping head. His parents are sitting across from us holding hands like we're about to tell them the meaning of life.

"Not sure how much you need filled in on. We're together," Kieran dismisses the question. Rick scowls and Clare rubs his hand in a calming motion. I remain silent.

"Okay, let's try this. My phone starts runnin' off the hook this mornin' with every person I've ever known askin' about my grandkids and their mother. Wantin' to know why it's been kept a secret. Wantin' to know how nobody knew all this time."

"I fucked up. Quinn didn't put up with my shit. She's offerin' me another chance now."

"Kieran!" Clare admonishes. "You can't be serious?"

"I'm serious."

"That's all you've got to say for yourself? You expect me to believe that you've had two children and never told me? That you would keep my grandchildren away from me for years with not so much as a word? I don't believe you, Kieran Michael Delaney. Not one word," she huffs.

"If she's in some kinda trouble and you need help, I'll do everything I can. You just have to be straight with me," Rick says, his eyes pleading with his son to be honest.

"They're my kids, Pop. I'm sorry this is hard for you guys. I don't wanna hurt you, but that's the truth," Kieran says emphatically.

I can't even look his parents in the eye so I study my hands. Kieran is a lot of things but a liar isn't one. I can't turn him into one just to keep me safe. Lying in the streets for our benefit is one thing, but lying to the people that he loves is crossing a line. Dílseacht. Here goes nothing.

"My name is Darcy Quinlan," I say, raising my gaze to his parents. Both of them pale, remaining completely still and wordless. Kieran goes rigid beside me. I let that information hang in the air for a long time before I continue.

"The O'Boyle Brothers would pay a lot of money for that information alone. So yes, I'm in trouble, but you can't help me. I appreciate the offer, though."

"Darcy Quinlan is dead," Rick mutters, trying to figure out what's going on.

"That's the rumor," I snort. My uncles spread that a few years ago after they couldn't hunt me down. I'm sure they were hoping it would make me feel safe enough to pop my head out from behind whatever dumpster they were searching so they could chop it off. It only made me that much more diligent.

"Is that why you kept these kids from us? You thought they'd be safer if they weren't known about?" Clare asks with a pained expression. I go to tell her the truth as Kieran painfully squeezes my shoulder, letting me know I need to shut up.

"Yes," he replies simply.

160

"And it's safe for them to be known now?" Rick asks, disbelief on his face.

"No one knows her real name. People believe Darcy Quinlan's dead. I want my family so we're takin' the risk. I can keep her and the kids safer with me, anyway."

Clare and Rick look sick right now. They believe the lie, which kills me, but I'm following Kieran's lead. These are his parents and I have to trust he knows what's best when it comes to them.

"Your father was a good friend when we were young men," Rick explains, his face lost in memories. "We lost touch over the years, but I've got some great memories with him."

"Maybe you can tell me about it sometime," I offer, wanting to know more about my father.

"Kieran, Quinn, I'd really like the opportunity to spend some time with the kids," Clare whispers in a sad voice.

"You can have as much time with them as you want, Clare. I'd love that for them and for you," I respond kindly, Kieran remaining silent. I can't tell if he's pissed or just working my sudden bomb through his head, but he's more stoic than usual.

"Thank you," she says through a weak smile.

A silence falls over the group and I get nervous.

"The O'Boyles will figure this out eventually. You need to make sure you're ready for them when they come lookin' for their long lost niece," Rick says to Kieran with a protective ire to his voice.

"I'll be ready."

Chapter 18

Kieran

After Quinn dropped her bomb I got her and the kids out of my parents' house quickly. We put the kids to bed and I dragged her into my bedroom.

Quinn's curled up in a ball against the headboard, her knees pulled protectively in front of her chest. I'm sitting facing her on the edge of the bed waiting for her to explain.

"Time to talk, Shorty," I urge in a low tone. I'm not pissed, but it's coming.

"What else do you wanna know?" she whispers, staring at the comforter.

"Why have you lived on the streets for the last eight years?"

"To keep myself alive."

"Need a little more than that."

"I was in the house the night it happened. My parents told 'em I was out for the night as I hid under some floorboards in our living room. I listened as my mother was tortured, raped and murdered by her own brothers' gang. I listened as my father screamed through his gag to make them stop. I listened as my father's men betrayed him for scraps of money. I listened to every single sound and word until it was silent. Then I laid there until my blood ran cold and my soul died," she finishes with one tear sliding slowly down her cheek.

163

I feel puke rise up the back of my throat. The O'Boyle Brothers are a crime organization that mainly run guns and drugs, but in recent years have started human trafficking. They're nasty motherfuckers to deal with. I worked with them for a while, maybe five years ago. I did a few hits for them and then got out, not people you want to be in bed with for long. If Quinn is a witness to the shit she just described, no wonder they want her.

Patrick Quinlan was convicted of his wife's murder with quite a bit of fanfare. The lifelong financial whiz for the mob was blinded by money and drugs, according to the State. Her uncles framed her father for her mother's murder and then he was killed in prison. Everyone believed it was a revenge hit for killing their sister. FUCK!

"So they want you because you're a witness?" I clarify, hoping this story doesn't get any worse.

"If only it were that. My parents left everything to me. House, money...everything. My father laundered and moved money for them. When the O'Boyle Brothers decided to start trafficking people my father wanted out. They didn't take kindly to his lack of loyalty to the family so they decided to eliminate my parents. They underestimated my father, though. Apparently he had a computer system set up that he had to check in with every twenty-four hours. If he didn't check in, it took every dime from the O'Boyle companies he had access to and filtered all of the money into a bunch of different places before it ended up in a bank account. The age of technology fucked the O'Boyle Brothers hard. I found a file with the account information before I left the house that night, memorized it and burned it as instructed by a sticky note on the front written by my father. His last words on that note said run. So I've been runnin' ever since."

I climb further into bed and scoop her tiny frame into my lap, forcing her legs around my waist.

"I'm sorry you went through that. I'm sorry you lost your parents. I'm sorry you were on your own for so long. I'm sorry your uncles are worthless fuckin' pieces of shit. I'm sorry I didn't find you sooner," I say softly, peering into her icy eyes that are shimmering with unshed tears.

"Now you and your family are in danger. I should just run, Kieran. I should take my kids and go before something happens."

"Absolutely fuckin' not. I just got you and I'm not lettin' you go. I can keep you and the kids safe. We need to figure some of this shit out and I'll broker some kinda deal with them. If they want their money they'll deal. They may be the scum of the earth, but they're smart enough to arrange somethin' with me and get their money."

"I'm sorry about your parents. They probably hate me now," she huffs burying her head in my chest.

"They don't hate you. They're pissed at me and I don't give a shit. They'll get over it. We need to get birth certificates for the kids with my name on 'em. Do you have Jack's?"

"I don't even have an ID for myself," she mumbles in my chest.

"I know a guy at the DMV. I'll get your license tomorrow. Did you have a license before? Shit, do you even know how to drive?" I ask, realizing she was really young when she hit the streets.

"Yes, I know how to drive and I had my license," she says in a chuckle, sitting up to face me. "I also graduated from high school before everything went down."

"Okay, we'll get your license and then go to Vital Records and get the kids' birth certificates. A paper trail like that'll be good for us."

"'Kay," she says in a yawn. "I'm gonna go to bed. Ash'll be up in a few hours."

Quinn peels out of my lap and scoots to the edge of the bed before I pull her back to me. I lay her down and climb on top of her, holding my weight off of her with my forearms on either side of her head. I pepper her face with kisses before pressing my lips to hers. She wraps her tiny arms around my neck and opens her mouth without hesitation.

I tangle my tongue with hers, enjoying the flavor of her mouth mixed with mine. I move my hand under her sweater and knead her tit as she moans and arches into me. I break from her mouth, sitting up on my knees while I grab the hem of her shirt. I slowly pull it up her body and over her head. I stare down at her petite frame as a flush works its way up her chest to her cheeks. Reaching behind her back I unclasp her bra and throw it across the room. Her tits are perky with raspberry nipples standing at stiff peaks.

"You're fuckin' amazin'," I groan. I reach behind my head and pull my shirt off before I bury my face in her chest.

I pull her tiny nipple in my mouth, nipping and sucking while I work the other between my thumb and forefinger. Quinn hisses at the feeling, pushing herself toward me. Her fingers twist and pull my hair, encouraging my exploration. I kiss and lick my way down the plane of her perfectly flat stomach, marveling at the smooth, soft skin.

I pop the button on her jeans and slowly pull down the zipper with my teeth, pinching her nipple hard as I go.

"Ahhh," flows from her throat.

I pull off her jeans and panties in one fast motion and then settle between her legs. I kiss her inner thighs, causing her to whimper. Her pussy is shaved completely bare which I was not expecting. I don't remember her being shaved when I washed her, but I'm loving it. I blow a cool stream of air against her and she shudders from head to toe, goosebumps rising on her skin.

I push her thighs apart wide until they're lying on either side of her chest. Holding her there I take one long lick from back to front, savoring her taste. A gravelly, sexy moan rattles in her chest and I get to work.

I fuck her with my tongue hard, thrusting in and out of her tight little hole, lapping up all of the juices spilling from her. She rocks her hips furiously back and forth. I move my mouth to her clit and suck, gently, massaging it with the flat of my tongue and her legs begin to shake. I pick up my speed and harden my tongue, flicking and licking her clit. She slams her head back and whimpers my name as she comes in my mouth shuddering and jerking violently.

I gently ease my mouth from her, kissing a trail back up to her mouth before kissing her deeply. She licks her come from my mouth, mewling and clawing at me for more. If she doesn't stop I'm going to take her right now. So I pull back and rest my forehead against hers.

"Stay with me tonight," I whisper.

"Yes."

I pull the covers back and pull her naked body against mine after I remove my jeans. My raging hard-on settles against her back and she starts to move.

"Be still or you'll have a mess on your back," I warn.

"Do you want me to take care of you?" she asks sheepishly.

"I'm good. I just wanna hold you in my arms."

"'Kay," she sighs and falls asleep a few breaths later. I follow not long after.

I wake up to an empty, cold space next to me. My pillow smells like milk and honey, but that's all that remains of Quinn. I climb out of bed, rubbing my dílseacht tattoo which, over the years, has become a calming motion for me. The house is silent, eerily so. As I pass the open, empty bedroom doors my heart begins to pick up in pace. When I hit the living room a trickle of fear creeps up my spine.

As I'm turning to run back to my room and get dressed, I hear Jack squeal outside. I hastily move to the back door to find Jack outside in the back yard jumping around in freshly fallen snow while Quinn watches, holding a snowsuit-clad Ashling. My pulse slows as I watch their smiling faces for a few minutes before moving back to my room to get dressed.

I take a quick shower before pulling on jeans and a black sweater. Making my way down the hall I hear the three of them coming in the back door.

"Can we go out later and build a snowman?" Jack asks hopefully.

"Sure, Baby," Quinn coos.

As I round the corner I find Quinn struggling to juggle the baby and peel Jack out of his wet snowsuit.

"Mornin'," I call as I make my way to them.

"It snowed!" Jack exclaims.

"I see that. Did you have fun out there?"

I sweep Ashling up into my arms and put a big wet kiss on her chubby cheek.

"I made snow angels. Mommy said we can go out later and make a snowman."

"Love makin' snowmen. Can I come too?" I ask, peeling the baby out of her puffy suit.

"Yeah, you can come. Do we have carrots?"

"I think so, Baby," Quinn answers, pulling the last of his suit off before taking it into the utility room.

"Do you think Rick and Clare would come build a snowman with me?" Jack asks walking over to the dining room table.

"I'm sure they would. I'll call 'em and ask, bud."

"Cool."

Quinn comes back and starts making hot cocoa. I tag her arm as she slides past me, pulling her into my chest. She tips her head up and I place a soft kiss on her lips.

"Mornin'," I murmur against her mouth. She grins.

"Gross," Jack mutters, causing us both to chuckle before she slips out of my hold and goes back to the cocoa.

We spend the morning together lounging around the house, playing with Jack and Ashling. Jack is non-stop energy, but he's happy doing pretty much anything. He never complains about picking up or playing on his own.

He's always content. I know it's because everything is new to him and he's got things he's never had before, but it's also because he's a good kid.

Ash is the quietest baby in the history of babies. She fusses a little when she's hungry and that's about it. Otherwise she's sleeping or staring at you with her big blue eyes that seem to hold millions of questions. She's absolutely stunning and she'll probably get me arrested when she's a teenager. Teenager? Fuck me, am I really that invested in this already?

I guess I am. I don't want them to leave. I want them here with me and the thought of them being in danger only solidifies that fact. I'll do anything I can to protect them from the demons lurking in Quinn's past. I need to start fishing around to find out more about the money that was funneled away from the O'Boyle Brothers.

Money is always the answer to the questions of criminal organizations. Respect and loyalty fall in there too, but it's always about the bottom dollar. Dead bodies don't pay bills at the end of the day. If I find a way to get their money back, they'll leave Quinn alone. I'll make fucking certain of that. No one is taking my family from me.

Chapter 19

Quinn

April has brought the rain with it, along with some headaches. Kieran has been working tirelessly to figure out a way to access the O'Boyle Brothers' money. Things have changed in the world since my father died. Having the account information is a small part of the equation in accessing and moving what we're guessing is millions of dollars. Kieran has some teenage hacker looking into ways of moving the money safely.

"Ian!" I yell down into the gym from his office. I've been working here two days a week, helping Ian with his books and things. Turns out my father's financial skills rubbed off on me. Kieran watches the kids while I come into the gym to help out.

I work while the fighters are here and no one pays Kieran Delaney's woman any mind. In fact, most of them don't even make eye contact with me. His reputation goes much further than I originally anticipated.

Ian ambles over to the stairs before answering, "Yeah?"

"Call for you."

Ian climbs the stairs quickly. His beating resulted in a cracked rib and a mild concussion, both of which he called bullshit pussy injuries and went right back to training fighters when the hospital released him. He's been on a mission to figure out what the street gang wanted with my kids, but so far he's come up empty handed. I'm hoping Kieran's message has run whoever was searching for them off for good.

"You wanna fight, Quinn?" Connor yells up to me from the grappling area. He's dripping with sweat and standing with Owen who looks a little worse for wear after sparring for an hour.

"You wanna get beat up by a girl?" I call down as I make my way to him.

"It's my favorite pastime," he says with a cocky smirk on his lips, his green eyes glowing with mischief.

I've been learning to protect myself for the last month at Kieran's request. Connor and Owen have taken on the job to personally turn me into some kind of ninja assassin. It's a good workout and I've learned a lot from them.

I get to the bottom step and tie my hair in a bun before Connor scoops me up and heaves me to the ground. I do the release moves he's taught me and he lets me off easy. I'm covered in his sweat and mine when I hear a voice from my past.

"Darcy?" he calls.

Connor stops his movements when my body goes rigid. I wait for a long moment, hoping I'm having some kind of weird auditory hallucination. I look up from where my face has been buried in the mat to see I'm not hallucinating.

"Sean?"

Connor slides off my back and picks me up off the floor, setting me in front of him, leaving his hands around my waist. Owen has stopped jumping rope and slides next to us.

"I had to see if it was true. Where have you been?" Sean asks, shaking his head from side to side, trying to figure out if he's hallucinating.

"Around. You shouldn't be here."

"What? After all this time that's all you've got to say?" he asks with a tinge of anger to his voice. Connor's hands constrict against my skin, but he remains silent.

"I'm not sure what you're here lookin' for. I can see you've moved up in the organization," I say, nodding toward his neck. The O'Boyle Brothers mark men with a Celtic cross on the back of their necks that wraps around the sides. I can see Sean's peeking around from beneath the collar of his jacket.

"I've done all right for myself. Can we talk alone for a minute?" he asks, eyeing the men protecting me.

"No," Owen growls.

"Last I knew her, she could answer for herself," Sean growls back.

Sean was a kid when I left, seventeen and lanky. He's now filled out and scarred up from a life of crime. His sandy hair is swept to the side, revealing a small scar on his forehead. His green eyes are stormy from a life of seeing torture and death. Sean's muscles flex and twitch below his tight T-shirt and jeans, itching for a fight. He's as big as Connor and Owen.

I see the familiar bulge under his jacket revealing his gun. I don't want trouble. I knew they'd find me eventually. No time like the present.

"Let's step outside," I say calmly.

Connor pulls me roughly into his chest, indicating he doesn't like my answer.

"Connor, can you grab my jacket from the office please?" I ask sweetly, patting his hands. Reluctantly, he pulls away from me and stomps up the stairs. Owen takes the opportunity to pull my body in front of his.

He leans into my ear and whispers, "Kieran won't like this." I nod my understanding. Kieran won't like this, but Sean won't do anything to me. I can see it in his face. He still has a soft spot for me.

Connor returns with my jacket and by the weight I can tell both my knives are hidden in the inside pocket. Good man. I slide it on and walk to the back door of the gym, Sean in step behind me.

The metal door slams shut as I lean against the brick wall across from it, waiting for him to say whatever it is he needs to get off his chest. He steps in front of me, a little close for my liking, but I remain relaxed. Or at least I look relaxed as I cross my arms across my chest and palm my Yarborough.

"Eight fuckin' years and you never came to me. Eight fuckin' years I thought you were dead. Now I find you and you're here. You're fine. Explain this shit to me, Darcy," he growls into my face.

"I am dead as far as you or my uncles are concerned."

"Jesus, you still got a fuckin' mouth. You think you bein' Kieran Delaney's woman is gonna stop me? You're wrong. I don't give a shit how bad that motherfucker is. You've been mine since you were born. It's time to come home."

Wow. I was not expecting that. Sean was my one and only boyfriend. I've known him my whole life and our parents pretty much raised us to be a couple when we grew up. There were always conversations of our future wedding and the grandchildren we would give them. Shit changes when people are tortured and murdered at the hands of the family Sean now loyally serves.

"I have a home, Sean. It's nowhere near you or my uncles. Don't lie to me and tell me you've been laying alone in a bed waitin' for me," I scoff.

"Pussy's pussy. *You* are mine."

"Fuck, you're delusional. You think you can come here and tell me what to do after all this time? Go to hell, Sean. Tell my uncles to join you there."

I push off the wall, nudging him with my shoulder. Sean flattens his body against mine, slamming me hard against the brick.

"You've forgotten how I work," he purrs against my ear. "Maybe you need a reminder."

The metal door across from us bangs open and Sean turns to see who's interrupting. His body is ripped from mine, thrown to the ground, as Kieran wails away at his face. I remain where I am, watching the blood bath.

Sean gets a good hit on Kieran and flips him to his back, returning the crushing blows. Kieran quickly shoves Sean off and tackles him back down to the ground. They roll around for a while before Kieran slams Sean's head into the concrete, knocking him out. Heaving and panting he gets to his feet, slowly trying to calm down his rage.

"Get inside now!" Kieran roars. I quickly move around Sean's body and go in the gym. This is not the time to argue or dig my heels in about being bossed around.

Connor is throwing Jack in the air while Ian is pulling Ashling out of her car seat as I enter the gym. Owen side swipes me carrying me into the therapy room.

He sets me on a table and starts feverishly looking for any marks on my body.

"Owen, I'm fine. Just a conversation," I insist, pushing him back a little.

"Kieran's gonna fuckin' kill me. I can't believe we let you walk out there with him. I didn't recognize him," he huffs, scrubbing his hands over his face violently.

"I'm okay. Kieran'll get over it. I'll keep you safe," I tease a little.

He grunts a weak sound in his throat as Kieran barrels through the door, pulling me off the table by my waist without pause. Once he has us in the bedroom he slams the door shut and heaves me onto the bed. Pacing at the side like a caged animal rubbing his dílseacht tattoo over his shirt, his face marked with pain and fury, I wait.

"You're not that fuckin' stupid," he growls in a low, menacing tone. "You're not stupid enough to go in an alley by yourself with an enforcer for the O'Boyle Brothers. YOU. ARE. NOT. THAT. STUPID!!" the caged animal roars.

I remain silent. There's no point talking to him when he's this wound up. So I wait for the beast to subside.

"Don't fuckin' move," he instructs and stalks into the bathroom again, slamming the door with such force I'm surprised it's not falling off the hinges.

As I hear the shower start there's a small piece of me that wants to leave the room to show him he doesn't run me, but I won't do that to him. I'm not playing games with Kieran. If he needs me to stay put right now I will. Not because he told me to but because he needs it and I can give it to him.

He makes quick work of his shower and stomps out of the steam filled room with only a towel around his hips. His entire upper body is covered in tattoos. I love looking at the black and grey ink, almost fluid as his muscular frame moves. The man in front of me is power personified. I feel safe with him even when he's looking at me like he is right now...pissed.

"Sean was my boyfriend," I start to explain and Kieran flinches like I just slapped him across the face. "He apparently feels that I'm still his and came back to take me home. That's what you walked into. Him attempting to stake his claim. He wouldn't hurt me, Kieran. That's why I went to talk to him alone in the alley. I would have cut him before he knew it was comin' because he still thinks of me as the high school girl I was."

"He was your boyfriend?" Kieran asks like he's finally seeing me through a thick fog.

"Yes."

"Sean Casey was your boyfriend?"

"Yes."

"Your parents knew this?" he asks shocked.

"We were practically betrothed. I've known him my whole life, grew up together. He lived five houses down from me. It was expected that we'd be together. I didn't have a choice, really." I shrug.

"So you have a thing for criminals?" he asks in a snide tone.

"No, I grew up with criminals. The typical dating pool wasn't within my grasp as a teenager. Sorry to disappoint you. Would you prefer I had a wholesome preppy boyfriend? Is that a better option for you?" I say with irritation in my voice. Why does this matter to him?

"He was touchin' you," Kieran grumbles, taking a few steps toward the bed.

"He was thinkin' about touchin' me and gettin' ready to get cut."

"He was in your space. Had you pinned against a brick wall in an alley. Quinn, I don't give a shit if he's part of your past, you can't be alone with him or anyone else that used to know you." Kieran's finally starting to calm down as he sits on the edge of the bed.

"I'm sorry I worried you. I was fine. I *can* take care of myself. Been doin' it long before you came along. Sean Casey doesn't scare me."

I wrap my arms around his shoulders from behind, inhaling the scent of the industrial combo in his damp hair. His muscles are taught and straining, still hyped for a fight. I rub my hands across his chiseled chest, kissing his neck softly.

I'm stopped when I hear a commotion out in the gym. Kieran growls, stepping out of my embrace and dropping his towel as he walks butt ass naked into the therapy room. I scamper behind him. He stops and pulls on some sweats from a storage bin in the corner. That's when I see the commotion and break into a sprint toward my kids.

Chapter 20

Quinn

"Jack!" I scream. He fights to get to me, but can't break from the embrace of the man holding him. Guns are aimed at all of the fighters trying to get to my son. Ian is panting and growling, smashing Ash to his chest, a gun pointed at her head.

I haul ass, not flinching at the guns until I'm right in front of him.

"Put my son down, now," I seethe. A cocky smirk stretches across his face as Jack struggles and fights.

"Is that any way to say hello to your uncle after all this time, Darcy?" my uncle Connall asks with warning in his tone.

"Put. My. Son. Down!" I roar. His dark brown eyes narrow at me before he slides Jack down his body. Where the fuck is Kieran? I thought he'd be right on my heels. He's nowhere to be seen.

Jack heaves himself into my arms, shaking violently. I shush and rub his head, kissing his face over and over, glaring at my uncle.

"Brogan!" Connall barks. "Bring me that baby."

"Fuck you, O'Boyle!" Ian roars.

I turn to Connor who's pumping his fists violently, shooting daggers from his eyes at my uncle, a gun pointed at his chest by Sean (who looks like shit).

I pass Jack to Connor, stepping in front of Sean's gun.

"You point that thing at my son, it'll be the last thing you do in this life," I fume at Sean who lowers his gun with shock on his face at my boldness. I turn back to Connor and give him a knowing look to hide Jack's view of what I'm about to do. He puts a hand on Jack's head, pressing it firmly into his neck. I glance at the therapy room to find Kieran, but he's not there. Would he really abandon me in my hour of need? This feels too familiar. I shake the feeling off, keeping my head in the game.

I spin quickly, pulling my Yarborough out as I move, ending with the tip pressed firmly against my uncle's heart. His face pales for the briefest moment before a broad smile splits his face.

"I see you've developed a skill set in your time away from me. You'll make Sean a suitable wife after all. Not a coward like your mother," he snorts.

I spit in his face and pierce his skin slightly with the tip of my blade. A mask of rage slips over his face. He moves to raise his hand to wipe his face and I move my knife again, halting his movement.

"She'll need to be trained, Sean. Gone a bit feral in the streets," he says calmly, never leaving my gaze.

"Get your men outta here now or I'll gut you," I whisper, my voice sounding foreign to my own ears. The threat of wrath in my tone is unmistakable.

"Time to come home, Darcy. You can bring your bastard children if you must."

I snort.

"I am home. Get. Out. Now!"

The back and front doors of the gym fly open, men in black tactical gear racing in, weapons drawn, screaming at people to drop their weapons. I hear the resounding clunks of metal hitting floors and mats around the gym. I keep my knife drawn, never removing my eyes from my uncle. They can arrest me if they must. I'm not letting him go.

From my periphery I see an official-looking man walk in the front door, striding confidently toward me.

"Ma'am please lower your weapon," the man says calmly near my side.

I don't comply with his request. My uncle smirks at my defiance like he's proud. I want to finish what I started. I want to plunge this knife through his chest until the hilt bruises his flesh.

"Quinn, put it down," Kieran's voice quietly filters through the rage in my brain.

My hand relaxes slightly as Kieran runs his hand over mine, helping me lower my weapon.

"Connall O'Boyle, you're under arrest for..." the official next to me rattles off a bevy of charges, but my ears stop listening. I quickly spin away to find my kids. Kieran has Ash curled into his chest while Jack is still clinging to Connor.

Sean is on his knees with his hands on his head being read his rights. I spit on the floor in front of him. He shrugs his shoulders and smiles at me, like that turned him on.

I pull Jack into my arms from Connor's chest. He clings to me tightly as I move through the mass of people into the therapy room. I set Jack on a table and start inspecting every inch of him the same way Owen had done to me only a half hour ago.

181

"Did they hurt you?" I whisper. Jack shakes his head no, but his chin trembles.

I'm going to make what I did to that Russian look like child's play when I'm done with my family.

"Quinn, he's okay," Ian soothes from behind me. I feel tears welling up in my eyes. They almost got my kids. Fuck!

I nod my understanding and pick Jack back up as three men enter the therapy room. It's Collin, his twin brother (hot times two) and, I'm guessing, their father, who looks damn good for an older man.

"You all right?" Collin asks Kieran.

Kieran offers him a chin lift. Connor, Owen and Ian stand behind me as Kieran sweeps a protective arm around my shoulders. I want to punch him for leaving me out there alone. I don't do it, though; I just stand there holding Jack.

"I'm Stephen O'Sullivan. These are my sons Collin and Hugh," the older man introduces.

I nod.

"I understand you're Darcy Quinlan. The O'Boyle Brothers' niece?"

"I am."

"I'm sorry," he apologizes for my unfortunate relations.

"Me too."

"I have a medic with us if you'd like to be looked over. They could check the children if you're concerned."

"Thank you, but we're fine."

I know these people are Kieran's family, but they're still cops. I don't do well with cops. When you grow up the way I did, you're trained from a young age to smile and say nothing other than "I want my lawyer". Living in the streets has only made me more wary.

"We'll need to take your statements before we go. Why don't you sit tight while we clear the scene? I'll send in Collin and Hugh to talk in a little bit."

"Thanks," Kieran speaks for me.

"No problem, Kieran. Thanks for the call."

Kieran nods and the cops leave the room.

"Quinn," Connor's voice shakes from behind me. I spin around and furrow my brow. He looks guilty as hell. "I'm sorry. Jack was runnin' around when they walked in. I couldn't get to him fast enough. I tried."

"This isn't your fault, Connor. You kept Jack safe for me. Thank you. Thanks to all of you," I whisper, clutching my son a little tighter.

Owen's face is sporting a nasty bruise above his brow. He's been pistol whipped, no doubt trying to get to my kids. Ian's perma-scowl is deeper than usual and his hands are shaking. I bury myself in his chest, smashing Jack's body between us. His strong arms sweep around my back pulling me in tight. I don't have my father anymore. Ian's the closest thing I've got.

"You did good out there, Quinn," he murmurs into my hair. "Scared the shit outta that fucker."

I nod against his chest and pull in a shallow breath. Jack's breathing has evened and his body's limp. He's asleep. I move back from Ian's arms and gaze up into his honey hued eyes. I pull his head down to mine and press a soft kiss to his cheek.

I haven't spoken words of love to anyone other than the kids in a long time. Those words have been tainted in my mind for the last eight years. But looking at Connor, Owen and Ian right now, I know I love them. They've shown me over the last few months that they'd do anything for me in a way I didn't know existed. They've shown me love.

"I love you guys," I whisper after I pull back from Ian's cheek. I make eye contact with each of them after I say it. Ian beams a smile at me that washes away his perma-scowl. Owen furrows his brow because he doesn't do mushy love stuff, but the corner of his mouth tips. Connor looks at me with giant round eyes in shock before a lazy grin captures his mouth.

I smile sweetly at the three of them before I move past Kieran into the bedroom, his footfalls following closely behind. Once in the room, I slide Jack into the bed and take Ashling from Kieran, placing her near her brother. I tuck them in before I turn to face Kieran.

I reach my hand back and slap him across the face with every ounce of strength I've got.

"You left me."

Chapter 21

Kieran

The sting ripping through my skin shocks me. I was not expecting that.

"You left me," Quinn seethes, staring ferociously into my eyes.

"Never," I say definitively. "I couldn't go out there with you. I'd have fucked up and it woulda gotten messy. Couldn't take that risk with you three out there. I called my cousin. It was the best option. I had your back, Quinn I fuckin' swear. If shit woulda gone south, I was there. I promise."

She nods and one tear slides down her cheek. I quickly swipe it away with my thumb. I wanted to be at her side out in the gym. When I saw what was going down my vision blurred and the murderous, violent criminal within me awoke with fervor. Then my logic kicked in and I backed down. If I'd gone out there running my mouth and waving a gun, people would have gotten hurt, most likely Quinn and the kids. I couldn't take that risk. As a result, she thinks I abandoned her in a time of need.

I pick her up under her arms, pulling her tiny frame against mine. Quinn wraps her arms around my neck and her legs around my waist, burying her head in my neck. The feel of the warmth of her body against mine relaxes me. I've been a live wire since I found motherfucking Sean Casey pinning her against the wall in the alley. That was a bad moment for me.

Then I was a dick to Quinn about him being her boyfriend. I was a jealous little bitch and I'm not afraid to admit it. The idea that he's been inside her before me turns my stomach. I know she's been with other men (she has two kids), but that fucker—hell, no. I'll take pleasure killing him when the time comes. And that time is coming, don't doubt that.

There's a soft knock at the door before Connor and Owen fill the doorway.

"O'Sullivans are ready for you," Owen whispers. Connor walks around us and slides in bed with the kids, pulling them into his side. He has guilt all over his face. I don't blame him, I'd feel like shit too if it were me. He didn't do anything wrong, though. I'll sort him out later.

Owen walks past us, a mask of frustration covering his face. He wants action. I'll make sure we get the action we're all craving. He climbs in bed on the other side of the kids, snuggling into them with a gentleness I didn't know he possessed. I know they love Quinn, but what they feel for her kids is beyond love. I don't have words for it.

I carry Quinn from the room in search of my cousins. I find them in the kitchen, sitting at the table, chatting quietly. It's just Hugh and Collin. These two could be twins. There's hardly a difference between them with their dark hair, chocolate eyes, same height, same weight and same bravado that marks the O'Sullivan clan.

They eye Quinn's back with concern as I approach the table. She slides down my body and climbs into a chair which I slide flush against mine, pulling her tightly beneath my arm. Hugh looks at the table and smirks. They've never seen me like this...I've never seen me like this. Collin clears his throat, bringing his younger brother's features back to professional.

"Miss Quinlan, I'm Collin O'Sullivan and this is my brother, Hugh. We weren't introduced the last time I was here," he says softly.

"It's nice to meet you, Detectives, please call me Quinn," she responds professionally. Her upbringing in a crime family is showing. She knows how to play innocent and sweet. She doesn't have to do that with my family, though.

"Quinn, please call me Collin."

She nods.

"Are the kids doin' all right?" Hugh asks sweetly.

"They're asleep," she whispers. I know she's afraid this thing will have fucked Jack up. It may for a while, but that kid's resilient. He'll be okay sooner rather than later.

"We won't keep you long," Collin assures her and goes about asking regular cop questions. Quinn answers them all truthfully for the most part. She says she doesn't know why her uncles are after her (lie) and that she's been laying low because she wanted out of the criminal lifestyle she'd grown up in (lie number two). Other than that, she tells the truth.

I remain mostly quiet throughout the process, just letting my presence support her.

"I think that about covers everything, Quinn," Hugh finishes politely.

"Thank you for comin' when Kieran called. I don't know what woulda happened if you all didn't show up," she says sincerely.

"We're family. It's what we do." Collin offers me a pointed look. I smirk at him. I'm the reason Collin and Hugh were left out of Shannon's rescue mission back in December. They're still holding a grudge.

"From the sound of it, you're our family, too. Here're our cards. If you ever need anything don't hesitate to call," Hugh says, pushing two business cards at Quinn. Her cheeks flame and she studies the cards like they hold all of the answers to the world.

"I wrote my cell on the back," Collin finishes with a panty-dropping smile. He did not just hit on my woman. Quinn's cheeks go from pink to crimson, her eyes bug out and then she giggles.

"We done here?" I growl at my cousins who are both pleased as shit to have irritated me.

"Yup," Hugh says, popping the *p*. "You want me to put my cell on my card for you, Quinn?"

"No," I answer for her. She may burst into flames if her cheeks get any brighter.

The O'Sullivan brothers chuckle as they stand from the table.

"Nice to meet you, Quinn. Hope to see you around again soon in better circumstances," Collin says nicely.

"It was nice to meet you, too. Both of you. Thank you again for your help," she says, beaming a smile at them.

Hugh fucking winks at her and then they leave, clapping me on the shoulder as they each pass by, gaining growls in return. Fuckers.

"You want some ice water to cool down?" I snarl.

188

"Sorry, but wow. They have a way about 'em that makes me nervous," she apologizes with a lie.

"Don't think that's nerves, Quinn," I admonish.

She furrows her brow, looking at me with sincere confusion.

"They were flirting with you."

"I know."

"And you liked it," I prompt.

"It makes me nervous."

"You don't like it?"

"I've never been flirted with. I've been propositioned more times than I can count, but flirting is new for me. Are you mad?"

Well, not now. How can I keep forgetting she's been living in solitude on the streets her entire adult life? I'm sure no one flirted with her in high school because of that chump, Sean. He probably didn't flirt with her because they were going into a modern-day arranged marriage.

"I'm not mad. I don't like men flirting with my woman."

"I didn't flirt back," she says defensively.

"You giggled," I growl, pulling her into my lap. "Your giggles are mine, too."

"You're a bit of a caveman. You know that, right?" she huffs, snuggling into my chest.

"Yeah."

"Don't be too ashamed of yourself," she snarks.

"I'm not. I turned into a caveman the first time you held a knife to my back. It's not changin' so get used to it, Shorty."

She rolls her eyes but doesn't comment for a long while.

"Let's go home," she finally whispers and I do as she commands.

Jack was really fucked up from the O'Boyle fiasco. After making a few calls I found a therapist that treats kids like Jack within criminal organizations. Money is a good motivator. He's been in therapy twice a week for a little over a month and is doing really well. He's clingy when we're in public and he won't set foot in the gym, but the nightmares have stopped.

Calling cops has never been my go to, but it was a smart move that day. Most of the men that were there will be spending a few years behind bars other than Sean Casey, who got off because he wasn't armed when the raid happened. He was just in the wrong place at the wrong time, according to his attorney. Connall O'Boyle got off for the same reason. He was unarmed and had no warrants.

Because so many of the O'Boyle Brothers' men are behind bars, the streets have been quiet. I'm not stupid enough to think they're done with Quinn, but they're nursing a slow bleed right now. The hacker teenager I hired to try and move the stolen money around called me this morning with a plan. I don't begin to understand it, hence the reason I hired him, but he thinks he can move the money with ease once I need him to.

Now I have to decide my move. I'm not confident they'll let Quinn go even with their money back. She's a liability for them and Sean Casey has a thing for her. It would serve their organization well in the streets if the long lost mafia princess came home and married the promising enforcer. Over my dead fucking body.

I leave my bedroom. Quinn still won't move in here with me. She sleeps with me occasionally, but she's usually in the guest bed with both kids. I'm trying to be patient. Trying being the operative word. We haven't had sex, either. This is the longest I've gone without pussy in my life and it's making me a little cranky. Quinn and I fool around a bit, but with two small children it's rare. Since she won't sleep with me, my opportunities are few and far between.

My parents are watching the kids tonight so I can take Quinn out. She deserves a nice night. It took me two weeks to convince her, but she finally agreed with some help from my mom. Quinn and my parents get along really well. They were pissed at me for a few weeks when I first lied to them, but they bought the lie and have taken to grandparenting like champs.

Jack and Ashling love them. My parents spoil the hell out of them every chance they get. Tonight they're going to watch movies and make fudge. I can only imagine the mess we'll come home to. It'll be worth it to hear Jack's stories tomorrow.

I walk down to the basement where Quinn is playing with the kids. Ashling is cooing and kicking, lying on her play mat while Quinn and Jack put together a puzzle.

"Hey, Daddy!" Jack exclaims like he hasn't seen me in days.

"Hey, bud," I say with a smile, plopping down on the ground next to Ash and blow a raspberry into her cheek. She squeals and giggles, which is my new favorite sound in the world. Jack got her first laugh making faces at her, but I get them the most often. She's a daddy's girl through and through.

"What's *Girls Gone Wild*?" Jack asks, not looking up from his puzzle. Quinn doesn't look up either, but there's a smirk playing at her mouth.

"It's a movie about crazy people," I lie.

"How come you have so many?"

"Uh, I didn't know I had a lot," I lie again, feeling like an old pervert.

"You have twelve. I counted 'em. You like lookin' at ladies' boobies a lot, huh?" He looks up at me with a curious gaze. I should have hidden my shit better when he started playing down here.

"Uh." Thank Christ the doorbell rings. I fly up the stairs, taking them two at a time.

"Go help your dad with the rest of the bags," my mother instructs as she places a soft kiss on my cheek. I do as I'm told, happily avoiding my son's awkward questions. That kid is too smart for his own good.

My dad and I lug way too many bags for just making fudge into my kitchen. He grumbles something about turning into a donkey as we start unloading the confections.

"Kieran Michael Delaney!" my mother screams up the stairs from the basement.

I burst into deep belly laughs imagining what Jack has told her. I hear her heavy clomps up the stairs as I wipe away tears from my laughter, my father staring at me with a mischievous grin.

"You had best get that smut outta this house where *my* grandchildren live!" she screeches, smacking my ass like I'm five. I fight off another round of laughter, knowing it'll buy me the business end of a spoon.

"Your son has porn in the kids' play area," she complains to my father.

"I doubt he put it on while they were in the room, Clare," he says with a smirk.

"He asked me why his daddy likes to look at boobies. He asked me if you like to look at boobies!" She stomps her foot in frustration.

My mother is a strange combination of old fashioned and modern. She knows what my father is and always has. She took him willingly into her life and loves him more than anything in this world. Well not really, but he's in a tie with me and the kids. But being married to a thief didn't turn her into a hard edged crime lord's wife. She bakes, sews, knits, goes to book clubs, volunteers at charities and generally lives in the 1950s most of the time. Me having porn in the house is a violation of her good values.

"I do like lookin' at boobies," my father teases and stares at hers.

"Jesus, I'm leavin' the room," I say with a fake gag. I don't really give a shit, but I play the part well.

"You two are incorrigible!"

She thuds back down to the basement, no doubt to vent to Quinn about how awful my father and I are.

"Should probably hide the porn, son," my father says through a snicker.

"I thought I did."

"Kids find everything. Best place to hide that kinda shit is in the trash until you're ready to talk about it." Wise words from the old man.

193

Quinn tops the stairs, giggling, and breaks into a full laugh when she sees me.

"It's not that funny," I admonish her.

"If you coulda seen your face," she stutters between chuckles. "Your mother is about to have an aneurysm."

"She'll be fine," my father dismisses, placing a quick peck on Quinn's cheek before heading downstairs.

"So you like young drunk girls that take their shirts off in public?" Quinn asks teasingly.

"I'm not talkin' about this," I grumble.

"If I flash you will you give me a free T-shirt?" she asks in a squeaky high pitched voice.

I growl and glare at her until she pulls the hem of her shirt up, flashing me her black lace bra. I move to grab her and she takes off down the hall in a sprint. I easily catch up, heaving her over my shoulder, stalking into my bedroom and locking the door for good measure.

I dump her on the bed, covering her tiny body with my own.

"My rules are different. You flash me, I get your shirt," I purr in her ear.

"Kieran, your parents are here," she whispers in my ear, making no move to push me away.

"Good, they can watch the kids and I can get some nookie."

She giggles.

I drag my nose along her jaw before smashing my lips against her roughly. With no preempting she opens her mouth and thrusts her tongue in my mouth with a pleading moan. I growl and rip my mouth from hers. I pull her T-shirt over her head with little finesse. She sits up and unclasps her bra while I divest her lower half of yoga pants and boy shorts. She yanks my shirt over my head while I push my sweats past my ankles.

I can't wait any longer to be with her. The wait is killing me. I don't want our first time to be while my parents are here, but I'm done jacking off like a teenager. I'm getting calluses.

I climb further into the bed, dragging her with me, my mouth melded to her soft, sweet lips. Her naked body beneath me is silky and warm, begging for my touch. Once her raven hair is covering my pillows I begin my exploration, tasting and licking her neck and collar bone until she glistens. My large hand palms her tit while my mouth devours the other, scraping my teeth against her peaked nipple until she shudders from head to toe. I switch and offer her other tit the same treatment as she moans and tugs at my hair, urging me to give her more. With her raspberry nipple solidly between my tongue and top teeth, I trace my hand down her body, rubbing one long finger between her folds.

Coated in her juices I rub her clit slowly, watching the flush creep from her chest to her cheeks as her body begins to quiver. When she's breaths away from coming I pull back, causing a frustrated moan to escape her lips. I return the pressure and bring her to the brink again before backing off just in time.

"Kieran," she complains and encourages simultaneously.

I smile around her nipple and move up her body, capturing her mouth in mine, keeping my body off to the side of hers. She reaches out with her small hand and grasps my cock firmly. Her tiny fingers barely reach around my girth as I thrust into her hold three times before pulling away.

"I'm not comin' in your hand," I whisper against her lips before she can argue.

I move across her body and settle between her legs, nudging her thighs apart to accommodate my larger frame. My dick lies over her pussy and I move my hips slowly across her clit causing her icy eyes to roll back in her head. When her orgasm is beginning to tremor through her I palm my cock and barely breach her entrance, shocked at how difficult it is to enter her.

Using a little more force, I surge forward until I'm stopped. Stopped by something a woman with two children shouldn't have. I look down at her face, a question (fuck that, a thousand questions) in my murky blues. Her crystal eyes shimmer up at me and I know. She lied. She lied about those kids.

Quinn runs a shaky hand up my neck and cups my cheek.

"They're mine," she says through a sob.

We hold each other's gaze for a long while, me still inside her and Quinn's legs wrapped around my waist, waiting. She lied to keep those kids safe. I know like I know I did the same thing. She's their mother no matter how they came to her. She sacrificed eight years of safety for two kids that I'm guessing she didn't know. It's in this moment I know for sure.

"I love you," I whisper.

"I love you too," she whispers back.

I press a soft kiss to her lips as tears leak from the edges of her eyes and thrust my hips forward, carefully breaking the barrier of Quinn's virginity. Once I'm fully seated within her I stop. I've never fucked a woman without a condom and certainly not a virgin. This isn't going to last long.

Quinn's face grimaces in pain for a few moments as I rest my forehead against hers and slowly begin to rock. The furrowed brow of pain changes to the blush of pleasure and I pick up my pace. Slowly stroking the length of my cock in and out of Quinn is the most fantastic feeling my dick has ever experienced. I bury my head in her neck and thrust harder as her nails begin to score my back, causing a feral growl to rumble in my chest.

I nibble her neck up her jaw to her mouth. Kissing her with the passion of the love we're making, I cup her cheeks in my hands and pound into her. As her legs quake and her breath hitches, I pull back to watch her face beam in pleasure as she gasps my name.

A few more thrusts and I come so hard my balls ache and my entire body tremors. I slow my strokes bringing both of us back to reality, panting heavy breaths against each other's skin until I collapse on top of her.

Quinn keeps her arms and legs wrapped around me tightly as I nuzzle into her neck, licking a bead of sweat from her milk and honey skin.

As my come starts to leak out of her I have the strange desire to scoop it back in. I want every bit of me inside her, marking what's mine. What has only ever been mine. What will only ever be mine.

"I'm so sorry, Kieran," she sobs and a violent tremor erupts down her body pushing my dick from within her.

I roll to my side and pull her into me as the tears pour down her face. The emotion wracking her body causes me pain. She's carried this load for months on her own and now that she can share it she's overwhelmed. I shush her and kiss her hair, stroking her naked back.

Once her crying subsides I tip her face up with one finger under her chin.

"I love you, Quinn."

"I love you so much, Kieran."

She surges forward, smashing her lips to mine, almost choking me with her tiny arms around my neck. We languidly tangle our tongues while our hands explore each other's skin. As my dick gets hard again, Quinn reaches around it stroking me slowly from base to tip, squeezing and relaxing. For a virgin she gives a mean hand job.

She lifts her leg over my hip and guides my tip inside her. She's still coated in my come, but tight and swollen from our recent sex. I move to pull away from her when she forces her pussy over me, shuddering through the pain.

"Quinn, it's too soon. You need to heal first," I murmur against her lips as she rocks her hips slightly.

"I want you inside me again."

I'm not one to argue, so I roll her beneath me and make slow, sweet love to the woman that's captured my heart until I come inside her again as I call out her name, worshipping the Irish goddess surrounding my body.

Chapter 22

Quinn

I'm not a virgin anymore. Twenty-six years of waiting, guarding my body against the filth in the streets, and now I've given it to the first man I've ever loved. I feel so many emotions I don't know where to begin sorting them out in my head. Kieran climbed out of bed a few minutes ago, dragging me with him to the shower.

He gently washed and caressed me while kissing and holding me. He takes care of me, not because I need it, because he wants to. There's a need within him to make sure I'm happy. And he makes me so happy I can't begin to describe it. Kieran's a criminal, a murderer, a fighter and probably a bad guy to the outside world. But with me and the kids, he's a loving father, protector, partner and savior. He's everything I could have wanted in my life and more. It scares the shit out of me.

After changing the sheets, Kieran pulls me into bed, arranging me against his side with my head resting on his dilseacht tattoo. I lazily trace the patterns that cover his chest and six pack, marveling at his body's strength.

"No more guest room," he murmurs into my hair. I nod and keep tracing. "Still wanna go out?"

"No," I whisper. I didn't want to go out in the first place, but now I'm tired and sore. I'd rather stay in, make fudge with Clare and watch movies with Jack. I'm a super cool person.

"You feelin' okay?" he asks, quietly tipping my head back with his fingers beneath my chin. His murky blues are sated and calm in a way I've never seen them look before. Kieran Delaney looks peaceful.

"I'm okay," I say through a small smile.

"You sore?"

"A little."

"Liar."

I am a liar. In so many ways that when he says it, guilt washes over me. He must see it in my eyes because his peaceful face turns into a scowl.

"Don't. Don't you fuckin' dare, Quinn," he growls, draggin my naked body beneath his, forcing me to look into his face with nowhere to run and hide.

"I'm sorry." The words barely make it past the lump in my throat.

"Me too," he says softly, causing my brow to furrow.

"Why are you sorry? I'm the one that lied."

"I should have known. It was obvious you hadn't just given birth. I wasn't payin' attention. Ian knows, right?"

"Yeah."

"I should've known. I could tell he was shocked. I thought it was because you were finally lettin' him help you out. It was because you showed up with two kids. I'm an idiot. And then with the Russian. You didn't know who he was because you weren't around when he tortured Jack. Fuck, I thought...I don't know what I thought. I wasn't payin' attention."

"Are you serious right now? You're blamin' yourself for not knowin' a stranger was lyin' to you? Thank you for tryin' to make me feel better, but this is my fault. I've had months to tell you the truth, but I didn't want to. I didn't want to say the words because the kids...they're mine. They even look like me. I know it sounds crazy, but it feels like they were supposed to be my kids all along."

"I do blame myself. It's my job to read situations, to know what's goin' on around me. I fucked up. But Quinn, I don't give a shit. I don't care how you got the kids. They're yours. Whatever the reason, those are *your* babies."

"They're yours too, Kieran. You've been in their lives the same amount of time I've been," I say confidently, wanting him to know how much that means to me...to all of us.

"Yeah," he breathes out, rolling off me. He lays his head on my chest and lightly trails his rough hand across the flat of my stomach. "Speakin' of kids...we didn't use a condom."

My entire body goes rigid. I'm obviously aware that he didn't use a condom. I figured if he was willing to do that he knew he was clean because he wouldn't put me in danger. I'm clean for apparent reasons. To be honest, I don't care if I get pregnant. I've already got two kids, having another doesn't bother me, but Kieran sounds worried. Maybe another kid is too much for him. Shit!

I move from beneath him, scooting off the edge of the bed. I grab my discarded clothes pulling them on quickly.

"Quinn," Kieran warns. "What're you doin'?"

"I'm gonna head out and get a morning after pill. I should've thought about it. Sorry," I grunt, pulling my Bears T-shirt over my head. Before it clears my face, I'm yanked hard back onto the bed, causing me to yelp.

"You're what?" Kieran growls, pulling the shirt off my face, balling it up and throwing it with force across the room.

"Don't worry. I'll fix it. I'd rather do the morning after pill instead of an abortion."

Kieran's face twists in rage, causing me to back away from him until my back slams into the headboard. He follows my movement, bringing his face inches from mine.

"That is the cruelest, most fucked up thing you've ever said to me," he whispers in a menacing tone, glowering at me.

"You sounded worried. I'm tryin' to fix it," I explain in a whimper. I don't know what I've done, but he's furious with me.

"I'm not worried. I was just talkin'. It's what adults do," he chastises me.

"So now I'm not an adult?" I take offense.

"That's not what I said."

"It's what you fuckin' alluded." I cross my arms across my chest and close my eyes. I can't look at his face when he's angry at me. He can cut straight to the quick with his eyes and his words.

"Open your eyes, Quinn," he commands in a throaty growl. I don't comply.

"I wasn't tryin' to hurt you," I whisper.

"Am I so horrible that you'd rather have someone else's kids instead of mine?"

My eyes fly open.

"What?!"

"You're willin' to take on two children that aren't yours, but you're runnin' outta my bed to end any possibility we may have just created one of our own. You explain that shit to me."

He starts to move away from me so I grab the sides of his face, pulling his forehead to mine.

"I thought it's what you wanted. You sounded worried. I don't care if I'm pregnant. I'd be happy if I was. It's early in our relationship, but we haven't done this the normal way. I'm not worried about carryin' your baby. I'm concerned about you."

"I wasn't worried. I've had a fucked up life full of mostly shit. I'm not complainin' about the life I've led because, as far as I'm concerned, it's been a good life, but it hasn't had much good in it. I've got the people I'm loyal to and that's it. I'm not gettin' any younger, Quinn. I'll be thirty-five in a few weeks. I want a family. Shit I *have* a fuckin' family and I want more...with you. Don't ever question that." His rage is gone and the soft, sweet Kieran is back.

"So what you do want me to do?"

"Lay here in my arms. Let me take care of you. Let me figure things out for us. Let me be what you need in life. Let me put a baby in your belly. Let me give you a few more after that. Let me grow old with you. Just let me."

"Okay."

Kieran presses a tender kiss to my lips before laying us down in the bed. He strips me out of my clothes and pulls me against his chest again with my head covering his dílseacht tattoo. Let him, just let him. I haven't let anyone do as much for me as Kieran already has. I'm ready for someone else to carry the burden alongside me, a partner. Kieran's not so much a partner, more a leader. He wants me to relinquish some of myself to him...let him. I don't know if I can do it the way he wants, but I'm willing to try.

"Love you," I whisper.

"I love you, Quinn."

Before we can drift off to sleep, there's a crisp knock at the door.

"Kieran, get your ass out here quick!" Rick bellows through the door.

I know that tone. Something's wrong, bad wrong.

We both leap from the bed, dressing quickly before racing from the room. In the living room there are two uniformed cops and a woman looking professional yet sloppy with a bad haircut that makes her mousy brown hair look like a helmet, an ill-fitting navy pantsuit that doesn't close around her wide middle and a worn black leather briefcase clutched in her hand.

"Kieran Delaney?" the woman asks.

"You are?" he responds harshly.

"My name is Bridget Foley. I'm a social worker with the Department of Children and Family Services. I have a court order to remove the two minor children, Jack and Ashling O'Boyle, from the premises."

"No!" I scream moving to run to my kids. Kieran sweeps an arm around my shoulders, pinning my back to his front. This can't be happening. How the fuck did my uncles do this?

"Declan O'Boyle has only just learned of his childrens' existence and wishes for them to be reunited quickly. I'm here to facilitate that transition. If you could, gather up a few of their belongings. It helps for children to have some items they're familiar with."

Rick is off in the kitchen speaking in hushed tones into his cell phone holding an official-looking document. The kids must still be in the basement with Clare. I can't get them out of the house unseen. I don't know what to do. I look up at Kieran with tears streaming down my cheeks, begging him with my eyes to make this stop. But I can see in his face he can't fix this. He doesn't have the power to stop two cops and a DCFS social worker.

A sob breaks from my chest. Kieran tightens his hold around me as my legs begin to give out. How do I do this? How the hell do I do this?! I can't. I can't give my children away. This can't be happening. Please, this can't be happening. I thrash my head side to side hoping it will wake me up from this nightmare. But I don't wake up.

I stay in this nightmare, trapped with no hope of breaking free. The light and love Jack and Ashling have brought to my life is stripped away, only to leave my soul shrouded in blackness.

Chapter 23

Kieran

"Shannon Kelly's office," Karl answers in his eternally kind voice. Karl is Shannon's assistant and best friend. I've only met him a handful of times, but every time I've liked the dude more and more. I hope like hell he likes me.

"Karl, it's Kieran," my voice rasps with emotion.

"Kieran, what's wrong? Do you need me to get Brian?" His voice is full of alert.

"I was kinda hopin' you could help me out."

"Of course, whatever you need," he says emphatically.

"Has Shannon filled you in on my situation?"

"Yeah. I mean I think she has. Is something wrong with Quinn? I can't get Shannon for a few hours. She's in court. I could try to go and grab her in between hearings."

"I don't wanna bother Shannon or my cousin. They've got enough goin' on. I need some fuckin' help, though. Quinn's kids were taken by DCFS yesterday," I groan, slamming my head back on the couch. Quinn's in bed where she's been since the kids were taken. She hasn't eaten, she hasn't slept, she hasn't moved. There's a veil of blackness around her that I can't see through.

"On what grounds?" Karl moves into professional mode quickly.

"On the grounds they're not hers. Her uncle, Declan O'Boyle, had paternity tests run on the kids and the courts say they're his. Him and his brother run a fuckin' crime syndicate here in Chicago. I can go in, guns blazin', and pull the kids out, but I'd have to run for the rest of their lives to keep 'em safe. You got anything for me?"

"How'd they get DNA samples from the kids?"

"They raided a gym last month that Quinn and I work at, guessin' it was then. We were in another room when their crew stormed in. Her other uncle, Connall O'Boyle, was holdin' Jack when we found 'em. Don't know how they got Ashling's."

"I suppose Declan is claiming he had no knowledge of the children prior to this?"

"Yeah."

"The biological mother?"

"Dead. Don't know much else about her."

"If we can prove Declan knew about the children prior to this, we could make a claim that he abandoned them. Abandonment is grounds for parental rights to be terminated. I can do some research, see what I can find. We'll have to get Shannon involved with this. She'll kick my ass if I don't. You may be willin' to take on the wrath of Shannon Kelly, but I prefer to stay on the good side of her gun."

"She's got her own shit to worry about with her man and his kid. She doesn't need my shit on top of it," I state emphatically. I don't want to cause her any trouble.

"Kieran," Karl admonishes. "You know her. It doesn't matter what's goin' on, you're her family. She'll wanna know. She can help you better than anyone. Shannon's as good in a courtroom as she is behind her gun. Let me talk to her."

"Just figure something out for me first and then I'll tell Shannon."

"I'll get on it. I've got a couple friends at our Chicago firm that can dig around for me. I'm really sorry, Kieran," his voice drops in a sad tone as he finishes.

"Thanks for the help, Karl. I owe you. Anything you ever need."

"You're Shannon's family. Makes you my family, too."

"Thanks, man."

"No problem. I'll call you later when I know something."

We hang up and I throw my phone into the side of the couch. Of all the things I could be doing right now, calling Shannon's assistant is my least likely choice, but it's a smart move. I don't want to burden Shannon with this, but she's a family attorney. If anyone could get the kids back to us legally, it's her. Karl's the next best thing.

I'm meeting with the O'Boyle Brothers in two hours. I've got their money ready to move. If this was their play to get it back, it's fucking working. The hacker kid has everything set up to move the money from the offshore bank into various fake charities he's set up. He assures me it's the best way to move the money and keep Quinn's name off everything. Anonymous donations are a good way to avoid federal scrutiny.

I walk into our bedroom and I'm shocked to see Quinn out of bed pulling her jacket over her shoulders.

She's wearing her green cargo pants, a white T-shirt and her black biker boots. Shit.

"Quinn," I say in a warning.

"I'm gettin' my kids. I can't fuckin' lay here and wait another second. I don't care what they want from me. I want my kids back now!" she yells.

"I have a meet with them in two hours. They'll get their money back and give me the kids. This was just a ploy to force our hand. You can't go in there alone with nothing to trade."

"They're gonna kill you, Kieran. They didn't do this for money. They did this for me. My uncles want me back for the street cred. They look bad now with me out here with you. It makes them look weak. I'll trade myself for the kids and you'll keep them safe until I can get away."

"No fuckin' way! You're truly insane if you think I'd allow you to do that," I growl, taking two steps until I'm right in her face.

"I can protect myself. The kids can't. You can be pissed at me all you want, but you know I'm right. I'm goin' for my kids and you're gonna let me," she seethes. "If you love me at all you'll let me do this. I can't live without them, Kieran. If you keep me from them you might as well put a bullet in my head."

"Quinn, please. Let's talk this through," I plead. I fucking plead like a little bitch because I can see she's already made her mind up. She's doing this with or without my consent.

I grab her face and crush my mouth onto her soft sweet lips. Quinn pulls me into her, fisting my shirt roughly. I tangle our tongues, tasting every surface of her mouth and lips, drinking her in, knowing this could be the last time. If things go south her uncles will kill her. She pulls away and looks up at me with her piercing blue eyes.

"I love you, Kieran. No matter what happens, know that I love you," she says with no waver in her voice.

"I love you, too. Come back to me. If you don't, I'm comin' for you."

She nods once and then leaves our room, our house and our world.

It's been four hours and no word from Quinn. I didn't go to the meet. I sat in my house like a little bitch, letting my woman do the work. My parents, Ian, Connor and Owen are here waiting with me. I called Collin an hour after Quinn left and filled him in. He's doing everything he can to watch out for her and the kids. He told me there are a few undercover cops within the O'Boyle Brothers that he would get word to. His hands are pretty tied beyond that.

If something doesn't happen soon I'm going to lose my fucking mind. I've paced, I've worked the heavy bag until I couldn't move my arms, I've puked, I've tried to cry, I've screamed. Anything and everything I can think of, I've done.

"Kieran!" Owen bellows from the kitchen. I leap to my feet and run to the back door. Collin and Hugh are striding up my path each with one of the kids in their arms.

"Jack!" I yell, jumping off the stairs to meet my cousins in the yard. Jack heaves himself into my arms from Collin's.

"Daddy," he whimpers, shaking and crying.

"I'm so sorry, bud. I'm so sorry," I apologize, rubbing his back, kissing his hair.

I reach out with my hand and grab Ashling's car seat from Hugh before stalking toward my house. My mother has tears streaming down her cheeks watching us from the deck where everyone is huddled together. I move past them into the house, not stopping until I get to the couch. I keep Jack in my lap while I pull Ash out of the car seat. She looks up at me and beams a smile that almost stops my heart. I crush both kids to my chest, just breathing in their sweet smells.

When I finally compose myself, I ease the pressure off the kids' backs, looking down at their beautiful faces.

"I want my mommy," Jack whispers, his big blue eyes rimmed in red, begging me to get him his mother.

"I know, bud. I want Mommy, too."

"Go get her," he demands with a furrowed brow.

My mother slides onto the cushion next to us, brave face in place. Jack doesn't need our tears right now.

"Can I get a hug?" she coos at Jack.

"Grandma," he says shakily, climbing into her lap. My mother does the impossible and keeps herself from breaking into the sobs that are choked in her throat. My father leans over the back of the couch, kissing his wife's cheek before resting a hand on Jack's head. I had to break my parents' hearts twice with this shit, once telling them about the kids being taken and again telling them the kids aren't mine. They took it in stride, considering the situation. They love the kids like their own...nothing will change that.

Ian, Connor and Owen take the other half of the sectional and I pass Ashling over to Ian who kisses her chubby cheeks before passing her off to the Doyle brothers.

I stand up from the couch and head into the kitchen where my cousins are watching and waiting.

"Thanks, guys," I breathe out and ring them both around the neck, hugging them tightly.

"One of our guys on the inside called us twenty minutes ago sayin' he'd offered to make the drop for the kids. Thought it'd be better if we did it," Hugh explains, his chocolate eyes boiling with rage.

"Gave us some good intel too. Apparently since Quinn's come back to life, there's been dissension among the ranks of the O'Boyle Brothers. The old school members aren't good with the rumors about Quinn's parents. It seems they felt some loyalty to Patrick Quinlan and there are rumblings that they're talkin' retribution for what happened to him and his wife. The uncles are tryin' to pull Quinn back into the fold to maintain control," Collin explains, his chocolate eyes just as stormy as his brother's.

"Fuck," I hiss under my breath, looking over my shoulder at my kids who are still being passed around by the people who love them. Jack's sitting on Connor's lap while Ash is in my father's arms, smiling at him with her deep dimple puckering.

"If you're thinkin' about goin' in after her, we're with you. No more keepin' us outta the loop," Hugh demands.

"You're cops. I can't ask you to risk your careers for me. I appreciate it, more than you know."

"Fuck that, Kieran! We're family before we're anything. You do this, we're there," Collin snarls under his breath, mindful of my children only yards away.

I relent and nod. If they want to help me, who am I to argue? They're my blood and they'll have my back no matter what.

"I've gotta get the kids settled before we move. Any idea where they've got Quinn?"

"I'll find out and let you know," Hugh says.

Buzz, buzz.

Shit!

"Hey," I answer softly.

"Kieran Delaney," Shannon barks. "You ever try to keep somethin' like this from me again, I'll beat your ass bloody!"

"I guess you talked to Karl?" I say through a snort.

"More like interrogated. I knew somethin' was wrong. He tried his damnedest to cover for you, though. What's goin' on? Where're the kids?"

"Just got 'em back."

"Thank fuck. How'd you manage that?" she asks, relieved.

"Quinn traded herself for the kids," I admit sheepishly.

"WHAT?!"

"She's who they really want. It's a long fuckin' story. I'm gonna get her, just figurin' out the details with Collin and Hugh right now. Probably should get off here and round up the boys. Wish you were here, Shannon."

She's silent for a long while.

"I'll be there in an hour and a half. Wait for me before you do anything!"

And then she hangs up. Shit!

214

"Uh, apparently your sister's comin' to Chicago," I say, shocked, staring at my phone.

"Fuck. It's on now," Collin says through a giant smile.

Shannon Kelly's coming to Chicago to work. This just got interesting.

Chapter 29

Quinn

Just as I thought, my uncles let the kids go when I agreed to stay. I don't know why they want me back, but it's what they want. I was immediately separated from the kids after I made my deal. I kissed them both, told them I loved them and watched some lackey carry them out the door. It was easier this time because I know I'll see them again. If I have to stab my way out of here day by day until they're all dead, I will.

Uncle Declan threatened to take the kids from me permanently if I leave so I have to play this smart. It could take months for me to get away, but I will get back to Kieran and my kids. My uncle can't take them from me if he's dead, so he's at the top of my hit list. Unfortunately, I was divested of my weapons upon entering the pub where my uncles run their organization. So for the moment, I'm stuck.

Every member of the O'Boyle Brothers seems to be here tonight. Old familiar faces keep coming by the table where I'm sitting, welcoming me home. I keep a broad, fake smile on my face and say thank you each time. Maybe I should go into acting because they all seem to be buying what I'm selling.

I'm in a booth, smashed between my uncles and Sean Casey. When I agreed to come home Sean immediately smashed his lips against mine, causing the room to bloom with hoots and hollers of congratulations. I almost puked in his mouth. He now has his arm possessively slung around my shoulders and his other hand is creeping higher on my thigh by the minute.

If I have to have sex with him, it'll be torture. I don't want another man touching me. Although, I can use the opportunity to smother him afterward while he sleeps, so there is an upside if it comes to that.

The celebration of my return is curious to me. I'm trying to listen to the conversations nearby, but it's too loud to gain any real information. I did hear one guy say he hopes me being back settles shit down for a while.

"See how much your family missed you?" Declan murmurs in my ear.

I cut my eyes to him, offering a menacing glare. He's the reason the kids look like me. I have my mother's eyes which Declan also shares. I should have figured it out sooner...the eyes, the Irish names, all of it pointing back to my family. I'll be damned if he gets to raise my children. Now that I know they're his, it makes them feel that much more like mine. They share my blood. They share my heart. I'll do anything to get back to them.

As the evening turns to night and the Guinness begins to flow like water, my nerves start to take over. I should have talked this through more with Kieran. I don't know how I'm going to get through tonight much less however many nights I have to spend with Sean. He keeps whispering in my ear about us spending the night getting reacquainted, which is turning my stomach. I spent eight years fighting off scum like him and now I'm going to have to give myself to him willingly.

As much as I'd like to see Kieran burst through the doors, guns blazing, I don't want him to. If he dies, I don't know how I'll go on. I'll have to raise the kids with Sean, and Jack will become a monster like him. Kieran may be a criminal, but he's a good man and will raise Jack to be a good man. I need to stop thinking like this. Everything will be fine. I just need some time to get a plan in place and get my hands on my knife.

"Think it's time to call it a night," Sean purrs in my ear before dragging me out of the booth by my arm.

"I'm kinda disappointed, Darcy. I was hopin' Delaney would show up here tryin' to be your knight in shining armor. His head would look great on my wall. Guess you weren't all that important to him after all," Connall rasps through a sinister chuckle.

"I'm sorry, Uncle Connall. Maybe you'll see Kieran tomorrow," I say sweetly, playing my part. He snorts at my fakeness.

"Go easy on her, Sean. She needs to be able to walk tomorrow," Declan instructs blankly. A shiver sneaks up my spine.

"I'm sure she's been worked in already," Sean says, suggestively eyeing me with a question in his eyes. He wants to know if I'm still a virgin. I keep my gaze on my hands, letting him draw his own conclusions.

After a few moments of silence, Sean drags me by my arm up the stairs at the back of the pub. They lead to apartments. Sean pushes me to the door at the end of the hall before unlocking it and forcing me through.

It's a studio apartment with a bed and a kitchenette. It doesn't look like it's been used recently for anything other than quick sex. The sheets are rumpled with stains marking the black comforter. I feel puke creeping up my throat as Sean nudges me toward it.

"Sean, please," I whimper. I'm losing the battle to stay strong. I don't want this. I'd do anything for my kids, but I'm scared.

"You'll be sayin' that all night, Darcy," he purrs in my ear.

He pushes me hard in the back when we get to the foot of the bed, sending me flying face first into the foul bed that reeks of sweat and bodily fluids. He covers my body with his, pinning me to the mattress, squishing the air from my lungs. His dick is hard, grinding into my thigh through his jeans. This is really going to happen.

Sean lifts his body slightly off mine and I try to wiggle from beneath him.

"If you fight, I'll make sure it hurts," he threatens.

I go completely still at the evil tone in his voice. Sean's not the kid I grew up with anymore. This life, working for my uncles, killed that boy long ago. The man lying on top of me is an enforcer for the O'Boyle Brothers and nothing more.

Sean's hand reaches beneath, me ripping my cargo pants open. He jams his hand into my underwear, roughly rubbing my folds. I'm drier than a desert, making the friction hurt. He forces a finger inside me and I wince at the pain.

"Fuck, you're tight," he groans against the back of my neck.

For some reason, I think about Connor and Owen in the moment. They would want me to fight. They taught me how to fight. I can do this. Or at least I can try.

"Get this pussy wet for me," Sean demands, getting frustrated with the drought between my legs.

"Turn me over," I whisper in the sexiest voice I can create. To my ear it sounds closer to holding back vomit, but it must work because he lifts off me to roll me over.

I take the advantage, swinging my elbow back and catching him in the side of the head. I move from beneath him as he shakes off the stars he's seeing. I run to the door only for Sean to grab a fistful of my hair, ripping me back across the room.

"You're so fuckin' stupid! You think you can fight me? Fine, let's fight," he growls as he knees me in the face. My nose starts spilling blood as I try to scramble away from him.

Sean drags me to my feet by my hair. He leans down into my face, ripping my head back, forcing me to look into his face.

"You still wanna fight me?"

I shake my head no. Connor and Owen taught me a lot, but I can't fight Sean. He'll end up killing me.

"Get on your knees and show me how sorry you are," he growls, leading me to the floor his fist still in my hair.

I assume the position and brace myself for what's to come when the apartment door slams open behind me.

"Who the fuck are you?" Sean bellows.

"Your worst fuckin' nightmare," a woman's voice threatens in a tone that makes me nervous. "Let her up off the ground and I'll let her kill you herself. Keep her there a second longer and I'm doin' it my way."

Sean hesitates for a moment and I hear a gun cock. As the sound reverberates through the room, Sean's hand releases my hair. I jump to my feet and back away from him, never taking my eyes off his face.

"Quinn, I'm Shannon, Kieran's cousin. You can turn around. He's not goin' anywhere," she says confidently. I trust her based on the timbre of her voice and the look of rage and confusion on Sean's.

I turn around and am taken aback with the most beautiful woman I've ever seen. She's really tall with long auburn hair and stunning green eyes. She's got two guns drawn and looks like she could take a nap she's so calm. I'm in awe.

"I brought you a present. Behind my back," she indicates with her chin.

I move behind her and spot a large hunting knife sheathed in the back of her jeans. I pull it out and take a breath. My hands are shaking, but I know I'm safe with Shannon here.

"You wanna do this up here? Kieran's waitin' downstairs with your uncles if you'd like to make this a family affair."

"Let's go down," I say in a stronger voice than I thought I'd have.

"You heard her. Move you fuckin' ass. Don't even think about grabbin' that pussy piece you've got in your pants. I'll blow your fuckin' head off before you have the chance."

Sean keeps his hands raised in front of him and takes tentative steps toward us. When he gets within arm's length, Shannon puts one of her guns in a holster before smashing her fist into his nose. I hear the bones crush, causing me to cringe and smile at the same time.

Sean cradles his busted nose in his hands.

"You fuckin' bitch. You'll pay for that," he threatens.

Shannon rolls her eyes, rips Sean's gun from his pants, throws it across the room and puts her gun to his head.

"Move!"

She leads him out the door. As we exit, a gigantic man steps up from the wall he's leaning against. He's the size of a house. I stop and stare at him, not afraid...curious.

"I'm Thomas, Shannon's bodyguard," his deep bass voice rumbles. I can't imagine why Shannon needs a bodyguard based on the skills she has, but I nod and follow Shannon when she reaches back for my hand. I put my palm in hers, letting her guide me down the hall with her gun barrel smashed into the back of Sean's head.

"Your kids are okay," she informs me in a kind voice. This woman is some kind of weird, sweet and scary at the same time.

"Thank you," I whisper.

She squeezes my hand, offering me her comfort and strength. I'm sure Shannon intimidates pretty much anyone she comes in contact with, but I feel safe walking behind her. It's the closest thing to having Kieran with me. I also feel safe because Thomas is looming behind me silently.

When we get to the bottom of the stairs I stop, trying to get my brain to register what I'm seeing. Half of the O'Boyle Brothers are holding the other half at gun point on their knees. Connor and Owen are hovering above two men that I met tonight, high ranking men in the organization. Ian is ominously scowling at another man next to my uncles. Hugh and Collin are standing on either side of Kieran who has two guns drawn, one pointing at each of my uncles.

I want to run and throw myself in his arms, but I stay beside Shannon as she leads us into the group. When we reach the back of my uncles, Shannon kicks Sean's knees out from under him causing him to crash to the floor. Keeping her gun trained at his head she moves her and I around to his front, past my uncles, stopping in front of them as Thomas weaves around toward the door.

"Now that we're all here, it's time to get down to business," Kieran commands from behind me. His voice is gravelly and haunting, raising goosebumps on my skin.

He takes a few steps, bringing his body in full contact with my back, his arms straight out around my sides, guns trained on my uncles.

"I'm endin' this tonight. This is your opportunity to do it yourself. You use that knife on anyone in this room you want," Kieran whispers in my ear.

I nod my understanding and stare down my uncles. I want to slit their throats. I want to watch the life seep from their eyes. I want them to pay for what they did to my parents. I can't do it, though. I'm not Shannon. I'm not a killing machine. What I did to the Russian was for Jack—a mother's vengeance. At this moment I just want to go home and hold my babies.

"You don't deserve my vengeance," I tell my uncles in Irish.

I turn and face Kieran, sliding the knife in the back of his pants.

"Dilseacht," I say loudly, placing a kiss over Kieran's T-shirt covered tattoo. There are murmurs of dilseacht ringing from the men in the room as I pull away from Kieran and walk out of the pub. I hear footfalls behind me as I reach the curb.

Hugh, Collin and Shannon are behind me when I turn around.

"Let's get you home," Hugh says softly.

I nod and follow them to a black Mercedes with Thomas waiting at the side near the end of the block. As I climb in the backseat next to Shannon, I hear the gunfire begin. I shut the door knowing that Kieran just became the head of a new organized crime family. I'll take my place at his side with pride.

Chapter 25

Kieran

She's letting me. Quinn is letting me carry the burden of these deaths so she doesn't have to. As she walks out of the pub, a broad smile splits my face—time to play. Shannon, Collin and Hugh leave with Quinn, as discussed. Two cops and an attorney can't be a part of what we're about to do. I was fairly confident Quinn wouldn't take me up on my offer, but I couldn't be sure. I thought she might take out Sean. It looks like Shannon got to him before he could do any damage to Quinn. He did fuck up Quinn's face, though. He's last on the list tonight. I'll make his death last the longest.

I fire a round into each O'Boyle in rapid succession, right between the eyes. As soon as I squeeze my triggers, the room erupts in gunfire. Not one life will be spared tonight. Every person loyal to the dead bodies on the ground in front of me will meet the same fate.

When silence falls over the room I turn to admire the mayhem. The room smells like gun smoke, vengeance, beer and death. The fragrance of victory. This is the moment I become the head of a crime syndicate. I won't run drugs, guns or people. I'll offer protection and continue with the illegal fighting. With the money I now have from Quinn's father I can run this crew almost legitimately.

This pub will burn to the ground tonight, taking the bodies of traitors, monsters and murders with it. I nod to Connor who hoists Sean to his feet, dragging him up the stairs, Owen following closely behind.

"Go home to Quinn," I instruct Ian. He shoves his gun in the back of his pants, offering me a small proud smirk before returning his perma-scowl to his worn face and leaving the pub, kicking a few bodies as he goes. My new crew goes about dousing the place in gasoline while I head upstairs to torture and murder the piece of shit that touched my woman.

As I enter the room, Owen and Connor have already started. Sean's barely conscious on the floor. I crouch in front of his bleeding and broken body, smiling.

"Did you touch Quinn?" I ask in an easy voice.

"Fuck you, Delaney," he chokes out. "Just kill me. I'm done playin' your fuckin' games."

Connor and Owen laugh from behind me as I pull out the knife Quinn shoved in my pants before she left.

"Killin' you is gonna be the best part of my day," I inform him with an evil snicker.

I start with his fingers, severing each one while Owen holds Sean's chest to the floor with his knee and Connor sits on his legs. Once I'm done with his fingers I remove both ears since they were able to hear Quinn's sweet voice. By this point, Sean's mostly unconscious so it makes cutting his tongue out easy. This punishment is for allowing his sick words to touch Quinn's ears. I'd like to take his dick but that would require touching it and I'm not in the mood, so I just stab him in the crotch repeatedly. I'm pretty sure he's dead as I finish sinking the knife into the area that used to house his dick. He doesn't seem to be breathing as I straddle his body, plunging the knife into his chest. I make quick and messy work of removing his heart, palming its warmth in one hand as I stand up. I spit on his body before Connor and Owen cover him in gasoline.

I'm drenched in Sean's blood from head to toe, relishing his death. With his dead heart in my hand, the three of us return to the pub which smells like an engine. I hold the heart in the air for all in the room to see.

"This is what happens to men who forget loyalty!" I bellow.

I drop the heart to the ground and smash it beneath my heel to the raucous applause and cheers of my new crew.

"Dílseacht!" I scream.

"Dílseacht!" the room returns in chorus.

I move to the door as matches drop, setting the pub alight. We stand across the street and watch the building glow in the blackness of the Chicago night. No cops, no firemen, no one will come to save the O'Boyle Brothers. The Dílseacht Crew has claimed the block, the neighborhood, the city and the respect that comes with it.

Planning meetings for the coming days before I bid my crew good night, I decide to stop at the gym with Connor and Owen before I head home. I don't want Quinn and my kids to see me like this. As I stand in the shower, shedding the layer of thick dried blood, I clear my head from the evening's events.

After Collin and Hugh told me there was a fracture in the O'Boyle Brothers, I made a call to the oldest member, Ronan Carey, who I dealt with years ago while I executed hits for the Brothers. We made a deal quickly: I take over as head of the crew and they get out of drugs and human trafficking. I wish I could say I'm doing this for the greater good, but that's not the case. People will still be trafficked and drugs will still be in the streets, just not facilitated by me.

When Shannon showed up in Chicago, we moved out. Every man I've ever done business with was at my side when we entered the pub. It was an easier take-down than I had imagined it would be. The O'Boyles underestimated me and the loyalty people have to me. I'm not a good man, but I'm loyal above all else. That matters in the streets where your word is your currency. It will take some time to restructure the crew and change the flow of income. These men have been waiting for someone like me to take over for eight years. A few more weeks won't be an issue.

I cut off the shower and pull on a Brogan's T-shirt and sweats before driving home to get my hands on my family. As I enter my garage, I nod at Connor and Owen who followed me, sending them on their way. They will be my right and left hand in the organization.

Ian meets me at the back door with a question lingering in his honey eyes. I nod, answering the unasked question...it's done. He claps my shoulder twice and moves toward his car to go home and get a restful night's sleep.

When I walk in the house Collin, Hugh, Shannon and Quinn are sitting on the couch. Thomas is sitting at the dining room table reading a book. He makes me look like a pussy, he's so unaffected. I'm glad he's got Shannon's back.

Quinn has Jack asleep against her side and Ash sleeping on her shoulder. The smile on her face is intoxicating. I stride quickly toward my woman and capture her lips in a searing kiss before pressing soft lips to my kids' sleeping heads.

I flop down next to my family, scooping them into my side.

"Gotta get back to the jet," Shannon announces. "Didn't tell the boys I was makin' the trip."

"They're gonna kick your ass when they find out," Hugh snorts.

"They're not gonna find out." She offers the brothers each a pointed look.

"We'll drive you," Collin states, trying to change the subject.

"Can't thank you enough for what you did tonight," I say to each of them, holding Shannon's green eyes the longest.

"You did the same for me," she says softly.

I stay silent. I'm in awe of the woman in front of me. She's a warrior in every sense of the word. Shannon flew through the pub, shot three guys that got in her way and crested the stairs to get to Quinn before most people knew what was going on. She did that for me. Eventually, Shannon will get to know Quinn and the kids and she'll love them. But tonight was her protecting me, not knowing what state Quinn would be in. She took that burden from me without me ever expressing the thought.

I stand up and pull Shannon off the couch into my arms, squeezing her thin frame with everything I've got in me. She returns the hug just as fiercely. After a long minute, I push her back by her shoulders and remove my shirt. Her brow furrows until she sees it. The tattoo that graces Shannon's ribcage, a four leaf clover in the form of a Celtic knot, dots the *i* of my dilseacht tattoo. Everyone in Shannon's family got a version of her tattoo after we rescued her in December. I hadn't told Shannon

231

I got the tattoo along with my cousins. It's a symbol that we're always together, endlessly bound to one another.

I stayed out of Shannon's life for a long time, almost ten years, before she was abducted. She's an attorney fighting for good and I'm a villain. I didn't want her to have to look the other way when I was committing crimes so I kept my distance. I regret those years without her in my life. I should have known Shannon wouldn't care. She's loyal to a fault.

As a seventeen-year-old girl, she showed me a light within myself that I didn't know existed. If she hadn't given me that glimmer, I wouldn't be able to accept the blinding light that Quinn offers me.

"Kieran," Shannon breathes out, tracing the symbol lightly with her fingertips.

Her face breaks into a beaming smile as she heaves herself into my arms, almost knocking me over.

"Love you," she murmurs in my neck.

"Love you, too." I kiss her hair before letting her go.

She steps out of our embrace, still beaming.

"Bring your family to Kansas City soon," she instructs. "It was great to meet you, Quinn."

"Shannon, I—" Quinn starts with an emotion choked voice.

"Not necessary," Shannon cuts her off. "I take care of my family. You and your kids are part of my family now. You ever need anything, you call that number I gave you."

"Thank you," Quinn breathes out. Shannon nods, her gaze lingering on the kids for a moment and then turns on her heel to leave, Thomas silently trailing her.

"It's hard for her," Hugh explains. I get it. Shannon's here helping me get my woman and kids back while her man and his unborn child are being held captive in Seattle by a she-devil. I swear, I'll do anything in my power to get them back to her. As soon as I have the crew in place, helping Shannon will become my focus. She deserves to have her family in her arms.

"Thanks for everything, guys," I say appreciatively to my cousins who I've also neglected for a decade. That stops now, too.

"Anytime, cousin," Collin replies, slapping me on the shoulder twice. Hugh pulls me in for a man hug before they both turn and leave. Alone at last with my family.

I haul Jack into my arms and pull Quinn down the hall by her hand to our bedroom. She climbs in bed with Ashling settling in next to Jack. I strip down to my boxer briefs and climb in bed, constricting my arms around the three of them, relaxing at the feel of Quinn's back pressed to my front. I need to be inside her as much as I need my family in my arms right now. So I compromise.

I pull her yoga pants down and thread my hard cock out of the flap in my underwear. Gently, I seat myself to the hilt in her wet pussy with a shudder.

"Kieran," she whispers.

"I just need to be inside you. Go to sleep. I love you." I press my lips to her hair and will my hips to remain still.

Her breathing evens out and the last of the tension drifts off my shoulders as a peaceful sleep claims me. My family is safe in my arms, my dick is buried in the woman I love and the threats to the people I love are glowing embers under a pile of rubble. Best night ever.

Kieran

"Daddy, I have to pee," Jack's whining voice wakes me.

"Huh?" I grunt.

"Daddy," Jack huffs, wiggling beneath my hand that has him captive against his mother's chest. I release my grip and Jack leaps from the bed, running into the bathroom.

"I don't know how you sleep that deep," Quinn says through a giggle, reaching back to pull her yoga pants over her ass. The movement makes my morning wood ache.

Jack thumps back in the room and climbs into the bed behind me before slinking across our bodies to sit facing Quinn and me.

"Mornin', bud," I say through a large smile.

"Mommy says no more bad guys. She said you're our hero, like *The Avengers*, and you got rid of all the bad guys," he says, hope glimmering in his bright blue eyes.

"You think Thor would hang out with me?" I ask, teasing him, not wanting to answer his question directly.

"He's too busy to hang out," Jack admonishes.

"Is that right?"

"Yeah, he has to guard Asgard, Earth, the nine realms plus his brother's a pain in the butt."

"He sounds busy."

"Can I go wake up Grandma? She's gonna make me French toast!"

"Sure, bud. I'll go with you."

"Stay put," I murmur into Quinn's hair.

I pull on my sweats and scoop Ash off the bed. I can smell that my mother doesn't need a wake-up call. The house is enveloped in cinnamon and vanilla.

"Grandma!" Jack squeals, running into the kitchen.

"Good morning, Sunshine," she coos, picking him up into a big hug before setting him on the counter where she's cooking away.

"Hey, Pop," I call to my dad who's at the dining room table reading the newspaper, drinking a steamy cup of coffee.

"Son," he says with a voice full of pride. He knows what I did last night and is offering me his approval. I beam a cocky smile at him. He snorts and shakes his head.

"You think you could feed Ash for me? Need some alone time with Quinn."

My dad pulls her from my arms, blowing raspberries in her neck. I guess I have my answer as she giggles away at her grandfather.

"Be out in a bit," I call over my shoulder. No one responds. Grandparents always get the good stuff.

I walk back into our bedroom and lock the door before diving into the bed. Quinn giggles as she turns to face me, both of us on our sides.

"You doin' okay?" I ask, softly brushing her inky hair out of her face.

"I'm good," she responds with a giant smile, her icy blues glinting with happiness. I gave her that.

She has two black eyes and her nose is bright red. I know she's happy—everything O'Boyle is gone—but she's far from good.

"I need you to tell me what happened."

"He kneed me in the face when I tried to get away. It looks worse than it feels."

"Did he do anything else to you? Do you need the doctor to come by?"

"I think I'm okay," she whispers, averting her eyes from mine.

"You didn't answer my question."

"He tried...to...well...uh...he couldn't," she stutters, trying to get something (something bad) out.

I tip her chin up, attempting to calm her with my gaze.

"He tried to get his fingers in me, but I was all dry so it didn't work very well. It hurt," she whispers. I'm glad that motherfucker is dead and I did him the way I did. I would've gone slower with his torture had I known.

"I'm sorry I wasn't there sooner," I apologize. Maybe I shouldn't have waited for Shannon. That's not true. It took me that amount of time to make the deal and round up my men. I was there as quickly as I could have been.

"Don't do that. It's not your fault. I'm okay and Shannon gave me the number of a therapist she knows. Said it helped her a lot when she needed it."

"I love that woman."

"I think I do, too. You shoulda seen her with Sean. He was so fuckin' scared and she was calm like she was doin' laundry."

"Her uncle trained her to be like that. It's not normal. She's a freak of nature with that shit."

"Something really bad happened to her, huh?"

"A lot of bad things. Shit's still fucked up for her, too. I'm gonna help fix it, though. I owe her for comin' here and gettin' you."

She nods and pauses for a moment.

"Thank you for what you did last night. I needed you to do that for me," she breathes out softly.

"Thank you for lettin' me."

I roll, pulling her body beneath as I settle between her legs.

"I love you," I whisper against her lips before taking her mouth.

I ravage her lips passionately, conveying how much love I feel for her. She returns the sentiment, threading her fingers into my hair, tugging me closer as our tongues lap at each other. Quinn hums contentedly in the back of her throat as I move down her jaw, feasting on the sweet spot just beneath her ear.

Her tiny hands roam my naked chest until she finds my nipples, pinching them firmly. I growl into her neck, nipping the skin before removing her shirt to get better access. I take a moment to remove her pants and underwear along with mine.

Fully naked, I cover her tit with my mouth, teasing her nipple with my teeth before flicking it with my tongue. I pinch her other nipple hard causing her back to vault off the mattress. I love how she responds to my

238

touch. Her skin warms beneath my hands as shivers of ecstasy creep up her spine.

I kiss my way down her ribcage, laving her with my tongue. When I get to her pussy I inhale through my nose deeply, breathing in her scent. I push her legs out wide, sweeping my tongue from bottom to top over and over, licking up every drop of juice she's spilling. I spear my tongue inside trying to coax more of her into my mouth. She bucks and moans as I hold her firmly to my face. I could eat her pussy for every meal and still be hungry for more.

I move to her clit, nipping it gently before sucking it into my mouth. Quinn whimpers with need as I let off my suction, licking rapidly. Removing one hand from her hip, I gently ease my index finger inside her, testing to see if Sean hurt her more than she's telling me. Her tight pussy clenches around me as she rolls herself further onto me. Slowly, I work my finger in and out as I continue my assault on her clit. Two strokes later she's muffling her screams in the pillow as her come drips down my chin onto my hand. Hottest fucking thing ever. So I go at it again. Her second orgasm rips through her minutes later.

I kneel between her legs, swiping my hand down my face as she watches me through hooded eyes. After I've captured all of her come in my palm I wipe it over my cock, rubbing her into my skin. Her breath hitches at the action as she leans up onto her elbows to watch the show.

Quinn reaches forward with her small hand, grasping my dick firmly. She strokes my wet cock slowly, gathering my pre-come with her thumb. She releases my cock and places her thumb in her mouth, moaning as my come touches her soft mouth. If I were a weak man

I'd blow my load right now. Instead, I palm my dick and press my head inside her. Quinn's so fucking tight it almost hurts.

Inch by inch, I sink into her, rubbing her clit with my fingers to give her pleasure through the pain. When my hips are flush with hers I lean forward and pull her fat bottom lip between my teeth. Quinn slants her head and shoves her tongue in my mouth, yanking my hair with such force I'm pretty sure I'll have a bald spot. I grin against her mouth, pulling my dick out slowly before plowing back in.

"Yes," she moans, arching her neck. I take the advantage, dropping my head next to hers and set a punishing pace. The room is filled with moans and skin slapping together. I pull her legs over my shoulders, sinking deeper until I bottom out inside her. Quinn's breath hitches at the sensation. Her icy blue eyes roll back in her head as she takes everything I've got to give her. My balls tighten as the pressure builds within me, driving deeper and harder.

With every thrust, Quinn's tits bounce until she reaches up, cupping them and pinching her nipples.

"Fuck," I gasp at the sight.

A flush blooms on her chest, working its way up to her cheeks as her orgasm thrashes through her body. Breathless incantations of my name stutter from her lips as her pussy leaks with pleasure. I drive into her once more before filling her to the brim with my come. I grunt and shake, thrusting every drop as far inside her as I can get it before lowering my body onto hers.

I keep my cock buried like a cork, trapping all of me within her. If this doesn't get her pregnant I'll have to get my swimmers checked.

"Shit, Kieran. You didn't use a condom again," she says, climbing out of her post orgasmic fog.

"I know," I grunt, surprised I'm able to form two words. "Never gonna."

"Oh, really? I should probably get on the pill then," she says through a snort, pushing a little of me out. I growl and thrust my hips forward.

"No," I grumble.

"No pill or no pushing you outta me?"

"Both."

"I'm gonna get pregnant."

"Yeah."

"Can you give me more than one word answers?"

"No."

She tumbles into a fit of giggles which pushes my dick out of her, causing me to get mad. Irrational caveman behavior? Yes. Do I try to hide this? No.

"Quinn," I warn.

Her giggles turn into full belly laughs until I take two fingers, swipe up all of my come leaking from her tight pussy and shove them inside her. She stops laughing and strokes my hair sweetly.

"Can't knock you up if it's running down your legs," I murmur into her neck.

"You really want another baby?" she asks in an inquisitive tone, not scared or annoyed, just wanting my answer.

"I want everything with you."

I sit up on my elbow, keeping my finger plug in place as I peer down into her bruised and battered face. She

241

offers me a small, almost timid smile, which makes my brow furrow.

"His fingers were in me last night like this." I immediately begin to remove my fingers, feeling like a monster. Quinn traps my wrist lightning fast, holding my fingers knuckle deep within her.

"I'll never feel them inside me again because you just took the memories and replaced them with the memory that your fingers could be holding in our third baby."

"Fuck, I love you," I groan and start working my fingers in and out of her, sliding my come all over her folds. My cock springs back to life and I bury myself inside her. I move to wipe my hand on the sheets, but Quinn catches me and guides my fingers in her mouth, curving a seductive smile around them. She sucks them clean, popping them from her lips as she finishes.

I crush my mouth to hers, tasting the tangy remnants of each of us on her tongue as I pound into her, fiercely driven by the primal need to mark her again. Growling and panting, sweating and grunting, thrusting and rubbing until she begs me to stop. I thunder into her pulsing hole, filling her just as I did before. This time she leaves my dick, allowing nature to do its job. Probably because she passes out before she can make a different choice.

Chapter 27

Kieran

"Yeah?" I bark into my phone.

"Just saw the most amazin' fuckin' thing in my entire life," Collin says softly.

"Tell me."

"She's sittin' there with her son on her chest. She's glowin' like the sun. Swear to God, I almost cried."

That crazy bitch in Seattle went into labor six weeks early with Kellerman's baby. Shannon and the rest of our families hopped flights to get there, not knowing if the baby would make it. Sounds like it all worked out in the end because Shannon's got her son and the crazy fucking ex died from complications. Complications she caused by taking cocaine while she was pregnant! It's a good thing she's dead, otherwise Shannon would be looking at a murder charge.

"Don't turn into a pussy on me, cousin," I snark, knowing full well what the sight of a woman and her child causes in a man.

"You are what you eat," he quips back. Touché.

"Give Shannon our love. We'd be there if Ash didn't have this ear infection. Quinn doesn't wanna put her on a plane."

"It's all good. You guys can fly into Kansas City once Ash is better. They'll have to be here in Seattle until the baby's released. You wouldn't believe how tiny Johnny is."

My breath hitches at the baby's name. That's Shannon's dead father's name.

"Johnny?"

"Jonathan David Kellerman."

I'm not a pussy, so I won't cry. Jonathan for Shannon's dad. David for Kellerman's also-dead father. Best fucking name ever.

"Hell, yes! Brian just texted me pictures. I'll send 'em to you."

"Do that," I say through a grin at how excited Collin is to be an uncle. He spends quite a bit of time with my kids, so I know how much this means to him.

"You're all domesticated, now the Kellerman family's together—who's next?"

"You?"

"Fuck that. I like pussy too much to settle on one flavor."

"You just haven't found your favorite yet. Once you do you'll do anything to keep that flavor on your lips morning, noon and night."

He chuckles loudly in the phone as I do the same.

"I'm gettin' love life advice from Kieran Delaney. What's goin' on in this world?"

Fuck if I know. If you would have told me six months ago I'd be in love and have two kids I would have laughed in your face. That's how life works, though, never know what's around the corner.

"Just got to our hotel. I'll call you later and fill you in once we know more."

"Thanks for callin'."

"Sendin' the pictures now."

We hang up and my phone dings. There she is. Glowing so bright I'm surprised they captured her on film.

"Quinn!" I bellow through the house, knowing I shouldn't.

"Shh," she scowls, striding into the room. "I just got Ashling to sleep. I swear to God if you—" I cut her off, holding up the screen of my phone.

Her scowl melts into an endearing, soft smile. She cradles the phone near her face as though she can climb into the phone to be with Shannon and Johnny.

"He's so little," she coos. "Is he okay? How's Shannon? When are they bringin' him home? How much did he weigh?"

"Quinn," I stop her never-ending questions.

"I wish we could be there."

"Me too," I say as I wrap her in my arms and pull her into my lap on the couch. "We'll fly to Kansas City once Ash's better and they're settled back in."

"Is that Kellerman?" She holds up the screen, showing Kellerman sitting next to Shannon, beaming with pride.

"Yeah."

"Wow."

"What?"

"Well, look at him. He's massive. Kinda hot, too," she says the last part with a mischievous grin on her fat lips.

"You're gonna get it." I throw her on her back on the couch and start tickling her throat with my stubble while she squeals and tries half-assedly to push me off.

"Daddy, did you know that dinosaurs make the gas in the car?" Jack says, climbing on the couch. I stop my assault and sit us up.

"I do know that."

"It was in my lesson today. Dinosaurs are instinct."

"Extinct," I correct.

"That's what I said."

"You wanna see something cool?"

"Sure."

I show him the pictures of the baby and Shannon. He's impressed for about two seconds before he goes back to telling me all about dinosaurs.

"Are you excited about your birthday, Daddy?"

"Yeah, bud."

"Mommy got you the best present ever, but it's a secret so I can't tell you."

"Is it *Avengers* pajamas?"

"No," he says rolling his big blue eyes at me.

"Is it Legos?"

"I'm not tellin'," he says seriously, crossing his arms over his chest. Jack looks more and more like the six-year-old he should. He's gaining weight and growing like a weed. Quinn had to go buy him a whole new wardrobe last week because he'd outgrown everything.

"Grandma says I get to sleep in your old room tomorrow night," he says excitedly, changing the subject.

The kids are staying with my parents' tomorrow night after we have a family dinner for my birthday. I'm not big on celebrating, but it's important for Jack to see these types of things. I've been planning all the surfaces in the house I'm going to have sex with Quinn on while the kids are gone. Happy birthday to me!

"I've got some work to do today, so Uncle Ian's gonna come over and hang out with you guys."

"Cool. You think he'll play video games with me? Mommy can't play 'em. She always dies and then kills me."

"Hey. I try," Quinn feigns offense. She doesn't try.

"How 'bout I play with you now?"

"Yeah!" He jumps up and runs down into the basement.

"I'm gonna go take a nap while Ashling is still out. I'm worn out from bein' up with her all night," Quinn says through a yawn.

"I'll wake you up before I head out." I press a kiss to her hair before jogging down the stairs to act like a kid for a few hours.

"Hey boss," Connor calls out as I walk into The Castle. I bought the building next to Brogan's to run the Dílseacht Crew out of. We named it The Castle, our fortress from the streets. It's taken some work, but things are coming together in here. There are offices and small studio apartments on the second level. The main floor is similar to Brogan's, set up for training and fighting.

"What's goin' on for the fight tonight?" I ask as I make my way up the metal stairs to my office.

"Lotta money comin' in for the Russian, Vetrov. He's fightin' that Italian kid, Barzetti," Connor informs me, taking the leather chair across the dark wood desk from me.

"Seen either of 'em fight?"

"Watched Barzetti a few weeks back. Kid's quick—got a lot to learn though. Heard Vertrov's a beast. Got the potential to go pro. Russian's are lookin' to line their pockets to make that push for him."

"Doesn't sound like much of a fight," I snort.

"Barzetti's the only one willin' to fight Vetrov."

"Why's that?"

"Vetrov killed a guy a few weeks back. Some say it was an accident others are sayin' he did it to prove a point."

"And that would be?"

"Don't fuck with him."

I quirk an eyebrow, signaling I need more fucking information than that.

"Apparently the guy he was fightin' had been runnin' his mouth for weeks. Spouted some shit about fuckin' Vetrov's woman. Don't think that's what set him off, though, because from what I've found out, Vetrov doesn't have a woman."

"Doesn't seem like the kinda thing a fighter would lose his shit over. You know that."

"I haven't found anything but that. No one seems to know about it."

"Who'd he kill?"

"Castro."

"That motherfucker was a punk."

"I know," Connor scoffs.

Castro was a pain in the ass fighter that also worked as a low level enforcer for the Mancini Crime Family, the same crime family that kidnapped Shannon back in December. Ever since her rescue, a lot of the Mancini Family have been arrested or are in the wind. There are a few hanging around trying to remain in power in their territories, but it's a failing effort. Russians are taking over along with some street gangs. I stay out of their shit, mostly drugs and guns. Vetrov could have killed Castro for family reasons. It wouldn't be the first time.

The fights I run are not refereed. You fight until you can't. People die in fights, but it's rare. Beating someone to death takes time unless you land a lucky blow or someone's fighting injured. Trainers can stop fights if they feel their fighter is done. Again, that rarely happens. Most fights end with someone unconscious or so beaten they give up.

"Russians got any beef with Barzetti or his family?" I ask. I don't want business running my fights. If families have issues, they can deal with them in the streets like men, not in my house.

"Not that I know of."

"Make sure. If the Russians are tryin' to use Vetrov as their long sword they can do it somewhere else."

"You got it, boss," Connor says as he ambles out of my office.

I peel out of my clothes and throw on some shorts before strapping up my hands, feeling the need for a workout. I miss fighting. It's been almost two years since my last fight. I'm too fucking old to fight, but it's hard to convince my heart. Fighting is the only thing I ever did well when I was a kid.

When my dad was in prison I had to hold my own and that meant a lot of fights. I was good to begin with and even better once Ian found me. He rode my ass hard and didn't take my angst-filled shit. Instead, he beat my ass and then beat my ass again for good measure. Once I was fifteen he let me start fighting for him. I've never lost a fight. Had the shit kicked out of me plenty of times, but I always came out on top.

As I approach the heavy bag, Owen steps behind it, bracing for impact. I start out slow working up a good sweat before I unleash punishing combinations, pushing Owen back off the bag. I get in a zone when I train. Just me and the bag, no thoughts.

Owen lets go and I stop, offering him a glare.

"Boss," he says, nodding behind me.

I pivot on my foot to find a Hulk-like man gliding across the room toward me. Owen steps in front of me just as Connor does the same. The Hulk guy may be big, but Connor and Owen together could take him.

The Hulk stops a few feet away, maintaining eye contact with me, ignoring my men.

"Mr. Delaney?" he asks in a professional voice.

"Who the fuck are you?" I respond with a warning in my voice.

"Alex Vetrov, sir."

Mr. Delaney? Sir? This kid has to be joking.

"Your fight's not for a few hours. You here to warm up?" I ask in a slightly nicer tone.

"I'm here for you." There's a threatening tone to his voice but not his posture.

Connor and Owen puff up at the sound. I laugh a loud bark.

"You wanna get your ass kicked before you fight Barzetti?" Owen growls.

"I need to speak with Mr. Delaney," Vetrov replies.

The kid's piqued my interest. It takes balls to walk in here unarmed and call me out.

"Let's go to my office," I say, moving past the Doyle wall.

Vetrov follows me while the Doyle brothers follow him. The rest of my crew are standing at the ready, though no one would know that to look at them. They look like a room of fighters and trainers, not armed criminals.

I open the door to my office and signal with my head for Vetrov to go ahead of me. Once he's in, I offer Owen a pointed look, letting him know to be ready for whatever goes down. He nods and shuts the door behind me.

"Have a seat," I order, coming around my desk and taking my chair.

Quinn painted the office a dark grey and bought black leather chairs with dark wood furniture. She said it was to make the space feel masculine. It does, and it feels a little like a bat cave, dark and foreboding. My guest doesn't seem intimidated, not that I expected him to be. The Russians' walls are probably decorated in blood and trophy heads.

"They want me to kill you," Vetrov says in a professional, cool voice.

"Wouldn't be the first time someone's wanted to kill me," I respond with a shrug.

My nonchalance at his admission gives me a first glimpse of a crack in his steely demeanor. He looks like Dolph Lundgren, short blond hair, massive body, square face and menacing, deep blue eyes. His tight set lips twitch at my shrug, barely, but it was there.

"You plannin' on killin' me now?" I ask with a quirked brow.

"No, sir."

"You gotta quit that shit. My name's Kieran. You say sir or mister, I start lookin' around for cops and attorneys."

"It's a sign of respect."

"Respect never comes from words, it comes from actions."

"I don't wanna kill you," he says, hunching his shoulders forward, leaning his elbows on his knees, dropping his head to his chest in defeat. Kid's got me curious.

"That's good since you couldn't if you wanted to," I snark. He snorts but keeps his head bowed. I wait for him to say something. He doesn't, just sits in the same position.

"All right. You're here to warn me for a reason. I've got two ideas as to why. One, you're not in the habit of killin' people so you have some moral objection. I doubt that's the case, though. Two, you have an issue with your family and you wanna use me to get you out."

His head pops up at the last sentence and I know I've hit the nail on the head.

"They're not my family," he seethes. There's the fighter Connor was telling me about. "Do you know anything about me?"

"Nah, just that you're a fighter and you killed Castro a few weeks back. Not much else."

"My name is Alexei Vasilyevich Vetrov. I'm guessin' you don't know anything about Russian names, so I'll spell it out for you...Vasily Rostov was my father," he growls the last part.

"Why's any of this important for me to know?"

A knowing and sinister grin sweeps across his lips.

"Because I know what you did to him. My mother was a whore...is a whore. I'm the well-known-secret product of their relationship. I think you know what that means, about how I was raised, what he did to me."

A long tense silence stretches between us. Rostov was a fucking monster. I'm happy Quinn fucked him up like she did. The man across from me is a warrior, but the wounds that piece of shit inflicted on him are lurking behind his haunting eyes. Now I feel bad for the kid, which isn't a normal thing for me, but I see Jack in him. What Jack could have become without Quinn. I'm hooked.

"Rostov got what he deserved," I state firmly, offering Alex a kind gaze.

"I want out. I don't want anything to do with them. I've been tryin' to find a way for a long time. I'm a good fighter. I love it, but I don't want to fight for men that fed me to a monster and keep feedin' kids to monsters just like him. Can you help me?"

"You want me to go to war with the Russians because you want out?" I ask, shocked. That's a big fucking favor.

"I want you to fight me."

"Huh?"

"I want you to fight me tonight. Make a deal with the Russians that if you win you get me. If I win, they get the territories you run that they want. They'll make the deal because they're certain I'll win."

"And how do I know this isn't the plan? You come in here with your sad fucked up story and I agree to climb in a ring with you so you can fuck me up?" I grumble, feeling set up and played.

"Because I saved your son," he states plainly, staring hard at my face.

"Come again?"

"I found your son when Rostov was passed out. I got him the fuck outta the house, paid his whore mother never to come back and made sure that happened."

"Shit," I breathe out, throwing my head back against the hot leather, rubbing my dílseacht tattoo.

After about five minutes of burning my skin with friction and calming myself down I clear my throat.

"You can't throw the fight. Everyone'll know if you do. If we fight, we fight. There's already a shit load of money ridin' on you, a last minute change could cause issues."

"You can beat me," he says encouragingly, like I need the coaxing.

"I will beat you," I snort.

"I'm a lot bigger than you."

"You'll hit the canvas harder."

"I'm a lot younger than you."

"Means you're fuckin' stupid."

"I'm undefeated."

"So is my older, smaller ass. Call me when you hit your twenties undefeated and I'll give you a high-five for your shitty accomplishment. Call me when you hit thirty undefeated and we can talk," I finish, offering him a pointed look to shut the fuck up.

"I'll be twenty in six months."

"Good for you," I snark.

"If I keep working for the Russians I won't see that birthday," he states solemnly.

"I'll beat your ass tonight to make sure you don't work for them another day. If this plan of yours is gonna work, I need to start makin' some calls. Did they send you in here to get me to fight?"

"Yeah. They said to do anything necessary to get you in the ring. Then I'm supposed to end you."

"Anything necessary bein'?"

I know the answer before he offers it.

"Threaten your family. There's a car outside your house, waitin' to take your woman and kids if you refuse."

"Motherfuckers!" I roar. Connor and Owen blow through the door guns drawn.

"Go to my house, now. Get my fuckin' family here!" I instruct.

Owen offers a chin lift since Connor's already running down the metal stairs barking orders at men while he moves.

"You good here, boss?" Owen asks, motioning the barrel of his piece at Alex.

"Get my goddamn family here and I'll be fine. You bring anyone you find outside my house to me. Don't let Quinn or the kids see shit."

"On it."

He slams the door and he stomps down the stairs. Pissed off Doyle brothers are fun to watch. Not now because I'm fucking fuming, but generally it's a good show.

"If you ever know there's a threat around my family again, you lead with that shit," I growl at Alex with a threat of bodily harm in my eyes.

"You wouldn't have listened to me if I'd told you upfront. You'd have put a bullet in my head," he responds pointedly.

"You're right. Don't do it again."

"I won't let anything happen to your family," he growls in a territorial manner that catches my attention.

"See that you don't."

He nods and I start making phone calls. The Russians may just want some territory, but they just bought a war. No one fucks with my family.

Chapter 28

Quinn

Connor comes into the basement with a scowl on his face that looks like it hurts. I quickly climb out of the recliner I was in, approaching him with caution. Please let Kieran be safe.

"Need you to pack up the kids," he whispers, trying not to alarm Jack. Jack is oblivious, watching *Transformers* for the second time today.

"Okay," I whisper back, hoping he'll give me more information, but he just stands there with a look on his face that says *move quickly.*

"Jacky boy. Let's go see your dad," Ian says, understanding what's going on without so much as a word passing between him and Connor.

"Cool," Jack responds and runs up the stairs to get ready.

When I get in the kitchen, Owen is loading Ash into her car seat. I didn't even hear him on the monitor—stealthy bastard.

I quickly pack everything we need for a night out and dash to the bedroom to get dressed. I know there's a fight tonight so I need to look presentable. I throw on skin tight black jeans, a slinky bright blue racer-back top and a pair of black and blue heels. I rip my hair out of the bun on top of my head and run my fingers through it. I want to put on some make-up, but I doubt I have time. I do a quick sweep of mascara and pink lip gloss. Done.

"You can't wear that," Connor informs me as I step into the living room.

I look down at myself and crinkle my brow. I think I look nice.

"Why?"

"I don't know. You just can't."

"Huh?"

"I don't know the rules of how girls are supposed to look, but you look too good to be out in public."

My cheeks flame and I look away.

Connor's phone buzzes as Jack joins the room with Ian in tow.

"I'm ready. Uncle Ian helped me pack up some toys and games," Jack tells me, threading his hand into mine.

"Gotta go. Can you put on a jacket or something?" Connor asks me.

"It's June Connor," I chastise, moving toward the kitchen, pulling Jack along.

Owen quirks an eyebrow at me as I move past him. Jesus, they're like two older brothers.

"Ready?" I ask, avoiding his disapproval of my completely normal outfit.

He snorts and nods.

We all pile into the SUV. As I'm maneuvering to get in the driver's seat, Connor leads me around the car and puts me in the passenger seat. I guess I'm not driving. Connor climbs in after, grumbling about how close the seat is before moving it all the way back. I'm short—what did he expect?

Owen leads us to The Castle in his truck while Ian follows behind us in his car. The ride is silent save for Jack talking every once and a while. I'm nervous. I know something is wrong, but I can't tell what.

We park on the street in front of The Castle next to Brogan's. It's a large red brick building that looks plain and unassuming, a perfect place to run the Dílseacht Crew from.

Connor scoops Jack out of his car seat while Owen grabs Ashling. Jack hangs on his hip as Connor pulls me into his side firmly. He's nervous. His massive body is tense and his eyes are scanning the street feverishly.

We walk into the gym area and find it's pretty empty. There are a few men setting up tables and chairs, but other than that, all is quiet. Connor leads us to the grey metal stairs that rise to Kieran's office just as he steps out of the door.

Kieran's face is masked in fury. His hands are balled into fists at his sides. He's also not wearing any clothes other than a pair of shorts. I'm sure it says something about my perspective in life, but damn he looks hot right now.

"Daddy," Jack yells, climbing off Connor and running up the stairs.

Kieran's fury melts instantly as he pulls Jack into his chest.

"You're all stinky," Jack says with a crinkled nose, making no move to get away from the stench.

"Thanks, bud." He rumples Jack's hair before setting him down, leaving a hand on Jack's shoulder.

"Ian, can you watch the kids for a few?" Kieran asks with a bit of fury creeping back into his gaze.

"No problem," Ian responds, taking Ash's car seat from Owen before plodding up the stairs. He pulls Jack away from Kieran and they disappear into the office next to Kieran's.

"Quinn," he growls in a throaty voice I've never heard. I quickly ascend the metal stairs, my heels clacking loudly as I go. When I reach the top, Kieran grabs my hand and drags me behind him down the hall toward the apartments. I have to basically run to keep up with him.

He opens the door, pushes me through roughly and slams it. I stand in front of him in the middle of the room, waiting. Either I'm in trouble or I caused trouble.

"I'm gonna take a shower. All I want to do right now is rub my sweat all over your body so everyone knows you're mine, but I have the feelin' that'll piss you off, so I'm takin' a shower. You wearin' that fuckin' outfit is makin' this real hard. Don't. Move," he orders and stalks into the bathroom.

I don't move. Kieran's a live wire right now, so I bend my rules of not being bossed around. His temper has been better since the night he became the head of the Dilseacht Crew, but only a little. I knew what I was getting into when I stayed with Kieran. He's mean, surly, quick tempered and tolerates no bullshit. I can live with all of that because underneath he's the kindest man I've ever known. He would never hurt me or allow anyone else to. I'm safe and loved when I'm with him and that's all I need in this world. I don't need rainbows and romance, I just need Kieran.

He steps out of the bathroom a few minutes later with a towel wrapped around his hips and steam rising from his shoulders. There are beads of water dancing over his skin and I feel a flush creep over me as I realize I want to lick them off. I'm out of my mind right now. I shake it off, but not before Kieran notices.

"Like something you see?" His voice is sultry and sex-filled.

"Everything." My voice is breathy and almost a whimper. I wish I could pull off sexy, but I can never quite manage.

"I'd love nothin' more than to get my dick in you, but I can't right now. I'm fightin' tonight so I need the motivation."

Sex haze gone.

"You're what?!" I screech.

"I'm fightin' tonight."

"No, you're not," I order, puffing my chest up for an argument.

"I am," he says plainly, taking a few steps toward me. I take a step back from him, halting his progression.

"Why? You haven't fought in two years. You run your own crew. Why the hell are you fightin'?"

"Business," he responds pointedly.

"Ah, so this is the moment where the woman is supposed to stand by her man and let him take care of business?"

"Yes. You know this life, Quinn. I don't have to explain it to you."

"Fine. I'm not watchin', though. I'll go over to Ian's with the kids."

261

I know my place and if he says it's business, I won't push. He's with me because I get this and I'm usually okay with it. I don't want him to fight. He's wound up, meaning this is important—something's riding on this fight. So I keep my mouth shut. Not happy, but silent.

"No, you'll stand next to the ring and support your man," he demands harshly.

"Don't make me do that, Kieran. I've seen enough bloodshed to last two lifetimes," I whisper, looking at the ground.

Shannon's therapist—my therapist—has been really helpful over the past few weeks. She thinks I'm doing well, considering what I've been through. I haven't given her all of the details about the last few months or even the last eight years, but she knows about Sean and my parents. That's enough for now. I don't want to add any new topics, especially not Kieran fighting.

"Quinn, look at me," he says in a hushed tone, moving into my personal space.

I lean my head back and gaze into his murky blues. They're angry.

"If I'm fightin', certain things are gonna be expected and you bein' by my side is one of those things. Me comin' out with a win is the other. You're not afraid to watch me fight. You're afraid to watch me lose. I'm not gonna lose, Quinn. Don't doubt me."

"Never. I've never doubted you and I never will. Fights aren't a sure thing, though."

He cups my cheeks with his rough hands and presses a soft light kiss to my lips.

"You've never seen me fight, Shorty," he murmurs into my mouth with that cocky Kieran Delaney swagger.

Then he kisses me, drinking from my mouth. He ravages my lips with his teeth before plunging his tongue in my mouth. His minty, sweaty, sweet taste sucks me in, causing my legs to tremble with want.

I sink to my knees, removing his towel in one brief snap of my wrist. Before he can think, I open wide and sink him to the back of my throat.

"Fuck!" he roars, grabbing my head by a fistful of my hair and tips my head back slightly so that I look up into his eyes. I keep my lips wrapped around him tight as I make eye contact and slide to the tip and then back down as far as I can get him in my throat. I set a slow pace, torturing him. Quickly he takes control, holding my head in place stroking himself deep. I flick my tongue and moan as he fucks my throat.

I run my hand up his inner thigh before cupping his balls. His breath hisses past his teeth, his head falling back in ecstasy. He plunges deeper into my mouth causing me to gag, but he keeps going. Something changes in his demeanor as he pounds away at me, becoming forceful and harsh. He growls and pounds deeper. I try to stay calm but the roughness and lack of care he has is starting to make me uncomfortable. Before I can push him away from me and make this stop, Kieran rips himself from my mouth stepping away on shaky legs. I look up at him, confused and hurt.

"Always feels good to get in the back of a throat. Thanks for the work up," he says in a cruel tone, panting and heaving with his dick standing painfully tall.

I climb to my feet glaring at him.

"Did you have fun usin' my mouth as inspiration?" I glower.

"Quinn," he says like he just came out of a haze.

"Fuck you, Kieran. How's that for motivation?" I run from the room before he can grab me. He won't chase me through The Castle naked. I get two steps before I run into a solid wall of muscle.

"Sorry! Are you okay?" a deep dark voice asks.

"I'm fine. Sorry," I grumble. "Excuse me." I move around him without ever looking at his face. I know he's a fighter based on the god-like sculpted frame he sports. No point looking at him, the only fighter I want to see just made me feel like a fluff girl on a porn set.

I walk into the office where Ian is playing with the kids.

"Come on, Jack," I order harsher than I mean to. Jack jumps at my tone, but moves quickly toward me. I scoop him up on my hip after grabbing Ashling off her play mat on the floor.

"Quinn?" Ian calls cautiously.

"I'm not feelin' well. I'll see you later," I lie.

I stomp from the office and fly down the stairs, searching the area for Ash's car seat. I find it up against a wall under the stairs. I buckle her in quickly and heave the handle into the crook of my arm, slide my purse across my chest, set Jack on my hip and make my way to the door.

There are a few more men here, but the place is still mostly empty, making my getaway easy. I kick the door open forcefully and unlock the SUV. Once Ash is loaded in, I get Jack in his seat.

"Mommy, are you okay?" he asks in a small timid voice.

"My tummy hurts, Baby. I'll be fine," I coo softly, rubbing his dimple with my thumb.

After Jack's safely strapped in his seat I shut his door and pull my knife out of my purse. Kieran brought me my Yarborough after he took out my uncles. He'll be sorry he did if he comes for me. I never got the story from Kieran, but I'm guessing I'm not safe right now so I feel better armed. I hear the door of The Castle open behind me and spin quickly to confront whoever is exiting.

"Whoa," a gigantic man says, holding his hands up in the universal "don't shoot" pose.

I keep my knife pointed at him as I move to the front of the car.

"I don't think Kieran would want you to leave," he says softly.

I remain silent as I round the hood. Once the SUV is between me and the Hulk, I lower my knife and climb into the driver's seat. I sit, moving the electric seat forward so I can touch the pedals. Of course, before I can get myself situated, Kieran tears out of The Castle, seething. I hit the locks and jam the seat-moving button harder as I turn the car on.

"Open the car, Quinn," Kieran demands as he yanks on the locked handle. I keep my eyes straight forward, willing this damn seat to move.

"Quinn!" Kieran barks.

"Mommy?" Jack's voice quivers. Kieran's scaring him which just pisses me off more.

"It's okay, Baby," I try to soothe him.

The locks click open, startling me. Kieran rips the passenger door open, heaving himself in before turning off the SUV and snatching the keys. He throws them to Connor who's standing on the curb holding another set of keys. Damn it! Connor comes around to my side of the car to the back door, no doubt to get Ash out. I throw my door open pressing my back to the SUV, my knife in Connor's chest.

"Don't. You. Dare," I seethe.

"Quinn, you're not gonna stab me," Connor says in a defeated voice.

"Try me!"

"Mommy!" I hear Jack scream in a panicked voice from the other side of the car. I kick Connor in the shin and sprint toward Jack's voice.

Ian is holding a screaming, fighting Jack.

"Give me my son," I growl.

Ian looks at me, shocked by my clearly mentally unstable state. I feel Kieran approaching my back and spin on him, my knife pointed at his dílseacht tattoo.

"You're scarin' my kids. Tell Ian to put my son back in the car, now. Tell Connor to give me the keys. Tell yourself you're an asshole and to leave me the hell alone!"

"Ian, put Jack back in the car. Connor, hand Quinn the keys, carefully so she doesn't stab us."

Both of the men comply quickly.

"Give us a minute," Kieran instructs his men as I begin backing away from him the same way I did the first night I met him.

There's a shuffling of feet behind me and the metal door slams shut.

"Quinn—"

266

"Don't. I have nothing to say to you."

"I have something to say to you," he growls.

"You said plenty. Leave me alone, Kieran. I've had enough of your words for the day."

"I love you."

"You've got a fucked up way of showin' it," I say through a snort, continuing to back my way to the front of the car.

"Let me explain," he demands.

"Go inside and get ready for your fight. You know, it's moments like this I realize I'm still in this world alone. I can't go to my parents' house to get away from you and have someone to comfort me. I don't have girlfriends to call and bitch about how my boyfriend just treated me like a common whore. I don't have a dad that'll come down here and threaten you for hurting his daughter. I have my two kids that are now freaked out because you're scary as hell when you act like this."

Kieran's jaw drops open as I clear the hood and run to the driver's side door. He's still standing there like a statue as I pull away from the curb. And he's still standing there as my vision of him fades in the rearview mirror.

"You're really mad at Daddy, huh?" Jack asks in a quiet voice.

"Yes, I am," I answer honestly.

"Are we gonna move away now?"

I don't know how to answer that question. I want to run right now, fade into the streets and alleys where I can be invisible. The feeling in my chest right now is painful. It hurts to take a deep breath. I'm guessing Kieran fucked my face and pulled out of my mouth because he wanted to be sexually tense for the fight. If he would have just told me that I wouldn't be so hurt. It's the force he used and the words he growled and the tone in his voice when he said it that crushed me.

Kieran's always been kind with me during sex. Dominant and a little caveman-like, sure, but always kind. In that room just now, he was cruel and heartless. I can take a lot of sides of Kieran, just not that one.

"I don't know what'll happen, Jack."

"You won't leave me though, right?"

"Never," I say firmly, locking eyes with him in the rearview. He nods.

I drive around for about thirty minutes, calming myself down. Deciding Jack could use some fun, I head to Marquette Park. As we pull up, I feel better already. Some open space with kids and families running around is just what we need. I unload the kids and settle at a picnic table with Ash while Jack runs around the playground laughing and playing.

What happened with Kieran today was painful. I've seen women used and discarded in the streets like trash. That's what that felt like today. The way he used me followed by the way he spoke to me, ending with that look on his face like I could have been any woman (mouth)...ripped me in two. I can be a lot of things in life, but I can't just be a thing that gets used. I fought for eight years to make sure I was never that. I'll be damned if that's what I become just to be with Kieran.

I know the man he is and what he'll always be. I don't have an issue with any of it. But I can't be an object to him when he loses himself. My kids deserve a mother that has the self-worth to not be a thing. I may be a murderer and a woman with a lot of baggage, but when

I'm with these kids I'm the best version of me that I can be. So that's what I choose.

I feel a ghost of a smile sweep across my face as I hold my baby and watch my son. I'm okay.

Chapter 29

Kieran

"Follow the tracker on the SUV. Don't let her see you," I order Owen.

Yes, I have a tracker on my woman's car. Yes, it's an invasion of her privacy. Yes, I feel like a stalker. Yes, it's for her safety.

"Should I punch you in the mouth first?" Owen grumbles.

"Probably," I huff.

He offers me a wry smile before heading out the door to track my family. I fucked up. As I've mentioned...I'm not a good man. I got too inside my head while I was plowing into her throat, which I never should have done, and treated her like trash. Not my finest moment.

Now I can't even go after her because I have a fight to get ready for. She looked sick when she left the apartment. She was in pain when I got into the SUV. She was murderous when I had Ian get Jack out of the car. She looked done before she drove away from me.

After all this time, she still feels alone in the world. I've kept her so isolated she hasn't started a life yet. Her life is all about me and the kids. I've been trying my damnedest to get her pregnant on top of everything, too. While I want to feel bad, I don't.

I want her isolated and safe with me. I don't want to share her with girls' night out and slumber parties—or whatever women do. I don't want her hitting the clubs and getting grinded on by yuppie pricks. She belongs in my house, at my side or in my bed. Wow, I'm a bigger asshole than I give myself credit for.

The thing is, Quinn doesn't seem to mind. She's been happy in our little world. I've never heard her complain in all the months we've been together. If anything, she's been agreeable to all the walls I've put around her. She feels alone now because she feels trapped with a monster within those walls.

After everything she's been through, I was an asshole during sex. The one place where she needs safety I made her feel unsure and dirty. I need to fix this, yet here I am staring at my hands resting on my desk doing nothing. I won't do anything, either. I have to go win this fight and then…

Buzz, buzz.

"Yeah," I bark into my phone.

"They're at Marquette Park," Owen growls.

"Got eyes on her?"

"Yeah. Jack's playin' and Quinn's holdin' Ash watchin' him."

"She made you yet?" I ask, hopeful she hasn't.

"Probably. She's palmin' her blade in her bag, lookin' around a lot."

"Shit," I say gruffly.

"What's my move here?"

"Keep eyes on her. Let me know if she runs."

"You think she'll do that?" Owen asks, shocked.

"Don't know. I fucked up. She might," I say, defeated at the realization that I may have lost my family.

"You want me to stop her if she does?"

"No."

"No?!"

"If she needs to go, let her."

"Fuck that, Kieran. I'm not lettin' her go anywhere. She's been alone long enough. If you fucked up that bad, I'll take her until you can pull your head outta your ass long enough to fix this shit. Fuck you for givin' up without a fight!"

"Owen," I warn.

"You can growl at me all you want, I don't give a shit. She's *my* friend. I'm not lettin' her spend another day in this world feelin' alone. Go fight, I've got this."

He hangs up.

I'm on a roll, pissing people off today. I want to call Shannon so badly right now, but she's got her hands full with a premature baby. She doesn't need my fuckery. I could call Collin, but he'll chew my ass worse than Owen. Treating women poorly doesn't fly in my family, so I'll get no sympathy. Not that I deserve any.

I slam my head down onto my desk, hard. The pain feels better in my head than in my heart. The worst part of this is Jack. I scared him. I scared my son like I never believed I would. I just wanted to stop her. I knew she wouldn't leave without the kids. A bad move in hindsight because she got stabby. Now they're playing at a park without me. I've never wanted to swing on a swing so badly in my life as I do right now.

"Time to get you warmed up," Ian growls in my doorway. He's pissed too.

"Ian—"

"Save it. I know you'll win, but I hope this kid beats your ass for whatever you did to her." He thuds back down the stairs without another glance at me.

I pick my pathetic ass up and plod down the stairs into the locker room where Ian and Connor are waiting for me. Ian straps up my hands so I can warm up, never looking at my face. It's a bare-knuckle fight so the straps will come off before I get in the ring.

I jump rope, shadow box, hit the pads a little and stretch intermittently for an hour and a half. Now I'm ready. I've got a good sweat going and I'm pissed the fuck off. Alex doesn't have a chance in hell. I walk out of the locker room to the screams and chants of about 250 people. This revs my blood and spikes my pulse. I've missed this. There's nothing like a fight, nothing makes me feel this tension mixed with relief. Except it feels empty and hollow when I see Quinn's vacant seat.

I shake it off and keep my head in the fight. Focus, Delaney! I hop in the ring and jump around a bit before taking my corner and getting greased up. Everything in my head goes silent as I eye Alex across the ring. His eyes are closed as his trainers bark at him in Russian. His long arms are loose and relaxed in his lap. As I watch him, his eyes snap open and meet mine. There's understanding in his eyes mixed with determination.

It's time. Alex and I touch fists in the middle of the ring and wait for the bell.

Ding!

Alex shoots his fist out quickly, brushing me back. As I shuffle back on my heel I offer him a classic cocky grin and shake my head no at him. He remains stoic, waiting for my move. I fake with my left and land a hard body blow to his ribs. The whoosh of air exiting his lips is music to my ears. He catches me twice with a left hook before we back off each other, moving our feet a little.

Bare-knuckle fighting is generally concentrated on body shots. Hitting someone in the face with your fist for five rounds does more damage to you than them. Alex and I meet in the middle again and trade body blow after body blow, heaving and swaying in tandem.

Ding!

Round one done. Ninety seconds of ass whipping and I still feel spry. Alex looks good, too. We need to stretch this fight the full five rounds to make it look as good as possible. The Russians are screaming at him, while Ian and Connor are silently rubbing me down and dousing me with water.

Ding!

Alex comes at me hot, taking a shot at my jaw and landing it. I spit a mouthful of blood on the canvas and swing widely, catching the big man in the nose. The bone cracks and he stumbles back a few feet. I back off, letting him regain his sight. He heaves a giant breath, clearing the bleed, spraying blood like a fire-breathing dragon.

We spend the rest of the round trading body blows, crushing each other's ribs. As I feel the round winding down I unleash some power, driving my fist upwards into Alex's liver, knocking him to the canvas.

Ding!

Alex lugs his body to his corner, wincing as he takes his stool. His trainer smacks him across the face like a bitch. The kid doesn't flinch, just stares me down. Another guy sets his nose back in place, again no reaction from Alex. He's a warrior, fighting for his freedom.

Ding!

Alex drives hard-hitting fists into my chest, driving me into the ropes. I cover my body as best I can as he works me over. I feel my first rib crack. I slam my body into his, knocking him back as I spin away when his fist plows into my kidney, dropping me to my knees. Alex backs off per fight rules. No hitting a man down, no matter the protests from his corner.

I take a breath and climb to my feet as Alex charges at me. He works me into the ropes again, leaving nothing off his punches, punishing my torso.

Ding!

I stagger to my corner as Ian jumps in front of me.

"Stop fuckin' around," he bellows over the roar of the crowd.

I nod, knowing I'm not fucking around. Alex is a talented fighter and he's currently kicking my ass. I feel old and tired right now. Not good.

Ding!

We both come out swinging from the fences. I catch his jaw and then his upper lip, splitting it open. He lands a crushing blow to my brow, slicing it. We're both drenched in blood, slipping and sliding on the canvas, doing more dancing than fighting. We're tired.

We meet in the middle and I swing powerfully, missing his face and losing my footing. It's his opening and he takes it, snapping my head to the side with a damaging blow to my cheek. My legs go out from under me as I topple to the canvas. I lay there in a puddle of my own blood, knowing my fate if I don't climb to my feet...I'll be dead by morning. I can see it on the Russians' faces. This fight is about taking my respect from my men, shattering my hard-earned reputation. Squashing me into a weak pussy with no fight left in him.

I weakly push to my knees and hoist myself to my feet as I see Alex charging in from the left. Just as he swings for my head, a hit intended to end the fight, I duck, sending him sprawling on his ass as he slips through my blood.

Ding!

I collapse onto my stool and Ian gets to work trying to stop my bleeding brow. Ian grabs my chin, jerking my face to look at his.

"You get your ass out there and fight for your son. Those motherfuckers did that shit to him. You fight for him! You fuckin' fight the fight he couldn't!"

Ding!

I have to go for broke now. I'm done. I'm fucking old and tired. I can't run around this kid. I have to stand up and fight him. I have to fight for Jack.

My body absorbs Alex's first blow, easing me away from him. I return the hit, pushing him back. And so we go about trading punches blow-for-blow. Battering the other's body with no concern for our own. Smattering the canvas with blood, fueled by the fight for little boys we couldn't save.

Alex knocks me off him one last time before landing a body-head combination, leveling me to the ground. I'm done. I can feel the fight leaving my body for the first time in my life. I've got nothing left to give. I close my eyes and allow the defeat to swallow my soul, shrouding me in blackness. I won't recover from this loss. I've lost my family.

Chapter 30

Quinn

"Quinn," I hear Owen's deep voice at my back. He's been here for an hour watching us. I don't think he was really trying to hide, though.

"It's gettin' late. Let's get the kids home," he suggests softly.

"Where exactly is that, Owen?"

"Where do you want it to be?" he asks sitting down next to me on the bench of the picnic table.

"Home is where you feel safe," I murmur into Ashling's hair.

"Then I'll take you where you feel safe."

"I don't feel safe anywhere. Not after what he did today."

"He hurt you." It's a statement not a question.

"Yes." I turn my head and gaze into his light brown eyes. He's worried about me, it's etched in his features, but his eyes look tortured.

"I'll take you home with me," he whispers.

"I can't do that to the kids. They've had enough. I need to give them stability, not another change."

"So take 'em home. Make Kieran sleep on the couch. You'll work it out."

"He hurt me, Owen. Why? Why did he do that?"

"I can't answer that. He's a lot of things, Quinn. Bein' a fighter makes you into somethin' else in life. His head was back in that mode today. That doesn't excuse whatever he did to you, it's just how that shit works."

"So I just let it go until the next time he has to fight or whatever else turns him into the cruel, heartless man that I was with today?"

"NO!" Ashling jumps as his voice booms. "Sorry."

"He used me like a whore. And you know, that's not really what bothers me. If he needed to work up some sexual tension before his fight I woulda done it for him. Owen, he looked at me like I was trash, spoke to me in a tone reserved for scum. I've never..." I trail off with a shudder.

"I'm gonna fuckin' kill him," Owen growls. He pulls me roughly into his chest as Jack runs up.

"Hey, Owen!"

"Hey, little man," Owen murmurs against my hair.

"How come my angel was with Daddy?" Jack asks as he plops down at the table, his sweaty raven hair stuck to his forehead.

"What, Baby?" I ask, shifting into Owen's arms a bit more. My racer-back shirt isn't doing much for me now that the evening is cooling off.

"When you and Daddy were havin' your fight I saw him. He's a lot bigger now, but that was my angel."

Owen and I share a mutually confused look. Then I remember the gigantic blond that came out of The Castle and told me Kieran wouldn't want me to leave.

"Who was that huge blond guy at The Castle today?" I ask Owen before looking back to Jack.

"Alex Vetrov. He's the guy Kieran's fightin' tonight."

"What?!" I hiss under my breath. That guy looked barely twenty years old and is a good four inches taller and forty pounds heavier than Kieran.

"Tell me about it. I never got the full story, but Kieran's makin' some kinda move with the Russians."

"Jack, how do you know that man?" I ask quietly with the slightest edge to my voice.

"He saved me from the bad man. I was all alone and then the angel came in and took me away. He told me he'd never let the bad man get me again, but I never saw him after that. That's how I figured out he was an angel," Jack explains quietly.

"Wow," I whisper, not having any other words in this moment.

"You think Daddy needs my angel right now?"

"I don't know, Baby." I glance up at Owen who seems to be putting pieces together faster than I am.

"You wanna go see Grandma and Grandpa?" I ask, changing the subject. I need a minute to process this.

"Yeah!" Jack exclaims, jumping up from the table.

"I'll follow you," Owen grumbles in my hair.

Once I have the kids loaded into the SUV I call Clare, who happily agrees to take the kids. She can tell something is wrong but doesn't push me for answers. Rick is away on a "job" so she'll be alone with the kids. That makes me nervous until we pull up in front of her house and I spot two of the Dílseacht Crew sitting in a car.

"Why're they here?" I whisper to Owen as he pulls Ash's car seat out of the SUV.

"I called 'em. Need to be sure you and the kids are okay."

"I'm goin' back with you."

He nods and scoops Jack out of his seat. Clare meets us at the door, offering me a sad smile. A mother always knows. Owen takes the kids in the house as Clare wraps me in a tight hug.

"You stay here tonight," she whispers in my hair. "We'll eat chocolate and watch movies."

I almost crumble at the loving gesture. Maybe I'm not alone in this world after all. Owen's here to support me, just me. He's not here to do Kieran's bidding. Now Clare is holding me to her chest like my mother used to hold me when I was sad. These people love me. I know Connor and Ian love me too.

Instead of letting this epiphany turn me into a puddle on the porch, I let it steel me. I need to get to Kieran. I don't know what kind of deal he's struck, but if he's fighting the man that saved Jack, something is wrong.

"I'll be back in a bit. Keep the chocolate ready for me," I say through a small smile, squeezing her one more time. She crushes me a little harder before letting me go.

As she enters the house I kiss Jack and Ashling, telling them each I love them before running back to the SUV. There's a feeling of dread creeping up my spine as I speed toward The Castle. What if Kieran doesn't know Alex saved Jack? What kind of game are the Russians playing? Why do I think I can do anything to help?

I screech the SUV to a halt in the middle of the street and tear into The Castle. I'm struck by the roar of the crowd pulsing with energy around the ring. I weave and slice through the mass of people, using my small size to my advantage. The sweat and blood wafting through the room makes my stomach churn as I can hear fists slapping against skin.

I break through the crowd stopping at the edge of the ring. The canvas is stained red, marked with swirls and footprints. Alex and Kieran are trading blows in the middle of the ring. They look tired. I can't tell which is bleeding from where, but they're both drenched in blood.

Alex pushes Kieran back, landing two quick hits, one to the ribs and the last to the jaw. Kieran's legs go out from beneath him and he falls. He's not getting up. His body is going slack as Alex returns to his corner. I look into my son's angel's eyes. They're willing Kieran to get back up. The pain and intensity marring his face spurs me into action.

I move to the ring and slam my palm as hard as I can against the canvas.

Kieran's eyes flutter open and lock on mine. The man standing next to the bell is counting down, readying to end the fight. The Russians are screaming in jubilation. This is about more than a fight. I don't know Russian, but this is an effort to end Kieran. I know the posture, the tone, the venom...it's the same feeling I had when the O'Boyle Brothers taunted my father. Only tonight, I'm not hiding.

"Fight!" I scream over the thundering crowd.

Slowly, Kieran drags his hips off the canvas, his arms shaking as he pushes himself up on all fours. He sprays a mouthful of blood, speckling his hands. As he hauls himself to his feet, Alex charges at him from his corner. Kieran closes his eyes, waiting for the impact. He looks beaten and broken until his murky blues spring open. There's the fight.

Alex swings wildly at Kieran's head. Kieran ducks, taps Alex lightly in the shoulder with his right fist before driving his left fist into the side of his face. Alex's head snaps violently from the impact, blood and sweat misting the air. His body goes limp as he topples to the canvas unconscious. The crowd roars to a deafening level, muting the sound of the bell dinging. Kieran wins.

Before I can make eye contact with him, discontent rages in the room and fights begin to break out around me in the crowd. I'm jostled a few times, wishing I'd grabbed my knife before running in here. Strong arms scoop me off the floor and I recognize Owen before I start to struggle. He cradles me to his chest, moving us through the fists and fury.

I'm suddenly sprawled on the floor beneath Owen before he scrambles off me. As he gets to his feet, he keeps me guarded behind his massive frame as he wails on the guy I'm assuming attacked him from behind. I remain as close to Owen as I can without getting in his way as he beats the man ferociously.

As the mêlée continues, I search for Ian or Connor, but neither of them is anywhere to be seen. Not that I can see much from my low stature in a room full of mostly men brawling like teenagers. From the corner of my eye I spot a woman around my age being screamed at by two of the Russians that were celebrating when they thought Alex had won. She looks terrified.

The fight taking place next to me catches my attention as Owen arches his neck and connects his forehead with the man's he's fighting, knocking him clean out. When he's satisfied his opponent isn't getting back up, he turns to me, shrugging his shoulders. Fighters.

I roll my eyes at his nonchalance with a smirk on my lips. He smirks back, nodding toward the door. I move ahead of him as he holds his arms on either side of me, clearing a path. Once we're outside, I find the SUV still running in the middle of the street with a few people standing around staring at it.

Owen ushers me to the passenger's side before climbing in and driving us away. The back door bursts open.

"Drive!" a woman screams.

I rotate in my seat to find the woman the Russians were yelling at. Her face is red with fury and chest is heaving in panic.

"Shit," Owen mutters.

I look over at him to see him training his eyes on the door where the Russians are running at the SUV.

Owen slams on the accelerator, burning rubber down the street.

"Thank you so much," she breathes out raggedly.

"Where to?" Owen barks.

I cut my eyes at him, but he doesn't say anything or even act like I'm not giving him the stink eye.

"Are you okay? Did they hurt you?" I ask softly, turning in my seat to get a good look at her.

She's got chunky bangs and thick platinum blonde hair that hangs just past her shoulders, stick straight. Hazel eyes are peering at me from beneath her fringe. There's a small spot of blood peeking from the corner of her wide mouth.

"Here," I say, offering her a napkin from the console.

"Thanks," she replies, dabbing at her wound.

"I'm Quinn and this is Owen. Can we take you somewhere safe?"

"I'm Sofia. Thank you guys so much for gettin' me outta there."

"No problem," Owen snorts. He's such a dick sometimes.

"I guess I could go wait at my brother's apartment, but I doubt he'll be there anytime soon," Sofia says, looking out the window, her nose scrunched in thought.

"Will it be safe at your brother's? Do those men know where he lives?" I ask quietly, trying to remove the tension Owen's oaf-like behavior has created.

"Yeah," she snorts "they know where he lives. They bought it for him."

Owen slams on the breaks in the middle of the street and spins in his seat to glare at Sofia.

"Owen!" I protest again getting ignored.

Sofia's eyes are bugging out at his behavior and his aggressive demeanor.

"Who the fuck are you? If you jumped in this car to start some shit you've just fucked up," he growls.

My stomach flips at his suggestion. If she's here to relay information about me to the Russians, she definitely picked the wrong girl to fuck with. I pick up my bag from the floorboard and palm my knife.

"I'm Sofia Vetrova. My brother's Alex Vetrov. Our 'family' is pissed he lost the fight. They think he lost on purpose. They grabbed me as leverage or something before the fight. When I tried to get outta their hold, Uri backhanded me. I kicked him in the nuts and ran. I ran straight into this SUV. I don't know who you are or why you're nervous about me. I'm not tryin' to do anything

286

other than get away from them. Alex promised he'd get me away from them," she finishes in a whisper.

Owen and I stare her down for a few moments after she's done explaining. There's not a hint of a lie in her body language or her pretty face.

"Should we take her back to The Castle?" I ask, turning my attention back to Owen.

He huffs and turns around in his seat, driving off without responding. We sit in silence a long time as Owen thinks through everything. We're basically going around the streets in circles. I've learned with these guys not to push in these moments. So I wait.

"Can't go back to The Castle now," he finally grumbles.

"Well I'm not takin' her back into Russian territory, Owen. Where do you suggest we go?"

"Your place."

"No," I growl. I'm not going back there tonight. I don't care if I went to the fight and had a moment with Kieran. I'm loyal to him. I always will be after everything we've been through. But I'll be damned if I walk back into his house after the shit he pulled today.

"Clare's?" I suggest in a kind tone.

"No," he barks.

"Runnin' outta options. As you know, I'm not a social butterfly," I scoff.

"I'll go to a hotel," Sofia speaks up. "Shit! I don't have my bag."

"It's probably better that way. I can check you in so you can't be tracked," I say, thinking back to my invisible days.

"I don't have any money and I'm in this damn dress," she grumbles.

She's wearing a slinky black long sleeved jersey dress with a high neck. The neck opens almost all the way to the edge of her shoulders giving the slightest peek at her golden skin. It's also really freaking short, maybe to her mid-thigh. Her feet are covered in high, silver stilettos that make my feet hurt just thinking about them.

"I think you look nice," I compliment her. She offers me a slight smile, almost embarrassed. "I've got cash. Don't worry about it."

"I can't let you do that for me. I'll be fine. Just take me to Alex's place." She says the words, but there's little-to-no conviction behind them.

"No way. They'll look for you there and you said your brother won't be there. If you're worried about the money, you can pay me back. Let's just get you somewhere safe tonight," I insist.

"Thank you, Quinn," Sofia relents.

"Take her to the Downtown Hilton. They won't look for her there," I say to Owen who's rivaling Ian's perma-scowl.

His phone keeps buzzing in his pocket, but he's made no move to answer it. Owen's livid at Kieran so I'm guessing that's whose calls he's ignoring. That won't go over well.

"You should answer it," I murmur.

"No," he grunts.

I leave it at that. I'm not his mother. Honestly, I don't want him to talk to Kieran while I'm around. Kieran's probably freaking out, though, so I made the suggestion...that's enough for me.

The silence in the car is tense, only more punctuated by the continuous hum of Kieran's request to be answered.

Chapter 31

Kieran

"God-fucking-damn it!" I roar, launching my phone across my office. It hits the leather couch with a thud, saving it from my wrath.

"He's not answerin' me, either," Connor grunts.

"You're positive he left with Quinn?" I growl.

"Yeah, boss."

"Why the fuck are they at the Downtown Hilton?!" I'm seething, irrational, exhausted, adrenalized and just about every other emotion you can imagine that resembles pissed off.

I had lost, given the fuck up. Then she was there, screaming at me to fight. I thought I was hallucinating at first until her icy blue eyes cut through to my soul. That was all it took. I dragged my sorry old ass up and ended the fight. I won. So why do I feel like I lost everything with that win?

The Russians were scheming, as usual. The Castle broke into an all-out shit show as soon as Alex hit the canvas. Ian and Connor forced me to stay put in my corner until my men shut everything down. I never saw Quinn again.

Alex has been downstairs in a therapy room getting worked on by a doctor for the last half hour. I got the same treatment. Stitches and bandages galore, I look like hammered shit.

My office door flies open and Alex barrels through the door, looking about as happy as me.

"Sofia," he growls.

"Nah, man. I'm Kieran. Must've fucked you up somethin' fierce if you think I'm a chick," I snark.

"My sister. She's fuckin' gone. I had her layin' low until after the fight so I could take her with me. Right before the fight I see Uri Pavlenko walk in with her all dressed up. No one's seen her since the fight!" Alex roars.

"You didn't mention a sister before," Connor interjects suspiciously.

"Yeah. Havin' people that are important to you makes you vulnerable. I'm not stupid."

"Call your fuckin' brother again. He doesn't answer we're takin' a field trip," I instruct slowly, standing up pathetically from my chair. I'm too old for this shit.

"You stupid motherfucker!" Connor snarls into his phone. "Yeah? Well next time, answer a fuckin' call or better yet, fuckin' tell me what you're doin'!"

There's a long silence while Owen does his own roaring. I can't make out his words, but I gather he's pretty pissed off. I'm also aware that he's filling Connor in on what I did to Quinn when his gaze pins me where I stand, a promise of uncompromising pain in the near future.

"What room?" he grunts, never leaving my gaze. I would attempt to glare back, but my face can barely move, it's so swollen. So I take the eye-murder and wait.

"Don't leave! We'll be there."

Connor hangs up and stalks to an inch in front of my face.

"If Alex didn't just beat your ass I would fuckin' end you right now!" he roars.

He stands in front of me shaking until he can't take the tension of being in the same room with me anymore. As he prowls from the room, he stops next to Alex.

"My brother has your sister. Let's go," he growls.

I move to follow Connor when he holds his arm out in protest.

"You're not comin'."

"The fuck I'm not," I bark, finding the end of my rope with his shit.

"You're not fuckin' comin'. She doesn't wanna see you. Owen's strugglin' to keep her at the hotel as it is. You show up and Quinn's gone. You've fucked up good this time. If she takes the kids and leaves, I'm done. I'll follow her around and make sure she's safe until she's old and grey. I can't fuckin' believe you," he says with disgust before leaving me in my office alone in a timeout like a damn toddler.

I sit in timeout for about five minutes before I climb into my Camaro and head for the hotel. I don't give a shit if she wants to see me. I need eyes on her. I need to know she's okay. This shit with Alex was just an excuse for the Russians to start a war and they'll use any means necessary to get to me. Quinn and the kids are the only things they can use.

The kids are at my parents' with four men guarding the house so I know they're good. Quinn is with Owen, but I'm guessing she'll take off as soon as Connor and Alex show up. She can't be alone right now. This all sounds well and good, but it's a load of bullshit. Owen and Connor will keep her safe and, because of that, she's in no real danger. I just have to see her for my own selfish reasons.

When I get to reception, I realize my usual charm isn't going to work on the woman at the desk. I look like shit smeared on crap crackers. Money's the name of my game. I find a bellhop who willingly gives me the room number. It's scary what two hundred bucks can buy you.

When I step in front of the door, I turn into a bucket of nerves. I haven't really thought this through. Connor may have reined it in with me, but I doubt Owen will. I can't fight him tonight, not after the beating Alex handed me. I'm so exhausted I can barely stand upright, so I lean against the doorframe and lightly rap.

"Who is it?" Owen growls in a deep, menacing voice.

"Housekeeping," I snark back.

There's a commotion on the other side of the door before it opens, Alex staring at me with wide eyes. I ease past him into the suite to find Connor restraining Owen against the far wall while Quinn and Sofia—that must be her—sit next to each other on a couch holding hands. Sofia looks nervous while Quinn looks defeated. I was hoping for pissed or hurt or something other than the look on her face right now.

Her emotionally devoid eyes scan my body and my injuries, wincing a little as she takes it all in. Once she completes her inspection, her face goes blank again.

"You've got some fuckin' nerve showin' up here," Owen chokes out since his brother has his forearm to his throat.

"Never been one to back down from a fight," I quip, never leaving Quinn's crystal blue eyes.

"It's your funeral," he growls, throwing Connor off him.

"Don't!" Quinn screams, halting Owen's progress toward me.

"Owen, please don't," she whispers, climbing to her feet. She looks right through me like I'm not in the room, coming to a stop in front of Owen, whose upper body is heaving through his panting. She puts her two tiny hands on his chest and I feel a fight building in me. An irrational, psychotic fight because she's touching Owen. Alex must have done a number on me.

Owen wraps his massive arms around her small body, pulling her protectively into his chest.

"Sorry," he murmurs into her hair as she nods. "Wanna get outta here?"

"Yeah," she mumbles into his chest.

I feel like I'm in the fucking *Twilight Zone*. I'm watching the woman I love seek comfort in another man's arms and just standing here like a bump on a log. He unfolds her from his chest but maintains a proprietary arm around her shoulders.

"I'll come by tomorrow and we can go for coffee," she says sweetly to Sofia.

"Thanks for everything, Quinn. You too, Owen," she has a slight flush as his name flows from her lips. She's a pretty girl, not gorgeous or beautiful, but pretty. I don't really care; it's just an observation.

Quinn turns to face Alex who's wrapped his sister in his arms, relief soothing his battered face.

"Alex, I'd like to talk to you about my son if you have the chance in the next few days."

"Sure," he says with a tight smile.

"Bye, Connor," she says through a sad smile.

Then she walks to me, stopping flush with my side so she doesn't have to look at me.

"I'm glad you won your fight. The Russians were tryin' to unman you in front of your crew to make it easier to take you out and maintain control of your territory. I'm sure you know this already, but I wanted you to tell you myself that I understand why you fought. Not just about Jack, but about business, too. I'm goin' to your parents'. You can come and see the kids whenever you want. Just call ahead so I have some warning. Goodbye, Kieran," she says with strength and conviction. Then she's gone without as much as a glance in my direction.

"Daddy!" Jack squeals as he launches himself into my arms.

I crush him to my chest, grimacing in pain as my broken ribs get caved in under the pressure. I only squeeze him tighter.

"Your booboos look better."

"They feel better, too," I murmur into his soft black waves. "What's Ash doin'?"

"She's rollin' around in the livin' room. She thinks it's the best thing ever!"

"Let's go watch her for a bit," I say, carrying him into my parents' house.

Sure as shit, Ashling's rolling around on the floor giggling and spitting with glee. My parents are sitting on the floor with her, laughing at the show she's putting on. Quinn's nowhere in sight. That's because she leaves when I visit. It's been five weeks since she left me and I haven't seen her once. I've heard her voice in the background a few times when I'm on the phone with Jack. Once, I heard her full belly laugh and I almost lost it. The only thing getting me through any of this is my kids.

Quinn's been true to her word. She lets me see them whenever I ask, and I ask every day. I call one of my parents to ask because she still won't speak to me, but the answer is always yes. I haven't gone more than twenty-four hours without seeing them. It's not the same as having them in my house. It's a sad, lonely, distant second to them being with me all the time.

The war with the Russians is slowing down. Mainly because we've killed enough of them off that they don't have the strength to come at us as hard as they were. Having Alex with us is a big help. He's a bevy of inside information that we've used tirelessly to beat the Russians before they see us coming. At this point, my territory's safe and my life is a fucking mess.

The front door opens behind my back and I hear the sound my ears have been fantasizing about for weeks, Quinn's giggle.

"Mommy!" Jack exclaims, rushing to her.

I look up from Ashling's spot on the floor and lock my gaze with hers. She's shocked as shit to see me. Horrified is probably a better term. I had The Crew drop me off while I have some work done on the Camaro, so my car wasn't outside to stop her.

"Hey, Mike," Jack says, breaking the stare down between Quinn and myself.

Standing behind her is a man. A man. That's all my brain can process.

"Hey, Jack," *Mike* responds cheerfully. I hate him.

Quinn sets Jack down and Mike high-fives him, leaning over her shoulder to reach him. As his front presses against her back, all I see is red...blinding, raging fury choking out all reason in my brain.

Just as I'm about to do something monumentally stupid, Ash rolls into my thigh, simmering me down immediately. I pick her up and blow raspberries into her chubby neck while she squeals and laughs. The best distraction in the fucking world!

"Mommy, you wanna watch a movie with us?" Jack asks, moving back into the living room.

"I'd love to, Baby, but I'm goin' out tonight, remember?" Quinn answers softly.

"Oh yeah," Jack says with a shrug. He's not bothered that she's going out with Mike, meaning she must go out with Mike often enough for it to be normal for him. The rage monster is building again.

"I just came back to get ready," Quinn says apologetically to the room. "We'll be in my room if you need me."

Quinn moves through the room silently with Mike's hand pressed in the small of her back. When she's safely down the hall and out of earshot, I pin my father with a gaze that could set his hair on fire. It's time to talk. Now.

"Jack, why don't you go downstairs with Grandma and Ash? I need to talk to Grandpa about some boring grownup stuff. We'll be down when we're done, okay?" I talk in the most normal voice I can muster.

"Don't forget the popcorn," Jack says, bounding toward the stairs. "And don't eat it all before you come downstairs, Grandpa."

"You think I'd steal your popcorn?" my dad feigns shock.

"You ate the whole bowl last time and it gave you the farts. Grandma made you sleep on the couch," Jack says pointedly, causing the room to erupt in boisterous laughter.

When my mother stops heaving with amusement, she leads Jack down the stairs, carrying Ashling on her hip. I wind up to go at it with my father when I hear the basement door close, but he shuts me down.

"Outside," he instructs in a parental tone I haven't heard since I was ten.

Once we're on the back deck with the door tightly closed, I hit him where it hurts.

"You're *my* father. How could you not fuckin' tell me she's seein' somebody else?"

"I may be *your* father, but I'm also a grandparent now. You're a grown man, Kieran. It's not my job to manage your love life, a love life you fucked up all on your own."

"Apparently, I've fucked it up more than I know since she's seein' that prick," I scoff.

"What do you expect her to do? Sit here alone and wait for you to pull your fuckin' head outta your ass and fight for her? Quinn's a young, beautiful woman, men are gonna be circling her until she's unavailable. Shit, even then they'll still sniff around."

"She's made it clear she doesn't want me around her. How am I supposed to fight for her without breakin' the boundaries she put up?" I huff, flopping into a lounger.

"I don't know, son. But if you don't figure out somethin' soon, she won't be around to fight for anymore. She's lookin' at places for her and the kids to move into. They went lookin' in the 'burbs last weekend."

"Who's 'they'?" I ask, not wanting to know the answer.

"Her and Mike. He's a real estate agent," he says softly before flopping into the lounger next to me. We both pull out our cigarettes and light up together. My habit has kicked into high gear since Quinn left. I'm also back to drinking whiskey like prohibition is threatening to take it from me.

"They look pretty cozy for a real estate agent and a client," I snark.

"I'm not gonna talk to you about her relationships. She trusts your mother and me. I won't fuck that up. You want answers about Quinn's life, you ask her. And don't you dare try gettin' information outta Jack. He's not a pawn," he finishes pointedly, pointing his cigarette at my chest like it's a weapon.

"I would never do that," I growl at the insinuation.

"Heard she's teachin' self-defense classes at Brogan's." Change of subject, much?

"She's still runnin' the books for both of us. She asked Ian about startin' the class a few weeks ago. Her and Owen teach together on Saturdays. First two have been so packed they're gonna add another time slot," I say with pride.

Quinn's finding her way in life. She's still sticking close to the gym, The Crew and my family, but she's branching out on her own. I love that and hate it equally. I can see now that isolating her was doing her a great injustice. I should have encouraged her to find her place in life. Her working at Brogan's is perfect because she's close and protected, yet doing her own thing.

I hate it because she's doing it without me. I'm not involved with anything. She's running my books, but the only proof of that is her handwriting coming back to me when she's done with things. Other than that, there's no interaction. Yeah, I fucking hate it.

There's a light tap on the glass sliding door behind me. I turn simultaneously with my father to see Quinn standing at the door looking...un-fucking-believable.

She's got on a dress. I'm a dude so work with me here. It looks like she stretched out a tank-top and made it into a dress, I should say. It clings to her body like a second skin with a deep neckline showing off a good bit of cleavage. It's a pale blue color, making her eyes pop against her porcelain ivory skin. She has on the perfect amount of make-up and her hair up in some sleek wrapped-up way. My dick is rock hard. I'm guessing Mike's is too based on his gaze being firmly placed on her ass.

She slides the door open just a crack.

"We're headin' out to dinner. I don't know what time we'll get back. I'll text when I'm on my way," Quinn says, looking directly at my father.

"Have a good night, sweetheart," he replies in the softest voice I've ever heard the man speak in.

"You too, Rick."

She slides the door shut and glides into Mike's side who wraps his arm around her shoulders, leading her away. Away from me.

Chapter 32

Quinn

"You all right?" Mike murmurs into my hair before he puts me in his Mercedes.

"I'm fine," I lie.

Damn Kieran Delaney! Of all the nights he has to show up, it's this one. I'm already nervous as hell and then he's there in the house, all cool and nonchalant.

"This'll be fun," Mike encourages as he pulls away from the curb. Ronan and Cormack follow behind us. They're always with me. Never close enough to talk to or interact with, but close enough to keep me safe. I haven't had any threats or attempts by the Russians, but I know they could just be lying in wait. I don't mind The Crew following me around. I feel safer knowing someone has my back at all times.

"This will be fun," I repeat, trying to convince myself.

As we walk into Little Goat, a great new restaurant that I love and picked for tonight due to its relaxed old school diner feel, my legs begin to shake and my stomach turns. I relax a fraction when I see Sofia waving at us from a booth. I can't see his face because his back is to us. I can do this.

"Hey babe," Mike purrs as he pulls Sofia into his arms for a sweet kiss. Mike is Sofia's boyfriend. It's a new relationship, but they're amazing together.

"Sorry I couldn't come get ready with you, Quinn. My boss is a pain in the ass," she huffs plopping down into the booth. Sofia works at an art gallery that may or may not also deal in stolen art and artifacts. She's become my best friend in the last month. We come from the same world and have similar-yet-different personalities. She's more outgoing where I'm reserved. I'm more confident where she's insecure. We work well together.

"Quinn, this is my friend, Craig," Mike introduces professionally.

I finally turn my gaze to him as he stands up. He's an impeccably manicured man. His light brown hair is styled to perfection, sweeping over to the side and held in place with product. His jaw is shaved so close I want to run my fingertips across his skin to inspect for any signs of growth. Green eyes are shimmering at me as he rises and extends his hand toward me.

"It's a pleasure to meet you," his cool, aloof voice brushes across my ears as I place my palm in his. He gently presses his soft lips to my knuckles, gazing up at me as he does. A bright red flush lights my cheeks and renders me speechless. I offer him a small smile before sliding into the booth, cursing Sofia for making me wear this damn dress. I feel naked!

There's tense silence between Craig and me as Mike and Sofia dissolve into their own world.

"Great choice for dinner," Craig whispers near my neck, causing me to jump. He smirks at my reaction and goes back to perusing the menu.

I feel like an idiot. I haven't said a word since we got here. The problem is, my brain can't think of anything to say. I don't know why I let Sofia talk me into a blind double date. I have no desire to date, blind or otherwise.

I guess it's because I've been lonely without Kieran. Having someone to talk to about the kids or how my day at work was, I miss that.

I miss seeing him with the kids. My kids light up when they're with Kieran in a way they don't for anyone else. It's one of the most precious things I've ever witnessed and I miss seeing it. Now that I'm looking for houses in the suburbs he'll see the kids less, which I hate. I don't want to take them from him, but the suburbs are safer now that we're on our own.

By some miracle I never ended up pregnant. I don't know what I was thinking allowing that (it was what I wanted). I suppose I was in love and wanted to make Kieran happy. I miss that too, damn it. I don't want to admit it, but making him happy made me happy. I was isolated and alone, yet I was also full and content. I couldn't go back to that now. I have friends and a life now that I love and deserve. But I sure miss making Kieran Delaney grin that cocky smile he gets when he's truly pleased with himself. He'd have one plastered on his face right now knowing I'm on a date and thinking about him. That's all it takes to push him from my mind and take a chance on Craig, the well-mannered, good looking, professional mortgage broker to criminals. Here goes nothing.

So, maybe not nothing, but Craig is not the man for me. He's what I suspect men call women like him: high maintenance. The way he ordered his food made my skin crawl. Just order your damn food and let the chef cook it without your instructions. Jeez! This type of thing continued throughout the evening—him insisting on driving then beseeching me to be careful with the leather and my high heels. What was I going to do, exactly? Shit in his car and then grind it into his carpet with my shoes? Then we got to the club and let's just say he was obnoxiously handsy after a few drinks. I got my fill of fondling and took off, saying I needed to pee. I texted Sofia and let her know I was out and then hopped a cab home. Never again.

I tiptoe in the front door at Kieran's parents' house trying not to wake anyone. It's 2:30 am, so everyone should be out cold.

"Hey," his voice cuts through the silence, causing me to jump and rip my knife out of my purse.

"Jesus Christ, Kieran you scared the shit outta me!" I rage in a whisper.

"Sorry," he responds without an ounce of apology in his tone.

I snort and go back to ignoring him like I have for the last five weeks. I move through the living room to the kitchen to get a glass of water, leaving my purse—and knife—on the island. Sofia and I had a blast together when Craig wasn't around to dampen the mood with his weirdness. I'm a little tipsy. I only had two drinks, but I only just started drinking a few months ago. I'm a cheap date. I giggle at the thought.

"Is that water funny?" Kieran snarks from behind me.

I roll my eyes even though he can't see me. I'm not doing this with him.

I gulp back the last of the water and rinse my glass, never turning to look at him. As I spin around to make my way down the hall, he cages me in with his arms around my sides, his hands resting on the edge of the counter.

"We need to talk, Quinn," he growls.

"I'm movin'. Mike found some nice houses in La Grange. I'm goin' back tomorrow to do a second viewing of two of them. We'll have to work out visitation with the kids since we'll be further away. I don't really want them to stay with you overnight at first. I'd like them to get used to the new place so we can do visitation here at your parents', if you want. Maybe once school starts for Jack we can do the every-other-weekend thing," I finish with a shrug. The whole time I've been rambling, Kieran's face has gone from hard to diamond-crushing solid.

"Mike found some nice houses?" he repeats in a venom filled tone. Out of everything I just said, that's what he focuses on?

"He's a real estate agent."

"Will Mike have his own room until Jack's comfortable with him bein' in your bed?" he drones sarcastically. Why the hell would Mike be at my house? Oh shit, he thinks I'm with Mike. This thought causes yet another giggle. Kieran scowls at my inappropriate laughter.

"Mike won't have his own room," I respond, a little short of breath from the laughter.

"So he's just hoppin' straight into bed then?" he snarls, leaning into my face.

"Kieran, you lost the privilege to decide who's in my bed over a month ago. I didn't do this to us, you did. Whatever I decide to do is just that...my damn decision. Now get outta my face before I get stabby."

"Quinn," he says in a defeated voice.

"I'm done, Kieran. Move."

He does. He steps away from me and I walk around him into my room without looking back. That was him just trying to piss on his territory, clinging to the hope that I would melt into him and take him back. Not happening.

I flop onto my bed taking deep breaths, trying to calm my anger. How dare he think he can tell me what to do? Screw him, even if he's so far off base he's playing hockey!

My door swings open as Kieran quickly steps in, shutting it with a soft click.

"I'm sorry. I'm so fuckin' sorry, Quinn. That's all I wanted to say to you tonight," he says with regret in his voice, rubbing his dílseacht tattoo. I sit up and try to cover my business that's surely hanging out at this point.

"The way I treated you the day of the fight was disgusting and I hate myself for it more than you hate me. I wasn't thinkin' and that's no excuse, but it's the truth. I disrespected you and our relationship, but worse than that, I ruined the trust you placed in me. I'll never be able to forgive myself for that. If you've found that again with someone else, I'm happy for you. I'm not fuckin' happy about it, but I'm happy for *you*. Because you deserve nothing but the best in life. It's clear to me that I'm not that for you, but you gave me something amazing with Ashling and Jack that I'll never be able to thank you enough for.

"Please don't make me the every-other-weekend dad. Work with me to figure out something better than that for them. I need them in my life every day, Quinn. I can't do twice a month. I'll come to you if I have to. I'll leave you and Mike alone, I promise. Just let me keep seein' the kids. Please," he pleads.

I'm in complete shock right now. Kieran Delaney has just blown me away. And now I'm just sitting here like a fish on a dock, sucking in air through flapping lips.

"I would never take the kids from you, Kieran. There just as much yours as they are mine," I whisper.

"Once you figure out which house you're buyin' I'll get a schedule together for us to agree on. Thanks for bein' open to this. You don't owe me anything, so thank you. I'll see you later."

Then he's gone. As quickly as he entered my room, he leaves it. Leaving me with a shit ton of questions, a little sadness and some hope that we can finally move forward.

Chapter 33

Kieran

"Shannon Kelly is currently unavailable. Please press one to be routed to another attorney," the polite message sings in my ear.

I press the button and wait.

"Aaron Kavanagh's office," Karl answers curtly.

"Hey Karl," I say, trying to sound…nice.

"Kieran Delaney, I hear you're nothing but a pain in the ass," he snarks.

"Nothin' new there."

"Oh, this is new. Shannon's gotten an earful from your cousins in Chicago, which means I've had lots of great gossip sessions in between changin' diapers and feedings with Johnny."

"What can I say? I'm happy my shitty life is causing you enjoyment," I grumble back.

"Don't go all sensitive on me. I take no enjoyment from your idiocy."

"Well, I've got some new developments you can share with the gang. I need a custody agreement and visitation set up."

"Shit. Kieran, I'm sorry. I had no idea it had gotten that bad. What happened?" he says with real remorse in his voice.

"She met someone else. She's movin' to the 'burbs. I've been assured that she doesn't want to take the kids away from me and I don't think she will, but I want my bases covered."

I let out a huge sigh. God, this fucking sucks!

"And you're just lettin' her go?"

"What choice do I have? She's made it clear we're done. I fucked up, Karl. Quinn's hurt and I did that. I want her, but I can't be with her knowin' I'll fuck up again."

"That's a cop-out. If you want somethin' you have to be willin' to fight for it. Look what Shannon and Dylan just went through. If you want Quinn, you don't throw in the towel at the first sign of trouble. Don't be a pussy. This is your family, Kieran. Aren't they worth more than a few weeks of waiting?"

"They're worth everything. That's why I'm backin' off. I'll ruin them."

"Hang on a second," he says, moving the phone around.

"Hello?" a familiar deep, smooth voice glides through the receiver.

"Kellerman. What're you doin' there?" I say kindly to my friend. After everything we went through together to get Shannon back in December, Dylan Kellerman and I have become friends. He's the only non-criminal friend that I have. Shannon doesn't count because she's not my friend, she's my family...I have a lot of non-criminal family.

"Lunch with the boys."

"How're Shannon and Johnny?"

"So good, man. Like I was tellin' you last week, I'm in awe of how amazing Shannon is. Blows my mind every fuckin' day." He sounds so happy it makes my stomach hurt.

"That woman of yours is pretty good at most things she does. I'm not surprised she's good at bein' a momma."

"Speakin' of mommas, what's goin' on with your baby's momma situation? Quinn and Shannon were on the phone for like two hours last night. Of course, Shannon won't fill me in because I'm *your* friend. What's up?"

"She met someone and is movin' to the 'burbs to live a happy white-picket-fence life."

"Shit," he hisses.

"Yeah," I grunt.

"You're just givin' up?" he asks, disbelieving.

"What the fuck am I supposed to do?" I growl, getting annoyed by this same question being asked over and over.

"Be Kieran Delaney."

"Bein' Kieran Delaney got me in this mess."

"No, bein' a fuckin' idiot and not usin' your brain got you in this mess. When you're bein' *you* that's never an issue. You're just like Shannon, always aware and in control. You had a moment where that went out the window and unfortunately you fucked up. That's not a death sentence, man. Put your big girl pants on, quit bein' a pussy and go get your woman and your kids. You're not gonna be able to bully or charm your way in, though. Just be present. If she needs help, help. If she needs a break from the kids, give it. If she's had a long day at work, offer her a ride home…not on your dick. Be there for her. She needs to trust that you're there for her no matter what. She has to be the one to come back to you. Quinn needs that power."

"When did you get so fuckin' smart?" I ask, shocked at the change in him over the past half year. He was a shell of a being when I met him. I'm aware that was due to some truly fucked up circumstances in that his woman had been kidnapped. Then he's torn away from Shannon only days after getting her back and forced to live some bizarre lie with his ex to ensure the safety of his unborn child. Shit like that would crush most people and definitely fuck up relationships. Shannon and he seem to be stronger because of it.

"Shit, I'm not smart. I've turned into a goddamned caveman since we had Johnny. I speak in mostly grunts and gestures at home. But I almost lost her in December and then was removed from her for six months. I know the hell you're goin' through without Quinn. Difference is, you can do somethin' about it and I couldn't. Fight for what's yours. You're good at that, don't lose sight of it. She'll come back to you in time. And don't fuck anyone else!"

"I couldn't if I wanted to. Rosie Palm and her five sisters have been holdin' me down. I feel like a fuckin' teenager."

"Again, I feel your pain. At least you don't have a psychotic pregnant woman tryin' to jump your bones at all hours. I had to sleep fully clothed and wrapped in a separate blanket for six months. I looked into buying a chastity belt at one point," he says through a deep laugh.

"Well, now I just feel bad complainin'."

"You should," he snarks.

"I'll let you get to lunch. Thanks for talkin' to me."

"Anytime. You should call Shannon. She'll surely rip you a new one, but she's always good to talk to."

"I'll let her cool off a bit. I don't feel like gettin' shot."

He laughs again, but he knows I'm right. His woman wouldn't hesitate to shoot me.

"All right. Hey, I'll call you later this week. We're startin' to plan Shannon's birthday party."

"Let me know if you need anything. Thanks again, man."

"No problem. Later."

As we hang up I feel better. Karl will work on the custody agreement while I try to behave like a normal human being and get my family back. No problem, right? To hell with it.

"You've got some balls callin' me, Kieran Delaney," Shannon chides as she answers.

"Hey, you know I'm hard up. Your voice is the closest thing to real I'm gettin' these days," I snark.

"Let me put Johnny down so I don't scare him while I yell at you."

She doesn't wait for a response as she sets the phone down to deal with the baby.

"I'm back," she says in a sigh. "So you've run her off to the suburbs."

"I didn't run her off. I've left her alone like she asked. Kept my distance as best I could. Fuck, I didn't see her once in the last five weeks until Saturday. How is this my fault?" I grumble like a child.

"You want this straight or soft? I can tell you're strugglin', but if you need this soft you gotta call Karl or Kel. I can't do soft normally, but I'm sleep deprived, my boobs hurt and I don't know how much more puke this shirt can hold before it's declared a natural disaster area. I've only got the straightest of straight to offer you. So how do you want it big boy?"

"Could you make shit like puke and sore boobs sound more sexual? Fuck, woman, how do you do that?"

"It's a gift. Ask the cavemen I live with about it. I got in trouble for smiling and sayin' thank you to the pilot on the way here from Seattle. Apparently, my charm knows no bounds."

"You're so full of shit I can smell you from here. Kellerman called me and told me what you did on the plane with that pilot. He said you pulled out the dazzling make-your-dick-so-hard-it-hurts smile and then purred thank you. Get your lies straight before you come at me lady."

"Fuck you. I'd been locked away in a hospital and smiled at some dude young enough to probably put me in prison. I can't help if I'm naturally appealing to you idiots. And we're not talkin' about me. You're the one in trouble."

"It's nice to talk about somethin' other than what a fuck up I am. Connor and Owen will barely look at me. Ian's offerin' new, more sadistic versions of his scowl. I got this kid I'm trainin' and he's the only one talkin' to me. His sister's Quinn's new best friend so I can't really talk to him about Quinn, thank fuck for that. My parents are Team Quinn so they're on my ass, too. I just talked to Karl and Kellerman who each informed me that I'm a pussy. You got anything other than all that shit for me?" I grumble, wondering why I called Shannon in the first place.

"You scared her," she offers, softer than I expected.

"I wasn't in my right mind when she was tryin' to leave—"

"That's not when you scared her," she cuts me off.

"Huh?"

"Really? You're not so good at watchin' the signs with her are you?"

"I seem to struggle when it comes to Quinn."

"I'm the same with Kel. When people like you and I are in love, it dampens some of that high alert we're always at. It's a good thing for the most part, until you fuck up and can't get yourself out of it."

"So I scared her?"

"You took care of her with no benefit to you. You allowed her to make the decision about what happened to her uncles. You stood by her side while she killed a man that hurt her son. You made her world safe to trust again."

"And then I broke that," I say with a moment of clarity.

"You didn't just break it, you cheapened and tarnished it before shitting on it and then shattered it."

We're both silent as we let that visual sink in.

"She spent her entire adult life keepin' herself from bein' raped or assaulted. Kieran, even I couldn't do that," she whispers that last part.

"Shannon," I try and soothe.

"I'm fine. It's true, though. If the guys hadn't found me when I was seventeen I woulda been raped. And God only knows what woulda happened in December..." she trails off. "Anyway, my point is I'm pretty fuckin' self-sufficient and I ended up in vulnerable positions. Quinn didn't. Yes, that's partly due to the fact that she made herself into a ghost and rarely interacted with people. It's also because it was the only thing she had left to protect other than her life. She gave you that, Kieran. That is some scary shit for people like Quinn and me.

"I didn't have my virginity to give away, but I guarded my heart like Quinn guarded her first time. When you finally decide to give something away that you've spent a lifetime holding back from the world, it's fuckin' terrifying. You used her like some slut-bag ring bunny. You took the one thing she had left to give you and made it dirty."

"My head wasn't in that space. I know that doesn't excuse what I did, but I was in fight mode. It took me back to a time where I used women like that on a daily basis."

"Yeah, don't ever say that to Quinn. Makes you sound like a bigger asshole than you are."

"Thanks," I snark.

"No problem," she snarks right back.

"Thanks for layin' that out for me, but I know that already. I'm aware how bad that move was and what a fuck up it was. It's why I'm backin' off. This is me, Shannon. I'm an asshole. I want to be more for her, but I know I'll fuck up again. You don't spend a lifetime bein' one way and just stop because you find a girl."

"Would you ever do what you did to her again?"

"Never."

"Would you do your damnedest every day to make sure you leave dickwad-I-run-this-shit Kieran in the streets and be the good man that you are in the home?"

"Every day."

"Then you have your answer. You're good enough for Quinn. That woman is so loyal to you, it makes me love her that much more. She doesn't want to take the kids from you. Quinn's tryin' to run to the 'burbs because isolating is all she knows. Out there, she can avoid the discomfort of havin' to tip-toe around you. She loves you. That hasn't changed," she says encouragingly.

"I guess she hasn't told you about Mike," I scoff.

"I know about Mike. What about him?"

"Well if she's movin' to the 'burbs with that preppy nightmare, I don't think she's spendin' sleepless nights lovin' me."

Shannon's full-belly, raspy laugh bursts through the phone, causing me to pull it away from my face.

"You really have no perspective when it comes to her," she says, reining her laughs into smiley words.

"Anyone ever tell you you're a pain in the ass?"

"Your cousin says I'm a pain in the dick," she deadpans.

"He's right."

We both fall into laughter.

"You can get them back if you do this the right way. Trust that. Don't be a pussy and give up. It's just not your style."

"I swear, if one of you calls me a pussy again I'm flyin' to Kansas City and beating some ass."

"Yeah, you go ahead and try that...pussy," she finishes, taunting me like a younger sibling.

"I'm callin' Kellerman back and tellin' him to get your ass in line. You're a mother now. Who talks like that with a baby?"

"Uh, me. You go ahead and call Kel. I'd like to see him try to put me in my place. Maybe he'll put his dick in my place, instead."

"Wow. You're like talkin' to a dude, Shannon. You never cease to amaze me."

"I aim to entertain," she finishes with one of her classic lines.

"Kellerman said I need to just be there for Quinn. Show her that I'm trustworthy again."

"He's a smart man. I'm no relationship expert, so I can't offer you much. Kel and I have been together a total of nine months and spent the majority of that time separated. Now we have a newborn. He's my first and only boyfriend and I'll be thirty-one in a few weeks. I'm no beacon of relationship wisdom, that's for damn sure. And as you just pointed out, I'm more like a guy than a girl so I don't really have great perspective on what to do for a girl, per se. But Quinn's more like me than not. She needs to know unconditional love. When she sees she has that from you and with you, she'll come back. Take Kel's advice. He got me and that's no easy task."

"No shit," I grunt.

"Fuck off," she says in a way that I can almost hear her rolling her gorgeous green eyes at me.

"Thanks for talkin' to me. I know you're wiped dealin' with Johnny. It helps to talk things through with you.

Makes me sick that I lost ten years of this bein' a stubborn dick."

"You were protecting me from your life. No regrets. We have each other now and that's not goin' anywhere, cousin. You're stuck with my ass."

"And it's a fine ass."

"I know, right?" she jokes.

The woman is stunning in a way that should be illegal and she could give two shits about it.

"I love you, Shannon Kelly."

"And I love you, Kieran Delaney. Go get your family back so you can come here and see me."

"I'll try my best."

"Then it'll happen."

"Talk to you later."

"Bye."

Now that I've had my Kansas City pep talk I feel better, exceedingly better. Time to get my family back.

Chapter 39

Quinn

At the end of a long work day and a longer work week, I'm still not done. Clare just dropped off Jack and Ashling here at Brogan's. I've decided it's time for Jack to meet Alex. I've talked to him about who Alex is, but they haven't met face to face again. I wanted Alex's face to heal completely first, plus I wanted to feel him out. He's a good guy. I can only imagine the life he had to live with a predator for a father, but he turned out good despite all that.

Sofia was "lucky" as she tells it. Their father's predilection was for boys, so she was untouched by him. Instead, she was passed around to other men until Alex got big enough to put a stop to it. According to her, that's when he was about twelve. That's a heavy burden for a child to carry. I've never heard him complain.

Alex strides in the back door with Sofia under his arm as Jack rolls around the grappling area with Owen.

"Jack," I call out, stopping the wrestling. His little head pops up from holding Owen in a headlock. I nod toward Alex and Jack climbs to his feet.

"Hey, Alex," he says through a giant smile.

"Hey, Jack," Alex responds softly.

"You wanna wrestle me? Careful, I'm really good," Jack stretches "really" as long as it can go.

"If you promise to go easy on me."

"No way. Daddy says it's all the way or nothing."

"He tells me the same thing," Alex says with a wink.

"Cool."

And that's it. Jack leaps onto Alex's back, attacking him like a spider monkey as Owen instructs him from the mat like a trainer.

"You're gonna have your hands full with that one in a few years," Sofia says, saddling up to my side, looping her arm through mine.

"Gonna?" I tease.

"Will you let him fight when he's old enough?" she asks, laying her head on top of mine. I'm tiny and she's in sky-high heels as usual, making her almost a foot taller than me.

"I won't get a choice in the matter. This will be his world. I can only hope that he's as good as Kieran," I admit with a shrug. "And I'll hate every damn minute of it."

"Maybe he won't want to."

Jack lands a hard elbow to Alex's gut to the applause of Owen. His dimple bursting smile breaks across his face.

"No such luck," I say with a prideful grin.

Kieran strolls in through the back door a few minutes later with his cocky swagger and cool smile. He offers me a chin lift before diving into the mêlée with his son and Alex.

I talked with Owen, Connor and Ian last month after my night with Kieran. I asked them to back off him and go back to being friendly (as friendly as they were). They grumbled a little, but I think they were happy to hear that I was loosening the reins on everything. Things aren't back to normal with them, but they will be.

I called Shannon after my night with Kieran, too. That woman is a beacon of information and understanding. She also called me out on my shit. Informed me that all I was doing was running away from things with Kieran by moving the kids to the suburbs. I was going to isolate like I have for my entire adult life. It sucked to hear and I argued a little until I realized she was right. Running is my go-to when things get difficult. So, I'm staying in the city, fighting the urge to take my kids and hide behind a white picket fence.

Now that Shannon has Johnny, I feel more like an equal to her. She would never make me feel less than her, but it's hard not to. Shannon Kelly is a super hero, the kind of woman women dream of being and men dream of being with. I'm lucky to call her my friend. I also got to see the super hero crack a little when she first became a mother. It was hilarious, sweet and endearing all at once. We've talked a lot about mom stuff over the past two months and it's been so fulfilling for both of us. I wish we lived in the same city so we could see each other and have the kids get together.

Shannon's birthday is in September, just a few weeks away now. We're all flying down to Kansas City for her birthday. Kieran, Collin, Hugh, their parents and the rest of Shannon's family that lives here in Chicago. I'm looking forward to it so much that I've already started shopping for clothes and gifts. Shannon and I do a lot of video chatting so I've "met" her man and her roommates—not roommates, family. She lives in a house of god-like men. It's unreal how hot the guys around her are. I'll be beet red for the entire week we're there.

Sofia and I flop onto the couch to watch my son do his thing. Ian comes out of his office with Ashling, food covering her face. After wiping her up, Ian sits on the floor with her between his legs and encourages her to watch the fighting. She's more interested in eating her toes. I stifle a yawn as the front door opens.

Mike walks in with a huge smile on his face when he spots Sofia. I guess Kieran's about to find out I'm not with Mike. Kieran watches as he crosses the gym. I can see him willing himself not to attack Mike, which causes a slight grin to ghost my features. Mike offers Alex and the others a chin lift as he strolls by.

"Hey, babe," he says softly leaning down to kiss Sofia before scooping her into his arms. Kieran's face drops, goes rigid, slaps with confusion and ends in that Kieran grin. I smile at him with a slight shrug.

Sofia and Mike say their goodbyes, leaving quickly to go have crazy monkey sex. Her words, not mine.

I stifle another yawn and lean my head back on the couch. A few minutes of rest and then I can drive us home.

"Quinn," I hear through a fog of sleep. "Jack's hungry. Let me get you all home," Kieran's tar and whiskey voice brushes across my face.

I flutter my eyes open to find the gym empty other than Kieran and the kids. I must have passed out.

"I'm good. I'll drive us," I say, stretching my arms over my head and yawning again.

"Let me take you. You're tired. I just wanna make sure you get home safe," he says in that soft Kieran way that's impossible to ignore.

"'Kay."

He loads us into the SUV quickly and drives us to his parents' house. I really need to move out, but I'm having a hard time making the effort. I want to do it the right way for the right reasons. It feels safe at their place for now, so I'm not rocking the boat just yet.

"Thanks for drivin' us," I whisper as we enter his parents' living room. Jack springs into the kitchen to eat whatever is making the house smell decadent.

Kieran sets Ashling's car seat down and pulls her out, eating her cheeks as he does. She squeals and giggles at her daddy with such love it makes my heart flutter. I miss this life with him. I miss it so much it hurts.

For the last month, Kieran's been doing little things like driving me home or watching the kids so I can go out with Sofia. He hasn't pushed me to talk or engage with him at all. He's just been present. His presence is impossible to ignore when he's like this. I'm losing the battle with myself to remain removed from him. The battle still exists, though. Every time I think about going back to him, I remember the day of the fight and I stop myself. I don't know if I'll ever get over that day.

"I like drivin' you guys home," Kieran responds, passing Ashling to me. "Jack asked me to stay for dinner while you were asleep. If you don't want me here, I'll take off and take him out tomorrow to make up for it."

"No, it's fine. If Jack wants you here, it's where you should be."

He offers me a sad smile before turning and walking into the kitchen.

We eat dinner as a family for the first time in months, laughing and talking. It feels so good I'd almost forgotten this feeling existed. Not forgotten, denied. Jack's his usual storytelling self, entertaining the table. Now he's in his room playing while Kieran puts Ash to bed. Yeah, this feels good.

"Mommy," Jack calls to me as he enters the living room where I'm lounging.

"Yeah, Baby," I say, extending an arm so he can curl into my side.

"I made you a present." He hands me a piece of white paper with a drawing on it.

"Tell me about this," I encourage, taking in the picture before me.

"It's our family. You, Daddy, Ashling and me."

There on the paper are four six-year-old-drawn, messy stick figures standing in front of what I assume is Kieran's house, based on the color and shape. A lump forms in my throat as I try to hold back the tears. Not just because my son obviously misses his family being in one house, but because I miss it too. I want that picture to be real as much as Jack does.

"It's beautiful, Baby."

"Will you show it to Daddy? I'm gonna go take my bath now. Grandma put in a lot of bubbles."

"I'll show him."

I rub my thumb across his dimple before he reaches up and kisses my cheek.

"I love you, Mommy," he murmurs into my skin.

"Love you too, Baby."

He thuds down the hall to the bathroom, excited for his bath. It's still one of his favorite things in life, so he gets one at least once a day.

"Ash is down so I'm gonna take off," Kieran says, moving into the room. "Jack's in the bath. He wanted you to show me somethin' before I went."

I hand him the picture and watch his face as he looks at it. It hurts him as much as it hurts me. I can't hold back the tears anymore and let them roll down my face. Kieran's murky blues glisten with emotion as he looks down at me from the picture.

"Quinn," he says through choked emotion.

"I can't, Kieran," I say as a sob breaks from my chest.

He drops to his knees in front of me, not sure what to do. His hands hover in the air before resting in his lap. He's afraid to touch me.

"Can't what?" he asks softly, studying his hands.

"Be without you," I whisper, wiping my face.

His head snaps up with surprise and caution in his eyes.

"What does that mean?"

"I don't know. I want our family back as much as Jack does. I miss this life," I say gesturing at the paper. "But I don't know how to get past what you did to me."

"I'm not gonna apologize to you again because those words mean nothing in the long run. But I swear to you I'll never again in this lifetime treat you like that. I give you my word on the lives of our children...I'll never ever disrespect you."

The conviction in his face is hard to argue with, but my defenses aren't that easily shed.

"I don't want you to change who you are to be with me."

"I'm not. I'm still an asshole. I'm still a criminal. I'm still a fighter. I'll always be those things. But I'm promising you to not be those things with you."

"I want to believe you so badly."

"Let me show you."

I pause and search myself for the internal battle that's been raging, but it's not there. I'm ready to try to trust him again. I want my family back enough to try.

"Okay," I whisper, wiping more tears from my cheeks.

Kieran lets out a relieved sigh.

"I'm still me, Quinn. I'll be possessive and dominant, aggressive and bossy, rough and harsh. That's who I am. But when I'm with you I fuckin' swear I'll be the best versions of those things that I can be. I want you and the kids back home right this instant, but I'm not gonna do that. I'm gonna give you time and space to see me for more than my words. I wanna kiss you and hold you in my arms, but I'm not gonna do that, either. Until you trust me again, completely, with everything that you have, all physical contact will have to be initiated by you. I won't make any attempt to push you."

Blown away. I'm blown away and can't find words to respond. Kieran's smooth with words. It's what makes him successful in life. I can see for every pore on his body, he truly means everything he's saying.

"Okay," is all I'm able to form, along with a tiny smile. I'm scared out of my mind right now.

"I love you," he says confidently.

"Thank you." Kieran jerks like I just slapped him. I don't want to hurt him, but I can't say those words in this moment.

"Daddy!" Jack squeals, running into the room in his hooded pirate towel. So damn cute.

"Hey bud," Kieran says through a huge smile, turning to catch his son's launching body.

"Did you like my picture?" Jack murmurs into Kieran's chest.

"It's awesome! Do you think I can take it home with me?"

"Sure," Jack takes a long pause before finishing. "I wish I could go home with you."

Jack whispers it so quietly I'm certain he didn't want me to hear, which crushes me. He doesn't want to upset me with his words. That's too much responsibility for my son to carry and I swore he would get to be a normal, happy kid when I got him.

"Baby," I coo, leaning forward on the couch.

He looks up at me with his stunning husky-like eyes, timid and worried.

"I'm sorry," he whispers to me.

"No, Baby, I'm sorry. You can say anything you want to me or your daddy. Don't ever be afraid of tellin' the truth. Do you wanna go home with Daddy tonight?"

"Will you come with me?"

"Not tonight. Ashling's already asleep so I need to stay here with her. But if you wanna go, you can."

"Are you gonna be mad at me?" he asks in a furrowed brow.

"No."

"Are you gonna be mad at Daddy, more mad than you have been?"

"No, Baby. If you wanna go, I'll be happy. I promise you," I say through an encouraging smile.

"Do you want me to come home?" Jack turns his wide eyes up to his father's.

"More than anything," Kieran responds emphatically.

Jack's smile bursts across his face, making his dimple almost look painful. Kieran presses a soft kiss to it before standing Jack up.

"Go get in some PJs and I'll take us home."

"Cool."

Jack flies down the hall to his room, jabbering to his grandmother about his plans.

"You okay?" Kieran asks without looking at me.

"No," I reply honestly. I feel like the worst mother in the world right now. I can't be with Kieran just to make the kids happy. But I've been keeping the kids here with me for two months without once considering how not returning to Kieran's would affect them. It makes it that much worse knowing I want to go home with Kieran just as badly as Jack does.

"I don't have to take him with me," Kieran mumbles in defeat.

"I'm not okay because I feel like a shitty mom, Kieran. Not because he's goin' with you."

"Why do you feel like shitty mom?" he asks harshly, turning his murky blues at me encased in a scowl.

"Because Jack was hurting himself to protect me," I mumble into the knees I've drawn to my chest.

"We can't be together for the kids. It'd be worse than what they have now. Someday Jack'll get that. You're not a shitty mom, Quinn."

I nod.

Jack comes flying into the room, as close to literally flying as he can get, with his Superman pajamas on and his matching blue cape flowing in his wake. He looks like a miniature Christopher Reeve with the same piercing blue eyes and curly black hair. My son, the super hero. He wraps his arms around my neck from the side of the couch and I heave him into my lap.

"Love you," I coo into his hair.

"You're squishin' me," he complains but remains in my tight grip.

I release him from my chest, just a little. Jack pushes up and lays a loud lip-smacking kiss on my mouth.

"Love you, too." Then he dives from my lap into Kieran's always waiting arms.

Clare enters the room with tear-stained cheeks and an overnight bag in her hand. She looks so happy it makes me feel even worse. I've had my head planted in my own ass for the last two months, hurting the people I love.

"Bye, Grandma."

"Bye, sweet boy. I'll see you tomorrow."

"Bye, Mommy."

"Bye, Baby."

Kieran offers me a chin lift and then carries our son out the door. As soon as it shuts I run to my room, throw myself on the bed and weep like a little kid. I cry for the guilt, the pain, the hurt, the happiness, but mostly for the love I have that I never thought I'd experience again. When there are no tears left to cry, I fall asleep dreaming of a stick figure family living happily ever after.

Chapter 35

Kieran

There's a soft knock on the back door as Jack and I put the finishing touches on our biggest Lego creation to date.

"I'll get it," I say through a grunt, standing up. I sound like my father.

I open the door to find Quinn standing there, nervous as hell, holding Ashling on her hip.

"Where's her car seat?" I ask, taking the baby and chomping down on her fat, soft cheeks. Ash squeals, giggles and spits all over me as I do it.

"She outgrew it. Had to buy a new one that stays in the car," Quinn explains, making no move to come in the house.

"You comin' in?" I ask, stepping back to clear the way for her. She glances over her shoulder and I do the same to find a guy sitting in the passenger's seat of the SUV. I can't tell who it is from here with the glare of the sun, but it's definitely a man. I wasn't expecting that. I school my features and wait for her to turn back around.

"I have plans this afternoon. I thought I'd leave the kids here with you and then come get 'em when I'm done," she says sheepishly.

"Okay," I lie. I don't give a shit about having the kids. If I could keep them here permanently, I would. Her driving off with some dude without me and the kids makes me want to hurt something, badly.

She reaches her hand out and rubs the baby's back before turning on her heel and leaving. She doesn't just leave, she runs. As she drives off I see her usual tail of Ronan and Cormack following closely behind. I haven't ever asked them to give me updates on her, but fuck if I'm not battling that at this moment.

Quinn told me last night she wants to be with me. I really thought we were headed back to each other, but I can't be in a dating pool. I can be soft with Quinn, and I will be. I will not share her, though. I'm Kieran Delaney, not some pussy yuppie willing to hang around and collect scraps. She's mine. She's been mine since February. Being a good man is a fucking struggle!

I go back to building Lego towers and enjoying my children. They're still my focus in life. I won't fuck this part up, no matter how strong the urge.

We actually have a perfect day together. Grilled cheese sandwiches and tomato soup for lunch was a hit with Jack. We worked hard trying to encourage Ashling to crawl, which ended in her laughing and rolling around instead. Jack and I worked on his wrestling while Ashling took her afternoon nap.

My son is a natural on the ground. I know Quinn will hate it, but the kid's a fighter. He's quick and thoughtful as he moves and takes direction without question. The smile he gets when he completes a maneuver or breaks out of a hold fills me with pride as a father. I never knew feelings like this existed. Now I can't imagine life without it.

I was successful with lunch, but dinner was a bit more of a struggle. Jack wanted roasted chicken and vegetables which apparently his mother makes him on the weekends. I informed him if I tried to roast a chicken and vegetables, we'd have to eat a burnt dinner. He laughed at me and we settled on hamburgers and hotdogs on the grill.

Quinn pulls up in the SUV (alone, thank fuck) as I'm loading a plate with our manly dinner. Jack bounds off the deck into her arms almost taking her to the ground. The slight boy that she found in February is nowhere to be seen. He's gained a lot of weight and has grown at least a couple inches. She absorbs the hit and wraps her arms around him with a glowing smile on her face.

At least she's not wearing that skin-tight dress. Now that I know she's not with Mike, I have a shit ton of questions about who she was dressing like that for. I would know if she was dating someone seriously, right? Someone in my crew or in my family would have the decency to pass that information along. I haven't pried into her life while she's been at my parents. If I wanted information on her it would take all of one, maybe two, phone calls. She wanted to be free of me though, so I've let it go. I'm a tough motherfucker to have accomplished that.

"Have a good day?" I ask politely.

"I did," she says through a huge smile. "How were things here?"

She sets Jack in a chair at the outdoor table before making him a plate. Who knew a white tank top, jean shorts and some white canvas sneakers could be a turn on? I find myself mindlessly ogling her ass as she leans over the table to grab…something, I'm not paying attention. She clears her throat, pulling me from my reverie.

337

"I asked if Ash ate yet," she prompts with a raised brow.

"Nope," I respond, popping my *p* like I wasn't just perving all over her perfect ass.

"I'll feed her while you two eat, then."

"You're not hungry?"

I take the seat next to Jack and shove a giant mouthful of burger into my face, grinning at Jack with a mess on my lips.

"I ate while I was out," she coos in her baby talk voice, spooning a mouthful of green shit into Ash's mouth.

I grunt in response. So she went out and at least shared a meal with another man today. I really want to ask if he enjoyed *her* as a meal, but I won't. It's tickling my lips, though.

"What do you wanna do tonight, Baby?" she asks as we're all finishing up.

"Daddy said we could have a movie night!" he exclaims. This kid loves movies like no other. We've been catching him up on all the movies he missed while he lived in the streets. That's a lot of movies.

"I didn't know what time you'd be back," I offer in a small apology in case she's offended I've made plans with Jack for the night.

"What movie are we watchin' tonight?" she asks Jack, ignoring my response completely.

"*Girls Gone Wild*," he deadpans.

I spit out my beer as Quinn pales. Jack bursts into laughter at his own joke, not knowing why it's funny.

"You got all the food wet, Daddy," he says through his giggles.

"You made me," I feign blame at him.

"That was funny. Can we watch *Teenage Mutant Ninja Turtles*?"

"Sure, bud. Why don't you go play for a bit while I get dinner cleaned up?"

"'Kay."

He climbs out of his chair and races inside, slamming the door shut behind him. At least he got it shut.

"Sorry I made plans with him. I thought you might be out late again," I apologize as I pick up our dirty plates.

"Again?" Quinn asks confused.

"The last time you were on a date you came home pretty late." I shrug.

"I'm not dating Owen. You really think I'd date one of your friends?" Her tone is skirting toward pissed and now I feel like a dick. I couldn't tell she was with Owen.

"I just saw a dude in your car and assumed it was a date. I didn't know you were out with Owen."

"You must think I'm a real bitch," she scoffs, standing up to get Ash out of her highchair.

"No, I don't think you're a bitch. I think I fucked things up with us a long time ago and you have the right to date someone else if that's what you want. I know you're not with Mike, but you were out for a date the night you left with him. What else am I supposed to think?"

"I didn't know you thought I was with Mike until I got home that night. I should have set you straight, but I didn't think it mattered. I did go on a double date that night with Mike and Sofia."

"Are you still seein' him?" I ask with pain in my voice.

"No. I told you, I wanna be with you. That's what I want," she says emphatically and still a little pissed off. I figure I'll push my luck because I'm an idiot.

"Did you sleep with him?"

"Fuck you, Kieran. I went on *one* date! I'm not a whore!" Now she's raging. The only reason she isn't screaming is because Ashling is on her hip.

"I didn't say you were a whore."

"You didn't have to. I don't wanna spend the evening fighting with you so let's get this outta the way."

"What?"

"You obviously need to ask me some questions, so go ahead," she barks.

I don't really have anymore. She didn't fuck anyone else and she's single. I'm good.

"I'm good," I say with a cocky grin.

"Did you sleep with anyone? Are you still single? Are there thongs hidden in the couches that you need to rid the house of?"

I drop the plates with a clang and stalk over to her. I grab Ashling off her hip and take her inside. I put her in her ExerSaucer and turn on the baby monitor. I can see her from the deck so she's safe in the kitchen alone for a few minutes.

I shut the door to find Quinn cleaning up dinner in an exasperated state.

"I haven't touched anyone but you since February. I can't even think about touchin' anyone but you. I've fuckin' tried. I don't know how to do this, Quinn. I wanna wrap you in my arms and hold you against my chest until you can't stand another second. I want you in my house, in my bed and by my side every minute of every day. I'm in love with you. That hasn't changed. It's killed me to leave you alone."

"Good," she seethes. "You think this has been easy on me? It's been goddamn torture! I've never been with anyone besides you. Sean was nothing compared to you. I can't even make the comparison. What you did to me that day crushed me, scared me, hurt me and made me think I was stupid to fall in love with a man like you. I knew what you were when we started this and I accepted you for every part of you. Then you face fucked me and treated to me like a whore afterward. How could I love someone that would do that to me? What does that make me? What does it make me that I still wanna be with you?"

I step as close to her as I can get without touching her. She cuts her icy eyes at me with tears brimming.

"I was a monster that day. I've been a monster for thirty-five years. I'll be one until the day I die, but I will *never* be a monster to you again. I've learned my lesson. I've paid the price of losing my family for months. I've had to watch you blossom into an amazingly independent woman from afar. I've had to listen to your laughter from behind closed doors. I've had to miss Ashling learning to roll and sit up for the first time. I missed Jack reading his first book on his own. I can do nothing to get those moments back. I'll do everything in my power to make certain I never miss another moment in your life or the kids'. I love you and if you still want me that makes you a fuckin' saint. I don't deserve you. I

341

don't deserve how good you make me feel. But please don't think badly of yourself for wantin' to be with me. I can't stand the idea that you're doin' somethin' you hate because you can't fight against it."

"See, there you go," she pokes at my chest as tears roll down her cheeks, "sayin' the right thing, makin' me feel better when I really just wanna be mad. I don't hate that I wanna be with you—it scares me. I can't be that woman that signs up for a life of hurt because the good times feel better than anything I've ever felt."

"I fuckin' promise I'll never hurt you like that again. I'll make you mad. I'll make you stabby. I'll annoy the shit out of you. But I'll *never* hurt you again," I finish emphatically, knowing I'm dead serious.

"You can't scare the kids again, either," she whispers.

"I swear I won't."

She studies me for a long time, her wet eyes dancing around my face.

"I love you. I *want* to be with you. This is your last chance to make me yours, Kieran Delaney. I won't come back again."

"I love you, too," I purr through a small grin.

"Kiss me."

She barely gets the words out of her mouth before I smash mine against hers. I grab her under her arms and hoist her up so I can have better access. Quinn wraps her tiny arms and legs around my body as I support her weight with my hands on her glorious ass. I work my lips in conjunction with hers savoring the flavor, sweet and minty. I move my tongue across the seam of her lips and she opens them quickly, slanting her head. I lap, lick, flick and massage against her until I'm struggling

342

for air. I don't stop. I can hear Ash cooing and happy inside so I keep going.

As our tongues tangle, Quinn moans and rubs her hips against my torso trying to relieve the building pressure. I want inside her like I want my next breath. It's taking every shred of human power I have not to slam her against the house and fuck her into oblivion. I keep my hands on her ass, not kneading her cheeks like I want. I continue to drink from her mouth, not moving down her jaw and neck like I want. I make no move to take this beyond the kiss she requested. It's frustrating her.

She takes my bottom lip between her teeth, biting down hard, trying to spur me on. I pull hers into my teeth, gently nibbling before plunging my tongue back into her mouth. Quinn lets out a frustrated growl and yanks my hair with vicious force, bruising our lips together. I remain steadfast and maintain the kiss. She rips her mouth away from me.

"Kieran," she chides.

"Yeah?"

"I don't like this," she growls.

"I'm sorry," I whisper and go to set her back on her feet. It was too much, too fast. Shit!

"No," she barks, wrapping herself around me tighter. "I don't want you holding back with me. Thank you for givin' me the power, but please take the lead. I miss you leading me this way. I've craved it."

"The last time I led, things didn't go so well," I say quietly in shame.

"Will you ever do that to me again when we're havin' sex or otherwise?"

"Never."

"Then please be yourself with me. I need you. I need this to be real with you. I don't want a different Kieran. I want the man I fell in love with, not some pussy who's afraid to touch me without permission."

And I'm being called a pussy again. That's all it takes.

"I am what I eat. And your pussy's for dessert," I purr in her ear before biting the lobe then caressing it with my tongue.

"Yes," she moans.

I drag my teeth along her jaw and then down her neck as goosebumps cover her ivory skin. My dick is so hard it burns with painful pulsing pressure.

"I want inside you," I groan against her skin.

"Yes," she purrs.

"All night."

"Yes."

"Until you can't fuckin' walk."

"Yes."

"Mommy!" Jack yells in the house, breaking our moment.

I kiss her lips long and hard before placing her on the deck. Her face is flushed bright red, her lips are swollen and her eyes look drugged with lust. Never a hotter sight in the world. Quinn moves around me with a small seductive smile playing on her mouth before heading inside to deal with our children. I'll wait until tonight, then all bets are off. She'll be mine in every way I can get her before the sun comes up.

Chapter 36

Kieran

I spent a normal, happy, loving evening with my family and I'm on cloud nine. *Teenage Mutant Ninja Turtles* was a massive hit with Jack. Quinn and I sat next to each other holding hands like a new couple. She's letting me again. Letting me love her, care for her, be my all for her and she's loving it. I wish I could be the sweet, loving, romantic guy that would light candles and whisper sweet shit in her ear before I take her, but I'm not.

I climb into bed naked with her after laying Ashling down and checking that Jack is out cold, which, of course, he is. I strip Quinn out of her clothes in record time before launching my attack.

I kiss her with all the passion in my soul until she rips her mouth from mine to nibble my neck and ear. I return the favor, fighting the urge to give her the biggest hickey known to man. Instead, I work my mouth down the valley between her perky tits, salivating at the chance to devour them.

I wrap my lips around one raspberry nipple and firmly pinch the other. Quinn's back comes off the mattress as her hands drive into my hair, smashing my face into her supple flesh. I suck on her nipples so hard I'm shocked she's not screaming in pain. I pop it free from my mouth and switch tits, offering this one the same aggressive suction as the other. She rocks her hips against my chest spurring me on.

I want to kiss and lick my way down to her pussy, but I've lost my self-restraint. I scoot down the bed on my knees before grabbing her hips off the bed. Forcing her legs to remain together I lift her up to my face and drag my tongue from her ass to her clit, long eager strokes. Quinn wraps her arms behind her knees, holding them to her chest, encouraging our position for my feast. I continue to stroke her with my tongue until every drop of juice is gone before planting her hips back on the bed.

I pull her knees from her chest and smash them on either side of her body. Quinn grabs behind her legs opening herself even further for me. I spear my tongue inside her with force as she moans and says words that resemble English. Moving up to her clit with my tongue I insert one finger and pound away. I suck her clit and add a second finger, curving them upward. She comes whispering my name, shaking from head to toe violently. I'm drenched with her come and I keep going.

I finger her and lick her clit until my tongue cramps and my fingers are pruney. She's had three more orgasms and is limp and sated as I crawl up her body. Quinn licks my lips clean before ramming her tongue down my throat with a guttural moan. I palm my dick and feed it into her tight pussy slowly. Her breath hitches as I move into her, but she never stops kissing me. Once I'm so deep in her I've bottomed out, I growl in caveman satisfaction.

I begin to move slowly in and out as her walls clench around me. That lasts about four strokes before I begin to pound into her, dropping my face to the crook of her neck. Quinn wraps her legs around my waist as an orgasm crashes through her. She scores my back with her nails and I relish the burn of her marking me. Running my arm beneath her lower back I tip her up just a little so I can move deeper within her. She cries out in another orgasm almost immediately, her pussy crushing my cock.

I slam into her as I come, filling her so much that it flows out around my dick, slathering my balls. I slow my strokes, bringing us down while kissing her lovingly and soft. Once we've both caught our breath, I leave my cock in her like the first time we were together and collapse on top of her.

"That was…" she trails off.

"I know," I mumble into her neck.

We lay joined together caressing each other's skin, kissing and playing for a long while.

"Tryin' to get me pregnant again?" she asks teasingly.

"Yes," I grunt.

"We just got back together."

"Uh huh."

"Think that's a good way to start stuff off?"

"Yup," I say popping my *p*. "Givin' myself a late birthday present."

"I thought I was pregnant in June," she whispers.

I push up on my elbows and peer into her flawless face.

"I was relieved at first when the test came back negative. Then I was sad. I cried in your parents' bathroom for a half hour lookin' at the damn test."

"I'm so fuckin' sorry, Quinn. I don't ever want you cryin' in a bathroom alone again. I can't believe…you were sad?" I ask, a little shocked. I figured she'd be relieved like she said she was, not sad.

"I want all the things you said you wanted before. I want more babies with you. I wanna grow old with you. I wanna be by your side in life. When I realized we weren't together anymore I was hopin' I'd at least get a piece of both of us to remember what we had," she whispers, tears threatening to spill.

"I'll never be able to take back that time, but I still want all of those things with you. More so now than before. I'll have sex with you every minute of every day if it means givin' you what you want. It'll be a tough sacrifice, but I'm up for the challenge."

Quinn barks out a loud, sexy laugh, launching my dick from within her. I scoop up all of my dribbling come and shove it back in her, working my fingers in and out until I'm hard again. Then I go about my sacrifice, spending the night filling her with enough come to get her pregnant with a litter.

"Mornin'," I groan as I slide my red raw dick into Quinn's tightly swollen pussy from behind, spooning her against my chest.

"Ah," she hisses.

"Want me to stop?"

"No."

I move in and out slowly, pinching her nipple and rubbing her clit. A shudder runs through her body as she comes quickly, whimpering in ecstasy. She's overly sensitive from a night of sex, so making her come takes barely a touch at this point.

I pull her thigh up so I can move faster and deeper, giving me better access to her clit. As I begin to pound into her, I nuzzle her neck before biting her flesh. She tastes like sweat and sex with a hint of her milk and honey.

Quinn rolls onto her stomach and I follow. She keeps her chest in the mattress as she raises her hips. Fuck yes! I slam into her, filling the room with wet slapping sounds. I trace her asshole with my index finger, causing her breath to hitch and an animalistic growl to rumble from my chest. She presses her hips back against me as I pound and play. I put a little more pressure on her ass and she comes, dropping her hips in exhaustion. I pick her back up, holding her to me as I ram into her a few more times before coming with a roar.

We collapse on the mattress, heaving and panting. I'm light-headed from all the exertion of our night together. My parents came and got the kids for us half an hour ago. Quinn doesn't know because she was dead to the world.

"My parents came for the kids thirty minutes ago. Let's sleep for a while before I make you mine again," I murmur into her neck, rolling us onto our sides, keeping my dick in her the best I can.

She grunts in response before passing out. Her soft snores fill the room and make me fall asleep with a contented smile on my lips.

"Kieran," Quinn's soft voice wakes me up.

"Huh?" I grunt.

"You need to let me up. I have to pee," she whimpers.

I have her caged beneath me. I always sleep with her wrapped up tightly. It anchors me somehow.

I roll off her and she flies from the bed. She's been trying to wake me up for a while, based on the speed of her run. The toilet flushes and the shower kicks on.

Hell, no—is she taking a shower without me? I climb from the bed and strip the sheets quickly. These things should be framed instead of washed. I leave them in a pile at the end of the bed before walking into the bathroom.

Quinn is standing motionless under the rain shower with her head tipped back, enjoying the steamy water. It's the most erotic vision my eyes have ever seen. I slide in the shower behind her and wrap my arms around her tiny wet body.

"I'm walkin' funny and it hurt to wipe. You've accomplished your goal," she says, pushing my wandering hands off her tits. "I don't think your pinky would fit in me right now."

"I'm sorry. I got a little carried away last night and this morning. Are you okay?" Now I feel bad and a little proud.

"Just tired and sore. It was a great night. Thank you."

She spins in my arms and reaches up with her arms around my neck. I lean down and place a small kiss on her lips before pulling back. If I don't I'll try to get my dick in her and that doesn't sound like it's on the menu.

We wash and kiss each other before climbing out. I dry her from head to toe before carrying her back to the bed. We put on new sheets before sliding in together. Quinn puts her head on my chest lightly, tracing my tattoos with her leg slung over mine.

My phone rings, bringing us out of our trance.

"Yeah?" I bark into the phone.

"Mancini's men are makin' a move toward Kansas City," Connor growls into the phone.

"Shit!"

I sit straight up, pulling Quinn with me.

"Don't know when, but there's a lot of chatter in the streets about Shannon killin' one of theirs while they had her."

"That's fuckin' bullshit. They could give two fucks about that. Watch those motherfuckers like a hawk. If they hop a plane, I wanna know before the wheels go up."

"Got it, boss."

We hang up.

"I've gotta make some calls," I murmur into Quinn's wet hair.

"Everything okay?"

"Fine. Just business," I lie. She's so close to Shannon, I don't want her worrying. I'm not too worried. The Mancini Crime Family is pretty much gone at this point. Shannon's case against them is coming to trial soon, I'm guessing that's why they want to try to take her out. Motherfuckers! There aren't many men left so I can track them easily.

"Get some sleep. I'll be back in a bit," I say as I swing my legs from the bed.

"I love you," she calls out sweetly.

"Love you, too."

She watches me as I walk away to get dressed. When I come back, she's soundly asleep. I head down to the basement and start making calls. I'll be damned if I let something else happen to Shannon Kelly on my watch.

Chapter 37

Quinn

Kieran woke me up at the crack of dawn to tell me he had to leave town on business. I didn't ask any questions because I could see on his face that I needed to just listen to him. He was full of fury and determination. Most people would be nervous in moments like this, but I feel calm. Kieran can take care of himself and any business he needs to deal with.

It's Labor Day, so that sucks. I wish Kieran was here so we could have our last day together before Jack starts school tomorrow, but Kieran assured me he'd be back as soon as he could be.

As I set Jack's waffles down in front of him, my phone rings. I grab it quickly, thinking it'll be Kieran telling me he's coming home, but it's Shannon.

"Hey," I answer happily.

"You won't guess where I am," she rasps in the phone, sounding like shit.

"Where?" I ask concerned.

"The fuckin' hospital."

"What? What's wrong with you?"

"I puked my guts out all day yesterday so Kel and the guys brought me into the ER last night."

"I'm so sorry. Do you have the flu or something?"

Please don't let it be something worse.

"Or something...I'm pregnant!" she squeals.

"What?!" I scream, making both kids jump. I smile at them to let them know that was a happy scream and they go back to enjoying each other's company.

"With twins," she says in disbelief.

"No way," I respond with my jaw hitting the floor. She's got a three month old at home. Holy shit!

"Yes. Fuckin' insanity, Quinn."

"Your man does quick work. When're you due?"

"March eighth. Can you believe that? Kel knocked me up the first time we went at it on the way home from Seattle," she huffs, like she didn't love every second of joining the mile high club.

"Don't tell Kieran, he'll make it a competition," I say through a laugh.

"Kieran? You're back together? What the fuck, Quinn? Way to leave your girl hangin'!"

"Sorry. I was gonna call you yesterday, but we haven't been very social if you know what I mean."

"No shit. I'm surprised you're not tied to a bed somewhere."

"I can barely walk, Shannon," I groan.

She bursts into raspy full belly laughs, dragging me along with her.

"I'm so happy for you both. This is awesome. If he knocks you up we can be pregnant and bitchy together. Kel and Kieran can complain about us to each other. Ooh, I hope he has good swimmers!" That's the girliest thing I've ever heard Shannon say. Pregnancy hormones must be making her more...I don't know what word to use. Girly?

"If he didn't succeed gettin' me pregnant, something's wrong with one of us."

"My caveman is givin' me the stink eye so I better get off here. I'll call you once they release me later today or tomorrow. Kiss the kids for me."

"Feel better and kiss Johnny from all of us. Tell Dylan congratulations for me. You wanna tell Kieran yourself or do you want me to pass on your good news?"

"Maybe Kel wants to tell him," she waits for confirmation. "Yeah, Kel says he'll call Kieran in a little bit to pass on the news."

"Okay. I'm so happy for you guys. Love you," I coo, brimming with joy.

"Love you, too. Talk to you later."

"Bye."

We hang up and my heart beats a little faster for the two lives about to join our crazy family.

"When's Daddy comin' home?" Jack asks around a mouthful of waffles, dribbling syrup.

"I don't know, Baby. Later today sometime."

"Are we movin' home now?"

"Yes. We'll move all our stuff while you're at school tomorrow."

"Cool. I like it at Grandma and Grandpa's, but I missed Daddy," he says honestly.

"I missed him, too. I'm sorry that our grown up problems made you sad."

I sit down in the chair across the table from him and spoon some baby oatmeal into Ash's mouth.

"You were really sad without Daddy, huh?"

"I was sad without Daddy, but we needed some time away from each other to figure out stuff."

"Will we have to go away again?"

"No, we're here for good now."

I say that confidently because it's true. I won't leave Kieran again. We can work through whatever comes our way. I'm ready for our life together to blossom and grow to its full potential. I won't run again. That girl is gone.

"That's good. I like my room."

If Kieran succeeds in getting me pregnant, we're going to have to move soon. The three bedrooms are already full and there's no room to add on to this house. At least, I don't think there is. The thought kind of makes me sad. I love this house. I don't want to have to leave it. There's a future talking point for Kieran and me.

It seems a little crazy to dive back into our relationship like we didn't spend months away from each other, but I think Kieran and I only have two speeds: all the way or nothing at all. I like moving at high speed with him. I feel like I was under a veil of blackness the last few months and the quickness of our reconnection blew it right off me. My world feels bright and full of life today in a way that I've been missing.

I'm happy with my new friends, working at Brogan's and teaching self-defense with Owen, but being without Kieran made everything feel a little less good. I missed everything about him. I'm excited to share my life with him. I'm finally starting to believe in happy endings.

"Daddy!" Jack squeals as he runs to the front door of Brogan's.

Kieran glides in with that winning swagger until Jack launches into his arms. They have an animated conversation as they walk back toward the group. We're having an unconventional Labor Day party. The alley is full of grills and food while the party is in the gym. Everyone is here, from fighters to The Crew. Ian, Connor, Owen, Sofia, Mike and Alex have been my main entertainment for the day waiting for Kieran to get back.

"Hey," Kieran purrs into my neck as he kisses it.

Jack climbs off Kieran and attacks an unsuspecting Connor, who topples to the ground dramatically with an *oof*.

"Did you hear?" I jump excitedly, wrapping my arms around his neck. He gathers me up against his torso with his cocky grin smearing his face.

"About?" he teases. I know he knows. I narrow my eyes at him, feigning frustration. He laughs a deep rumbling chuckle at me before pressing his lips to mine.

"I just got back from Kansas City. I know about the twins," he murmurs against my lips. I go rigid at his answer. Kieran pulls his face back from mine, offering a small smile.

"You had business in Kansas City?" Oh fuck, someone was going after Shannon. My heart pounds into my throat with fear and concern. She's in the hospital sick. No way could she protect herself.

"She's fine, Quinn. I got there in time. It was a fucked situation, but everything's fine now. That was the last of anything happening to Shannon Kelly," he states emphatically.

"I need to call her. I can't believe you didn't tell me! I coulda warned her!"

"I woulda told you had I known it would go as far as it did. I had to move fast and it left no time to tell you or Shannon. I tried gettin' a hold of 'em once I landed, but no one was answerin' phones since she was sick and in the hospital."

"Fine. There you go bein' all sweet and reasonable when I'm tryin' to be mad at you," I complain.

"Sorry," he says sweetly before capturing my mouth in a searing kiss that earns a few hoots and hollers from onlookers.

"I've gotta get you pregnant now. Kellerman knocked Shannon up with twins in one try. I can't let that pretty boy outshine me," Kieran whispers into my ear. "I'm shootin' for quadruplets."

"You're insane," I say through a snort.

Kieran smacks my ass and gives me a pointed look, letting me know he's serious about getting me pregnant before he dives to the floor to join Owen, Alex, Connor and Jack.

"I'm pregnant," Sofia whispers into my ear.

"No," I whisper, shocked, glancing at Mike who is nothing but pleased with himself.

"I know it's early, but I love him and it just happened. I was on the pill so I don't know how, but I'm so freakin' happy I don't care," she squeals, wrapping me in her long lanky arms.

"Hey if you're both happy that's all that matters," I murmur, squeezing her tight. "Don't tell Kieran yet. If he hears another man has successfully knocked his woman up he'll tie me to the bed. I can barely walk today as it is."

Sofia tips her head back in boisterous laughter, drawing the attention of Kieran who quirks a brow at us. I shrug. My vagina can take no more...at least until tonight.

I unwrap from Sofia and approach Mike with a dazzling smile plastered on my face. He enfolds me in his arms, dragging my feet off the ground.

"Congratulations," I whisper, kissing his cheek. Mike has become a good friend to me. He's sat and talked to me about Kieran for hours on end. He's been kind and supportive, never questioning my crazy ramblings. Mike's just been there for me.

"Thanks," he says through a broad smile. "I'm gonna set you down before those three come over here and pound on me." I assume he's referring to Owen, Connor and mostly Kieran.

"You can hug me if you want. I won't let 'em hurt you."

He crushes me in a tight hug as I hear a throat clear behind me.

"Yes, Kieran?" I say, annoyed, without looking away from Mike.

"I'd be more comfortable talkin' to you if he'd put you down," Kieran says in an attempt not to be bossy.

"I'm huggin' my friend right now. I'll talk to you in a minute."

Kieran snorts. Mike shakes his head at my defiance.

"You'll be a great dad, Mike. You've been amazing with my kids. I can't wait to see you with your own little one in your arms."

"Thanks, Quinn," he whispers and a little bit of the tension leaks from his face. I could tell he was nervous.

First-time dad jitters have already set in. He squeezes me one more time before setting me back down. Mike offers Kieran a chin lift over my shoulder before walking over to plant a big fat kiss on the mother of his child.

"I can feel you scowling at my back," I chide.

Kieran roughly pulls me backward, smashing me into his chest.

"You were in another man's arms," he growls in my ear.

"And it won't be the last time. Mike's my friend so are Connor and Owen, so get used to it, pal."

"Can I at least set like a five second rule or something?"

"No."

He snorts and presses his lips to my hair. I may say no, but Kieran will never sit idly by and watch another man hug or hold me. It doesn't matter if he knows nothing more will ever come from it. I'm his and that doesn't involve sharing. So he'll allow it to a point, but there will surely be a five second rule in place before the end of the day.

Chapter 38

Kieran

"That was a fun night," Quinn says, flopping onto the bed.

"It was," I grunt in exhaustion.

We're in Kansas City for Shannon's birthday. She had a party at local pub tonight and I'm wiped from the celebrations. Shannon is glowing with pregnancy and watching her with her entire family around her was something my eyes will never forget witnessing.

"I know it's Shannon's birthday but I got you a present, too," Quinn says, reaching into her purse and retrieving a small box wrapped in silver paper.

"Thanks," I respond with a kiss on her cheek.

I unwrap the box quickly, crumpling the paper in my fist. It's a rectangle plain white box. I pull the lid off and my hands begin to shake.

"No," I whisper in disbelief, pulling the stick from the box.

"Yes," she whispers back, sitting up on her knees with tears in her icy blue eyes.

"When did you do this?"

"This afternoon. That's what Shannon and I were doin' earlier."

"You're sure?"

"I took four tests."

"I love you so fuckin' much," I groan before tackling her to the bed. "Do we have to stop havin' so much sex?"

"I'd like to go back to walking normally," she teases.

I will admit, over the last month I've been an animal. I have had sex with this woman as many times a day as our bodies will allow. Since Jack started school we have more alone time so I've been hitting it routinely. I'm sure she's ready for a break. I won't give her much. I can't be in a room with her for more than a few seconds before I need to be inside her.

"You're pregnant," I say through a broad smile.

"That I am," she says, grinning back at me.

I wiggle down her body and pull her dress up until her flat belly is exposed. I press soft, feathery kisses to the place that will soon swell with the life I've planted inside her. I now feel the ultimate caveman within me surging to the surface. Kellerman wasn't joking about this shit.

Quickly, I remove her thong and press long wet kisses down her pussy causing her to shudder and groan. She immediately pulls her legs back like I want them, opening herself to me. I love that she knows how I like it and gives it to me without thought. It's not submissive, it's giving. She's letting me have her the way that I want.

I lap at her slowly, working her into a frenzy. With her clit between my lips I finger her until a quaking orgasm wracks her petite frame. Once she's calmed down she sits up and directs me back to the mattress. She removes my jeans and underwear before circling her tongue around my head.

I'm completely still. This is the first time she's put my dick in her mouth since I face fucked her before the fight. I'm nervous. Her warm mouth pulls my dick into her mouth and I groan in appreciation. Her small hand wraps around the base, stroking me as her mouth pulls me deeper and deeper into her throat. I'm not going to last long if she keeps that up.

She looks up at me through her lashes, pumping me into her mouth. Quinn moans with the eye contact and it breaks my resolve.

"I'm gonna come," I warn her.

She watches me intently and works me harder with her hand, bouncing my cock off the back of her throat. I gaze at her as my come pumps into her mouth and she swallows feverishly, attempting not to spill a drop. Once she's licked me clean she sits up on her knees, staring at my dick triumphantly.

I sit up and yank her dress over her head before removing my shirt. I spread her out beneath me and feast on her body like it's my last meal. When my fingers and face are drenched with her come after her fourth orgasm, I slide my dick in her tight wet pussy.

Up on my knees, I pull her into my lap and work her up and down my dick as we rest our foreheads against one another. Her breath hitches as another orgasm builds so I lay her down to pound into her the way she likes it. With our mouths devouring each other's a moan of ecstasy bursts from her chest.

The taste of my come in her mouth would usually be an issue for me, but it only makes my dick harder knowing she just gave me the last thing she was holding back from me. I have her now, completely. With our third child growing inside her, my life is as full as I ever dreamed it could be.

I growl with passion as I fill her with my come. I know it's a wasted effort, but I keep my dick planted, trapping myself inside her. I continue to lick and kiss her, waiting to get hard again and start all over. She can go back to walking normally next month. I'm not done with her yet, I never will be.

"Jesus Christ, Kellerman, that's a fuckin' statement," I say shocked, holding Shannon's newly adorned left hand.

"That was the intended goal," he states proudly.

I have no idea what kind of diamond it is other than to say it's the size of a planet. Every man that comes anywhere within a five mile radius will know she's taken. Good man.

"It's the most horrible thing I've ever seen," Shannon complains through a smile. Kellerman could have tied a piece of string around her finger and she would have been happy. Things like this don't matter to her. She'll wear it, though, because he wants her good and marked.

"It's pretty awful," I agree with a smile. "So when's the wedding?"

"No fuckin' clue. Kinda have my hands and uterus full right now."

"Let's hop a plane to Vegas and get it done," I suggest.

"Oh no, you don't," Karl elbows the in the ribs. "I get to see her in a dress once in my life."

Shannon rolls her eyes at her friend. Shannon's not one for dresses or girly shit. She'd be happy to get married in her backyard in jeans and a T-shirt.

"I wanna help plan it," Quinn chimes in with a smile.

"Good because I have no idea what I'm doin'," Shannon says, relieved by Quinn's suggestion.

Karl, Quinn and Shannon dive into baby and wedding talk while I slowly shift away. That conversation was making my balls retreat into my stomach. I smile at Jack who's playing with his sister on the floor surrounded by the grandparent types of Shannon's family. We told Jack that Quinn's pregnant this morning and he leaped with excitement, deciding immediately he was getting a brother. I'm hoping for the same thing.

Kellerman, all three of my O'Sullivan cousins and I congregate around the breakfast area of Shannon's massive house. It's like a fortress and a mansion wrapped into one. I'm going to have to buy a new house now that I've knocked Quinn up. I know she loves our home, but we need more space.

"I hear congratulations are in order, cousin," Hugh says as he slaps my back.

I offer him a cocky grin.

"The two of you are seriously ruining our fun," Collin complains. "All domesticated and shit."

"It's not so bad," Brian chimes in. He lives with Shannon and Kellerman so he's been domesticated a bit himself.

"You two should try it," Kellerman jokes.

"Fuck that. You two can carry the diaper bags for the family. I'm good playin' the field three times a week," Hugh says through a snort.

"I think Brian's next. He's all gooey when he's holdin' Johnny. He's been bitten by the baby bug. Another one bites the dust," Collin teases his older brother.

"I think I'd have to find a chick that I could fuck exclusively for more than a week for that to work," Brian responds.

"Your bed hasn't been as busy as it once was," Kellerman points out.

"Your kid cramps my style," Brian scoffs.

"You're so full of shit," Kellerman says through a booming laugh.

"Whatever. I've been busy," he lies. Brian O'Sullivan is settling down. Never thought I'd see the day.

"Busy thinkin' about a blonde," Kellerman murmurs, confirming my suspicions.

"No fuckin' way. You met someone?!" Hugh shouts.

"I didn't meet someone. It's just...oh fuck, I don't know."

"Sucks doesn't it?" I ask.

"What sucks?" Collin asks confused at our conversation.

"When you meet the girl, but you're still a piece of shit so you don't know what the fuck to do about it," I explain. Hugh and Collin look at me like I'm speaking a foreign language while Kellerman points at me and nods in agreement. Brian's so pale he looks like he might puke.

"If she's worth it, you'll figure out a way to quit bein' a dick so you can just give her your dick."

"That was fuckin' poetic, Kieran," Kellerman says, wiping fake tears from his cheeks as we all burst into chuckles.

"I have a way with words," I admit.

"Since you're all gung-ho on settling down, when are you gonna put a ring on it? You've got two kids and another on the way. You're slackin'," Collin chides.

"I was gonna do it this weekend, but Kellerman stole the glory and set the bar too fuckin' high with that rock," I huff.

"You were gonna propose this weekend?" Kellerman whispers to not alert the room.

"Yeah," I say with a shrug.

"Bullshit," Hugh says, disbelieving.

"Got the ring in my pocket right now."

"Holy Fuck! Do it. Do it right now!" Collin orders excitedly.

"Right now?"

"Yeah, do it now," Brian pushes.

I look at Kellerman for some guidance.

"Dude, I did it while she was half naked in the middle of sex. There's no right time," he informs me with an encouraging smile.

"That's a romantic story you have to tell your children one day," I tease. He offers me a cocky grin and directs a chin lift toward our women, daring me to do it.

I shrug and walk off. I can do this.

I grab Jack and Ash from the O'Sullivan parents who are in kid heaven here. I walk over to Quinn, rudely interrupting the wedding and baby conversation and pull her into the middle of the room. All my cousins have their phones pointed at me, recording this moment.

This room is full of people. Shannon's nine brothers, three fathers, two mothers, Thomas, her long-lost best friend from childhood—Nick, Karl and of course Shannon's new little family. It's a room filled with acceptance and unconventional, unconditional love. I wish our family and friends could be here for this, but they'll understand I couldn't go another day without doing this.

Once I have Quinn at the center of the room, her face flushes with embarrassment, I drop to my knee, holding both kids on either side of my body. Her eyes go wide and her hands begin to shake.

"Quinn, I've been informed there's never a right time to do this so I'm doin' it now because I can't wait another second. I wanna make the mother of my children my wife. I wanna spend the rest of my life with you by my side. I wanna grow old with you and watch our children become everything good in you and everything strong in me. I wanna give you the world. Will you let me?"

Tears stream from her beautiful eyes as she ponders my question.

"Okay," she responds sweetly.

"Yes?" I confirm.

"Yes!" she squeals, dropping to her knees in front of me as the room erupts in applause and shouts of congratulations. I pull her into my chest, smashing my family against me. I hand Ashling to her mother and pull the black velvet box from my pocket. I crack it open and watch her eyes double in size.

I may not have gone as big as Kellerman, but I went as big as I thought her finger could hold, a five carat round stone with a band made of a never-ending Celtic knot in white gold. It's perfect for my Irish princess.

"Jack, you wanna help me out?"

"Cool."

Jack holds his mother's finger for me as I slip the ring on her delicate hand.

"Kieran, it's perfect," she whispers.

"Dílseacht is engraved on the inside," I explain and she smashes her lips against mine.

"Gross," Jack groans at our side, causing us both to laugh into each other's mouths.

I climb to my feet, helping her up as the room converges on Quinn, staring at her ring and hugging her in congratulations. Shannon and Karl hang back so I approach them.

"Pretty good," Karl says kindly. "I never drew up those custody papers. I knew this day was waiting for you. You just needed to find it."

I wrap my arms around him in a rough hug. He laughs at me, pushing against my chest to be let free when I hold him too long.

"Stop hittin' on me. You're engaged now," he snarks. "I'm gonna check out your handy work with the ring."

"Happy?" Shannon asks, folding under my arm. I pull her tightly to my side and kiss her hair.

"Like I never thought existed. This is because of you, Shannon. Almost fourteen years ago you gave me a little light. Havin' that in me when I met Quinn allowed me to let her set that light afire. Thank you for that," I murmur into her hair.

"You had that light all along. It has nothing to do with me. You deserve the love and happiness you have. Treasure it always," she says sweetly, pressing a kiss to my cheek.

We stand there in each other's arms as Quinn and Kellerman talk, holding the babies. The smiles on both their faces are intoxicating. Two good souls have found their way into two troubled hearts, making Shannon and me the best versions of ourselves we can be.

I lived a life shrouded in blackness until a cold February night when a girl stabbed me and showed me the light. A light I can't live without now. With Quinn and my kids, life is full and bright. The veil has been lifted. The blackness is now a distant, faded memory chased away by icy blue eyes filled with love. My soul is at peace.

Coming Soon...

Into the Blackness
Nick Cooper's story available Summer 2014

Late Summer/Early Autumn 2014
Brian O'Sullivan's story available

The Blackness Series

Blackness Takes Over

Blackness Awaits

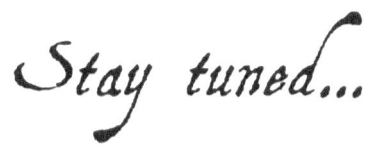

Stay tuned...

Follow me at one of the links below to keep up to date with my newest projects. *Into the Blackness* will have sneak peeks available throughout the summer available to those on my mailing list. You can sign up at my website below. I'm currently writing the fifth chronicle in the series to be quickly followed by the sixth. Thank you again for your support. Please leave reviews if *Shrouded in Blackness* made an impression on you. I take the good with the bad, appreciating honesty above all.

www.normajeannekarlsson.com

www.twitter.com/NormaJKarlsson

www.facebook.com/AuthorNormaJeanneKarlsson

www.goodreads.com/normajeannekarlsson

www.ingramcontent.com/pod-product-compliance
Lightning Source LLC
Chambersburg PA
CBHW030546180626
46816CB00005B/1416